Hootiecackle Chaos

by

Dyann Love Barr

Hootiecackle Chronicles

Hootiecackle Chaos Hootiecackle Chronicles

Cover Art by *Debbie Taylor*

The Wild Rose Press, Inc.
PO Box 708
Adams Basin, NY 14410-0708
Visit us at www.thewildrosepress.com

Publishing History
First Edition, 2024
Trade Paperback ISBN 978-1-5092-5624-2
Digital ISBN 978-1-5092-5625-9

Hootiecackle Chronicles
Published in the United States of America

Dedication

I couldn't have written this book without the encouragement of my husband, Dennis, my greatest supporter and cheerleader. My critique partners have always had my back and have never failed me. Also, not to mention Aka and Jinja my two marmalade cats who never miss critique night.

Chapter One

"Oh, my." Maisie McDermott adjusted the binoculars to get a better look. "That man's backside is sweet enough to make my teeth ache."

"That's impossible. You have a full set of dentures." Daisy, her twin sister, snorted and reached for the binoculars. "Here, let me see."

Maisie shook her head and continued to stare at the object of her fascination. "Doesn't matter. I'd still like to take a bite out of him. My Alfred always said he didn't mind if I lost all of my teeth—told me that my gums were magic."

"You *are* a pervert." Daisy wrestled the binoculars away from the protesting Maisie. "I take it back. Alfred was the perv in the family." She aimed the lenses in the direction of Hootiecackle's newest police officer, Sergeant Lachlan Briccio Donovan. "Oh, my…"

"Stop bein' such a hateful toad." Maisie's bosom heaved with an affronted huff as she slumped into the delicate bistro chair. It groaned in protest. "He's the one for Rory, isn't he? The Plan will work, won't it?"

Daisy continued her perusal of Sergeant Donovan's rear as he bent under the hood of his Ford Escape. "How could it not? Rory will fall head over heels once she gets a gander at him."

"Maybe we're pushin' too fast? She just got out of one disastrous relationship. He's been here a month and she's not even curious about him. What if they don't hit it off?" Maisie's chair screeched against the tile floor of the breakfast nook as she scooted around to get a better look. "You know how she feels about the Hootiecackle police department. She'd just as soon spit in his eye." She reached out for the binoculars.

"Trust me." Daisy slapped her away without ever losing focus on their new neighbor. "I have the brains, you have the charm, and Rory has the looks. The poor man won't know what hit him."

"What if Rory finds out?"

"I wouldn't have sold him my house if I thought we couldn't pull this off. God as my witness, he'll marry Rory, even if I have to sew their lips together." She looked up from the binoculars with a reassuring smile for Maisie. "The man is a perfect fit for our great-niece—tall, dark, handsome, and very Irish. And he can cook."

Maisie chewed her lower lip. She had doubts about The Plan.

"I sneaked over there while the workmen was redoin' the house. It's a modern wonder. At least Rory won't starve."

Maisie gave a sad little nod of her head. She cast a guilty glance over at the two loaves of charred banana nut bread resting on a cooling rack. "Even my bread came out a little toasty."

"If you mean you can use them to barbeque then, yeah."

"All the Callahan women are genetically flawed when it comes to the kitchen, but I swear, that girl can ruin a shit sandwich."

"Language, Sister, language." Daisy sighed, put the binoculars on the bistro table, and sat in the matching chair across from Maisie. "We can hire a cook once Rory gets married."

"That might be forever."

"Not if we stick to The Plan." Daisy drummed her fingers against the table. "She's been here goin' on six months."

"How is she goin' to meet him if she's at her business or in the work shop all the time?"

"We need to find a way to push them together. Leave it to me, I'll think of a way." Daisy's eyes narrowed in thought.

"How?"

"I don't know, but it'll come to me."

"I just found Ronnie Jackson is bein' transferred to Kansas City at the end of the year." Maisie pulled back the curtain and took another gander at the man across the fence.

"What!" Her sister's eyes widened with shock. "That means Sally Anne Schrock is goin' to be out of a place to work and stay. We have to grab the opportunity to get her. Do you realize how long we've been tryin' to hire her away from the Jacksons?"

"I live here you know. Good live-in cooks are hard to find. Darn it. We'll have to speed up The Plan but the only extra room in the house is Rory's" Maisie sighed with resignation. "I feel like I'm pushin' her out of the nest." Tears welled up in her eyes. "We are such bitches."

"I swear, Sister, I'm goin' to take a bottle of Listerine to that mouth." Daisy put the binoculars on the table. "This is God's will. The minute I laid eyes on Sergeant Donovan, I knew he would be the one to heal Rory's broken heart. She needed us, and to be honest, I think that poor man needs her—and that was even before we found out about Sally Anne."

"Poor man?" Maisie grabbed up the binoculars and craned her neck for a better look. "He doesn't look like he's sufferin'."

"He's lonely." Daisy stood, went over to the kitchen cabinet, and got out two tall glasses. "Cops can be lonely." She headed to the pantry, where she fished around behind the baking supplies to find Amos' special blend, or their *arthritis remedy* as they preferred to call it. A quick pop of the cork, a couple of splashes later, she filled each glass with iced tea. "Rory needs a good man—she doesn't know it yet."

The sound of clinking ice made Maisie lick her lips in anticipation. "How do you figure that?"

"Jenny Meyers spilled the beans." Daisy raised one auburn penciled brow and held out a glass. "Need you ask?"

"Of course." Jenny was the dispatcher at the police station. Maisie settled back into her chair and took the glass Daisy held out to her. Maisie shook her head in resignation. "Trust the Hootiecackle PD to arm the worst gossip in town with a radio." She took a delicate sip and sighed her approval. "So, what did she say?"

"He left the homicide division of the St. Louis police department to come here." Daisy swilled down half of her tea in one gulp. "She said that she overheard him tell Chief Nolan that he wanted a slower pace of life."

"You know she had her ear glued to Chief Nolan's office door." Maisie wagged her finger to make her point. "He'll get a *slower* life here. That's like going from sixty to zero. The initial force could kill him."

"Inertial force, you ding-a-ling. No wonder you

flunked science class." Daisy slit her eyes and pursed her mouth. "I hate to disappoint him, but Hootiecackle is a hotbed of crime."

"Oh, get a grip." Maisie swirled iced tea in her glass and drank. "Someone cutting off the heads of your prize roses doesn't constitute a crime wave."

"It's still an unsolved mystery, but I have my suspicions that it was Elmyra Jenkins." Daisy slammed her drink onto the table.

The memory of Daisy coming outside to prune her roses right before the big flower show made Maisie shudder. The poor things were snipped below the blooms. Her sister had vowed bloody revenge on the culprit.

"She's always been jealous of my roses—always comes in second."

Maisie nodded in agreement and warmed to the topic. "And then there was the broken window at Serena Moondancer's magic shop." She sighed. "I don't know why she had to buy that old, haunted bank buildin' and then convince Rory to rent out the other half. Maybe one of the ghosts knocked out the window. That's what she gets on callin' up spooks."

"I heard it was a stray rock from the quarry truck. Serena doesn't do magic—just sells candles and soap."

"And books about meditation and yoga." Maisie had listened, ever so innocently and covertly, to the Ladies of the Purple Hat Brigade at church. They whispered about crystals, tarot cards, and goings on in the curtained-off back room. "I heard she dabbles in *stuff*. And, don't forget the herbs she grows."

"It's called New Age. Don't think of startin' a witch hunt. If Rory says she's okay, she's okay."

5

"I was just—"

Daisy held up her hand. "You're repeatin' gossip. Lordy, you're worse than Jenny."

"And you're not? Well—" Maisie sniffed, "—I'll be glad when Sergeant Donovan pops the question. We're hirin' Sally Anne to cook for us when this is all done." She patted her rounded stomach. "I'm witherin' away to nothin'."

"Don't worry, you'll be eatin' weddin' cake before the end of the year." Daisy closed her eyes and Maisie knew she envisioned white tulle and pink roses. "Never lose faith in The Plan."

****

Rory Callahan breezed through the front door of her great-aunts' house with two sacks of groceries in her arms and a plastic bag from Walmart hanging from her right wrist. A whirlwind of dogs twisted around her feet. "Lucy, Einie, stop it."

Neither dog paid attention to her command. Avery, the large black and white barn cat sitting in the window seat, hissed out a warning. His claws snicked out on the off chance he'd get an opportunity to slice and dice one of the over exuberant dogs. On the other hand, Spook, Aunt Maisie's neurotic white cat fluffed up in protest and shot out of the room at light speed.

"Enough." This time her command got results. The dogs quit winding around her feet. They trotted beside her to the kitchen, the corgi on one side and the dappled dachshund on the other. Both glanced up at her with hopeful eyes. "Chill. I bought treats today."

Rory's trip to Holloway, the largest town near Hootiecackle, left her hot, tired, and in need of a shower. Her deodorant quit way before her errands were done.

No matter how bad she smelled, it couldn't compete with the foul, acrid smell coming from the kitchen.

She stopped at the sight of The Aunts sitting at the small bistro table in front of the bay windows. Her late Uncle Marvin's binoculars held a place of honor in the center. Both pairs of green eyes glowed with innocence. She knew it was an act.

"Okay, have you two been spying on your new neighbor again?"

"No." Aunt Daisy picked up the binoculars and made a show of putting them back into the cracked and worn leather case. "We were—"

"Communin' with nature," Aunt Maisie finished and took a sip of her iced tea. "Bird watchin'."

Daisy snorted and coughed.

Rory looked out the window, squinting until she made out a pair of broad, tanned shoulders and a well-muscled back that tapered down to a narrow waist. *Bird watching my ass.* She knew Donovan was handsome, muscular, and most women's dream, but she wasn't interested in men. "I'm so sure." Cops were off limit.

"What did you do today, Rory?" Aunt Daisy blinked and patted her short, white curls. Leave it to Aunt Daisy to divert the topic of conversation from a direction she wasn't willing to go.

Aunt Maisie giggled like a schoolgirl.

Oh yes, something was up, and they'd better not be on a match making spree. Glen Peters had doused any fire she had ever felt. The next-door neighbor was on the city police force. That by itself should've told The Aunts to butt out. They knew how she felt about the local police, especially since she'd spent most of her wild teen years getting in trouble.

Now her main focus was The Aunts and her shop on the main drag of Hootiecackle. The Funky Junk Shoppe had only been open a couple of months and already it was a hit with the tourists on their way to Branson. It was next door to Serena Moondancer's Moonshine Metaphysical Emporium. Location, location, location.

"I put the final touches on the Funky Junk Shoppe's window, then I went to Holloway for groceries and to get more supplies for Chandra's bachelorette party. It will be spectacular. Everyone in Hootiecackle will be talking about it."

"Oh?" Aunt Maisie looked wide-eyed. "How so?"

"I've hired a male stripper from Branson to show up about eight o'clock." Chandra's finance, Nick was on the Hootiecackle police force. He was the odd duck in town. Korean American, well over six foot tall, with a middle that had never seen a donut. "The dancer is going to come as a cop."

"Is that wise?" Aunt Daisy frowned and tapped her index finger against her rosy cheek.

"Why not?"

"Well, this is a small town. We respect our law enforcement."

Aunt Maisie's green eyes held worry. "People will talk."

"I'm inviting Jenny Myers. Of course people will talk, if they can get a word in edgewise."

"Maybe you ought to invite poor Lachlan."

Rory thumped the bags down on the counter and fished out the dog treats. "Lachlan is it?"

"He is our neighbor after all."

"This is ladies only."

"Maybe you can take him a loaf of banana nut

bread?" Daisy shot a knowing glance over at her sister. The Mona Lisa smile didn't fool Rory.

"So that was the stench I smelled when I came through the door." She shook her head. "I will not be implicated in manslaughter. You know what they do to cop-killers in prison, don't you?" Rory pried open the box as the dogs jumped up and down in anticipation.

"Victoria Shoiban Callahan!" Aunt Daisy's scolding overlapped Aunt Maisie's affronted, "Well, I never!"

Both dogs took this as a sign to howl and yap for their treats.

The noise level drove Rory to shout, "Stop it."

The dogs and The Aunts shut up at the same time. The dogs slunk down to the floor and The Aunts swelled like puffer fish. "Good. I'm only going to repeat this once." She dug into the box and threw a couple of dog treats on the floor. "I'm on to you two, so don't get any ideas of dragging that *poor* man into your web."

"You've never even met him." Aunt Daisy's squint was meant to intimidate, but Rory had outgrown its power.

She squinted back. "In case you haven't figured it out, I don't want to. There's too much to do in the shop for moonlight and magnolias. Been there, don't want to punch that ticket again."

"But—"

Rory slammed the box onto the countertop and held her breath until she could control her temper. She'd slice out her tongue rather than hurt her great-aunts. Right now, she had no desire to spend the rest of her life as a mute. "I love you two, but please, please, please—nip this in the bud. Excuse me, I have a cake to get out of the car before the icing melts."

****

Lachlan slammed down the hood of his SUV. The day had turned hot and humid, even for the end of May. He grabbed up his t-shirt and used it to wipe the sweat running down his chest and arms. If he weren't going on duty in a few hours, he'd grab a beer. A cold Coke would have to make do. He started toward his back door, but the sight of the Callahan Twins' great-niece trotting out of the house and down the steps of the wrap-around porch made him stop. Who wouldn't appreciate the way her long, curly red ponytail bounced with each step, or the slight jiggle of pert breasts? White crop pants covered a tight, round rear and her long legs made his body tighten with unwelcome need. If he were on the lookout for a date, she'd be the one, but he wasn't.

Life was too complicated to add a woman into the mix. Four years as beat cop and six on homicide left scratches on his soul—some way too deep to easily heal. His heart died along with his wife, Kate. That's why he decided to pull up stakes in St. Louis. His Chief recommended him for the job in the small town of Hootiecackle. Now he was one of seven officers under Police Chief Nolan who vowed to serve and protect the small burg of a five thousand souls on a good day.

His friends back in St. Louis wanted him to stay, try another occupation, but he liked police work, it was in his blood. Looking at corpses, the vicious things one human could do to another day after day—not so much. Now he only had to deal with petty shit. Stolen bicycles, parking tickets, and an occasional lookout for the odd meth lab. He'd already been told to overlook Amos Cunningham's venture into providing alcoholic refreshments for the community.

It was hard to do when Amos pulled up at the Gas-N-Go with the parts of a damned still perched on the back of his flatbed truck.

Lachlan shook his head and chuckled. Hootiecackle had more characters than the cable company had channels.

He liked the Callahan Twins. They were seventy-three, spry, nosy, and sweet as hell. It didn't matter that they had married the McDermott brothers, who were not twins. Hootiecackle still called them the Callahan Twins. He ought to know because Jenny Myers had the straight poop on everyone, including Rory Callahan. She arrived from New Orleans a three months ago to take care of her great-aunts. Jenny dropped hints that Rory was available and nursing a broken heart. He only caught an occasional glimpse of her because he worked the night shift. Lachlan might be the low man on the HPD totem pole, but he didn't mind. He was single and it gave the other officers of HPD more time to spend with their families.

Lachlan took one last look at Rory's enticing backside as she balanced a large, white bakery box. No, the last thing he needed was a woman who had just come off a bad relationship.

He slung his shirt over his shoulder and went into the kitchen for a coke and a few slices of cold pizza. A shower was the next order of business and then he planned on a nap before his shift.

****

The rest of the afternoon passed in quiet bliss. A gentle night breeze filtered through the window of his bedroom, bringing in the scent of honeysuckle. He finished dressing for work and reached into the bedside safe for his gun. The first hint of twilight muted the sunlight.

A loud bang and a flare of lights had him rushing to the window in time to see a shower of gold and red blossoms flickering in the sky. Fireworks? Why fireworks? It was only 6pm. Weren't they illegal before the 4th of July?

Another volley rocketed skyward. This time a series of feminine oooh's and ahhh's followed. Music cranked up and came close to drowning out the next bombardment.

The whole thing soured his mood. He bought the damned house because it was on acreage at the edge of town. Peace and quiet. Lazy days of summer. All of it blown to hell.

There was nothing he could do—the city limits ran down the fence line between the properties. He picked up the phone and called the Sheriff's office.

"Deputy Parker." The deep honeyed voice of Deputy Callie Parker trickled into his ear. Now there was a woman who could make a man stand to attention. But one wrong move, and the Afghanistan vet would have a person on the ground with broken fingers, as well as an ego to match.

"This is Sergeant Donovan over at HPD. There's a disturbance at the Callahan Twins' house. Fireworks, loud music, and cars coming and going."

"Oh, that must be Chandra Barrett's bachelorette party. Hear it's going to be quite the blowout. I'd be there, but I'm on duty."

"Why don't you send someone over to tell them to pipe down?" Lachlan hated the way his demand held a hint of a whine. Manly men didn't whine. They didn't even cajole. It had to be cut and dry, this needs to be done, so do it statement. Nope, he was headed for wuss territory if he didn't get hold of himself. All because of his red-haired neighbor. He couldn't see the Callahan Twins rocking out to ZZ Top's "Sharp Dressed Man."

"Deputy Carmichael is working on a complaint about someone cutting fences. That's more serious than some women letting off a little premarital steam. I'll radio him and let him know to check it out. In the meantime, why don't you go over there and ask them to take it down a notch?"

Lachlan rubbed the back of his neck in frustration. "All right, all right."

"Gird your loins, Sergeant Donovan." Deputy Parker's soft, knowing chuckle didn't bode well. "Rory was a hellraiser in high school. I doubt things have changed all that much."

"Will do." Lachlan ended the call and stared out the window. He could take down a murderer in a heartbeat, but the prospect of facing a room full of estrogen laced partygoers made him break out in a sweat.

There was only one solution. He drew in a deep breath and put on his best game face.

What was the worst that could happen?

Chapter Two

Rory glanced out the kitchen window to check on The Aunts. They scampered in the back yard, busily blowing up half of the Mega-Ton Pack firework selection she'd bought for later this evening. Aunt Maisie twirled in circles with a sparkler in her hand reminding Rory of a demented fairy. *Arthritis my Aunt Fanny, or in this case, The Aunts.* A hiss and sputter of a fountain shot bright white light into the fast-approaching darkness to the delight of Aunt Daisy. She crouched close by with a lit punk shoved behind her ear.

Who knew they were closet pyromaniacs?

Life would be lonely without The Aunts. In the three months she'd been here, they'd been involved in a scandal at the First Baptist Church when they nominated the town's bootlegger, Amos Cunningham, as a deacon. Aunt Daisy caused a near riot at the Plants-A-Lot Nursery over the return of some dead peony bushes. They were arrested for releasing the dogs at the pound. Aunt Maisie told the reporter from the Hootiecackle Caller that it had been a life-or-death mission. The city council wasn't amused and fined them anyway.

Jenny Myers and Althea Mackleson sat in lawn chairs, sucking on wine coolers, and egging them on. Rory would have to set The Aunts straight about the fireworks. The other—well, as aggravating as her aunts could be, she needed them as much as they said they needed her.

She filled the last deviled egg and put it on the appetizer tray. Out of nowhere a vison of her ex-lover, Glen Peters, wafted through her mind, his smile hiding betrayal. Her heart constricted with pain. She sucked in a deep, cleansing breath to calm the hard knot of anger brewing inside. This wasn't the time to let him get the better of her— there was a celebration to get started.

She grabbed up some pimentos to use as garnish and soon the eggs supported little horns with a matching red smile. It was the culinary equivalent of drawing a moustache on a picture or a voodoo doll. "There you go, Glen. I hope it hurts every time someone bites you."

Rory put the finishing touches on the rest of the appetizers with a small flourish and a smile. Chandra's bachelorette party had been a stroke of genius on her part. What better way to reconnect with all her old friends and catch up on life? The music grew louder, and she glanced up at the clock. It was almost seven and the male stripper should be here any moment. One day, over coffee at the Dinner Bell, Chandra had leaned over the table and whispered that she wanted to see a male stripper show in Branson before the big day. Her request puzzled Rory. Quiet, neat, and reserved, Chandra was the epitome of an elementary school teacher. However, she was the bride and tonight she would get her heart's desire.

A quick search on the internet and everything for the party was a go complete with the male stripper she'd hired. Rory had asked specifically for him to be dressed as a police officer. Chandra's eyes would bug out of her head. The girls were already laughing over the erotic party favors. The penis shaped lipsticks were a big hit.

Another volley went off in the back yard. Jenny held the punk and supervised.

Rory leaned over the sink and yelled out the window. "Hey, ladies, save some for later." She rolled her eyes knowing it was like herding cats.

Aunt Daisy waved her away in the fading twilight. "We hardly made a dent in these bad boys." She pointed to the array of fireworks laid out on the picnic table. "Black Cats, sparklers, and Maisie found some of the cutest little fountains at the bottom of the box."

Rory knew when to admit defeat. She hefted the heavy tray of food and headed out to the living room. The doorbell rang. *Right on time.* The Climactic Events agent promised punctuality and performance to write home about. The girls went out of their minds after she'd told them about the male stripper coming to give Chandra a big surprise.

Someone opened the front door and a loud shout and whoops of laughter greeted her, as well as the sight of a gorgeous man with black hair and the darkest eyes she'd ever seen. Her heart stuttered, her mouth went dry, and she was reminded once again that her lady parts were alive and well. The man looked oddly familiar, but she brushed the notion aside.

When the agency delivered, they really delivered.

Rory blinked and pulled in a deep breath to steady herself. The appetizers were drying out while she grew hot at the way his eyes scanned her. She forced one foot in front of the other until she made it to the refreshment table. The tray weighed a hundred pounds by the time she sat it down.

Darn, Chandra's isn't here to get a good first look at the dancer.

Another hoot and holler came from the ladies in the room.

She wove her way through the crowd to meet the stripper. It was imperative to get him out of the house and on the front porch because she wanted to introduce him to Chandra first.

Hope faded the moment Tanzy Anderson, the town librarian, spotted him and took the decision out Rory's hands.

Tanzy sidled up to him with a drunken leer. "Why, orificer, you forgot your gun." She slapped her hand against his crotch and gave it a friendly squeeze. "Or, maybe you didn't."

The poor guy jumped like a scalded cat.

Tanzy was not to be denied and tried to feel him up again. He whirled Tanzy around, leaned her over a wingback chair, and slapped handcuffs on her. Tanzy giggled and wriggled back against the dancer. "Oooh, a little rough play," she hiccupped. "Which shade of gray are you?"

"Hey, hey," Rory was mortified. The Climactic Events Agency had a strict hands-off policy and the dancer looked he'd blow hotter than Mt. St. Helens. "I'm sorry."

The last thing Rory needed was a lawsuit for sexual harassment from the agency. "Tanzy didn't mean anything by it. I'll make sure you get a very large tip. Really, really large."

Tanzy leered at him over her shoulder.

"Can we work something out? They don't know the rules," Rory whispered under her breath.

"Are you bribing an officer of the law?" He scowled, looking up at her from under his lids. Those darker than dark eyes pegged her lust-o-meter to overdrive.

"No, no." Rory beamed a smile at him and went along with role playing. "She's had one too many drinks. Please, take the handcuffs off now."

"I don't think so." He crossed his arms over his broad chest and raised one eyebrow.

Zing. Something snapped in her heart. She understood Tanzy's bad behavior. One look at the deviled eggs should've warned her against handsome men.

"Come on, Officer Good Body." Tanzy wiggled her fingers at him. "Be a sport. Fun's just starting."

"Shush!" Rory warned, but Tanzy squirmed even closer to the dancer.

"Yeah, take these off," Tanzy giggled and winked at him over her shoulder. "I'll really show you what I can do with my hands. Start strippin' baby."

The other ladies squealed their agreement. "Strip, strip, strip."

"I want to see that package." Tanzy's eyes widened. Her face turned a strange shade of green. "Oh no, I think I'm gonna—" She jerked up with a horrible gagging noise and vomited. Warm liquid ran through Rory's toes, and what might be the remains of several hot wings decorated her new wedge sandals.

Chandra came down the hall. "I go pee and it sounds like Armageddon out here. The ladies out back are blowing shit up and I can barely hear myself tinkle over all the commotion." The instant Chandra caught sight of Tanzy in handcuffs and the glowering officer, she clapped her hands over her mouth. "Oh, my god, oh my god," she mumbled from behind her hands.

It was difficult to tell if Chandra's was laughing or crying. Her face turned red, blue, and then white. Very patriotic. She lowered her hands. "Sergeant Donovan?"

"Sergeant Donovan?" Rory looked from Chandra to the gorgeous man in front of her. No, it couldn't be. But it was. Why hadn't she recognized him from the start? It might be the fact she never got a good look at him. He worked nights, she spent most of her time at the shop and she wasn't about to get chummy with the new neighbor. Chandra *had* downed several Captain Morgan's on the rocks. Maybe she'd mistaken him for the man next door.

"In the flesh." He whipped out his cell phone and made a call. "This is Sergeant Donovan at 309 Country Lane. Send someone out to the Callahan house." He frowned and pulled in a breath. "I know Deputy Carmichael is out on another complaint, but I want to report an assault on an officer." He glared at Rory. "And an attempted bribe."

Rory's lust-o-meter zeroed out in a heartbeat. "Wait, wait." She waved her hand in the air to signal he was all wet. "I didn't try to bribe you. No, no, wanted to give you a tip. I thought you were the stripper."

"Lady, do I look like a stripper?"

"Well." Rory couldn't help remembering the long, lean back draped over the inside of the SUV.

Before she could answer, Guns N' Roses' "Welcome to the Jungle" blasted from the doorway. The male stripper had finally arrived, waving around a night stick, and sauntering into the room. He ripped off his uniform shirt with a loud, *yee-ha.* The man sported an impressive six pack.

Her guests cheered him on. They quickly forgot the angry police officer in all the excitement of a handsome man getting down and dirty to an 80s hairband.

With one deft move, he snapped off his pants to reveal a leopard thong with a shiny star on the front. "Officer Studly Do Right will do right."

The dancer ground his hips in a circle and pointed at his crotch with his nightstick. "Cause, Studly Do Right is the *long* arm of the law."

****

Lachlan had as much as he could take without grabbing Studly's night stick and knocking him and the very drunk Tanzy upside the head. He usually tried to find a way to negotiate and deescalate a situation, but he could still feel Tanzy's steel grip on his privates. Heat washed over his face, and he knew it had to be bright red. He pulled a deep breath through his teeth and made a manly effort to calm down.

"Who the hell are you?" Studly stood with his hands on his hips and shouted at Lachlan over the blaring music. "I wasn't told there would be two of us. This is my gig. I go solo pal, or I don't go at all."

"I'm the cop who lives next door." A headache blossomed behind Lachlan's eyes. "Turn that damned thing off." Just then another bombardment thundered, and light burst through the windows. "And tell whoever's trying to start World War Three to cut it out!" The last thread of his patience snapped. He turned to Studly and tossed him the remnants of his pants. "Party's over pal. Suit up." He put his hands to his mouth and blew a New York whistle. "Quiet!"

The room full of ladies went deathly still, eyes bugged at his command. Tanzy alternately cried and giggled like a loon,

Nick's fiancée, Chandra, lay on the sofa, gasping for

breath. She pointed at him, cackling as loud as the woman who had groped him.

"I can't wait to tell Nick." She fanned her face with her hands as tears of laughter ran down her cheeks. "He is gonna *die*."

The Callahan Twins ran into the living room. Miss Maisie's hot pink capris and sequined floral top hurt his eyes, while Miss Daisy wore her ever-present khaki shorts and white t-shirt. They glanced from Lachlan and Tanzy, and over to the dancer.

"Oh, my," they exclaimed in unison. Both stared at the dancer, appreciation glowing in their green eyes, Identical, slow smiles spread over their round faces.

"Good evening, Lachlan." Miss Daisy ambled over to where he stood. "I'm glad you could make it. We told Rory that she should invite you to our little get together."

"Yes, yes, indeed." Miss Maisie nodded in agreement. "So nice to see you here. Rory said it was for ladies only, but I feel that's so un-neighborly of us." Her gaze raked over Tanzy as she *tsked*. "Dear, you know you don't handle drink well." She turned to Rory. "I should have warned you that our Tanzy is a bit of a tippler. There's nothing worse than a librarian who can't hold her liquor. It doesn't set a good example to the children."

Miss Daisy wrinkled her nose and looked around the room. "What *is* that smell?"

"Tanzy puked on my shoes." Rory grimaced and shook her foot. "Can someone get me a towel?"

"Thank god." Miss Daisy held her hand over the lower part of her face. "I thought maybe you decided to actually make the appetizers instead of buy them."

"I made the deviled eggs." Rory looked down at the

stern look from her aunts.

"Are you sure Tanzy didn't eat one?"

"No. She filled up on the chicken wings." Rory snorted and pointed to her shoes.

The relief on Miss Daisy's face would be comical if the odor of vomit and now weeping Tanzy hadn't stolen Lachlan's sense of humor.

"I'll get the towel." Maisie ran into the bathroom. She brought back the asked for towel, as well as a washcloth. "You might want to wipe down your feet with this."

"Thanks." Rory took both from her aunt and did a quick, squishy walk to a bright blue armchair. She gingerly removed her sandals and threw them to the side. "There's fifty dollars I'll never see again."

The sight of Rory scrubbing at her pretty, high arched feet hit Lachlan right in the pit of his stomach. He'd like to think it was the stench of Tanzy's round trip meal ticket squeezing at his gut, but in reality, he picked a heck of a time to find out he had a foot fetish.

Tanzy gagged again. This time Miss Daisy picked up a half-eaten bowl of party mix from the refreshment table and tossed the contents onto the floor—just in time to accept Tanzy's offering. She gave the woman a few comforting pats on the back. "Tanzy, sweetie, a town's librarian needs to be a bit more circumspect. Do your drinking at home, or the Hootiecackle Public Library Board will have to have a meeting."

Tanzy nodded and let go again.

Flashing red and blue lights shone through the open doorway. Deputy Callie Parker strolled through, assessing the situation. "Well, well," She took in the half-naked stripper. "What do we have here?"

"Officer Studly at your service. Just doing my duty, officer." He gave Callie a big, beaming smile and snapped to attention. "Just doing my duty."

"Save it, pal. That's my line." Callie tipped the brim of her official deputy's ball cap back and whistled through her teeth. Hazel eyes twinkled at the tableau. "Rory, you still know how to throw one hell of a party."

Chapter Three

Lachlan scowled and nodded toward Rory. "I got groped." He caught her withering glare. He half-expected snakes to slither from her mass of red curls.

"Our party crasher got a little more than he bargained for." A small smirk at the corner of her mouth twitched. If looks could kill, he'd be turned to stone and smashed into gravel.

"Now, Rory, I told Sergeant Donovan to come over here as a neighbor, not as a cop with a beef." Deputy Parker motioned for Rory to zip it. "Now what's going on?"

"I had everything worked out to the nth degree, but The Aunts started blowing up all the fireworks." Rory quit wiping at her slender feet and scowled in the direction of the Callahan twins. "I think Aunt Daisy got into the M80s."

Red flags of guilt stained Daisy Callahan's cheeks.

Deputy Parker nodded with a knowing chuckle. "I can imagine that could rock the neighborhood."

"Rock it?" Lachlan stared at the two in disbelief. "The place sounded like bombs were going off. I followed your suggestion, came over here to talk it out. I ended up being felt up by the librarian." He pointed to Tanzy who alternately sobbed and vomited into the bowl.

The low-level murmur of the room began to rise in

volume as each person began to voice their opinions about poor Tanzy and police brutality. "Pipe down, ladies." Deputy Parker vibrated with authority. One by one they hushed. "Thank you." Her gaze returned to Rory. "I don't think you need to add party consultant to your resumé."

"Yeah, well this one didn't work out as planned." Her grimace was aimed at him.

Deputy Parker's deep, throaty laugh held a hint of humor and resignation. "When do they ever? Remember the swimming party you organized at the rock quarry?" It was too bad he wasn't in a mood to appreciate the pretty shade of pink coloring Rory's cheeks.

"You and the mayor's son were caught running naked from a swarm of hornets."

"This is no time to be bringing up past errors in judgment," Rory hissed and turned even pinker. Her green eyes glittered with anger and embarrassment. "It's not funny."

Deputy Parker laughed even louder. "Oh, I don't know. The rest of us thought it was a real hoot to see Bobby Joe Henry shooting out of the woods and slapping at his pecker like nobody's business." She shot a quick look in Lachlan's direction. "Never try to do the horizontal mambo in the great outdoors, especially under a tree with a hornet's nest."

"We didn't see it." Rory frowned and went back to scrubbing between her delicate toes.

"Are you two finished reminiscing?" Lachlan raised a brow in question at Deputy Parker.

Her gaze scanned the roomful of women, and especially Tanzy, who sat on the sofa blubbering with her hands over her face. A very pregnant woman patted her on the back.

"It's gonna be okay, Miss Tanzy." The young woman rubbed her stomach and sighed. "We all make mistakes. Sometimes."

"Lachlan, why don't you remove Tanzy's cuffs? I don't think she's in any condition to make a break for it."

He had to agree with Deputy Parker. Tanzy's head rose from her lap and what came out, thankfully, were moans of distress rather than lewd comments, or vomit. "You've got a point." He went over to Tanzy. "Stand up."

The pregnant woman managed to heave herself out of the sofa and gave Tanzy a hand up. Tanzy stood as directed with a sniff, and snot bubbled from her nose with a pop. He'd seen things a hundred times worse but for some reason, tonight, his stomach gave a lurch. "Turn around." A few seconds later, the cuffs were removed and slipped into the case on his belt. "There you go."

Tanzy looked up at him with reddened, hazel eyes. Her lip wobbled and she went off into another bout of hysterical sobs. She plopped on the sofa and the Callahan Twins sat down, one on either side of her, rubbing her back and crooning.

Miss Maisie pulled a wad of tissue from a box covered by a crocheted frog. "Here you go. Everything will be all right." She glanced up at him, her eyes pleading Tanzy's case. "Just you see."

"Do you want to file a complaint?" Deputy Parker nodded her head in the direction of the drama being played out for the entire room. The women congregated around the sofa with coos of comfort and a few choice words for him. Why should they be upset, he was the one who'd been molested?

His jaw hardened at the memory. "I should."

Deputy Parker placed her hand on his elbow and nodded toward the door. "Come on, let's step outside."

He followed her out to the porch with the intention of throwing the book at Tanzy and Rory. Tanzy had quite a grip for a librarian. He swore he still had the imprints from her fingers on his nuts. She probably won every arm-wrestling contest at the county fair. As for Rory, it was her party. He was reluctant to toss the Callahan Twins in jail. He couldn't imagine the jolly faced duo in orange jumpsuits, but it was the principle of the thing. He had a right to peace, quiet and no manhandling.

They got as far as the front step. A scramble of feet could be heard and the slats of the blinds in the front room opened wider to accommodate several sets of eyes.

"We might want to go to the street." She pulled him across the lawn to where she had parked her four-wheel drive SUV. "I swear Jenny Myers has had a sonic ear implant. That woman can hear a snippet of gossip from a hundred yards away."

"What did you want to say?" Lachlan's irritation had grown with each step to the curb. Deputy Parker could argue until she was hoarse. It wouldn't do any good. Someone had to pay for his aching balls and ego.

"Don't get testy with me." She frowned, her expression hardening in the soft glow of the yard light. Her gaze swept down to his crotch and back. "I wasn't the one going for the glory."

"Sorry. Just don't say anything that even remotely sounds like testes." He jammed his hands into his pants pockets. "I feel—"

"So violated?" Callie raised one eyebrow in question.

Dyann Love Barr

"Pissed."

"Remember that next time you have to bust heads at the Cow Catcher Lounge." She leaned against the side of her vehicle. "It's not unusual for some guy to get too handsy with one of the girls. Now you know what a woman feels like when that happens to her." She sighed. "Thank God that headache is in your jurisdiction. Anyway, what I'm trying to say is it's unfortunate, it does happen. You're in your rights to have me haul Tanzy in for lewd behavior. I could arrest all three of the Callahan women for disturbing the peace, but would it be worth it?"

He rubbed the back of his neck in frustration. "Put like that, I guess not."

"Consider it a first move in public relations. You're new to Hootiecackle and those women," she pointed to the house, "are some of the community leaders, even if they are a bit eccentric."

"I've noticed." He couldn't help the small smile pulling at the corner of his mouth.

"This is a small town—you just don't walk in and get welcomed with open arms." She turned and opened the door of her SUV. "I've lived here for twenty-five years and I'm still on probation." She reached inside to pull out her ticket book. "I'll issue them a warning, all of them. I plan to give them the whole sexual harassment talk—you go on to work."

He glanced at his watch. "Yeah, I'm already late."

"Good choice."

****

Rory finished the last bit of cleanup on her aunt's hardwood floors. They'd taken Tanzy to the guest bedroom to sleep off her intoxication. Everyone else

28

remained just in case some new excitement broke out. They sat around the room, whispering to each other, peeking through the blinds, or eating the now limp appetizers.

The limpest appetizer, Studly Do Right, stood by the refreshment table, swilling down a beer. He eyed the blue recliner and made a move toward it.

"Hey, hey." Rory wagged her finger at him before he could sit his almost bare butt on the plush blue upholstery. "Your *long* arm is off duty. Drink up and get out."

Studly finished his beer in one long guzzle. "No never mind to me. I already got paid for this gig." He picked up his uniform and tapped his hat with the baton as he winked at Chandra. "You are shackled for life but call Studly if you want it done right."

Chandra's gaze was glued to Studly's impressive butt cheeks as he swaggered out the door. "Rory this has been the best bachelorette party, ever." She squealed and gave Rory a big hug. Chandra jumped up and down jarring every bone in Rory's body.

"My pleasure." It *had* been an interesting evening. Chandra had been the real surprise. Normally she was so cool, reticent about sex. Tonight, she dropped her inhibitions.

"No, I mean it." Chandra finally let go. "The party favors, the refreshments, a stripper, Tanzy blowing chunks, and an honest-to-God police bust right in the middle of the living room. Wow, I mean, wow."

The Aunts came into the living room. "We still have fireworks left over." The hopeful sound in Aunt Daisy's voice made Rory hold her breath and do a quick, mental count to ten.

"I think we've had enough excitement." She leaned down to twist the wringer on her mop. "Let's save the rest until the 4th of July. It's a little over a month away."

"Okay." Two sets of shoulders slumped in disappointment, but they eyeballed the way to the kitchen and backdoor. Knowing her aunts, they'd probably pocketed some firecrackers.

"How's Tanzy?" Rory hoped she'd passed out and wouldn't wake up until late in the morning. The woman had to be the sweetest person in the world, but drink wasn't her forte. Donovan could make her life a hell if he pressed charges.

The sound of boots had Jenny Myers and her cohorts trampling over to get away from the window and look as if they hadn't been spying on the goings on outside.

"She's fine." Aunt Daisy pointed down the hallway with her thumb. "Sleepin' like a baby."

Rory glanced up from wringing out the mop. She'd decided if she had to go to jail she might as well make it worth her while and smack the self-righteous Lachlan in the kisser with the string mop.

To her relief, and disappointment, it was Callie Parker.

Everyone stared and waited for the verdict.

"What's Donovan going to do?" She might as well get the bad news out of the way.

Callie opened her ticket book and scribbled. "I'm going to issue you, your aunts, and Tanzy a warning." She proceeded to give them the talk about life and sexual harassment in the Me Too era.

A shadow of memory darkened Rory's mood.

"You ladies are lucky." Callie stood, hands on her hips. "I talked him down."

"Oh, darn," Aunt Maisie pouted. "Spendin' the night in the stony lonesome was on my bucket list, even if I look horrid in orange."

Her sister plopped down in the blue recliner with a snort. She toed off her brown leather flip-flops and hit the recliner lever. "You just have that on your bucket list because I do. I did it first."

"Did not," Aunt Maisie protested. "You're the copycat. I wanted to go to jail first." She gave a delicate sniff and sat on the sofa.

"I could arrange it if you want." Callie smiled over at Rory. "You can ride in the back of the SUV."

Aunt Daisy shook her head. "Nope. Gotta get there on my own steam or it doesn't count. I don't want company in the tank."

"Tanzy will be grateful he's not pressing charges." Rory sighed. She could sleep easier tonight with the knowledge that Tanzy wouldn't be shamed by being hauled to the county jail.

"Not when she wakes up with a hangover." Callie handed her the tickets and closed the book with a snap. "Here you go. I hope you can talk her into taking it easy on the booze."

"That might have been our doin', dear." Aunt Maisie's gaze slid over to her sister. "Tanzy had a few beers before we went out back to set off the fireworks. And, well…"

"The punch was really lame, Rory." Aunt Daisy crossed her arms over her ample bosom. "That pink, fuzzy stuff needed a bit of a boost, so I added a bit of our arthritis remedy to it. Smoothed it out, gave it a nice kick, if I do say so myself."

"And you didn't warn anyone?"

"Why? They were suckin' it up like a pig does slop after we doctored it." Aunt Daisy did have the grace to blush. "Maybe I should've given Tanzy a heads up. Like Maisie said, the girl gets drunker than a monkey if you don't keep an eye on her."

Rory sighed and stood the mop in the corner of the room. "It's water under the bridge."

"Not water, our arthritis remedy!" Aunt Maisie sidled up to Callie to whisper in her ear. "You better go talk to Jenny." Unfortunately, her aunt must've turned down the volume on her hearing aid. The whisper carried throughout the room. "Tell her to keep mum. You know her tongue is loose on both ends with a spring in the middle."

Jenny's face bloomed pinker than Aunt Maisie's blouse. "I-I..." she sputtered.

Callie fixed Jenny to her chair with narrowed eyes. "Consider it a professional courtesy, Jennie. Sergeant Donovan wouldn't want to hurt the reputations of any of the ladies here tonight. He made it clear he intended to keep it to himself."

Jenny glanced around the room to all the women present and huffed. "Who would I tell? Everyone is here except you and Joy Nowell. She's on night shift at the nursin' home."

"There you go. Problem solved." Callie's gaze caught Rory on the way out. "I don't want to hear of anymore shenanigans on this side of the fence. Be sweet."

Rory hated that Callie knew her so well. Visions of ways to get back at the next-door cop flitted through her brain. None of this would've happened if he'd kept away from the party. *I'm the injured one here. It's not like he was going to bed or anything. Geez, he was going to work.*

One excuse after another convinced Rory of her innocence. She'd worked so hard over the last three months to repair her reputation. People still gave her the side-eye when she into Hootiecackle. She'd had one run in after another with the local law since she's come to Hootiecackle as a teenager. People said she was wild. The Aunts maintained it was nothing but high spirits.

Rory knew she wasn't an angel. She'd be the first to admit it, but now it would be impossible for the citizens of Hootiecackle to believe she'd changed after tonight's debacle.

"Did you hear me, Rory?" Callie stopped at the front door. "I said be sweet."

Rory crossed her fingers behind her back and nodded. "Will do."

Chapter Four

The sound of gunfire jerked Lachlan from a deep sleep and to his feet in less than two seconds. He pulled aside his room-darkening shades, shielding his face to keep the bright sunlight from frying his eyeballs. A quick glance at the clock on the nightstand showed it was only a little after one in the afternoon. Two freaking hours of sleep!

Another report sounded. This time he zeroed in on the direction of the noise—a large, detached garage of the Callahan house. He thrust his legs through a pair of denim shorts he'd thrown over the back of the chair by his bed. Again, the sound of gunfire.

He yanked the drawer to his nightstand open, pressed his thumb on the scanner of his gun safe, and pulled out his Glock. He sprinted out his back door, in the direction of the shots. He vaulted over the chain-link fence between the properties. Visions of carnage, blood covered Callahan women, raced through his brain at light speed.

The shots were coming from the garage. It was to the back of the property next to the fence line.

Lachlan eased against the wall and inched his way to the door. He peered into the depths of the old wooden building. Someone moved at the rear of the building. The perp was still popping off shots. He had to make his move. His nose picked up the acrid smell of cordite.

"Put the gun down." His shout filled the garage.

It surprised him to see Rory reach over to one of the steel studs propped against a wall. She hummed and danced to her own tune and acted as if she hadn't heard him. He tapped her on the shoulder and was greeted with a scream that rivaled the gunshots.

She pulled off her goggles and hearing protection with a mixture of fire and fear in her eyes. "What's wrong?"

"That's what I want to know." He slipped the gun into the back of the waistband of his denim cutoffs. For the briefest of seconds, he thought he registered a small smirk at the corner of her mouth.

"What does it look like I'm doing? Geez," She picked an orange and black tool from the floor. "Scare a girl to death, why don't you? You made me miss that last nail."

"Nail? It sounded like a massacre out here."

"It's a powder actuated nail gun." She pointed to lengths of two-by-fours on the concrete surface. "I'm turning this into my workshop, so I need to put up a few walls, gussie it up a bit."

"I was sound asleep when I thought I heard the shots." The inside of the garage was stifling in the late May afternoon heat. The humidity had to be close to a hundred percent. Sweat bathed Lachlan's body, partly from the greenhouse conditions of the garage, and partly from the awful sense of relief. "I thought someone had killed you and your aunts."

"Why, that's so sweet." Her voice contained enough syrup to drown a stack of pancakes a mile high. "Especially after last night." She laid the nail gun back on the floor and brushed her hands free of bits of concrete dust. "You really don't need to worry about us Callahan women. We've been taking care of ourselves for a long time, and in case you've forgotten, we're county. Not city."

For the first time, he noticed her denim short-shorts and the pale blue sleeveless blouse. Rory caught the hem up in an enticing knot just under her high breasts. His mouth went dry the instant he realized she had no bra on under the thin material. Perspiration drenched skin had plastered the fabric to parts of her body. He'd enjoy the sight if he hadn't been so damned tired.

"Okay." He held up his free hand in surrender. "I get it. No heroes need apply."

"Oh, are *you* my hero?" She kicked the saccharine level a couple of notches before picking up her noise protection and goggles.

He refused to get into a pissing contest with the redhead right now. His brain wasn't firing on all cylinders from a lack of sleep. In a few minutes his eyes would roll to the back of his head, and he would begin drooling. "I sincerely thought you ladies were in harm's way."

"Nope." She settled the googles over her slender nose. "You'll have to excuse me. I need to get busy."

Irritation made his cheeks flush with heat. "I'm trying to sleep. Can't you do that later tonight?"

She shook her head and replaced the noise protectors. "I'm way behind and I've got a load of dry wall coming in tomorrow." Her voice rose in volume as if to compensate for the headset. "You won't have to worry about this bad boy." She hefted the nail gun in her hand. "But I still have to crack out my power saw and drill."

Lachlan watched her fit a round and nail into the gun, and crouch down to position another length of steel on the floor. "I need my sleep." He shouted to make himself heard.

She lifted the right side of her ear guards. "What?"

"I need my sleep."

Rory positioned the gun on the stud. "Well, good night, don't let the bed bugs bite."

A deafening boom and concrete dust filled the air. The stench of cordite burned his nose once more. "Well, screw me harder."

He'd have to find his ear plugs if he expected to get any sleep.

****

Rory wanted to laugh at Lachlan's woebegone face and his weary trek back to his place, but her small victory tasted like crap. It hadn't been as appetizing as she'd thought it would be. She stood and laid the nail gun on her makeshift worktable of two sawhorses and a piece of plywood. The dark circles under Lachlan's eyes took all the fun out of her revenge. She was hot, sweaty, and out of sorts for no good reason. The goggles and hearing protection joined the nail gun.

In reality, she'd had all morning to start her project, way before she knew he would be home and trying to catch some sleep. A perverse sense of being mortified, of her guests' humiliation at the hands of this jerk had egged her on. She bit her lip. True, Tanzy had given his family jewels a buff and shine. It was wrong, horribly wrong, but the sting of being blamed for everything ate at her.

The *bad girl* returns home. Her wild child teenage years with multiple scrapes with the law would be rehashed with small town glee. No one knew the real reason she'd been sent to juvie at fourteen for a year. No on, not even The Aunts would ever know.

Jenny Meyers was bound to spill her guts to the first person who hadn't attended the party, she had to, it was her nature. A dog barked at cars, cats licked their rears and Jenny's mouth, and brain went on autopilot at the scent of scandal.

It wasn't The Aunts' fault she'd been a hellraiser. Her parents had washed their hands of her, saying it was either live with her great aunts or boarding school. Life with them had been a dream, even if she fell off the behavior wagon on occasion.

She yanked off her work gloves and threw them on the plywood surface. Salt stung her eyes from the sweat pouring down her face. She hadn't worn a headband to mop up the perspiration, instead she'd put her unruly hair up into a ponytail. The blouse and short shorts hadn't been meant to tease Lachlan. She knew the inside of the garage could double as a steam bath. Her skin still burned from the way he stared at her damp blouse. An air conditioner was the first order of the day once she had the inside of her workshop done.

She hadn't counted on her own heat level rising at the sight of his bare chest. The dusting of hair that arrowed down past the unbuttoned fly of his jeans unsettled her. One tug of his zipper tab, and—Rory shook her head. No, she wasn't going there. She refused to get hot and bothered over the guy. He might be The Aunts' man of the hour, but her new life had no place for a man. Not after her experience with Glen. Greek god or not, Lachlan was a cop. The last thing she needed was to get involved with the enemy.

Maybe she was being pissy because it was close to that time of the month, or it was the last email she'd received from Glen. He wanted to talk to her, explain things. She didn't need him, or his reasons for dumping her faster than a dog turd at a garden party. Glen had found a new woman, and he didn't want his old squeeze to mess up his pretty new world. Rory decided she'd be damned if he would show his face around her again.

"Damn all men!"

"What was that, dear?" Aunt Maisie came toddling into the workshop, carrying a tray of iced tea and what appeared to be chocolate-chocolate chip cookies, or maybe burnt oatmeal raisin. Either way, it was a pass on the pastries.

"Oh, men in general. Our neighbor in particular." Rory didn't want to get into it with her aunt. Her problems with Glen were just that, her problems. The last thing she needed was The Aunts to decide to come up with a way to make her happy. Happy to them meant married, which meant dealing with the opposite sex. Rory didn't need to be fixed up. All she wanted was to lick her wounds in private and get on with her life—without a man.

"I agree, men can be a trial at times." Her eyes twinkled in her round face. "But they do have their uses. Oh, yes, indeed." She set the tray down on the table and poured out a large glass of sweetened tea. "I thought that was poor Lachlan I saw as I came out of the house?"

"It was."

"He didn't look like he'd dressed for a visit."

"It wasn't a visit."

"Then why was he here?" Aunt Maisie's shrewd gaze bore into her.

Rory shrugged.

"Lachlan isn't the type to come over without an invitation." Aunt Maisie continued her relentless probing.

"Oh, for goodness sake. He was complaining about noise pollution, again." Rory took a tentative sip of the iced tea to make sure none of The Aunts had doctored it up. She couldn't drink it down fast enough once she'd ascertained it to be alcohol free. "That's wonderful." Rory ran the icy cold glass against her forehead.

"It's miserably hot in here." Aunt Maisie lifted the front of her white lacy shirt from her full bosom and fanned it a few times. "Why didn't you start your project earlier in the mornin' when it was cooler?"

"I had my reasons."

Aunt Maisie poured herself a glass of tea. The ice cubes clinked merrily as she gave Rory *the look*. "And those would be?"

Rory eyed her aunt. Had she figured out that Rory was out for Lachlan's blood? It was hard to tell, given the beatific expression on Aunt Maisie's face. That usually indicated she was up to something. "Do you want to get out the rubber hose and brass knuckles while you're at it?"

"Whatever do you mean?" Her green eyes grew round in question. "Hmmm?"

"Nothing, absolutely nothing." Unthinking, she grabbed up a mystery cookie and took a bite. Oatmeal raisin. The acrid char and burnt raisin taste made her tongue beg to spit it out. Instead, Rory womaned up and swallowed—hard. The sweetened iced tea only made the taste swirl around her mouth in a whirlpool of awfulness.

"What do you think? This is my best batch yet."

Aunt Maisie gave her a cherub's smile. "I think I'll take a plate over to Lachlan."

There was no way she'd inflict the oatmeal raisin horrors on anyone, even Lachlan. She shook her head, forced down the tea, and smiled. "These are so special. Let's keep them for ourselves. I'll run by Elmer's Donuts and pick up a couple dozen donuts for the guys at the police station. I'm sure Lachlan won't mind sharing. It'll be my way of saying I'm sorry for disturbing his sleep."

"That's a great idea." Her aunt's face turned pink with pleasure. "I thought you said you'd never set foot in the police station after tyin' Chief Nolan's lawn jockey on top of the water tower."

Rory grimaced at the memory of getting caught under the school bleachers drinking beer with a boy. Chief Nolan's not so subtle hints that he'd help her in return for a *favor* made his favorite racist yard ornament fair game.

"It was a degrading, disgusting awful thing."

"True, but it wasn't the right thing to do." Aunt Maisie wagged a finger at her. "You were a trial but such a lovin' child. I don't know what gets into you sometimes. Must be the Callahan temper."

She'd never tell The Aunts that a blow job would've gotten her out of doing time in juvie. If she had, the lawn jockey incident would've been minor after The Aunts got through with Chief Nolan. They didn't need any more grief from her and her shenanigans as they called her bad behavior.

They headed back to the house with the empty glasses and tray of horrors. She smiled at Aunt Maisie's round backside in deep purple capris. What would she have ever done without her and Aunt Daisy to work out the hurt that brewed inside her, then and now?

"I tell you what." Maisie hustled around the kitchen and pulled out a bunch of ingredients. "Why don't I send some of my special chocolate chip cookies along with you?"

Rory nodded, knowing when to bow to defeat. She planned on dumping the cookies of doom before they ever made it HPD. "Sure. Let's spread the love."

The rest of the afternoon passed in hot, sultry silence, except for the nail gun. To be honest, getting her project started late meant she had to hustle to get the wall done. It was the truth that Jackson Delio and his sons were coming early tomorrow morning to get the inside of the garage finished out.

She stood and surveyed the potential of her new workshop's space. Salt stung Rory's eyes again. A quick wipe with her forearm and she decided to call it a day. All she wanted right now was a cold shower to erase the grime from her body and the image of Lachlan's sweat slicked chest from her mind. The empty ache low in her belly told her a dive in the Arctic Ocean wouldn't do the trick.

****

Monday started with an army of customers and a decent number of sales, much to Rory's pleasure. "I think I want to put the credenza there." She pointed to a space that had recently been occupied by an antique umbrella stand made from an elephant's foot. It had been in a block of items she'd purchased at an estate sale, and it wasn't anything she'd buy on her own. As awful as the remains of the poor beast were, it sold the first day she put it out. At least the elephant hadn't given its life in vain. She'd be able to pay the light bill this month from the hefty profit. Now it was stored in the back room until the new owners picked it up on their way back from Branson.

Josie Tally frowned. "I don't think the credenza will fit."

"Oh, honey, I can squeeze a whale into a fishbowl." Rory grabbed a few odds and ends from different areas of the shop and placed them on the old wooden countertop. Her shop had once been the town saloon, one-half of the original bank where Serena had her metaphysical shop. Rory had kept the shelves and antique mirrors, along with a painting of a half-naked harem girl hanging against the back wall. Jars of penny candy sat next to the register.

A hat rack, along with several other pieces found a new home across the room. She soon had the refurbished credenza shoved into place, along with a tasteful array of plates, bowls of potpourri, and candles. "There, see, I told you." Satisfaction filled her. Those pieces would be out the door before she knew it.

"I never would've believed it, Miss Rory." Josie's round face broke into a smile, her dark eyes glowed with admiration. "You have a real knack. How do you take all that junk and make it look so pretty?"

"Trial and error, along with a degree in interior design." Rory eyed the credenza again. It still wasn't right. It needed something else to put the entire presentation over the edge. She pursed her lips in concentration and made a quick mental inventory of her store. Then inspiration hit her.

She pulled an old lace doily from one of the credenza drawers and placed it under an ornate chiming clock to add the finishing touch. "There we go."

"I think it's wonderful." Josie hesitated for a moment. "Do you think I could learn to do somethin' like that?"

"I don't see why not. You have a good eye and are better bookkeeper than I'll ever be." The clock chimed ten o'clock. "Oh, my, I didn't realize I kept you here for so long. Won't your family be worried?"

"Nah, my brother is pickin' me up in a few minutes."

"Let's shut down here and I'll wait until Theo shows up. How's he doing?" Rory knew her brother had come back from Afghanistan without his left foot.

"Oh, he's okay. At least he can drive now. He's just havin' a hard time finding a job."

"Hootiecackle isn't exactly awash in employment opportunities."

Josie laughed and turned off the lights over the counter. "Unless he wants to take up moonshinin' with Amos."

"What about over at the warehouse for the Large Mouth Bass Fishing and Camping Company?" Bryce Pomeroy, the town's largest employer, would want to welcome home a veteran with an injury with a job. "Pomeroy's got red, white, and blue bunting all over his store. He's always talking about the brave men and women who serve our country on his commercials."

Josie smirked. "No. He don't got no use for a one-legged kid, especially someone who's used to leadin' instead of followin'."

Rory couldn't hide her shock. "He hired Billy Franklin. He's missing an arm."

"Billy is one of *the* Franklin's. He's all yes, sir, no, sir, besides bein' so white he glows in the dark. Theo

44

would tell Pomeroy how to do his business in no uncertain terms. The last thing the Tally's need is to butt heads with the wealthiest man in town."

"There's got to be someone who will hire him." Disappointment and anger swelled in Rory's breast. "If there's anything I can do—"

Josie held up her hand and gave Rory a sweet smile. "You've done enough by hirin' me."

"Why wouldn't I hire you?" She went behind the counter and set the box of doughnuts out to take to the police station after they closed for the night.

"Oh, come on, I'm a Tally. You know how the town feels about us, especially with Daddy in prison. He couldn't prove he didn't know the Jonas boys were goin' to rob the gas station."

"Not hiring Theo is their loss."

A knock sounded on the door. Rory expected to see Theo, but instead she found a cop. Lachlan scanned the room before he stepped over the threshold.

"I saw the light from the street and decided to check things out."

Much to her chagrin, the unbidden image of him dressed only in denim shorts popped up. Her tongue stuck to the roof of her mouth as if she'd eaten ten peanut butter sandwiches without a glass of milk in sight. "I— ah—we were finishing up here. Josie's waiting for her brother Theo."

"Good, good. Then I'll say goodnight and have a safe trip home." He turned to go.

Rory bit her lip. She debated whether to tell him about her aunts and *The Plan*. She ought to, if only to be upfront—and polite.

"Wait." She ran to the counter where she'd set the

box of doughnuts. "These are for you. I had intended to drop these off at the police station a bit earlier, but we got busy."

Suspicion grew in his eyes as she held them out. "Why are you giving me doughnuts?"

"Don't worry," she huffed, and thrust them out again. "I didn't put a laxative in the chocolate icing."

Josie made a noise, half-way between a snort and a giggle. Rory gave her a major side-eye.

"Believe me, you'll want these instead of Aunt Maisie's chocolate chip, or maybe it was oatmeal raisin cookies. It's hard to tell one from the other. She's been on a baking tear this last week and asked me to deliver a dozen to you at the police station. I keep telling her that I'm not a cop killer."

A smile replaced his misgivings. "Nice to know. I'm glad you draw the line at psychological torture."

"Ah—un—about this morning." The heat of embarrassment crawled up her neck. It had been a childish thing to do, even if she thought Lachlan deserved every minute of his *psychological torture.*

"Yes?" His voice took on a low rumble that sent shock waves through her system. She wondered if it would show up on the Richter Scale as a small quake near the New Madrid Fault.

Josie glanced from Rory to Lachlan. She grinned and motioned toward the office. "I'll just go and get my purse. Maybe I ought to double check to make sure we got that back door locked."

Traitor.

"I was feeling a little peeved about last night and decided to make your afternoon a living hell." Rory held out her hands for his inspection. "All I got for my trouble

46

was blisters on my hands, heat exhaustion, and a bad taste in my mouth."

"One of Mrs. McDermott's cookies?" One black eyebrow raised in question.

Rory couldn't stop the smile if she wanted to. "Well, there was that too. I put a couple in there so I wouldn't be lying about bringing them to you. Avoid them like the plague."

"Will do."

"Ummm—if she asks, tell her the cookies were delicious."

"That would be lying." Lachlan nodded and took the doughnuts. "How about this? You tell her that I've never tasted anything like them before."

"Good. That should work, because believe me, you don't want to taste anything like them."

"Or maybe they had a distinctive taste all their own?" He rocked back on his heels, clearly enjoying the nuances of avoidance.

"No." Rory gave a delicate shudder at the memory of Aunt Maisie's cookie. "But if you think something that's a cross between asphalt and burnt tires is distinctive, go for it."

"Okay, I get the picture." His lips twitched with his efforts to keep from laughing. "Mrs. McDermott will never be the wiser."

"Around here she's called Miss Maisie. Aunt Daisie is Miss Daisie. I think it's a southern woman's attempt to keep the illusion of youth."

"Got it." He nodded. "Miss Maisie it is."

Rory liked Lachlan, despite their rocky start. Not only was he good looking, but he was sharp, able to think on his feet. Too bad she'd given up on men.

Josie came out of the back room just as her brother opened the door. "Hi, Theo." She leaned under the counter and pulled out her purse. "I'm ready to go."

Theo Tally's big body framed the door. He had the same finely drawn features of his sister and a smile that lit up the room. The only evidence of his injury was the cane he used to brace each step.

Theo raised his hand in greeting. "Hello, Ms. Rory." His gaze slid over to Lachlan. Sergeant Donovan."

"Mr. Tally." Lachlan nodded back. "How's the leg?"

Theo shook his head and tapped the side of his running shoe with his cane. "I wish my damn toes would quit itchin'."

"I have a friend who lost a leg in Iraq. Says the same thing. How's the job search going?"

"Not so good." Theo's smile dimmed. "No one wants to hire a cripple."

Lachlan shifted the box of doughnuts to one hand and reached into his uniform blouse pocket. "Here's my card. Come by the station tomorrow and fill out an application. You can use me as a reference. There's an opening for a night dispatcher. Frank Appleton is retiring, and Jenny Myers is going to days. Captain Nolan is putting an advertisement in the Hootiecackle Caller tomorrow. Maybe you can get a jump on it."

Theo took the card and slipped it into his jeans pocket. "Thanks. I'll get on it." He motioned for Josie to follow. "Come on. Mama's got a pot of stew on the back burner."

Rory waited for the two to leave before she turned to Lachlan. "That was a nice thing to do." She didn't want to be impressed or see him in a positive light. It made him too human and appealing.

"It was the right thing to do. He seems to be a good man."

Damn it. Why did he have to be so—heroic? "There might be some blowback since his father is in prison."

"Theo's not his father."

Lachlan didn't understand the way things worked in a small town. Once the brush of wrongdoing had made its mark, nothing could remove it from the town's mind. She didn't agree, but it was a reality he'd have to deal with—same as she had. "The good people of Hootiecackle might not see it that way."

"Then they aren't so good, are they?"

"No, I suppose not." She'd put off telling him about *The Plan* long enough. "Lachlan?"

"Hmm?" His intense, blue gaze bore into her, and one brow rose in question.

It was now or never. The awful truth had to come out, and it did, in one rushed breath. "I think you ought to know that The Aunts are trying to set us up."

"I know."

His calm reply threw her off kilter. "You know?"

"Yes. Don't worry, I'm not offended, and I'm not looking for a woman in my life."

"Not looking ever? Looking for the right guy, maybe?"

He shook his head and gave her an infuriating half-smile. "No one. I need time by myself to sort out some personal stuff."

A shadow passed over Lachlan's dark eyes. Whatever troubled him was more than getting dumped by a woman. One thing Rory understood was pain.

"Gottcha." She nodded. "I've got enough baggage

to give everyone in Hootiecackle a matching set of luggage."

"I need to go on my rounds." He hefted the box of doughnuts. "Thanks for these, and the warning."

A blush heated Rory's cheek. "Sorry about The Aunts' matchmaking urge." She brushed a long tendril of hair away from her face. "It's so embarrassing."

"Don't worry about it." He gave her a roguish smile that belied whatever ghost lurked in his eyes. "We're all good as long as you run interference on future cookies."

The tender swell of desire wound around her heart and radiated throughout her body. She couldn't allow him to wriggle under her skin like the chiggers which were so bad this year.

That was one itch she didn't need.

Chapter Five

Lachlan kept his head down but sneaked a quick glance at the wall clock. He spent part of his shift doing paperwork—not that it took long to do his reports. Nothing much happened in a town the size of Hootiecackle. Right now, he'd linger over traffic tickets if it meant he didn't have to hear Jenny's ramblings.

From the moment he showed up at the station, she worked the bachelor party into every conversation with him, other officers, and anyone who walked through the door. She hadn't mentioned Tanzy getting wasted or him being fondled, but it didn't matter. The rest of the town already knew what had happened. Even Amos, the bootlegger, honked and gave him a thumbs up from his pickup window.

The night dispatcher wasn't scheduled to take over from Jenny for another hour. It was all Lachlan could do to keep from stapling her mouth shut. It was a mean thought, but he'd rather eat one of Miss Maisie's cookies than listen to any more gossip.

"Word's out that the Callahan Twins have their eyes on you." She sat a cup of coffee in front of him. "It must be real convenient livin' next door and all."

"Real convenient—if I'd planned on becoming their boy toy." He winced at the unintended double-entendre, especially after last night's debacle. "Which I don't."

"No, silly. For Rory." She giggled with a knowing

smile on her lips. "Too bad her ex was such a jerk. Ruined her for men—or so she says." Her hip perched on the edge of her desk. She sipped her coffee, all the while giving him the hairy eyeball. "Glen Peters, that's his name. You know he dumped Rory for some blonde with fake boobs and a daddy with more money than God." She sighed and stared off into space with a dreamy expression. "I smell romance."

"The boyfriend and the blonde?" Lachlan knew he'd regret those words.

"No! Rory." Jenny stood and went back to the radio, adjusted her headset, and put her coffee on a coaster next to a half-eaten doughnut. "Haven't you been listening?"

How could he not have been listening? The constant drone of her voice had the same effect as a fly buzzing around a prisoner in solitary confinement.

"I really need to get these done before Nick takes over." He tapped his ticket book with his pen for emphasis. Hootiecackle's computer system was antiquated and much of the office still revolved around good old pen and paper. "Chief Nolan likes a tidy cop shop."

"What are you workin' on so hard?" Jenny snorted and swiveled her chair around to face him. "Amos spit tobacco on the sidewalk again, or was there a big bust over at the sand bluffs?"

Yes, he'd taken a trip to the sand bluffs at the edge of town—and near the old cemetery, to make sure no one had taken the term "lover's lane" too far. Lachlan preferred not to deal with crying girls and angry fathers on his watch. The kids might be rural, but they knew how to get whatever they needed to party. Beer and moonshine were usually the drugs of choice in

Hootiecackle. Everyone managed to find someone who grew marijuana in their garden. Meth labs were plentiful, but thank God, those were County's bailiwick.

"Nope. Everything is buttoned up tight. Quiet is good, but I still have to log my reports."

"Anyway, as I was sayin', Rory's ex is an up-and-coming interior designer in New Orleans. That's how Rory met him. He was one of her clients. Although how she expects to make a livin' in that junk shop on Main is beyond me. Did I tell you she's an interior designer?"

"No." He already knew everything about Rory, down to her shoe size. The Callahan Twins made sure to fill him in. They brought a large pizza from Guido's, the local pizzeria as a welcome to the neighborhood dish. They assured him it was a southern thing, but he was sure they came over to reconnoiter the remodeling of their old house.

"Look, Jenny, I really need to get this done." Lachlan glanced up at the clock again and prayed he could last another five minutes. Next time he saw her husband, Tom Meyers, at the tavern, he'd buy him a beer. It was the least he could do.

Lachlan made it through his nightly rounds until he clocked out into the late dawn. The air was already heavy with warm, moist heat. Lavender-gray clouds, tinted with hints of coral, smeared the horizon. He pulled in a deep breath of the honeysuckle scented morning.

He got into his SUV and headed south, slipping a CD into the stereo, and let the soft jazz smooth the edges off of his irritation. There was a steak at home with his name on it, along with hash browns, and farm fresh eggs. A couple of hours with the news and he'd hit the sack. He had the next two days off and he planned to work on a small vegetable garden. He'd picked out the perfect spot to plant tomatoes, cucumbers, along with some melons. Miss Daisy even offered the use of her old rototiller.

The gravel crunched under his wheels as he turned into his drive. He stepped out of his SUV to silence— country silence. The Callahan Twins' roosters crowed. The soft muted lows of cattle came from the field behind his house.

This was now home.

The noise of a screen door slamming brought him out of his reverie. He glanced over the fence in the direction of the Callahan Twins' house. Rory stood on the large veranda with a mug cradled in her hand. She took a sip before heading down the stairs and in the direction of her workshop.

The sunrise struck her long hair turning it into a fiery cascade that flowed over her shoulders and down her back. The image burned itself into his brain with the precision of a laser.

A punch of desire hit him with the force of a medicine ball to the gut.

When had the memory of Kate's face blurred?

He closed his eyes at the recollection of Kate taking her last breath. The anguish of loss squeezed his heart in a vise. Now his body hummed to life with a gnawing need he thought long buried. She'd been gone two years, but his betrayal felt fresh.

"Good morning." Rory's voice still held a touch of sleep. Warm, husky, and sexy as hell.

It would be unneighborly to ignore her. He opened his eyes to see her standing at the chain-link fence dividing their property. She leaned against it with one arm draped over the top and drinking her coffee. Luckily, her cotton housecoat obscured his view of her body. He didn't think he could deal with anymore visual aids.

"Yeah, it is."

"Tough night?"

He shook his head. "Jonas Cramer and Dick Woods were duking it out in the Cow Catcher Lounge's parking lot. They were so drunk they were mostly punching air."

"Those two have been at each other since high school." Rory gave a delicate snort. "All over a girl who wouldn't look twice at either one of them."

"You?" He hadn't heard any names mentioned, other than the ones they hurled at each other.

She shook her head. "Kelly Pomeroy. She was the most popular girl in school. Mean girl. I hear she's doing quite well in Hollywood." She gazed down into her coffee cup. "She's made to order. Tall, dark-haired, and daddy bought her some new boobs to jump start her career."

He remembered what Jenny said earlier this morning. "I prefer natural breasts and redheads myself." A demon must have possessed him. The words popped out before his tired brain could stop them.

Rory stared at him with puzzlement, and then she frowned. "Thank you—I think."

Lachlan cleared his throat. "I was just—hmmm— trying to tell you that not every man prefers blondes with big breasts."

Her green eyes lit up. "You're in the minority."

A smile tugged at one corner of his mouth. "Discriminating."

Rory shook her head and *tsked*. "No. Crazy." She pushed herself away from the fence with one hand. "I better go. The Aunts were threatening to cook breakfast. I've learned to scramble eggs and cook bacon without burning it out of self-preservation."

"That's good." He winced inwardly at his lame comment. The uncomfortable moment passed after he reminded himself that they'd both agreed to avoid the Callahan Twins matchmaking net. "Bon appetit."

"Try to get some sleep." She gave him a fast wave and hurried off in the direction of her house. "I'll keep the noise down as much as possible."

"Thanks."

Sleep was debatable as the sun came out in its full glory and blasted through the material of her thin housecoat. The silhouette of her rounded backside would haunt his dreams.

****

Rory stood over the stove frying up some bacon. She tuned out the sizzle and pop as it cooked in the pan. Her thoughts drifted off to the way the early morning light put Lachlan's face in the study in dark and light. It empathized the chiseled lines, gilding his high cheekbones. His black eyes looked tired.

She'd gotten another email last night from Glen. He wanted to talk to her. All she could think about was his parting shot about her lack of sex appeal and sophistication, especially to him. He'd said he'd always preferred blondes.

Lachlan's smile, the way he looked at her, sent chills of anticipation bubbling through her body. She hadn't felt sexy for a long time. Too bad it had to be with the out-of-bounds neighbor. Still, it had been nice—too nice.

The acrid smell of burnt bacon jarred her out of her thoughts.

"Well, I declare." Aunt Daisy stared down into the pan with disgust. "If I wanted charcoal for breakfast, I'd let Maisie have a go at that poor pig."

Rory dumped the contents into the trash. "I'm sorry." She grabbed up some paper towels to wipe out the hot pan. "I'm a little distracted this morning."

Aunt Daisy handed her the package of bacon. Rory pulled out six slices and started over. She turned the heat to medium-low and moved the pieces of bacon this way and that with the fork.

"What's eatin' at you?" Aunt Daisy plopped down onto one of the kitchen chairs and stared out the window. "Your face is longer than—wait, it's that fella again, isn't it?" She gave a disgusted huff and grabbed a piece of toast from the plate in the middle of the table. "No count, son of a biscuit-eater."

"Glen wouldn't be caught dead eating biscuits." Rory reached for a plate. She gingerly picked up each piece with the fork and placed it in precision strips across the paper towel. "He'll lower himself to eat an avocado toast or bagel because it's urban chic. Everything else must be haute cuisine."

Aunt Daisy screwed her face up into a good likeness of a dried apple doll. "Give me a nice fluffy biscuit any day. I've had those bagel things. Tastes just like one of Maisie's donuts."

"He wants to see me—wants me back."

"Why?"

"How should I know?" Rory slammed the fork onto the countertop and whirled around to face her aunt. She rubbed her hands over her eyes, all the while castigating herself for being so defensive. "I'm sorry. This is so out of the blue, especially since he's supposed to be getting married. The jerk made a point of showing me the ring he bought Fiona before he dumped me." She gazed up at the ceiling and squeezed her eyes shut to hold back the burning tears. "He never proposed to me. Now I'm glad."

"You don't have to see him."

"See who?" Aunt Maisie wafted in on a cloud of Shalimar and bedecked in a flowing floral robe. She snagged a piece of bacon before heading to the coffee maker. "I always get in on the tail-end of conversations."

"Glen Peters."

Aunt Maisie gave a gentle cluck of her tongue. "Oh dear, that's a pisser."

"Sister, that's an understatement—and watch your language."

"You don't have to get sassy with me, Daisy Marie Callahan McDermott. I can understand Rory gettin' her knickers in a knot, but you got no cause to take your bad mood out on me."

"You're right. It's a pis—infuriating." Rory caught the frown on Aunt Daisy's face. "Really infuriating." She beat the eggs so hard they splashed onto the countertop. She grabbed a handful of paper towels. It would be wonderful if they cleaned up life's messes as easily as the goopy mess left by the eggs. She gave the slime a vicious scrub. "I don't want to see him and told him so."

"Good for you." Aunt Maisie poured a cup of coffee for herself.

Aunt Daisy gave her thumbs up. "Attagirl."

Rory didn't have her aunts' confidence to ignore the still aching wounds in her heart. Later that evening she met Callie, Chandra, Serena, and their friend Joy Nowell at the Cow Catcher Lounge. She told them about Glen.

There would be murder most foul if he'd come to hand-deliver an invitation to his wedding. That ought to keep her friendly neighborhood cop busy for a while. Callie had offered to give Rory a glowing character reference if she ever ended up in the pokey for doing Glen in.

It paid to have friends in high places.

Chapter Six

The cold water sluicing over Lachlan's head and shoulders felt like heaven. He turned off the outdoor faucet and dropped the hose to survey his hard work. His garden was planted. Neat rows of tomatoes and peppers, along with a few melon plants, made him smile. In a few weeks the entire thing would be lush and green. He'd also put in beans, beets, onions, lettuce, and a few rows of corn. Herbs sat in giant pots on the brick patio. *Not too bad for a city boy.*

He pressed his hands over his head to squeegee the remaining water from his hair, toweled off, and went inside to pull on some dry cargo shorts. The soft breeze coming through the bedroom window called him outside again.

Snagging a cold beer from the fridge, he opened the screen door. This time to relax on the patio. Once settled in the lounge chair he opened the book he planned to read. Although he'd left the world of being a homicide detective in St. Louis, he still enjoyed a good mystery.

Off in the distance the sound of a drill hummed. It harmonized with the frogs and dragonflies in the pond at the end of his property. It gave him an oddly contented feeling to know Rory was next door in her workshop.

The crunch of gravel caught his attention. Curiosity got the better of him. He put the book aside and ambled over to the fence. Maybe it *was* rude to check things out, but he reasoned it was the neighborly thing to do.

He leaned down and pulled off the bright yellow heads of the dandelions that grew along the length of the fence. It gave him a good excuse for being here. For a moment he feared he and Jenny Myers were soulmates.

A new black Lamborghini Urus pulled in front of Callahan Twins' house. A foreign car that cost more than their homes would make anyone in Hootiecackle take notice. The driver, a man with blond hair and a lean build, got out of the car. The guy loped up the steps of the porch and knocked on the front door. He prowled the porch waiting for someone to answer. Moment-by-moment, his pacing grew more agitated.

The twins were home, but Lachlan wondered if they had their hearing aids turned down. Rory's power tools were probably distracting them from their afternoon canasta practice. No one messed with canasta practice. He still bore the scars of interrupting them the first day he moved in.

He kept his gaze trained on the man as he came back down the steps and turned toward Rory's workshop.

The hairs on the back of Lachlan's neck stood.

Anger twisted the man's face. He marched toward the workshop with clenched hands. Lachlan made a note of the pink shirt and khaki slacks. Deck shoes, no socks. Sharp features. The guy pounded on the door and yelled for Rory. That should've gotten the Callahan ladies' attention. Still no answer.

Maybe he *was* being too nosy by scoping out the stranger, but the cop in him resolved to serve and protect. The sound of pounding fists made every muscle in Lachlan's body tense.

"Goddamnit, Rory. Open up. We need to talk." Pink

Shirt slapped his palms against the door. He yelled so loud that it was easy to eavesdrop.

"No." Rory's muffled response came back just as heated.

"You open up now!"

Pink Shirt pulled at the handle. "I'll kick this son of a bitch in."

Lachlan had had enough of this asshole. He ditched the weeds and hurdled over fence dividing the properties. No time to use the gate. Before he could get to the workshop Rory opened the door and pushed past the guy. He grabbed her by the arm. She slapped at his hand with a shriek of anger.

Heat exploded inside Lachlan's chest. A red veil of fury slipped over his eyes. His first instinct was to take the guy down. Instead, he forced himself to stroll over to Rory's workshop. It was imperative to assess the situation and de-escalate.

"Hey, Rory." He gave her a wave. "What's up? Got company?"

The dude whirled around to face him. "Yes, she does." His sneer made it clear he considered Lachlan to be an uncouth hick.

"Hi." It took everything Lachlan possessed to work up a smile. "You must be, Gregg, no—Grover, no—oh, who the hell did you say he was?" He walked between the guy and Rory, placing himself on Rory's right. He slipped his arm around her shoulder and hugged her to his side. "Now, Peaches, you know how bad I am with names."

Rory looked shell-shocked for a second, but she quickly caught on. "Glen. It's Glen Peters." Her body relaxed in his hold.

"Oh, that's right, Glen." He snapped his fingers and held out his hand, all the while giving her a slight squeeze of reassurance.

Peters hesitated for a split second, but finally shook Lachlan's hand. The last thing a man like Peters wanted to do was to lose face. His gaze raked over Lachlan with disdain before he turned to Rory. "Aren't you going to introduce me?"

Rory snuggled in closer. It might be for looks, but it sent Lachlan's blood pressure skyrocketing.

"Oh." She brushed back a bright lock of hair captured by the warm afternoon breeze. "This is Lachlan Donovan, actually Sergeant Lachlan Donovan."

Lachlan straightened his shoulders and smiled. "One of Hootiecackle's finest."

Her smile, though he knew it to be fake, dazzled. "Yes, he is fine."

Glen snorted. "Rory, you can do better than this."

Her green eyes glowed with fire. "Better than what?"

"Barney Fife here."

That hit below the belt, but Lachlan let it go. He clenched his teeth so much from smiling that his jaws ached. His back molars were probably dust by now. "Barney only had one bullet. I have a license to kill if the circumstances warrant."

"Yes, I've seen his gun," Rory piped up and patted his chest. "Big and scary."

She may not have meant the double entendre, but Peters' face turned bright red. Lachlan decided to go for broke.

"Now you're making me blush, Peaches." He put one finger under her chin to tip her face up to his for show. "Big yes, scary, no." Before he could talk himself out of it, he kissed her. It was supposed to be short, sweet and to the point. Her breath feathered his lips a second before his tongue brushed over the seam of her mouth, demanding entrance. Hot, sweet, and spicy. He hadn't expected this explosion of desire to hit him way below the belt. He burned and all he could do to quench the thirst was deepen the kiss. He held her face in the palms of his hand, brushing his thumbs over the smoothness of her cheek while he tasted her fire. Her little moan of pleasure drove him harder. Her taste made thinking impossible. All he could do was feel.

Rory's hands pushed against his chest. She pulled away. "PDA, big guy. Glen's watching." She stepped back, gently touching her lips with the tip of her fingers. "I'm sure The Aunts are at the window somewhere. Let's not give them a show."

Lachlan didn't care if he had an audience, all he wanted was more. Peters could disappear—all he cared about was tasting Rory again. "You can't blame a guy when your kiss tastes like peaches." The only thing that kept him from leaning down to kiss her again was the firm set of her mouth and dark green fire in her eyes.

Peters glared at Rory, to him, and back to her. "Rory, we need to speak alone."

"You've already said your piece in New Orleans."

****

"You need to leave—now." Rory lifted her chin. "I don't want to hear what you have to say."

"Five minutes. That's all I ask." Sunlight hit the pale highlights in his hair. She wondered why the sight used to make her giddy. Now he came across as what he really was—a man trying too hard to put on a show for everyone.

"No. I don't think I want to. I've got better things to do." Five more minutes of her life was too much to waste. She'd already lost so much time crying over the speed in which he dumped her the instant Fiona entered the picture.

"Please?" He cajoled. His smile was as fake as his heart. She could scream for the number of times she'd worked her butt off to get one of his smiles. Now she knew his true nature. Glen sucked people emotionally dry and threw them away when they no longer provided entertainment for his sick psyche. Besides, she couldn't think straight. Her head still buzzed from Lachlan's kiss. His mouth held a wealth of wonders, giving and taking with a rich dark taste that made her hungrier for more.

She ventured a quick glance at Lachlan. He stood beside her, looking so primal, wearing nothing more than denim shorts and flip-flops. Her reaction forced her to cross her arms over the thin knit fabric of her tank top. It was the only way to hide the way her body betrayed her. The quicker she got Glen out of here, the sooner Lachlan could take his hunky self back to his side of the fence.

The Aunts were probably doing a jig behind the curtains and thinking their plan had worked.

"Come on. You owe me that at least. You're the one who ran away." Glen's wounded words no longer had the ability to twist her heart. "Come back with me," he demanded.

"What part of *I don't want to have anything to do with you* do you not understand?"

"I thought we could start over." Glen smiled and held out his hands in supplication. "Remember all the fun times? The plans we had? You know we're made for each other."

Lachlan snorted. "As if."

The side-eye she gave Lachlan should've warned him to butt out. He smiled but it didn't reach his eyes as he stared at Glen.

"I heard you already had another woman?" Lachlan was brutal and to the point.

Glen's cheeks flushed red. "I don't have to answer to you."

"Yes, but I have a right to know." She was curious about his change of heart. It was petty, but she hoped Fiona tossed his sorry ass out the front door. "What's about Fiona?"

"She's history. She's nothing compared to you." Glen held out his hand as if Rory would come to him. "Let's start over."

"No."

"Please, have dinner with me tonight."

"She can't." Lachlan shook his head. "We already have plans."

Rory stared at him in surprise. "Oh?" She didn't know what scheme he had this time, but she was in if it kept her from breathing the same air as Glen. "Did you finally decide what you wanted to do tonight?"

"Yeah. I've got some steaks we can throw on the grill. Invite The Aunts over for dinner, and then we'll shoo them home and watch a movie later on."

"Sounds like a plan. Should we bring anything?" Rory held back the laugh at the stricken look on Lachlan's face. The "Oatmeal Raisin Cookie Incident" had been enough to warn him away from The Aunts cooking. "Potato salad, or dessert?"

"No, no." He held out his hand with a laugh. "This

is on me."

For a brief instant, she forgot about Glen and enjoyed the easy give and take with Lachlan.

"Rory!" Glen all but stomped his foot on the grass. "I came all this way to see you."

"Go back to Fiona. Maybe she'll take pity on you." It would take one more word from him and she decided to bitch slap him all the way back to The Big Easy.

"You don't understand," Glen pleaded.

She raised her hand but found it in a firm grip before she could follow through. Lachlan gaze swallowed her whole. "Let go." Her demand came out in a breathless squeak.

"No." He soothed his refusal with a smile.

Second by second, she glared at him in defiance. Finally, she dropped her hand, even if she still itched to smack Glen.

"Now see, you made Peaches angry. I can't have that." Lachlan went over to the Lamborghini, opened the door, and motioned for Glen to get in. "It's time to go."

Lachlan smiled at Glen's scathing glare.

"This isn't over." A hint of panicked whine slipped into Glen's voice when he slid into the driver's seat and slammed the door. He backed up and squealed his tires the moment his wheels hit asphalt. It was a childish move but one she expected from her ex.

Relief swamped her. When the last bit of dust cleared in the drive, she hoped she wouldn't have to see or hear from the jerk again.

"Dinner's at seven."

"What?" Lachlan's voice finally penetrated her thoughts.

"I said, dinner's at seven." He motioned with his

thumb toward his house. "Grilling with The Aunts."

"You don't have to do that." She shook her head. The last thing she needed now that she'd rid herself of one man was another to give her sleepless nights. No more men.

"I don't know what he wanted, other than to talk to you. It's none of my business, but I know the type. He won't let it rest."

"You're being overly suspicious."

"Peters has stalker written all over him." He stared in the direction of the road.

"Don't be silly." False bravado filled her nervous laugh.

"I trust my instincts." He bent down and gave her a quick kiss and flicked the end of her nose. "Don't forget, seven." With that, he turned and headed back toward his house.

"Wait," she called after Lachlan.

He continued to stroll to the gate, acknowledging her comment with a wave of his hand. "See you tonight, Peaches."

Chapter Seven

"Oh, lordy, did you see that kiss?" Daisy kept her nose pressed against the warm glass of the window. Her sister opted to plant herself in one of the bistro chairs and fan her face with her hand.

"Did I ever! The Plan is workin', Sister." Maisie closed her eyes with a smile, no doubt dreaming of Sally Anne Schrock's smothered pork chops. Once she got hitched, they'd hire the county's best cook and set her up in Rory's room. "Now we have to figure out how ta move it along a bit faster. The Jackson's will be movin' at the end of the summer and someone else could snap up Sally Ann before we can."

The lace curtains snapped shut with a quick flick of Daisy's wrist. "Any faster and I'll have to find Marvin's shotgun. I don't know what prompted the fireworks, but I'm not goin' to get nosy, and spoil it by askin' a lot of questions. Still—I got that itchy feelin' between my shoulder blades that says something ain't quite right."

"Well, we couldn't have planned it any better. Thank you, Baby Jesus, for makin' Glen pop outta nowhere—even if he is a rat bastard." Maisie rose to take a peek.

"Sister! Language." Daisy shook her head. When she got to the Pearly Gates, St. Peter would be asking why she hadn't been able to curb her sister's swearing. If she didn't get into heaven, she'd drag Maisie to hell alongside her. They came into the world together. They'd go out the same way. She looked through the curtains again. Lachlan and Rory were still in an animated conversation.

Her sister lowered to the other chair and sat with her chin in her hands. "I can't figure out what happened to get Lachlan and Rory together, but I'll take it.

As far as Daisy knew, they'd sworn off the opposite sex. "I don't care what it was, as long as it puts a kink in Glen Peters' shorts." She smiled in contentment and wanted to do a victory dance in the kitchen, but her knees were acting up today. Instead, they'd celebrate with a package of Nutter Butters. "I'd hoped Lachlan would punch that jerk in his pretty face. I know Rory would've if Lachlan hadn't stopped her deckin' him." She placed the cookies on a small plate.

"That kiss nearly set my panties on fire." Maisie's face pinked and she picked up a cookie. "I'll bet Glen feels like Rory gave him the Callahan Bash a bit lower."

Avery, their big black and white cat, sauntered in, jumped on Maisie's lap, and stuck his huge head through the curtains.

"There's nothing to see, Old Man." Maisie scrubbed the top of his head. "The floor show's over, but I must admit, it was quite entertainin'."

He gave a cat's version of a huff and settled in Maisie's lap for the petting that should follow such a disappointment. She obliged.

Daisy couldn't resist giving the cat's head a good scrub as well. "You are spoiled something fierce." Avery slit his eyes open barely enough to acknowledge her presence with catlike smug smile.

"You know, I thought I'd die when that poop-head

of a boyfriend showed up at the door."

"Language, Sister, language." Daisy absently tapped her finger against the side of her glass of her iced tea. "I don't see how Rory ever got mixed up with such a sissy. Maybe that's what women are goin' for nowadays. When we were young, we wanted Paul Newman or Robert Redford."

"At least Lachlan doesn't wear pink shirts. Who ever heard of such a thing?"

"Glen's here to cause trouble. I just know it." Daisy sipped her tea and pushed aside the curtain with one finger. Rory stood unmoving, staring at Lachlan's retreating figure. She flicked the curtain in place when Rory turned and marched in the direction of the back porch. "Here she comes. Act natural."

The door slammed, and Avery shot out of Maisie's lap to head for safety. Rory stomped in and stopped in the middle of the kitchen floor with her hands on her hips. "Can you believe the gall of the man?"

"Which one, dear?" Daisy picked up a cookie and nibbled on the edge, all the while pretending she hadn't practically pushed her face through the glass of the bay window.

"Glen shows up on my doorstep, asking me to forget our little *tiff* in New Orleans. He wants me to come *home*." Rory went to the pantry, dug around until she found the brown bottle of Amos' special blend, and poured two fingers worth in the bottom of a water glass. She tossed it back with one expert move and poured another. "Who the *hell* does he think he is? Back in New Orleans he even showed me the engagement ring he intended to give Fiona. Jerk." She swallowed the next shot with a grimace and wiped her mouth with the back of her hand.

"Oh, that's plum mean." Daisy's blood pressure shot up. Her head throbbed and she was close to letting fly with one of Maisie's favorite swear words.

Rory poured another shot.

Maisie frowned and shook a finger at Rory. "You should go easy on that stuff. It's for medicinal uses only."

"My heart aches." Rory thumped her chest as her eyes welled with tears. "Does that count?" She slammed the glass back onto the counter. "And to top it off, Lachlan kissed me."

"Oh, my. What was it li—"

Daisy gave a quick little shake of her head to keep Maisie from following that line of questioning. She'd almost blown it earlier when she'd asked which man. Rory didn't need to know they'd been spying on her.

Rory's face burned bright red. It could've been from the alcohol or memories of the kiss.

Daisy imagined she'd have fainted dead away if Lachlan kissed her, but Rory was forty years younger, and her hormones were in tip-top shape. Their sexy neighbor probably kindled a fire that Glen Peters could never hope to put out.

"Oh, and to top it off Lachlan invited everyone for a cookout at seven in front of Glen." Rory rinsed the glass and put it in the sink. Her eyes widened for a second. "Woo. I think I better lie down for a while."

"Really? A cookout!" Maisie's face lit up like a kid being offered a year's supply of ice cream. "Should we bring somethin'?"

"We're not going."

"Yes, we are." Daisy nodded in agreement with her

sister. "It would be outright rude to refuse."

"Good. You go. I plan to stay here and nurse a hangover." Rory picked up the bottle again, along with the glass.

"No, you're not." Daisy hauled her round frame out of the chair and stood toe to toe with her great-niece. She gently pried the bottle away and set it on the counter. "Victoria Shoiban Callahan, you're too old to throw a tantrum. He's just bein' neighborly. Besides, there's no need to spend any more tears on that creampuff. You take a nap, and when six thirty rolls around, I'll make sure you have time to freshen up."

"I'll whip up a batch of my famous oatmeal raisin cookies." Maisie clapped her hands in excitement and went to the cabinet to pull out the ingredients. "Or maybe I'll try my hand at chocolate chips again. Oh dear, I'm goin' for broke and make a chocolate cake."

A sour taste filled Daisy's mouth at the memory of Maisie's attempt at chocolate cake last week. She could still taste the burnt chocolate lingering on the back of her tongue. "Maisie, I just cleaned the kitchen. You better not dirty a dish."

Crestfallen, Maisie shoulders drooped. It was for the greater good.

"Lachlan said we don't need to bring anything." Rory shook her head, scowled, and touched her temples. "He's a smart man, our neighbor. Quick on his feet. Maybe a bit too smart." Her steps were unsteady as she carefully made her way out of the kitchen.

"She'll feel better after a nice lie-down." Maisie smiled. "This last batch of Amos' was pretty stout."

Daisy sat back in her chair with a sigh and gazed through the lace curtains in the direction of Lachlan's house. "It takes more than a couple of swigs of Amos' white lightning to put a wobble in Rory's step. I think she's finally met a man who can deliver the goods."

****

Rory watched Lachlan turn the steaks with well-practiced moves. His large hands were surprisingly graceful. She tried to forget the feel of them as they held her head gently, yet firmly for his kiss, but it was impossible. His fingers had caught little strands of her hair, his mouth worked magic. He was a much bigger danger than Glen could ever be. It was a good thing he had no interest in beginning a relationship. *Yes, it's a godsend.* Her logical brain said men were of the devil, but her hormones ran amok with a hundred different fantasies.

"How do you want yours?" Lachlan's voice feathered through her daydreams.

Hot, naked, and horny.

"What?" His startled question drew her up short. A lopsided grin graced the corner of his mouth. The wicked twinkle in his black eyes squeezed the air from her lungs.

Sweet Mother Mary, did I say that out loud?

"Ah, medium well, hot, naked, you know—no sauce, and I'll have some of the horn—err—corn." Thank goodness, she came up with something on the fly. Amos' hootch hadn't completely fried her brain.

"I didn't make any corn—just salad, beans, and baked potatoes." He flipped a steak over. "And there's homemade ice cream for dessert."

"Potatoes then. Definitely potatoes." She jumped to her feet as if spikes had shot out from the seat of her chair. Appetizers, salad, as well as the baked beans and potatoes were set out on the cheery, red-checked covered table. Rory filled her plate and picked an olive from the assortment in a bright red platter.

"Just wait a second." Lachlan grinned. "I'll give it to you—hot and naked, just like you like it."

Rory nearly choked on her olive. She bit her lip to keep from groaning, both from embarrassment and the return of unbidden thoughts of tumbling around under the sheets with the guy. Sex with Glen had its moments, nice moments, but deep inside, Rory knew Lachlan didn't have an ounce of *nice*. The idea of having sex with him made her palms sweat and her body hum with anticipation.

That's not going to happen.

"Why, dear, you usually bury a good cut like that in steak sauce." Aunt Daisy zeroed in on her face in concern before she gave her steak a small cut and inspected the insides. "Oh, goody. Well done." It was charred on the outside and gray through and through. Lachlan never once complained about having to ruin a high dollar cut of meat.

Aunt Maisie cut into her steak as well. Her's was nearly raw. "Sister, there's no wonder you can't cook if you think shoe leather is good to eat." She gave Lachlan a wide smile. "Now, this is a steak."

Rory's stomach flip-flopped at the sight of blood pooling on Aunt Maisie's plate like the aftermath of a gruesome sacrifice. She sat down and glanced away to nibble on her salad without seeing her aunt slurping away like a vampire.

"At least I like mine cooked, not just warmed through." Aunt Daisy snorted and took a bite of her overdone meat. "Yummy, yummy. Lachlan, you're a man after my own heart. Too bad I got over forty years on you."

"Ladies, there is no wrong way to eat a nice cut like this." It was confirmed. The man could lie with a straight face.

Lachlan forked a steak onto Rory's plate. "This one is medium well."

The next hour passed with The Aunts in fine fettle as they ate and gossiped with Lachlan about the people in Hootiecackle.

Aunt Maisie leaned back in her chair and rubbed her round stomach. "That was wonderful. I don't know when I've had such a wonderful meal. We usually eat frozen dinners and pizza."

"Except when we go to the Dinner Bell for Sunday lunch." Aunt Daisy leaned forward and patted his arm. "Why don't you come to church with us on Sunday and we'll treat you to dinner?"

"That would be nice, but I have to work." He spooned a bit of vanilla ice cream into his mouth. "Weekends are for the family men."

Rory's heart fluttered at the sight of his mouth wrapping around the bowl of the spoon.

"Oh, that's too bad." Aunt Daisy pursed her lips and tapped them with one finger. "We'll think of something."

Aunt Maisie's face lit up. "I know. I can make my famous chocolate cake after all."

"No!" Rory and Aunt Daisy yelled in unison.

"That sounds ah—ah—delicious—I mean interesting." Lachlan held up his hand to wave away her suggestion. "But it's too hot to cook in the kitchen."

"That's not a problem." Aunt Maisie's green eyes glowed with anticipation. "We have air conditionin'."

Rory managed to hide her snort of laughter behind a

napkin. Lachlan needed to learn that it was impossible to outmaneuver a Callahan woman once she got a notion fixed in her head.

"Why don't you make me a pitcher of lemonade, instead?" He beamed a smile at Aunt Maisie that made her cheeks pinken.

"With, or without Amos?"

"Huh?" For once he looked out of his depth and turned to Rory for clarification.

"Never mind." Rory settled her napkin back into her lap. "You can make plain lemonade, Aunt Maisie."

"Good, good." She patted her silver curls. "I'm not one to be stingy with my ingredients, but I'm a little low on Amos right now, thanks to Rory here."

"That sounds great." Lachlan rose and leaned down to take Rory's hand in his.

She tried to pull away, but he held tight.

"Ladies, it's been fun cooking for someone other than myself." He helped Rory to her feet and did the same for each of her aunts. "I'm going to borrow your niece to help me with the dishes. We might watch a movie later."

"Oh, yes." Aunt Maisie clapped her hands in approval. "That sounds like fun."

Aunt Daisy gave him the hairy eyeball. "I suppose it will be okay."

"Rory, make sure you do a good job." Aunt Maisie grabbed her sister's arm to drag her away. *Good grief, could they be any clearer about their intentions to push her and Lachlan together.*

"I will." She glared at Lachlan. He knew what they were up to. Why was he going along with their madness? "I can't stay for a movie." The first excuse she could think of popped out of her mouth. "I need to get up early and strip the paint off that old dresser I picked up in Rockville."

"You told me you were done with that." Aunt Maisie narrowed her eyes.

What was going on here? Callahan women should stick together. The Aunts probably saw this as a golden opportunity to push The Plan.

"The *other* dresser," she shouted as they waddled across the yard and through the gate.

"When did you haul in another dresser?" Aunt Daisy yelled back over the fence. "You better not be lyin'. Should I look in the workshop or are you goin' to help Lachlan. Hmmm?"

"Okay, okay!" She knew when she'd been tag teamed. "Yes." She turned to Lachlan. "I will dry the dishes and watch a movie, but it better be an action-adventure. I'm in no mood for a chick-flick."

Chapter Eight

Lachlan slid the last dish into the washer and closed the door. He glanced over to where Rory stood, back against the granite countertop, with her arms and a small pout on her face.

"You didn't need me here to help you with the dishes." She straightened and headed toward the back door. "I'll pass on the movie."

"Okay, I admit it was a ruse, a dastardly plan to get you into my clutches." He twisted the knob on the dishwasher to start the cycle. "I thought you might like to relax, get away from the stress of this afternoon. Besides, it will get those two loveable, but insistent matchmakers off our case."

"How do you figure that? This will only throw gas on the fire. No matter how much you insist you're not looking for a woman, they have a target plastered right between your eyes." Rory's finger poked the middle of his forehead. "You've pulled the trigger. I'm convinced The Aunts saw the kiss. It's a self-inflicted wound, so don't blame me if Aunt Maisie shows up with some banana nut bread and ulterior motives. It would serve you right."

He gently removed her finger but kept hold of her hand. His heart twisted in the nicest way. She'd caught him off guard. "I've been shot in the line of duty." His thumb grazed over the top of it, amazed at the silkiness of her skin, considering how much she put them through. "I think I can survive a loaf of banana nut bread."

She gave a little tug, and he reluctantly released his prize.

"Considered yourself warned." Rory lifted her chin in defiance. "I want you to know the kiss meant nothing so don't read anything into it."

"Okay."

She swiped her hand in the air and shook her head. "Don't a think it's an invitation to, well—"

"Okay."

Her green eyes narrowed in irritation. He could tell from the thinning of her lush lips that she didn't like him agreeing so easily.

"I know you were pulling some *my dick is bigger than your dick* thing with Glen, but it was uncalled for."

He went to the refrigerator, pulled out a beer, and gave a quick twist of the top. No matter how calm he appeared on the outside, the word *dick* tumbling from her mouth made his temperature soar. A long guzzle gave him a few precious seconds to get himself under control. Rory was right, he wasn't on the lookout for a woman. This one would be big trouble. He could see it from the top of her head down to her toes. She was like a grenade, and he'd pulled the pin. "You don't know."

"Know what?" Rory cocked her head to one side as if he spoke to her in tongues.

"If my dick is bigger than his."

"Of all the—"

"Hey, you brought it up first." He shrugged his shoulders and swirled the beer around in the bottle. "I know what kind of guy you like—someone with a galloping sense of entitlement and an ego to match.

Urban, cultured, and with boatload of money."

The mulish expression on her face was both adorable and maddening at the same time.

"What's wrong with that?"

He raised his brow in question.

"Just because Glen is an asshole doesn't mean every guy who fits that description is one," she huffed.

Lachlan stepped closer until they were nose-to-nose. He put his beer bottle down and braced one hand on the granite counter, alongside her hips. The light floral scent of her perfume kicked his desire into overdrive. Her mouth tempted him as surely as the moment Eve reached out to Adam with the apple. Unable to help himself, he traced the line of her cheek bone with his thumb. Memories of Kate were overshadowed by the woman in front of him. He knew he would regret getting entangled, even for a few minutes, with Rory. The guilt would come later in the night. "I think you're lying."

"Lying?" Rory blinked and backed up a few inches until her rear hit the counter. "About what?" She moved her face away. Her chin went up.

"The kiss. How long has it been since a man, and I'm loosely including Glen in that description, got you fired up like you were this afternoon?"

****

Lachlan was right. She'd lied about the kiss.

His nearness threw what was left of Rory's brain right out the window. She couldn't think with him surrounding her. It threatened her on a primal level—one that left her giddy from the bubbling sensations coursing throughout her body. His intense gaze smoldered, nailing her to the spot. The simmering ache in her body grew stronger with each breath she took. She pulled in the tantalizing mixture of warm man, wood smoke from the grill, and the faint whiff of beer. His mouth was only a whisper away. If she made the effort, took that last step, she could taste him again, and thrill at the heady rush she'd experienced this afternoon. No, she wasn't about to give in so easily. Glen had won her heart, broke it, stomped on it, and left it to die. She couldn't afford another relationship. Not with anyone. But she wasn't about to let Lachlan have the last word about the kiss. "I followed your lead."

"That doesn't explain why you responded." Lachlan's smile lit up his dark eyes. "You put a lot of tongue into it for someone who was playing along."

"I didn't." Her breathless denial and refusal to look him in the eye ratted her out.

"Liar, liar, pants on fire."

Her chin tilted up a fraction, but she refused to look him in the eye. "That is so childish."

"Then kiss me again and prove me wrong."

"I don't think so."

Lachlan leaned down to whisper in her ear. "Coward."

His warm breath sizzled the skin of her cheek and neck. It would be so easy to turn her face to him and give him what he wanted. *No. No. No.* It didn't matter if he smelled like sin and barbeque. She had to keep some semblance of control. "It's an obvious ploy to get me to comply." She put her hands on his chest and pushed.

"I call it like I see it, but I'd never force you." Lachlan backed away and picked up his beer again. "No is no. Pure and simple." He smiled and pointed toward the back door with his bottle. "Go home. Tell your aunts we couldn't agree on a movie."

"I didn't agree to any of this." She threw her hands in the air. "My aunts pushing a man on me, especially a cop, and then getting kissed by said cop, wasn't my idea."

"That's Sergeant Donovan to you."

"If I wanted to be manhandled by a man in uniform, I can always call Studly Do Right, because he *always* does right." She hitched her hip up on one side and crossed her arms over her chest, as if daring him to touch her.

He wasn't about to take the bait. His mouth twitched with a hint of a smile. "I'll just bet. Could be false advertising."

"He gets top dollar." She gave him the sweetest smile she could muster. "I should know."

"I'm beginning to think Chief Nolan was right. You're nothing but trouble."

"He said that?" Disgust mixed with disbelief caused her to squeak. "About me?"

"I hear you were a handful in high school."

For the space of a heartbeat, her mind threw her back to those dark days after her parents died. No one wanted her except The Aunts. "Yeah, I was." She nodded in agreement. "I wore black, went totally Goth on The Aunt's. Poor things."

"Why?"

"Why not." She shrugged. "Long story."

"Life's full of long stories."

"What's so hard about your life that you ended up here? I heard you couldn't take it in the big city."

"You're right. I'd had it after years of watching people murder each other over nothing more than a few bucks." He waved his hand around in an all-inclusive motion. "Now I have the good life."

She knew there had to be more to his story. Nobody moved to Hootiecackle on a whim.

"You better go. There's the dresser that you need to finish stripping in the morning." He heaved a heavy sigh and went to the back door. He opened it with a gallantness that would do anyone named Jeeves proud. "I want an early start on the garden."

The hollow victory made the breath sink in Rory's lungs. Part of her wanted him to kiss her again. The other part wanted to charge out of the house with all the hair-flinging, *your're-not-the-boss-of-me* bravado of a bad romance novel. "I haven't been very gracious this evening. Thank you for helping me out earlier today. Even the kiss was—nice."

"Ouch. There goes the ego." He leaned against the counter. Lachlan's brow rose to challenge her. "Better go. If not, kiss me."

"Are you giving me an ultimatum?"

"I see it as a choice." He shrugged. "Unlike you friend, Grover—"

"Glen, his name is Glen." Little prickles of irritation ran through her. How had he managed to get her back up over a man she could no longer stand? "It's easy to remember—one syllable, unless that's beyond your," she pointed to her head and made little circles, "mental capabilities."

"Don't worry, my brain is fine, but thank you for the concern." He gave her a slow, panty melting smile. "You know where I live if you need help getting rid of him. Your aunts have me on speed dial."

She touched the bruise on her arm, above her elbow. "This is the first time he's been physical with me.

Believe me, I can take care of myself. I have a black belt in taekwondo.

"I never said you couldn't, but it doesn't hurt to have backup." He motioned her out the door. "Go on, go home. Sleep tight, don't let the bed bugs bite."

Rory was at a loss for words. No quick, witty response rolled off her tongue, instead, she glared at Lachlan, squared her shoulders, and started down the path to the gate. The door closed behind her and the kitchen light went out.

"Go home. Sleep tight." How was she supposed to do that when the man had her riled up? His offhand dismissal fueled the fires of her anger. Glen coming back, unannounced, and unwanted, along with Lachlan's lackadaisical attitude to *the kiss* stirred everything into an inferno. She got as far as the end of the patio before she turned around and glared at the back door. He was probably settling in with a movie without giving her a second thought. Well, she'd see about that. "Don't let the bed bugs bite."

Two heartbeats later had her pounding on his back door.

The light came back on and Lachlan opened the door. He stood in silhouette with his forearm resting on the doorjamb and a hip cocked to one side.

"Yes?"

Rory gave him a little push. He stood rock solid where he stood.

"Did you forget something?" The slight chuckle in his voice riled her up even more.

She narrowed her eyes and set her hands on her hips. "I'll show you who bites, you big jerk."

One kiss to rock his world, and I'm out of here.

She grabbed him by the front of his dark blue t-shirt and pulled his mouth to hers. For the briefest second, he stiffened, and then relaxed. She snaked one arm around his neck while her hand reached up to touch his cheek. His stubble raked against the tips of her fingers as they slid upward. The tingle of sensation sent little shockwaves of delight sizzling throughout her body.

She drew him closer.

The whisper of his breath heated her lips a second before she seared her mouth against his. Desire overwhelmed her until she couldn't catch her breath. His first kiss had made her knees weak, but this time, the first touch of his tongue against hers sent her into a tailspin of delight. She had to maintain control, fought for it. Waves of intense sensation, the emptiness that demanded to be filled overcame her. She melted and leaned forward into the kiss.

Despite her best efforts, she surrendered.

His mouth continued to work magic she'd only heard about but never felt before today. She couldn't stand it any longer—she needed to touch his skin.

Her hand worked under the hem of his T-shirt. The hard planes of his stomach made her gasp with pleasure. He was warmth and silk.

A deep longing throbbed between her legs. Her breath came in small pants even as his tongue tangled with hers in an erotic simulation of what she really desired.

He pulled back, his forehead resting on hers. "I want you."

"Good, I think we're on the same page." She threw back her head as his mouth lowered and grazed the tender skin under her jaw. Her hand reached for the snap of his jeans.

His hand covered hers.

"Don't start anything you don't intend to finish."

"I always finish my plate, never start a project in my workshop without giving it that last bit of polish." Her fingertips brushed over his denim-covered backside. "Believe me."

"Good to know." Lachlan kept his arm around her waist and walked backward into the kitchen. He closed the door. His mouth swooped down on hers, his hands on either side of her face.

The fire he kindled burst into full flame. Her earlier emotions were nothing compared to the clawing desire eating her alive.

"Shirt, shirt." His kiss muffled her words, but she tugged at the hem and drew it up past his chest. "Hurry."

He didn't have to be asked twice. The shirt flew over his head, her skirt followed, until their clothes left a trail to the bed. They fell together on the dark blue duvet and the mattress gave a healthy bounce.

Rory couldn't keep a giggle back. "Whoa! Is this a bed or a trampoline?"

Lachlan's laughter rumbled against her shoulder. "Want to find out?" His hand slid over the tender skin of her breast.

The smart-assed remark she started to make stuck in her throat. All she could do was feel—and moan in pleasure. Never before had she'd been so out of her mind with desire. Glen could walk around naked, hard as a rock, and with a rose clamped between his teeth and she'd laugh. One touch of Lachlan's hand and she'd turned to butter. She needed him inside of her.

"I'm going to die if you don't make love to me — right now."

Oh, no! That did not pop out of my mouth.

Chapter Nine

Lachlan's heart slammed against his ribs. He couldn't breathe.

He and Rory lay in a sprawled heap of arms and legs. All he could do was to hold on to her and nestle his head in the crook of her neck. Her veins fluttered against his mouth. The salt taste and the hint of her perfume did little to steady the aftermath of their explosive sex. He wondered if he'd ever be able to walk again.

"Ugh." Rory gave him an insistent push. "Got to breathe here, big guy." The distress he heard was real.

His little bubble of fantasy burst. It was all he could do to ease off her and flop over with his forearms over his eyes. "Breathing is good. Tell me when there's some oxygen in the air. I think we burnt it all away."

The bed jostled. A quick glance from under his arm revealed her sitting, gloriously naked, on the edge of the bed, bending down to grab her clothes. A pang of regret hit him. He should've taken more time with her. As fast as she was moving, he doubted there'd be another chance to prove he wasn't a complete clod.

"Damn, damn, damn." Her muffled words came from inside her blue green tank top. "I can't believe I did that." Her head popped out and she tugged her long hair out of the neckline. Bright red stained her peachy complexion. "No, I really can't—what got into me?" The panic in her voice grew stronger.

"I'd say that was obvious." He sighed in contentment. "It was spectacular."

"I didn't say *it* wasn't—*it* shouldn't have happened." She stood and wriggled into her panties. He had to hold back a groan of pleasure as two ivory globes danced in front of his eyes. "The plan was to kiss you and knock your socks off."

"Mission accomplished, along with everything else." His small attempt at humor fell flat. Her expression was stony. "Are you sure you don't want to use the bathroom to shower?"

Horror flickered through her green eyes. "No." She slipped the skirt over her hips and looked around the room. "I'll have to keep out of sniffing distance. The Aunts have noses like bloodhounds. All they need is the scent of fresh soap or sex to send them rocketing down the matrimonial path with us as the toppers on a cake."

"Well, I've got to take care of some business." He stood and started to the bathroom but turned around with the niggling sensation that she'd bolt at the first chance. "Don't go anywhere."

He returned, ready for a talk. His hunch proved right. She'd shot out of the house the minute his back was turned. The only thing left of Rory was the rumpled side of the bed.

After Kate he hadn't looked at another woman, even wanted to, for that matter. However, the sight of Rory being manhandled by Glen kickstarted his "white knight syndrome." as Kate used to call it. She'd always teased how he couldn't stand by and let the elderly, little puppies or any woman cry out for help.

The wave of guilt he expected had lessened. It wasn't gone but the ragged edges had dulled. He'd never forget Kate. Love was love. There'd been so little time after her diagnosis of pancreatic cancer. He'd gone from a lover to a caretaker, but he hadn't minded. She'd been his life. Now her memory was placed in a spot that only he could find. The crack in his heart had begun to mend.

That didn't mean he was looking for a woman to settle down with. There were some big potholes left in his soul that needed patching. The evening with Rory took him by surprise and the most surprising part was discovering how much he liked his crazy, sexy neighbor.

He lay back on the bed, in the spot left vacant by his on-the-run lover, with his arms behind his head. If he knew the Callahan Twins, they would be lying in wait. A smile twitched at the corner of his mouth.

Maybe I should've told Rory she had her tank top on inside out.

****

Rory grimaced at the groaning protest of the back door. She vowed to hit every door hinge in the house with a good shot of WD-40 in the morning. It hadn't made this much noise on the way over to Lachlan's—why now? It ratted her out like a convict with a juicy piece of incriminating evidence against a fellow inmate.

The Aunts had the hearing of bats.

She waited, holding her breath, and prayed for a quick trot through the kitchen without detection. A glance around the kitchen showed it to be aunt free. She breathed a quiet *hallelujah* and headed toward the stairway to go up to her bedroom.

A faint glow came from the living room. The Aunts always left it on for her when she'd gone out on a date when she lived here before. She made it to the darkened hallway leading to the stairs.

Lucy looked up from her doggy bed in the corner and yipped with excitement.

"Quiet, Lucy Loo." Rory's attempt to *shush* the dog failed. Avery sprawled on his belly, back legs out, with his head on his paws. One eye opened, giving her a baleful glance before it snapped shut.

"Is that you, Rory?" Aunt Maisie toddled from her bedroom hallway with a deck of cards in her hand. "Come on, join us. We could use a third hand. Daisy and I are gettin' ready to play two-handed canasta." She motioned Rory into the living room. "A third hand would be great. We have to hone our skills for the big tournament at the country club."

Aunt Daisy's head popped up over the high back of the Victorian, blue velvet sofa. She held up a plate of crackers topped with orange swirls of spray cheese. "Cracker?"

"No." Rory's refusal came out in a squeak.

"It's been—" Daisy's mouth snapped shut.

Two pairs of identical green eyes narrowed.

"What?" She did a mental check. Her skirt wasn't caught up in the back in her rush to get out of Lachlan's house, flip-flops were on the right feet, and she'd finger-combed her hair into some semblance of order on her way across the back yard.

They continued to give her the once-over.

"What!"

"Oh, nothin'." Aunt Maisie ambled over to the card table. Her sister got off the couch with a small *oomph* and carried her snack with her.

"Did you and Lachlan have a *nice* time?" Aunt Maisie's southern, butter-wouldn't-melt-in-her-mouth simper was The Callahan Twins' code for "did you screw your brains out?"

"Ah—yes—yes we did." She cleared her throat. "He's a very considerate host."

Geez, Louise. That sounds lame—even to me. She had the same gut-twisting, cotton mouthed sensation she had at fifteen when she'd been caught sneaking in late at night.

"Whad'ya watch? Action adventure, comedy, porn?" Aunt Daisy didn't hold any punches. It tempted Rory to say "all three" but there was no use in riling her up.

"Some science fiction thing." She shrugged and continued with her lie. "One of those Star Something-or-others. Part one or two."

"I'm surprised you didn't stay for part three, especially since you were havin' such a 'nice time.' "

Aunt Maisie handed her sister the cards. "I suppose you weren't distracted by his tasty lookin' hiney?"

Rory choked. She wanted to disappear. Her neck and cheeks heated with the flame of embarrassment, but that didn't stop the onslaught.

"Or those blacker than black eyes," Aunt Daisy sighed in appreciation. "I'd grab him up if it were me. Why, I saw him fixin' his car the other day and the man is built like a brick—"

"Stop it right there." Rory held up her hand and shook her head. "You guys are reading way too much into this. It was a movie. That's all."

"I'll buy that for a dollar," Aunt Daisy snorted.

"I'm going to my room. It's a hot shower and then off to bed for me." Rory flounced out of the living room and up the stairs to her bedroom. She kicked off her flip-flops and jerked the silver hoops from her ears, the whole time fuming about the lack of privacy and nosy old ladies.

Her sense of indignant outrage died a sad, horrible death the instant she caught her reflection in the mirror. It wasn't her overly bright eyes or flushed face that brought her up short. A few minutes with the Aunts caused that reaction.

Her tank top was inside out.

Busted.

****

A quick shower hadn't cooled his desire for Rory. *This was insane.* He paced the bedroom trying to figure when she'd gotten under his skin. One-night stands weren't the way he rolled, yet the rumpled bed and Rory's perfume on the pillow made a liar of him.

The Callahan Twins had been so apparent in their rush to push him and Rory together. He'd only wanted to oblige them by playing along for a bit. Maybe it might give them both a little breathing room from well-intentioned matchmaking. To be honest, he hadn't thought a bit of flirting would get so out of hand.

Not that Rory hadn't been complicit in the deed. He was lost the second he opened the door and she kissed him.

He ran his hands through his hair and headed out to the patio where he sank into a lawn chair and stared at the night sky. The smell of the extinguished charcoal mixed with the lingering aroma of the steaks rode on the slight breeze.

Hot, naked, and horny.

He thought he'd choke on his beer when the words popped out of Rory's mouth. At first he couldn't believe she said them but her horror-stricken face and fast save confirmed it. The tiny gasps from her aunts turned into the faked innocence of chattering about his garden but they cast sly glances in their direction.

Where did he go from here? It wasn't as if Rory was some unknown woman he'd picked up at a bar and could forget about. She lived on the other side of the fence.

The neat, nice plans he had when he first came to Hootiecackle were blown sky-high by a pair of green eyes. He'd taken a small bite from the apple—now he wanted the whole damn apple pie.

No wonder poor Adam was a screwed-up mess.

****

Maisie didn't know whether to be outraged or laugh like a loon. She shuffled the deck and swiftly dealt the cards

"I didn't have the heart to remind Rory to check her clothes after a romantic encounter. Lord knows my Alfred and I almost got caught by Mama when I ended up with my sweater on backward. It took a lot of fast talkin' to convince her that wearing the buttons down the back was the new Paris trend." She lifted her hand skyward. "Thank you, Baby Jesus, she believed me."

Surprise and understanding rounded Daisy's eyes. "So that was it! Mama was always a snob. No wonder the ladies in the choir were staring at you that Sunday morning."

"Come on. Let's play. I need to practice my bluffing technique. If I can fool you, the other players are toast."

"What a nice thing to say, Sister."

Maisie frowned and turned over a card. "Should we go easy on Lachlan and Rory? I feel they skipped over several steps in the courting process."

"That may be, but the deed's already done." Daisy

sighed and leaned back in her chair. "Let's see how things go. I hope Rory is really over that Glen guy."

"I'd be inclined to slap her silly if she isn't." The cards shuffled and snapped together in Maisie's expert hands. "Or, if she lets Lachlan get away. She's already baited the hook—she just has to reel him in."

"So right, Sister. So right. Now, deal."

Chapter Ten

The sight of Serena Moondancer standing in front of the Funky Junk Shoppe was a balm to Rory's tattered nerves. Between her irritation at Glen and the way she'd fallen into Lachlan's bed it was a wonder she could even function. Her night was filled with tossing and turning while questioning her sanity.

"Good morning." Serena raised a dark brow. "I'm sorry I missed the bachelorette party. Mom called and made it sound like an emergency. I hot tailed it to her place only to find she was having one of her spells."

"All I can say is the party didn't quite go as planned." Rory shrugged.

"That's because it was *your* party."

"Is your mom okay?"

"Yes. She keeps saying the grim reaper is around the corner, but she'd finished up her hot yoga class a few minutes before I got to Eureka Springs."

"She's always been a hypochondriac."

"You'd think a psychic would know when she was going to die, but that's not the way it works." Serena held out a cardboard carton of to-go cups from the local coffee shop with a wink. "Agnes suggested you could use a pick-me-up this morning." She nodded her head in the direction of her half of the old bank building. Not only was it Serena's business but she lived on the upper floor. "I left her and Henry arguing over which you'd want—

the caramel macchiato or a white mocha."

"Agnes and Henry?"

"My upstairs neighbors. You know. On the third floor." She pointed to the ceiling.

"If you say so." This wasn't the time to get into it over the reality of ghosts or anything else in the ether. Rory didn't believe in ghosts but as long as she'd known Serena her belief was as real as Rory's wasn't.

Josie Tally, Theo's younger sister, opened the door. She was eager to learn, and sharp. Rory went inside with Serena following. Early morning light shone through the display window and mixed with the light from the antique brass fixtures giving the shop the glow of times past. Vintage items from tea sets to clothing filled the space in a way designed to make the customer roam from area to area. This was her second home.

"Give me the macchiato." Rory reached out, wriggling her fingers in demand.

"Agnes is never wrong. Here you go, Josie. One white mocha for you." Serena handed Josie the other cup. She pulled the remaining drink from the carton. "Chai for me."

Serena looked every inch the owner of a New Age shop. Her black lawn cotton dress flowed down her petite, yet slender frame ending in a lace edged, handkerchief hem. Black button up shoes with purple roses embroidered on the toes completed the look. Most shoppers would say her clothes were designed to add atmosphere to the shopping experience. They would be wrong. Serena not only loved Goth, she lived it.

A chill rolled into the room. "Josie, can you go check the thermostat? It's cold in here." Goosebumps scattered over Rory's arms with prickly abandon. Every hair on her arm stood at attention. She swore there were little frozen puffs of breath coming from her mouth when she spoke. *For goodness sake. It's nothing.*

"Don't bother, it's only them." Serena pointed toward the ceiling before taking a dainty sip of her tea. "They decided to join us." Her friend swore much of her information about the residents of Hootiecackle came from her roommates, if ghosts could be considered roommates. Agnes and Henry Purcells had been victims of a bank robbery back in 1929 and refused to leave their home above the bank.

"Maybe you should've brought more coffee." Half the people in Hootiecackle believed Serena was the real deal. More likely it was nothing more than gossip gleaned while giving tarot readings and her friend's intuitive nature. It was hard for Rory to keep from rolling her eyes. "Serena, I'm used to your weirdness, but Josie just began working here. Don't start on your ghost stories."

"My granny says there's people like Miss Serena who got the sight. I know better than to argue with Granny. Besides, everyone in town knows all the Moondancer women are gifted."

"From the mouths of babes. I'm gifted. Josie, be a dear and put your hands over your ears." Serena leaned over and patted Josie on the hand with all the aplomb of a black draped southern belle. "I'm about to go R rated here."

"Hey, if I can get into R-rated movies, I can hear what you're goin' to say." Her smile beamed with anticipation. "What happened?"

Probing violet eyes focused on Rory's face. "Agnes says you and that delicious, her words not mine, Lachlan fellow partook in some horizontal refreshment last night. Henry was a little more graphic."

Heat rose up Rory's neck and into her cheeks. Even making a slashing motion across her neck to silence Serena had little effect.

"Agnes had to fan herself while giving me the juicy deets."

Josie cocked her head to one side in confusion. "Horizontal refreshment?"

"He rocked her world." Serena's smug comment came with a nod of certainty.

The girly *squeee* coming from Josie could've replaced the tornado sirens in town.

"Cut it out. Tell the Purcells to mind their own business, not that I believe in that mumbo jumbo. How the hell do they know this stuff?"

"I never asked." Serena leaned against a large walnut armoire with her hands across her chest. "They didn't tell me."

Rory reached under the counter for a pack of antique French tarot cards she'd found at an auction. It was meant as a gift for Serena's birthday next week. Right now, she needed a diversion. She thrust it at Serena. "Here. Go next door and play with your little friends. I have to open the shop."

Serena took the cards and turned them over in her hand. The way her eyes twinkled said Rory had made a big hit. "Oh, these are so cool. I have a reading this afternoon. Speaking of which, I have to clean and set up in the back room. The tourists like atmosphere but not dust." She headed for the door and waved. "Play safe, my friend."

"Don't worry. I plan to stay on my side of the fence

from now on." A quick glance at the clock said nine had rolled around. It was time to begin the workday. Josie raised the blinds and filled the cash in the register before Rory unlocked the door. Sightseers on their way to Branson were already glancing in the store window at the enticing array of wares she'd put there to attract attention. She turned to Josie. "You did not hear a thing."

"I wanted to let you know that Theo put in his application at the police station." Josie stuffed the last of the ones into the till. "We're keepin' our fingers crossed."

"He'll do fine." Rory crossed her fingers behind her back as well. Chief Nolan was a rat bastard, but she hoped Lachlan might be able to make him see Theo would be an asset to the department. "Maybe I ought to go next door and have Serena whip up a charm."

"I thought you didn't believe in that stuff."

"Let's say I'm skeptical but anything is possible. I went through a Goth phase when I was a kid, did the Ouija board and all that stuff. Serena, Chandra, Joy and I ran around all over town together. Chandra was Sandra Dee while Serena and I were Elvira and Morticia. Joy was, well, Joy. A strange combination but we had to admit Serena was—special. So I'll ask her for that charm."

"Don't bother. Theo doesn't believe in superstitious nonsense as he calls it, although he likes Miss Serena well enough." Josie's smile tickled one corner of her mouth. "He don't take crap off of Chief Nolan, either." She sprayed the counter with polish and ran the dust cloth over it. "By the way, we sold that Blue Willow place settin' after you left yesterday."

Rory frowned at the sight of a table filled with

various odds and ends. There was a glaring hole in the display that needed to be filled. "Would you go to the storeroom and get the antique spoons. I think—" she let her mind run through the inventory she knew she had.

"—and there's a pink teapot with matching cups. Bring those as well."

Josie gave her a friendly salute and went to the back of the store.

The *ding* from the small brass bell mounted on the front door of the shop made Rory look up from her task of re-arranging one of the displays. Glen stood there in tan designer slacks and a soft blue polo shirt. He wore his brown Ferragamo loafers without socks.

"Good morning, *Peaches.*" His practiced smile was designed to light up the room. She wasn't impressed.

"Very funny. Josie!"

The young woman raced from the storeroom with a fistful of silver teaspoons. "Miss Rory?" Alarm shone in her eyes. "Is anything wrong?"

"No. Why don't you take those spoons next door for Serena?" A quick nod in Glen's direction was all she needed to communicate with Josie to leave. "Now." She wanted to get the kid out of the store in case Glen did something stupid. She had to admit one thing that Lachlan said. Once someone begins getting physical, they could do it easier the next time. The last thing she wanted to do was to put Josie in harm's way. Rory had a black belt, even if she'd been caught off guard yesterday. Today she'd stay alert for any pushiness.

"Will do, Miss Rory." Josie hightailed out of the shop so fast the bell clattered against the old oak door.

Rory turned her attention back to Glen. His smug smile made her stomach roll. Anger coursed through her.

How dare this man come into a place she worked so hard to make her own.

"What do you want?" She wasn't about to give him any of her precious time. He had no idea of what she had to endure to uproot herself and start over.

He shook his head and *tsked*. "Don't be like that."

"Like what?"

"So bitter."

The snarky remark hit a nerve, but she maintained her cool. His infidelity had a bite with teeth that had rent her soul to pieces. Now she looked back on her anguish and realized it was for nothing. She smiled. Glen's startled reaction was a balm to the hurt he'd inflicted. "Not bitter. Informed."

Surprise and anger played over Glen's face. It was clear he hadn't expected her to be rational and collected. In the past she did her best to cajole him into a better humor to keep the peace, for the business and their relationship. No more.

"That's good." He glanced around the store to deflect from the conversation. "You have a cute place here. Very homespun." The jibe failed to hit its mark.

"I think so."

He frowned at her lack of response. "You've always had a knack for design." He reached out and repositioned a delicate Capodimonte floral centerpiece. "Come back to New Orleans. I'll make you a full partner. We worked well together."

"There's nothing for me there. My life is here. Friends, family, a good—social life." She put the porcelain centerpiece in its original position on the table. "Being a partner wouldn't suit me. Fiona might have some objections."

"Fiona is—this isn't about her. The clients want what we used to give them. With you gone it's not the same."

A smile touched one corner of her mouth. Her finger traced the pale pink rose of the centerpiece. "Really?"

She'd been the real talent behind the business.

A flush of red colored his artfully stubbled cheeks. He jammed his fists into his slacks pockets. "I need you," he ground out. "Some of my biggest clients have left."

Bingo. There it was. The reason for his visit.

"It's a good thing I didn't buy into the business—or marry you." She pressed her lips together and forced herself to smile. "If you need a boost to your career, just ask Fiona's daddy for help."

"I can't." His gaze dropped to the floor. "Fiona left me."

"Why?"

"I discovered how much I love you." His sigh was loud and long. "I was w—wrong." The strangled word sounded as if stuck in his throat. He was as transparent as the glass window showing the growing traffic outside her store.

Her snort of laughter had him dropping the mask of ardent lover. "Damn it, Rory—"

"You cheated on Fiona, didn't you?"

The expression on his face was priceless. "How did you—"

"Oh, honey, you're a one trick pony, but you do it *so* well." She turned away, but he grabbed her by the upper arm. "Let go." He chose to ignore her soft warning.

"I'll do anything." His grip tightened. "You need to get out of this small town. I don't believe for a moment you're interested in that hick cop."

She'd had enough. Glen was on his ass and staring at the beautiful tin ceiling she'd installed last month. A table with expensive Limoges teacups took the brunt of the damage. Shards of white and gold porcelain scattered across the floor along with delicate doilies.

"That *hick* is a former homicide cop from St. Louis. He could eat you alive if you pushed him too far." She shook off the adrenaline rush. "For someone declaring your undying love, it took you long enough to get around to talking about him."

"I'm the best thing that ever happened to you." He struggled to sit. His gaze wary as he stared at her. "If you'd only understand. None of this is my fault. You owe me."

"I don't owe you a damned thing." She rubbed her arm. "Don't ever touch me again. You forgot I earned a black belt in taekwondo last summer."

Josie came trotting in with Serena right behind her. It was good to see her backup arrive before Glen could escalate the confrontation.

"I've got a complaint." Serena's piercing gaze targeted Glen. He got to his feet, but it was clear from the way he wobbled his legs were unsteady.

"Oh?" Rory didn't know what Serena had planned but she knew her friend to be very inventive. She got her and Chandra into mischiefs that even now, people in town had no idea it had been them. A crop circle in Bill Shouse's wheat field. Alien sightings and ghostly encounters in the graveyard were only a few. Now it was time to follow her friend's lead.

"Yeah." Serena slapped a crude burlap doll on the counter. It sported a scrap of blue across the top and yellow straw sprouted from the head. Two googly eyes completed the unsettling object. "Agnes and Henry are upset and it's ruining the vibe in my shop." She took a step closer to Glen. "Bleed over, you know. Henry said it was an asshole alert." She scanned him up and down. "He was right." She leaned over to pluck a few hairs from Glen's neatly styled hair and stuck it in the rough straw of the doll's head. With one swift motion she pulled a long, sharp hair pin sporting an amethyst heart from her bun. She thrust it between the doll's eyes with an enthusiastic *yee-ha*.

Glen howled and grimaced. He slapped his hands on his forehead. "What are you, a goddamned witch? Take it out. Take it out."

Rory could only stare at him in amazement. *He believes this crap?* Maybe it had something to do with growing up in New Orleans. The town swam in voodoo.

Serena's expression of confused innocence could make her a contender for best leading actress in this year's Oscars. "I'm a shop owner, just like Rory. I sell bits and bobs to the tourist going to Branson. Rory—" she smiled and held up the doll. "—this came in with the new merchandise and I thought I'd give it a test drive. What do you think?"

"I think Henry is spot on, but your new toy is a little—er— unnerving" She had no words. However, the look on Glen's face was worth the horror show. "Oh, get over yourself, Glen. It's one of those migraines you get all the time." She was still surprised to find him to be so superstitious. "Go back to New Orleans. There's nothing here for you."

"This isn't over yet."

Serena poised the pin over the doll again.

His eyes bulged in fear. "I'll call you later." He groaned and held out his hand in demand. "Right now, I need an aspirin."

"There's a drug store down the street."

"You, bi—" Serena waved the pin closer to the doll. "—all right," he yelped and left without any need for further warnings.

"Henry's right. He is an asshole." She stuck the long pin back into her bun. "I'm glad I never got to meet him before."

Rory and Serena broke into giggles while Josie stared wide-eyed through the window at Glen's fast retreat. "I didn't know you could do voodoo."

"Oh, Sweetie, I don't. It was just a show for Rory's ex." She pitched the gruesome doll in the trash. "Although Henry had fun plunking Glen between the eyes." Her fingers made a flicking motion with her thumb and index finger.

"I don't believe in voodoo or Henry." Rory wiped tears of laughter from her eyes. "But thank him anyway."

"Well, I have to get back to the shop." Serena headed toward the door. "Call me later about your date."

"It wasn't a date," Rory called after her. It definitely hadn't been a date. They'd skipped that phase altogether. If she didn't watch it The Aunts would have Lachlan smooshing wedding cake in her face

"Miss Serena is really somethin'." A long sigh of appreciation came from Josie. She leaned against the countertop and her chin propped in her hands. "She's weird and all but a lot nicer than I thought she'd be up close. Most people in town steer clear of her."

"That's because they don't know her like I do. I spent most of my summers here and when I was fourteen,

I came to live with The Aunts. Serena hasn't always had it easy. All through school she wore heavy glasses and braces. The other kids made fun of the way she stayed by herself, except for Chandra and me."

"It's hard to think of any of you as—"

"That young?" This time Rory sighed. "I need to get some paperwork done. Knock on my office door if you need me to answer customer questions."

No matter how she tried to concentrate on the receipts and orders in front of her, she couldn't. The troublesome Glen kept popping into her head. They were chased away by the even more disturbing images of Lachlan's enticing smile, his kisses, his amazing abs, his—she shook her head to disperse the thoughts in a flurry like a snow globe she had once owned.

Last night won't be repeated. Ever. Ever. Ever.

Chapter Eleven

Daisy crouched next to one of her prize roses, patting the mulch around the base after its tri-monthly feeding. "There you go." She couldn't resist stroking a pale peach bud. "Now you grow nice and pretty so you can whip Lotta's butt all over the place."

Suddenly, a shadow loomed over her. She yelped in surprise but a quick glance over her shoulder showed Lachlan standing there with a familiar 70-foot hose coiled over his shoulder. His right hand was curled around the handle of her favorite two-pronged hoe.

"Lordy, you gave me a start." A few quick pats on her chest quieted the frantic beating of her heart. "I've become a little goosey since Glen showed up on our doorstep." With a few grunts and groans she used the handles of her kneeler to rise, but her knees were being crabby today and didn't want to cooperate. "Lordy, I'm not as spry as I used to be. Just a second."

"I'm sorry. I didn't mean to scare you." Lachlan held out his hand. "Here. Let me help you up."

She accepted his offer and with another grunt she made it to her feet. Her knees wobbled for a second and finally locked into place. *Good. At least I won't take a nosedive into my roses in front of a handsome man. Oh, to be fifty years younger and seventy pounds lighter.* "Thank you. I'd might've been stuck down here if you hadn't shown up."

"Well, I don't mind giving you a boost." A frown creased his face. "Maybe you need a medic alert bracelet. You know, 'I've fallen and I—' "

"Old people wear those." She narrowed her eyes, daring him to say any more about her age.

"Well, I—my mistake." He held out the two-prong hoe. "I wanted to return this as well."

"How's the garden goin'?" She leaned the hoe against the house. "We haven't seen you around much these last few days."

"I went crazy at the hardware store—even got a tiller and a composting system."

"My, my—" one by one, she picked up her gardening tools and put them in a bucket, "—you have been bitten by the gardenin' bug."

"I've lived in apartments my whole life. This has been enlightening." He eyed her roses before his glance traveled to the front porch. "You've got a good head start on me." It was clear he was looking for Rory.

"She's at the Funky Junk Shoppe, you know. Why tourists buy that old crap is beyond me, but it's flyin' out the door." She pulled off her gloves and gave them a few quick slaps against her jeans to remove the dust. "It does my heart good to see her make a success of things, especially after that good for nothin' ex of hers is still makin' a nuisance of himself."

A light flared in his eyes. It was a good thing Glen wasn't here right now. Her heart fluttered once more. *Rory better not let this one slip away.*

"I thought Grover left for New Orleans." With a quick flex of his muscles, he hefted the hose on his shoulder. "Tell me where you want this, and I'll put it away."

It was hard not to giggle at the way he intentionally said Glen's name wrong. She grabbed her hoe and pointed to the garden shed next to her greenhouse. "Follow me." The moment she opened the door, the smell of fertilizer, weedkiller, and petroleum products rolled from the sun-warmed building.

"I swear, it's rained every day. The sun pops out and everything turns into a sauna." It took a few seconds for her eyes to adjust to the dark. "Just put the hose there on the hook and prop the hoe next to the door."

Lachlan did as instructed. It was impossible not to enjoy the sight of his muscled arms and the fine sheen of sweat on his skin. She might be old, but it couldn't keep her from admiring one of God's creations.

Marvin would have a hissy fit if he were still alive. He'd always been the jealous type. Daisy couldn't help if she appreciated a handsome man, and all that masculinity was wasted at the moment. Her hormones were dried up, along with everything else, but the memories of her and Marvin in the sack could still make her a giddy—giddier than a shot of Amos' hooch. Marvin had been an absolute rock until his prostate went sideways. He still flirted with her like a fiend up 'til the day he died. She sighed and teared up.

There wasn't a day that she didn't miss that old coot.

"Everything okay?" The worried expression on Lachlan's face made her smile.

"Nah." She waved his concern away. "Just reliving the past a bit. A person tends to do that at my—er—age."

"You are timeless."

She didn't bother to hide her giggle. "You, sir, are a bald-faced liar and that will earn you some lemonade and cookies."

His eyes widened with, dare she say it, fright.

"Don't worry. Everything is store boughten."

"Then I'd be delighted." There was a hint of Rhett Butler in his voice. The boy was turning southern by the minute.

"Good. I wouldn't serve one of Maisie's cookies to a dying dog."

They passed another one of her America climbing roses on the trellis by the back door. She bent to sniff the fragrance. "Hang in there, Toots, I've got a date with a handsome man. Water after sunset."

"Toots?"

"Oh, she's my favorite climbing rose." Her chest puffed up with pride. "She won me a blue-ribbon last year."

"Where's Miss Maisie?"

"You mean it's awful quiet around here?" They went through the screen door to an enclosed back porch. She toed off her sneakers and stared down at Lachlan's flip-flops.

He followed suit.

"She at the hairdressers getting a permanent. I think she said she might stop off at Rory's shop and Serena's as well." She went to the pantry and pulled out a box of sugar cookies she'd purchased at the supermarket in Holloway. "Here we go." Soon she had the cookies on a plate and motioned for him to sit. "Dig in. We don't stand on ceremony around here."

"Thanks." He picked a cookie with white icing and took a bite. "Umm, tastes good."

A few minutes later she had two tall glasses of lemonade ready and set one in front of him. "Too bad you missed Rory."

For a moment or two he stared at the lemonade and finally took a tentative sip. "Tart. Just like I like it." He set the glass on the table. "I haven't seen Rory since the barbeque. Is she okay?"

"I'm sorry she's such a coward. I raised her better than that."

He picked up another cookie. "A coward?"

"Callahan women don't cut tail and run away over something like sex. She should've stayed and faced whatever had her panties in a wad."

Cookie bits sprayed across the table. His face reddened. "What?" he croaked out before drinking the lemonade down in two gulps.

"I'm just sayin', and it's really none of my business, but she needs to stop avoidin' you." She filched a pink iced cookie with unicorn sprinkles and delicately nibbled on the edge. "It's important to know where you stand. She's not givin' you that courtesy."

"I—ah—you have beautiful roses." He brushed the crumbs into a napkin, giving her the same look as when she caught Rory and Serena smoking behind the garage. They tried to change the subject as well. It didn't work.

"I give up." Daisy threw her hands in the air. "You are as love dense as she is. Get a clue." With a sigh, she reached for her lemonade. "Thank you for the compliment, even if it was to deflect the conversation. I'm entering my hybrid peach roses in the county fair. Lotta Charles thinks she has a lock on the prize but I'm going to win."

He blinked a couple of times before leaning back in his chair. "I'll put my money on you."

"My roses have stamina, just like the Callahan women. They don't drop petals in a light wind. They can withstand an Ozark tornado."

Lachlan laughed. "I'll buy that for a dollar."

"You're startin' to sound like a true Hooticakleian."

"I doubt it. Deputy Parker said it took her 25 years to be accepted by the townspeople."

"Nah, she's pulling your leg. It was only 20 years."

He laughed and stood. "I need to get going. There's a few things I have to do before my shift starts. Take good care of Toots."

"Oh, I will. I have a big pair of garden shears and I know how to use them if Lotta starts any trouble." With a quick wave, he was gone. "I like that boy better and better every day. He knows how *not* to ruin a steak unless he's cooking it for Maisie."

No one was in the kitchen to argue the point, so she grabbed another cookie. It was time to hatch a plan to protect her roses. Lotta would go down hard.

****

Lachlan decided to go into town to buy groceries. His fridge was empty except for a couple of beers and an out-of-date carton of potato salad. On the way he spied Rory's shop. *Okay, I took the scenic route to the supermarket, but I might as well stop by. It's almost closing time. Maybe we can get coffee before I have to go home to change for my shift.*

He parked in front of the old bank building and opened the door. A couple of customers passed him on their way out. A small *ding* sounded, and Josie rushed up to greet him. Her brother, Theo, followed close behind.

"Good afternoon, Sergeant Donovan, is this your first time here?" Josie's bright smile was infectious.

"Miss Daisy said Rory was probably here. I thought I'd drop by to say hi." It was a struggle to sound nonchalant.

"She's got a *do not disturb* sign on her office door." Josie's brow puckered. "It's closin' time and she's up to her neck in paperwork. We got a shipment of merchandise we didn't order. It's been crazy tryin' to get it sorted out." She turned the *open* sign over to *closed* with a quick flick of her wrist. "

"Sorry to hear that."

"Oh, did Theo tell you he got the dispatcher's job?"

"No." He held out his hand to Theo. "Congratulations." He knew Theo would be hired, even over the disapproval of Chief Nolan. He'd taken Nolan aside making it clear that hiring a vet would be a good move. Theo might be impaired, but he's a military man and he could handle himself.

"Thank you. I appreciate it" The young man's shake was strong and firm. "How hard could it be to dispatch in the middle of the night?"

"Well, a lot of stuff goes down after dark." Lachlan's mouth twitched. "We had an interesting night last week."

"What happened?" Theo's curiosity shone in his eyes.

The kid might as well know what he was getting into. "I was on my rounds Sunday evening when Frank Appleton called, flustered and scared." It was hard not to laugh although the situation could have gone egg-shaped. "About sunset, Milo Mendelbaum showed up at the police station, all 300 pound, six feet seven inches of him. He kept slapping that bald head of his, saying the laser beam in the sky was burning his brain. He wanted to show Frank the trunkful of knives he had just in case he went out of control because of the aliens."

"Aliens?" Theo didn't look convinced.

Josie's eyes went round. She clapped her hands over her mouth, either in shock or to hide her laughter.

"I heard he'd been committed to a mental health facility." Theo nodded. "The rumor is it's because he was running around the front yard, naked and shooting off guns at UFO aliens."

Lachlan hadn't a doubt that the kid's story was true. "He'd escaped the facility and wanted to make his way home. Frank was doing his best to keep him calm. Both Milo and Frank were happy to see me when I got to the station, especially Milo. He was very worried about his knife collection and didn't want to lose control and go back to *that place*. He started to pace and slap his head again."

"He said, 'My mama called 911. I tried to tell her about the aliens, but she wouldn't listen. EMTs strapped me to a board and put me in an ambulance. I told them to stop and let me go because I got so hot from the laser beams. They finally undid the straps at the hospital. The first thing I did was to run into the bathroom and stick my head into the commode.' Then he turned to me and said, 'You know what those sons of bitches did? They strapped me back on that board. This time I'm ready for the aliens.' "

"What about the knives?" Theo leaned against the counter with his arms over his chest and chuckled. "That's the craziest thing I've ever heard."

"It took some doing but I managed to talk him into letting me keep them safe for him. Doctor Marshall, the county counselor, was called in. His mother and sister finally convinced him to go back to the hospital. So far, no more fights with aliens from outer space."

"Forewarned." Theo tapped his cane on the floor. "I guess I'm going to have to be on my toes."

Josie gasped out, "Theo!"

"Hey, they're my toes." He pushed away from the counter and started toward the door. "I've got to get things lined up if I plan to start at the end of the week. See you later to take you home, Josie."

Rory came to the front of the store with a pile of papers in her hand. She shuffled them, putting them in order. "Josie, can you check the stock numbers on these receipts against what came in today? Something doesn't add up. I've been on the phone all day trying to get this billing straightened out."

"Will do, Miss Rory." Josie grabbed the receipts from Rory and went to the office.

It took a few seconds more before Rory acknowledged his presence. "Oh, hello."

"Am I that forgettable?"

Red coursed in her cheeks. "Look, I'm too busy to rehash our—interlude."

"Interlude?" It was hard to know whether to laugh or be insulted. "That's one way to describe it. I came by to see your shop, but I guess a guided tour is out."

"Not much to see except what's on the floor." She walked away, leaving him alone.

There was no way he'd let things stand as they were. He needed to define their relationship, or even if there was one to define. How did he get beyond the barrier she'd erected? She drew him. He was at a loss as to why, but he wanted to find out.

It wasn't because she was just pretty. She had a face that was both hauntingly beautiful one moment and could be described as plain the next. A red head with freckles gracing her nose and green eyes that could slice a person in half. He knew the feel and taste of her body, but the pull went deeper than that.

There was only one way to find out. Hit it head on.

Her office door was open. He knocked on the doorjamb to announce himself.

She looked up from her typing. "We're closed."

"What do I have to do to talk to you?" It was hard to keep it light. Frustration stained his words.

"Do I have to report you to the police for being a stalker?" She turned back to the computer, leaning forward to read the screen. "I told you, I'm busy."

"I'm not stalking." He held up his hands in surrender. "Okay, maybe a little. About the other night—"

"It happened. Over and done with, never to be repeated." Her exasperation mixed with irritation came through loud and clear.

"Okay. No is no." It was hard to ignore the way she bit her lower lip. He needed to talk to her without coming across as the neighborhood pervert. "I get it."

Her fingers hovered over the keyboard. She twisted her desk chair around to face him. "I'm not good with this." Her hands fluttered in the air. "I don't cling. I don't dissect the morning after—"

"Actually, it was about five minutes after. I'd say that was a record."

"Ha, ha."

"I've never had a woman rocket out of my bed before. Did I do something wrong?"

"No. It was sex, pure and simple. There's no way to gussy it up."

"Well, that's blunt and to the point, except not so

simple. That's one reason I came to town. I didn't want your aunts to listen in." His attempt to sit in the chair next to the desk was met with a glare. "I'm sure they have eavesdropping down to an art."

She sighed in exasperation. "Too true that. What was the other reason?"

"I need to buy groceries. There's not much in the fridge. I need to stock up or your aunts will try to feed me." He jammed his hands into his pockets. "I better get going if I plan to avert disaster. Maybe I'll see you tomorrow."

"I doubt it."

"I live next door."

"Stay on your side of the fence."

He smiled and waved goodbye. "Tell Grover hi if you see him again."

"It's Glen," she yelled as he went out the door.

****

Rory's heart fluttered and burned. It had to be Taco Tuesday at Los Flores that gave her this giddy feeling. *No more hot salsa.* She was a guacamole girl from now on.

That didn't answer the major question of why, oh why, did his smile play havoc with her hormones. The uncomfortable, excited anticipation whenever Lachlan showed up drew her in. Now she understood the old saying about a moth to the flame. She ached from head to toe with the need to be near him. He always appeared when she thought she'd got her rioting emotions under control. Her stomach churned with guilt. She'd been so rude to him and it wasn't his fault she was paranoid.

A pounding on the back door interrupted her worried musing.

"Rory, Rory, open up." Josie continued to bang on the door and yell. "We have another delivery."

"What?" Rory opened the door. "I thought you went home?" A large delivery truck backed into the alleyway with the *beep, beep* warning to others.

"I did but they pulled up to the back of the shop just as Sergeant Donovan was leavin'. The driver said they need to offload the merchandise before six thirty."

The driver jumped out of the cab. "You Rory Callahan?"

"Yes."

"Sign this." He thrust a clipboard at her all the while chewing on a wad of gum.

She stared down at the forms on the clipboard. The company sending the merchandise was known for its shoddy knockoffs. "This stuff isn't mine."

"Don't care." The stocky driver's gum snapped. "Your name, your address."

"Not my problem. I can't allow you to unload this. If I take this order, I'm liable." She used her phone to take pictures of the documents on the clipboard. "Have your company call me if there's a problem."

"Look, lady, we gotta unload this stuff and get to our next delivery." The guy took a threatening step toward Rory, but Josie stepped between them, shaking her head.

"Oh, no you don't." Josie stood toe-to-toe with the driver.

The nasty smile on the guy's face said he was aching for trouble. "Listen, girlie I—"

"If she says she didn't order it, she didn't order it." Josie pointed toward the entrance of the alley. "My boss knows Kung Fu and has already thrown one dude on his butt." Her voice held a boatload of *I-don't-take-crap-*

from-anyone sass. "Now get in your truck and haul yourself out of here."

The guy's eyes scanned Rory as if assessing a threat. "Actually, it's taekwondo. Second degree blackbelt."

"Taekwondo," Josie corrected herself. "Got it, taekwondo."

He gave them one last glare, grumbled under his breath, but got back into the truck.

An appreciative whistle blew between Rory's teeth. "Wow, I'm impressed."

"No one messes with a Tally, their friends, or bosses." She turned and went back into the store. "That's what got Daddy thrown in jail. He was with his friends the night Chief Nolan arrested him. He was hangin' with the wrong crowd and got caught for bein' the wheelman in a robbery. He thought they just went in for beer."

"I appreciate your enthusiasm but let me take care of things like that in the future. I don't want you to get hurt."

Josie's beatific smile belied the militant glint in her eyes. "Miss Rory, I might not know your taekwondo but I'm good with a knee to the nuts. Theo showed me how to protect myself before he went into the Marines."

"Thank you. I knew you were right for the job." Tiredness overwhelmed Rory for a moment. She needed a bit of time to figure out what was going on. She was at a loss. "I'll tackle this first thing in the morning. Let's go home."

Chapter Twelve

Rory's brain hurt from dodging questions all day about her *nice time* with Lachlan and working on the Glen problem. At dinner they slipped in sly comments designed to fish for information. She frustrated them at every turn.

They decided to have coffee in the living room. Rory stayed in the kitchen to put together the cookies and coffee for her aunts to nibble on while they watched television. It gave her time to pull herself together. Her fingers arranged and rearranged the vanilla wafers and chocolate chip cookies.

She understood her aunts were worried about her future. They still saw her as an angry, fourteen-year-old girl. Not that they'd be far from wrong. Lingering resentment nestled in her heart. The way the town treated her when she was young and now hot anger over the Glen situation plagued her. The Aunts had warned her a couple of years ago about Glen, but she'd blown off their concern. Now she was paying for her stupidity.

The tray was finally set to her satisfaction. She'd sucked in a deep breath and plastered a smile on her face. *Fifteen minutes. Fifteen minutes and I'm heading back upstairs.*

Aunt Maisie sat in her big recliner, knitting her never-ending afghan. It was in shades of every poke-you-in-the-eye color she could find at The Knotty Spot in Holloway. Meanwhile her sister was busy checking out her late Uncle Marvin's night vision goggles. Several shotgun shells littered the end table by her chair.

"I'm primed this year. Lotta even shows her face, or clippers, around my roses she won't be sitting for a week. I put salt in my shotgun shells." She cackled to herself and slipped the goggles on her head. "Oh, yeah." She took them off and blinked. "Whoa. It's a little bright in here, but these will work just fine. And to think I reamed Marvin for spending so much for these babies."

"I think we need to have Lachlan over for dinner sometime *next* week." Aunt Maisie stared at her knitting, tongue sticking out of the corner of her mouth as she slipped the needle under a loop of lime green yarn. "We don't want to look too eager."

"There is no *we*." Rory tried her favorite yoga breathing technique again. She'd had it up to her eyeballs with her aunts' meddling. Lachlan was the least of her worries. It would be difficult to prove Glen was the villain in her personal melodrama. Different scenarios of how to eviscerate him, in a multitude of satisfying ways, whirled through her head.

Dinner with Lachlan was a no-go—not after what happened last time.

"Go ahead, feed the poor man a last meal because that's what it will be. I love you two, but this has got to stop. Wild sex doesn't equate to happy ever after."

"Says who?" Aunt Maisie's pout made her bright pink lipstick spiderweb around her mouth. "Now I've dropped a stitch."

Expectation filled Aunt Daisy's eyes. "*Was* it wild?"

Her mind came apart at the seams. If they'd broken the proverbial camel's back with The Plan, tonight they steamrolled the poor thing into the ground. "Yes, it was mad monkey sex. We hung off the chandelier. The mattress was burnt to cinders."

"No need to get snippy." Aunt Daisy glared at her. "You're just upset because you won't admit you like Lachlan."

"Yes," her sister nodded in agreement. "I hope you used protection while you were hangin' from the chandelier, although I don't remember seeing one in the house."

There was no talking to them. She threw up her hands in surrender. "I can't handle you two right now. There's a bunch of paperwork I brought home. It's not getting done by listening to you plan Lachlan's demise."

"Why, we'd have it catered by Price Rite's Deli." Aunt Maisie put on her most innocent look. "They have a wonderful roast chicken dinner."

"I'm out of here." Rory rolled her eyes heavenward with a grimace. "You feed him. I won't be there."

"Victoria Siobhan Callahan, don't you pull a face with me." Aunt Daisy's *voice of doom* filled the living room. She might be thirty-two, but it stopped her dead in her tracks.

"I'm going to get some work done." True to her word, she spent two hours making a thorough search of the receipts and devising a plan of attack. Glen may have stolen her identity, but she wasn't about to let him take her business because of his childish revenge.

Her eyes started to blur. The letters on the computer screen looked like so much chicken scratching. Her bed called to her. There was nothing like the smell and feel of clean sheets to ease her into sleep. With a sigh, she let Morpheus take her.

Her dreams were filled with the taste and touch of Lachlan's body while Glen madly threw credit cards in the air and laughed at her. The dark seduction in Lachlan's eyes became impossible to resist. His mouth hovered over hers. A diabolical laugh rolled over them. The credit cards swirled in a tornado that tore at her, slicing her skin. One struck Lachlan. Blood poured downward until all she could see was his dark eyes staring out at her from a red face.

Her eyes flew open. Sweat plastered her hair to her forehead.

She checked her bedside clock. It was four in the morning. Unable to sleep, she pulled on a t-shirt, along with a pair of denim shorts that were liberally splattered with paint.

An antique bed waited for her. She'd picked it up at the same auction where she found Serena's tarot cards. The tall walnut headboard carved with floral garlands and fat cherubs needed some tender loving care. Even an hour of taking a cotton swab to the intricate details couldn't stop her mind from wandering back to her Lachlan/Glen problems. Exasperated with herself, she put away her tools.

"Coffee, I need coffee." It was still dark outside. It was that time in the morning when the sun hadn't come up, but she felt the excitement of a new day. Plans for Glen were already forming.

She'd call Serena first thing in the morning and have her send Glen a box of voodoo dolls with receipts pinned through their heads. It was petty. Very petty. If one voodoo doll made him nearly crap his pants, no telling what a whole box would do to his psyche. It still amazed her that she'd never paid attention to Glen's superstitious nature. He'd pick up a penny on the ground saying, "find a penny, pick it up, all the day you'll have good luck." It was a small thing, but it made her realize that their love was only the surface variety. She hadn't known Lachlan long, but she knew where to touch him to drive him mad, that he liked baked potatoes with chives and butter, no sour cream, and he had a soft spot for old ladies.

She went to the sink in her shop and turned on the faucet. Warm fur whispered against her ankle. Sadie, their barn cat, looked up at her with bright blue eyes that contrasted with her black coat.

"Taking a break from the kiddos?"

Sadie meowed in response.

Rory washed her hands and reached into the cabinet for cat snacks. It was hard to resist Sadie's pleas for treats. "Okay. I'll give you four tonight because you've got a clutch to feed."

The treats were gobbled up in record time and Sadie skipped, cat style, out of the door.

It was time for her to leave as well. The sound of tires on gravel and headlights caught her attention. From a distance she watched the man who gave her sleepless nights pull into his drive.

That pot of coffee looked better, especially if she put a shot of Amos' hooch in her cup. At least it would dull her taste buds by the time Aunt Maisie made breakfast. She turned off the workshop lights and stepped outside. A dull gray on the horizon was the only hint of day. Luckily, she knew the way to the house by heart, but putting in a yard light by the workshop was next on her list of things to do.

She got as far as the greenhouse that Aunt Daisy had built a few yards away from the house. Rustling came from the nearby bushes. She turned to see a black shadow race across the yard.

The loud bang that roared through the dark was followed by a shriek. She was pushed to the ground as someone whizzed past her. The faint scent of Glen's cologne whispered on the air. All she could hear was panting and footsteps tearing around outside of the house. A cat screeched and hissed in protest.

Her heart stammered, her breath caught, and she swore she was one Kegel away from peeing herself. She raised herself up to her hands and knees.

"Damn it, Rory, stay down." Aunt Daisy's command stopped her cold. It didn't matter. Her shaky legs refused to work.

Another report sounded. A string of profanities that would do her Uncle Marvin proud turned the early gray of dawn blue. "That cocksucker better not have touched Toots." Aunt Daisy crouched beside her. She glanced skyward. "Sorry, Lord. I got excited."

"What's going on?" Rory drew in a shuddering breath. It was more from fear of the shotgun her aunt cradled in her arms rather than the intruder sprinting across the yard.

"There's someone snooping around my roses." Aunt Daisy sniffed in satisfaction. "I knew Lotta would try something funny." She hunkered on the ground peering through her night vision goggles. "I couldn't make out who it was. Wore a hoodie. Who the hell wears a hoodie on a warm June night? Humidity is close to ninety percent."

"Someone who doesn't want to be recognized?" Rory's breathing returned to normal.

"Too tall for Lotta. She barely scrapes five feet."

Aunt Daisy gave a delicate snort. "Looks like it's safe to get up."

Rory finally managed to stand although her legs still had the consistency of overcooked pasta. "You scared the living daylights out of me."

"Oh, come on," Aunt Daisy snorted. "You're a Callahan. We're made of stronger stuff than that."

"Tell that to my bladder."

Satisfaction oozed from her aunt. "Whoever it was got a butt-full of salt."

****

Lachlan spied a dark SUV parked on the side of the road close to the Callahan's drive. It didn't belong there, so he decided to check it out. He pulled his own vehicle onto the shoulder and got out, taking his Maglite off his front seat. It might be a county problem, but he didn't want to ignore the second sense he'd honed over the years. The bar code sticker indicated it was a rental.

A gunshot coming from the direction of the Callahan's filled the early morning darkness. Instinct kicked in. Adrenaline pumped. He raced toward the fence, but the gate was too far away. Without breaking his stride, he clambered up and over in record time.

Miss Daisy's, 'Damn it, Rory, stay down," chilled him.

Another shot sounded.

The half-moon provided just enough illumination to make out the shadow of a person stumbling across the lawn. Lachlan trained the powerful beam on a tall figure dressed in black hoodie and dark clothes. The person gathered speed and ran toward the SUV.

Damn it. He was too far away to chase and concern for the Callahan's took priority. He turned back toward the house.

"Ladies," he shouted. "It's Lachlan. Don't shoot." He swung the beam toward the back of the house. Miss Daisy and Rory stood in its brightness.

"Over here." Miss Daisy slid a pair of night vision goggles to the top of her forehead. "Whoo-hoo, I got to get me one of those flashlights."

"Are you okay?"

"Fine as frog hair." Miss Daisy gave him a broad smile and did a little dance. "Yes, yes, yes."

"I'm still shaking but other than that—" Rory gave him a thumbs up.

He wanted to touch her, feel her from head to toe to make sure she was in one piece. "Did you recognize who it was?" His blood boiled at the sight of her scraped knees.

"Someone's trying to damage my roses, that's who." Miss Daisy shifted her gun in her arms. "They're paying the price. All I have to do is look for someone who's having a hard time walking. They got a load of salt for their troubles."

He reached out and motioned for Miss Daisy to hand him her shotgun. "I'm going to call the sheriff's department."

"Okay, okay." She gave it to him with a pout. "I have a right to protect my property."

Rory brushed her arms with her hands as if warding off a chill.

"Are you sure you're all right?"

"I think it was Glen." Rory brushed the dirt and grass from her shirt and shorts. "I could smell his cologne. It's been a crappy day, and this was the cherry on top of a shit sundae."

"Sundae?" Miss Daisy's smile grew to the point of scary. "That sounds good. I need something to celebrate my peppering our intruder's backside." She turned to go back into the house and motion for him to follow. "I got the fixings for a banana split."

Rory gave him a resigned smile. "Come on. I don't want to be alone with her and Aunt Maisie right now."

As if on cue, Miss Maisie turned on the porch light. She stood in the doorway wearing a pair of bright pink pajamas with coffee cups scattered over the surface. Her shirt had a cartoon coffee cup dancing around on her massive breasts. The cup stared at him with movable googly eyes. The slogan said, *"Coffee Saved my Sanity."*

He sincerely doubted it.

Chapter Thirteen

Rory made coffee while her aunts led Lachlan to the table. Aunt Daisy went to the freezer out in the garage and brought back enough ice cream to feed a kid's birthday party.

"My arms are frozen." It sounded more like victory than a complaint.

Lachlan jumped up from his chair. "Let me help." He picked up the cartons of butter pecan and the chocolate fudge that were precariously balanced on her chest and held in place by her chin.

"Why thank you." She managed to drop the rest of the ice cream on the counter without mishap. "I thought my bosoms were going to turn into icicles."

Lachlan's glance flitted around the room, anywhere except Aunt Daisy's ample chest. "I—ah—It's not a problem."

"Sister, he doesn't care about your boobs. Sit back down, Lachlan." Aunt Maisie scuffed around the kitchen in her pink fuzzy slippers, getting cups and bowls from the cabinet. "What happened out there? I heard Daisy shooting away with that gun of hers."

"Lotta was after my roses."

"You don't know that, Aunt Daisy." Rory didn't think it was Lotta. Glen had to be the culprit.

"It wasn't her, but I bet she sent someone to off my Peaches and Cream Special. Whoever it was ran into

Toots. I hope she scratched them good." Aunt Daisy opened a carton of vanilla and put a scoop of ice cream into a bowl. "Name your poison, Lachlan. We got vanilla, chocolate fudge, butter pecan, strawberry, and orange sherbet."

"I'm really not hungry." He moved toward the door. "I had a big meal at the Dinner Bell."

Aunt Maisie slipped her arm through his before he could make his escape. "Come on." It was a command wrapped in southern sugar sweetness. She led him to the table. "Sit."

"Really—"

"Eat some ice cream or be invited for dinner next week." Rory whispered his impending doom if he didn't eat the ice cream.

"Butter pecan." His quick response held a touch of self-preservation.

She couldn't resist giving him a wink. "You chose wisely."

"What do you want on it?" Aunt Daisy hauled toppings of every sort to the counter. "We got chocolate syrup, caramel sauce, strawberry, nuts, whipped cream—"

"Plain is fine." Lachlan jumped up and got his bowl of butter pecan before Aunt Daisy could glop anything on top of it. He manfully spooned it into his mouth.

Rory shook her head in disappointment. "Here I thought you were a man of adventure."

Lachlan raised one brow and stared at her aunt over his spoon. He shook his head and swallowed. "I came here to get away from excitement."

"There's big difference between excitement—" Aunt Daisy waggled her white eyebrows at him and nodded toward Rory. "—and adventure. Never a dull moment when she's around."

"You were the one doing the shooting." Rory didn't know whether to walk out in abject humiliation at her aunt's obtuse matchmaking. "And if you continue to throw me at Lachlan like a steak at a hungry lion—"

"I'm not hungry." He put down his spoon, pushed the bowl away, and got to his feet.

"Speaking of dinner next week." Aunt Maisie took up where Aunt Daisy had left off. "How about Tuesday—"

"I'm working—all week long. Ladies, I called the sheriff's office earlier. They'll send a deputy out." He made his way toward the back door. "I've had a long day and need to get to bed."

A knock on the door saved Rory from coming to Lachlan's rescue again. Her aunts thought they were being sly, even if The Plan had been outed, but they were as subtle as jackhammers on a Sunday morning.

Deputy Callie Parker stood on the other side of the door. "Hey Rory, I hear you had a dust up over here."

"I've got to go, Deputy Parker—" Lachlan double-timed it toward the door.

"Call me Callie. Everyone in Hootiecackle and Holloway does." She gave him a wry smile of understanding that wasn't lost on Rory. "I'll get a statement from you before you go on your shift. Good night."

Lachlan picked up his pace out the back door and Rory raced after him. "Lachlan," she called out. He practically broke into a speed race to the gate, not that she blamed him. The Callahan women could be a handful on a good day. "Lachlan!"

He stopped and turned. Even in the light of a half-moon she swore his eyes glittered like someone who had stepped on the devil's tail. "What?"

"I need to talk to you about something important."

"Nothing's more important than eight solid, but I don't see that happening."

"I'm sorry. I'm going down to Romeo's Adult Shop in Holloway first thing in the morning and buy ball gags for those two." She threw her hands up in the air. "I'm thinking about doing like Serena and move above my store if this keeps up."

"Why don't you?"

"Agnes and Henry."

He gave her a puzzled stare.

"Long story for another time." She wanted to ask for his help before she lost her nerve and pride. "I've got an issue with Glen—or at least I think I do, and it involves my store."

"What's happened?"

"Can I drop by the police station, or better yet why don't you stop by the shop after five. I'll still be there."

"Okay. I usually pick up something from the Dairy Freeze for supper about that time."

"Tell you what—I'll call ahead and have Melody put it on my tab. You're not on the payroll until six-thirty, right?"

He nodded. "I can do that."

"Good. Good. I didn't want to say anything back there." She pointed her thumb in the direction of the house. "Old pitchers have big ears."

****

Lachlan was surprised to have Melody thrust two bags of food into his hands.

"Here you go. Rory ordered a tenderloin and curly fries for herself." She gave him his coffee cup and handed him a bottle of Coca Cola. "This here is for Rory, on the house. She refinished my kid's dresser for me free of charge. It was the cutest thing. Pale blue with fish on it. Teddy's daddy surely loves to go bass fishing and hopes he'll take after him. All those cute little fish," she sighed. "I don't know how she comes up with that stuff." A horn blasted in the line behind him. "Anyway, Rory does love her Mexican Coke. I keep it in stock for her."

"I'm sure she'll like it."

"Tell her hello." Another blare sounded. Melody leaned out the drive-thru window and flipped off the kid causing the noise. "You keep your britches on, Henry Wilkins, or I'll tell your mama that you were neckin' with your girl behind the buildin'. Don't think I didn't see you." She pointed at Lachlan. "Maybe I'll have Sergeant Donovan keep a special eye on the property tonight."

"Food is getting cold." Lachlan hefted up one of the bags.

"My goodness yes." She beamed a smile at him. "Rory hates cold fries."

He took a break in her speech to hit the gas and make it out of the drive-thru lane and onto the street. A few minutes later he pulled up in front of the Funky Junk Shoppe. Somehow he'd managed to grab both sacks and the cola in one hand and his coffee in another. The fries were probably cold by now.

The problem of how to open the door was solved when a customer came out with a smile on their face. He slipped through the door, and it closed behind him with a ding.

Rory was in the middle of a transaction. Once she was finished ringing up her last sale and artfully hustling the customer out the store, she locked the door.

"Sorry I'm a little late." He placed the greasy brown paper sacks on the counter. His fingers were cold and cramped from carrying the bottled soft drink. "Ah—that's better." A quick shake helped to bring the feeling back into his hand.

She peered into the bags until she found hers. A sad, limp carton of fries followed a huge tenderloin that had to be the size of his hand. The grimace on her face said what he'd feared, the fries were cold. "Melody talk your ear off?"

"I'm going to have to count body parts later on to see how many I have left."

Her laugh filled the room. "Don't worry." She lifted the sorry looking fries from the bag. She put them back with a sigh. "I'll zap them in my microwave. Follow me."

Her office was compact with a coffee maker and the smallest microwave he'd ever seen. It sat on a wooden shelf above her desk. The only other furniture in the room was two chairs.

It took her a few seconds to move things around on her already neat desk. "Let's eat here." A second later two napkins were unfolded to use as place mats. "I know," she laid out her food. "A clean desk is the sign of a sick mind, or at least that's what Aunt Maisie says."

"I guess that makes us cellmates at the asylum. Mom swears I'm a pod person. She's the original Earth Mother. Nothing slows her down from any artsy thing that catches her eye. Her whole house is in chaos, but she knows where she's put everything. I like order." The smell of his Rueben sandwich made his stomach growl. The tartness of the sauerkraut and the earthiness of the rye bread was the aroma of paradise.

"What about your dad?"

"He's not in the picture. Mom said a baby wasn't in his life path."

"Oh." The understanding in her eyes both chafed and comforted him. "I guess we missed the Power Ball in the parent lottery." Her lids fluttered down as she opened the bottle of cola.

"What about you?"

"I'm sure everyone in town has filled you in on my past. My parents fought all the time, and I acted out. They couldn't handle me so they passed me off to whoever would take me. God bless The Aunts." She raised her soda in salute. "I made their and my uncles' lives a living hell and they loved me anyway."

"I went into the police academy as soon as I could." His first bite of his sandwich proved the aroma had only been a teaser. His taste buds were in heaven.

Rory pulled a fry from its cardboard holder. The once hot, crisp fry drooped in her hand.

"Story of my life." She gave him a wry smile. "Cold, limp and not worth eating."

He didn't know how to react to her statement, especially with his mouth stuffed with corned beef and sauerkraut. Memories of their evening together made it impossible to speak or swallow. He chewed faster. A swig of his coffee made the wad stuck in his throat finally go down. "So, what's up?"

"I think Glen is committing identity theft. I've got a lot of merchandise that I never ordered, would never think of ordering, being delivered. The bank said all but

$200 from my personal account had been transferred over to a new business account. "There was ten thousand in the bank, now I'm pretty much broke." She pushed her sandwich away. "So far I've found two other credit card accounts set up in my name. Thank God I can cover Josie's pay."

"What makes you think it's Grover?"

"Oh, come on. I lived with *Glen* for a year, worked with him for four. He's got my social security number, all my other personal information because he was my boss before he was my lover." The soggy bag of fries hit the bottom of the waste can with a *plop*. "The man is a narcissist with a grudge."

"Did you report this to the proper authorities?"

"Yes. The credit card companies are looking into it. The most disturbing thing is Glen, or someone he hired, has taken out some substantial loans from online banks in my name. He's trying to destroy my credit and reputation. Thank goodness Serena is lenient on the rent and I have enough in cash stashed away to keep afloat for a couple of months." She slammed her drink on the desk so hard it came close to fizzing from the top like Mt. St. Helens. "What worries me is the intruder. I don't know why, but I think Glen may have something to do with this mess." She grabbed napkins to mop the soda.

"I wouldn't put it past him." He leaned back in his chair, his mind whirring. "He struck me as stalker material and someone who hates to lose."

"This needs to be cleared up and fast, but there's no evidence to back up my suspicions." Vulnerability flickered on her face for a brief second to be replaced by a set chin and narrowed eyes. "It will take forever to set things right. I'll make him pay." She picked up the dill pickle that came with her meal and bit into it with a snap.

He instinctively crossed his legs.

"Whatever you have in mind needs to be legal." Sparks glinted in her eyes. "The law *is* sitting in front of you."

"Would sending a box of voodoo dolls to him be considered a death threat?" The expectation and excitement in her voice made him wary.

"It might be."

"Damn." Her shoulders slumped.

"Sorry. Besides, it's tacky."

"I suppose you're right." She got to her feet and began to pace in thought.

"Of course, I am."

"Ha, ha."

"If you do—send one big doll. Make's a bigger punch—you know, like a single red rose instead of a whole bouquet." He couldn't believe the words popped out of his mouth. It must've come from his visceral dislike for the man. All the red flags went up the moment he saw the guy grab Rory. He'd feel the same way if it were any other woman as well, or so he told himself. He believed in a good neighbor policy. Their evening together still had his brain and body twisted into a pretzel of confusion. It had worn and dulled his constant grief until he could breathe again.

Rory's warm and earthy chuckle poured over him. "Sergeant Donovan, I am shocked. Truly shocked at your disregard for the law." Her broad southern belle accent was accompanied by waving a napkin in front of her face. "I do declare, the idea has merit. I can see it now. Aunt Maisie could make a giant burlap doll, I'll tell them it's a gingerbread man, with big—" she demonstrated with her fingers, "—googly eyes for a sick friend in New Orleans. That wouldn't be a lie." She warmed to the subject. "I'll dress it like Glen, blue shirt and tan pants." Her smile faded. "No, Aunt Maisie would want to include The Ladies of the Purple Hat Brigade sewing guild in the project. They get together every Thursday morning. I wouldn't want to get them involved in homicide."

"Very thoughtful of you." Lachlan worked to keep his face neutral.

She nodded her head with queenly aplomb. "I'm a very thoughtful person."

"Maybe I should get a reward for the idea."

"I thought of it first, you merely improved upon it."

"We're partners in crime or will be if Grover keels over from fright." He decided to go for broke. "Hey partner, do you want to take in a movie at the Rialto this weekend? Discuss the particulars?"

She sat back in her chair, surprise and caution on her face. Her head cocked to one side as she considered his proposition. "Yeah, I want to see a movie with blood and guts and lots of revenge—research, you know."

"Your wish is my command. Revenge it is."

Chapter Fourteen

"Was there enough blood and guts to suit you?" Lachlan stepped out of the Rialto Theatre with Rory standing so close that he could take her hand if he thought it prudent. Instead, he closed his eyes and breathed in the night. The early summer evening was balmy with the scent of honeysuckle and fresh popcorn filling the air. Other floral smells joined in, but Lachlan could only identify the honeysuckle because it grew rampant on the south side of his property.

"Over-the-top villains deserve an over-the-top death. I suppose the steel rebar through the eye socket will do." Her smile turned into a grimace. "It's the everyday rat bastards that are hard to pin down, let alone punish."

"As a sworn officer of the law I don't condone violence—unless unpreventable." He leaned closer to whisper, "Don't tell anyone, but I liked the way the heroine took him out." It was time to take a gamble, throw the dice. He reached out and locked her hand with his. She didn't protest or pull away. It was stupid to feel so triumphant at this one small thing when they'd been all over each other a couple of weeks ago. Every line of her body, the taste and scent were etched in his brain, but this was enough for tonight. It might be the beginning of a real relationship. *Liar. Quit being so noble. You know you want her like crazy.* "How's it going with your identity theft problem?" They headed through the city park to get to their parked cars.

"Not so good. I mean, the credit card debts will be okay, they're covered. It's going to be harder to take care of the loans taken out in my name." The set of her shoulders slumped for a second. Just as quickly she squared them with the Mona Lisa smile she'd inherited from her aunts tickling the corner of her mouth. It spelled danger for whoever was in her thoughts. "I'm up to here in paperwork and calls." She slashed her hand across her nose. "I've got a sneaking suspicion that Glen may have hired a hacker to take care of the tricky stuff. Technology isn't his thing.

"I wish I could help, but it's not my field of expertise. If you found a body in your shop, now I could help you with that." The swing of their hands matched the pace of their steps. "However, I'd rather not find Grover lying in a pool of blood. I'd have to let Nick handle that mess."

"It's Glen. *Glen.*" She rolled her eyes heavenward. "You're doing that on purpose, unless you have dementia."

"Okay, I admit that he's on my shit list."

"I can take care of myself." Her gaze was fixed on their feet as they walked. "You know, once I met Glen, I tried to be the perfect partner—instead he cheated on me. I let myself believe that I had to keep the peace by giving in to him. All it did was to eat my self-respect away to nothing." She smiled at him with a martial glint in her eye. "I got tired of being a doormat. No more."

"Good for you." He gave her hand what he hoped was a reassuring squeeze. "If it helps, I never thought you were a pushover. Crazy, beautiful, but never a pushover."

"Ah, thanks. That's the dementia talking."

The soft night air sifted through her hair tossing the few tendrils that had escaped her ponytail. The breeze rustled against the soft cotton of her loose muslin blouse until the fabric hugged her body. There were only a few steps to his SUV and the evening would be over. He didn't want it to end.

"Did you fill out a complaint about the identity theft with Chief Nolan?"

"I'd rather talk to a vampire that hasn't eaten in a month of Sundays."

"I know you have a past with him." He tried to keep it light but the way she stiffened sent the red flags flying.

"You could say that. What about a forty-five-year-old man demanding a blow job from a fifteen-year-old girl?"

He abruptly stopped, letting her heated words sear into his brain. "Are you serious?" The moment he asked the question he knew he'd hurt her. The pain in her eyes stole his breath away.

"Why do people think the worst of me? Would I make up something like that for shits and grins? I guess I can understand why you'd ask since I fell into bed with you the moment we were alone. I chose to have sex." She snatched her hand from his and waved them in the air as if trying to erase the memory. Her words tumbled out in a torrent of anger. "I knew all cops were the same."

"No, we're not." Her words wounded, but then again she'd been the one betrayed and let down by the authorities. "Did you report it?"

"Sure. I'll come to the police station tomorrow morning to file a complaint if that makes you feel any better." She stared straight ahead, talking as if he were a stranger.

Together, they sat on one of the park benches. He could see Amos Cunningham perched on a bench across from the Funky Junk Shoppe and Serena's place. The man chatted away to no one in particular.

Lachlan couldn't let her revelation about Chief Nolan rest. It left a sour taste in his mouth. Gut deep he believed her. He had no trouble seeing his boss abusing his power. Anger pulsed through him.

"Did you tell anyone?"

"My aunts." She shook her head. "But they know less than nothing about identity theft. "

She kept zigzagging about the real subject of his questions like a rabbit being chased by a hungry fox.

"No, I meant about Chief Nolan." Clumping him together with a pervert or having the evening they spent called a romp irked him. He hadn't asked for someone in his life right now but there was no denying fate made him step into a cow patty of dilemma. Deep down he had to acknowledge she was worth the effort. "Maybe he's still doing it with other girls?"

"No doubt. Who was I supposed to tell? He's the law. My word, word of the town troublemaker, against his. That wasn't going to happen. I didn't dare say anything to my family. Uncle Marvin would've gone after him with that shotgun of his and it wouldn't have been salt in the shells. That's when I asked Uncle Marvin if I could go to Holloway for martial arts lessons." Her face beamed with pride. "I earned my second-degree black belt this last summer."

"See, you're not a doormat."

"The Chief is in the past. Best forgotten. Right now,

I have to focus on Grover—err—Glen." She sighed. "Strange what the illusion of *love* will do to you." Her wry smile tugged at him. "I thought it was the real deal. It exists—real love that is—I know it. My aunts and uncles were proof of it."

Lachlan knew love was real but could be easily snatched away. There was nothing he could do about Rory's past pain. However, the future was a different matter. Glen would be on his radar. When Rory sat next to him the world was filled with possibility. He decided he'd keep an eye on Chief Nolan.

"Tell you what—let's head over to the station and write out that report—about the identity theft."

She wrinkled her nose as if she smelled something foul. "I'd prefer to stay out of Chief Nolan's territory."

"As a former boy scout—" he held up his hand in a familiar salute, "—I promise you won't have to deal with him."

"How?"

"I have my ways." He planned to tell the chief it might be better if he took the case. Let the new guy handle the case. Less work for the chief.

For a moment he thought she would argue. Instead, she nodded. "Okay."

"I have a friend who works for the FBI. Cybercrimes. He might have some ideas. Meanwhile, why don't you file a complaint with the Federal Trade Commission?"

"I think one of the bank managers mentioned it in passing, but he acted like it wasn't important." She stiffened next to him. "Do you really think it will do any good?"

"Do you want to hang Grover by his ba—thumbs?"

****

Rory sat on the bench, unable to believe how she spilled her guts to him. He must've been an expert interrogator in St. Louis. A look, a few words and all the hurt and anger at Chief Nolan and Glen poured out in an emotional avalanche. It left her feeling vulnerable, something she vowed she would never be again. With Lachlan it was natural. The poison she'd held in for years eased until she could breathe.

Amazing.

She rubbed her hands together to relive the way they tingled when they'd walked down the street. It wasn't the same. There was heat from friction but none of the electricity that she felt at his touch.

"Is something wrong? Don't be nervous." He stood and held out his hand to her. "We're only going to fill out a report.

"I—ah—thank you." She smiled and looked straight ahead while they walked the few blocks to the police station, watching Hootiecackle pass them, street by street. Tall, three-story homes from days gone by lined their way. This was home. "Can your FBI friend really help?"

"His name is Caleb McGuiness. He wants to check out my new digs, so this will give him the perfect excuse to visit. It shouldn't raise any suspicions with Grover." They stopped in front of the police station. Lachlan turned to her, concern on his face. "Don't worry. He's the best in his field."

"Thank you." She didn't know what else to say. Confusion filled her. Being in a theatre with other people had made it easier to sit beside him. Now that they were alone it was hard to believe she'd practically ripped the clothes from his body and ate him alive. Not that he complained. They made the Kama Sutra look like an elementary school primer. It was amazing what the man could do in two hours. For her it had been climactic as well as cathartic.

Was this even considered a first date?

"This should only take a few minutes."

"That's good. I need to get home to keep Aunt Daisy from going on any more moonlight maneuvers. She's now calling last night's adventure Tootsgate because she's adamant one of Lotta's boys had to be the culprit. Callie might as well have saved her breath convincing my aunt otherwise." She followed him into the station.

Theo was on duty, and it looked as if he'd been doing the job forever. He was on the phone but raised his hand in welcome. "That's right. I'll have an officer drop by to check if the skunk is rabid. Goodnight, Miss Annie." He hung up and gave them a rueful smile. "Nick's goin' to have a fun night."

"How's it going besides rabid skunks?" Lachlan picked up the log sheet. "Looks like a quiet night."

"So far." The phone rang. "Hootiecackle Police Department. How may I help you?"

Lachlan led her to a desk and pulled out a pad of forms. He was right, it only took a few minutes to make a short statement about the identity theft.

"There. It's done. Why don't we go to the Dinner Bell and grab a cup of coffee—maybe pie?" He cocked his head to one side and gave her a smile that dared her to reject his offer.

"You're on." She licked her lips and enjoyed the way his eyes widened.

"Pie—ah—yes, pie it is." He got up to leave and

waved goodbye to Theo.

The phone rang again. "Busy night after all." He led her toward the front door. Before they got to leave Theo yelled out for her.

"Miss Rory!" The urgency in his voice made a hundred horrible scenarios kick into place. Her heart raced. Something had happened to her aunts. Maybe Aunt Daisy had actually hurt someone. That had to be the reason Theo sounded so upset.

She raced back to the dispatcher's desk. "What is it. Are my aunts okay? Did Aunt Daisy shoot someone again?"

The quizzical expression on Theo's face didn't help her apprehension.

"What's wrong?" Lachlan's clipped question brought Theo out of his daze.

"Well, it's Miss Serena. She said Agnes was doin' a bit of shoppin' and noticed someone in your shop." His head cocked to one side. "Josie wasn't supposed to work tonight—was she? Why would Agnes be there at this time of night?"

"No, Josie's not working." Her insides were a slip and slide of emotion. Queasiness gripped her. "Someone is in my shop." She didn't need this right now. Was it Glen again?. "Thanks." She grabbed Lachlan. "Let's go"

He followed but yelled over his shoulder, "Call Nick and tell him to get over there."

Theo's thumbs up was all the answer they needed.

The Funky Junk Shoppe was a block and a half away. She wasn't dressed to jog. Why had she decided to wear bright green pumps with her skinny jeans tonight? Looking nice wasn't a sin, was it? Attracting Lachlan hadn't been her goal. *Never.* Now she tottered as fast as she could over the cracked concrete of the sidewalk.

"Who's Agnes?"

She didn't have time for a complicated answer. "It's a long story." They stopped in front of her shop and she dug in her purse for her keys. The shop was locked up tight.

The faint light over the counter showed nothing appeared out of place. She went to her office to find her computer on, as if someone left in a hurry. The screen burned bright in the darkness. Her emails to her banks and vendors who sent the merchandise showed on the monitor.

Lachlan flipped on the overhead light. It washed the small office with unrelenting detail. The once neat desk was littered with papers, her pencil holder knocked over, and her mail was strewn over the floor.

"Oh my God." It angered her to think someone had touched her things. "I turned my computer off before I left this afternoon."

Fury built until it was impossible to speak. The sensation of violation grew with each breath. Her hands curled into fists ready to strike down whoever trashed her office.

"Is anything else out of place?"

A quick inspection showed her right desk drawer had been jimmied open. "Here," she pointed to the drawer. Scratches marred the once perfect Victorian piece. That could be repaired but not her peace of mind.

"What do you keep in here?"

"Receipts that need to go into the next day's accounts. Odds and ends. Sale and auction notices I'm interested in."

"What about the cash?"

"It's in a safe in the floor under my desk." She crouched to pull the wooden panel from the floor, but Lachlan stopped her before she could touch anything.

"My fingerprints will be all over this anyway," she insisted.

He helped her to her feet. "We don't want to smear any useable prints." The hard set of his jaw said he was all business now. "I need to make a call." He pulled his phone from his pocket and stepped out of the office, leaving her alone."

It didn't feel safe here anymore. The sanctity of her space was gone and now she'd worry if Josie or she worked past closing time.

Nick finally showed up with Lachlan following behind. "I brought the fingerprint kit like you asked. Miss Annie's skunk turned out to be a horny tomcat."

Lachlan pointed to the desk. "I want you to dust the keyboard and mouse. There's a safe under the floor, too. We'll check for any prints that aren't Rory's."

"Got it." Nick set to work on his task. "How did the perp get in?"

"I don't know. The front door didn't look like it was forced." Lachlan turned to her. "What about your security system?"

"Just locks and a key."

He gave her a look that said she should have Fort Knox security for her store.

"Hey, this is a small town. You ought to know by now that Hootiecackle isn't a high crime area. I have an electronic lock on the back door. Not even Josie knows the code." She couldn't help the smug smirk. "It's very high tech."

"The front door is the issue. What's your pass code for the back door?"

"I don't go around giving my code out to everyone. Isn't that the point of a lock—to keep people out?"

Lachlan arched his brow in question.

Yes, indeed. A master interrogator. She wrote down the code on a post it note and handed it to him. He took it and went through the back door to inspect the door frame. "No sign of forced entry here as well," he called out before coming back inside and closing the door.

"Told you." *Nanner, nanner, nanner.*

"*Someone* got in here and ransacked your office."

"Well?" That one brow went up again. His mouth firmed. Gone was the man with whom she'd enjoyed watching people being torn limb from limb. This guy was all cop. "Is it a new code or one you've used before?"

The uncomfortable need to squirm under his pointed gaze made her chin go up. "I've used it for years. It's easy to remember."

"Does Grover know your passwords?"

"He—ah—" she scrunched her face in frustration and annoyance. "—damn it. Yes."

"Whoever trashed your office was either Grover or an accomplice."

She wished he'd stop watching her. "I swear no one else would know."

A familiar *beep beep beep* sounded at the back door.

Chapter Fifteen

Rory's heart sounded like a bass drum in her ears as the handle of the door turned. Even with two of Hootiecackle's finest having her back, the hairs on the nape of her neck and arms stood at attention. No matter how much martial arts she'd learned, the fight or flight response had turned to plain flight.

Serena sailed into the back room dressed in black silk pajamas, purple fuzzy scuffs, and her long hair covered by a purple, bat printed scarf. "Hi Rory." Her smile drooped when she noticed everyone staring at her.

"How did you get in?" Rory frowned at her friend then glared at Lachlan. "You left the door open, didn't you?" *There, try to make me look like an idiot.*

"No. I made sure it was shut." His eagle eyes were now focused on Serena. "Why do you know the code?"

The question held a demand that even made Rory stand a bit taller. Guilt swamped her when she'd done nothing wrong. There were many times in her youth when she hated feeling the sensation of taking on another's wrongdoing.

"I need answers." Lachlan stared at Serena. "The perp may have had a local accomplice as well."

The air grew chill. The lights flickered for a second before Serena replied.

"I came over to see if Rory was okay. I saw the flashing lights and police car parked outside." She gave a delicate sniff, making the flooffy purple scarf in her hair flutter. "Henry told me the code."

"Oh, for God's sake, Serena." Rory palmed her forehead and groaned. "Not that again?"

Serena's violet eyes slitted, her mouth scrunched up in annoyance. "I'm telling the truth. Agnes said she literally ran into a blond dude in a black hoodie while she was looking at a calabash pipe."

"As if." Rory couldn't keep the skepticism out of her voice until she remembered Josie had just put the pipe in the display case right before they locked up for the night.

"Agnes said they both screamed the minute they made eye contact. He was dancing a jig like she'd scared the pee-waddin' right out of him when she skedaddled."

"What was Agnes doing here at this time of night?"

"Er—ah—shopping for Henry's birthday."

"Wait, wait." Lachlan looked totally lost. He glanced over at Rory. "You mentioned her before. Who's Agnes?"

"Oh, that'd be Henry's wife," Nick piped up as he affixed a piece of tape with a fingerprint onto a card. "Everyone in town knows they're Serena's roommates." He gave an amused snort but cut it short at Serena's cutting glare. "I'm going to check out the store front." He left as if she'd put a hex on him.

The chill grew stronger, and the lights faded in and out once more.

"I don't care who they are, I need to ask them some questions." Lachlan surveyed the room again. "It would clear a lot of things up if you asked them to come down to answer a few questions."

"Henry is still trying to get Agnes calmed down."

"Nick, call them to come into the station first thing

in the morning."

"Uh—I can't." Nick's expression was one of apprehension. "No. Body. Can."

"Why not?"

Serena cocked her head to one side, her smile more a grimace. "Not that easy. They don't have a phone."

"How do we contact them?" He glared at Serena.

She glared back. "Only if you have a Ouija board."

"What?" Lachlan looked even more lost than he had earlier. It appeared he didn't appreciate finding himself in this position—ever. "W-h-y?

Serena lifted her chin in a defiant pose worthy of any Gothic novel heroine. "Because they're ghosts."

"You're shitting me, right?"

Rory couldn't begin to explain her friend's insistence she had a connection with occupants from upstairs. She should've shut her down in high school when she took the Goth thing too far by claiming she could see dead people.

She groaned in frustration. She loved Serena dearly. However, tonight was one of those times she wanted to stuff her friend's mouth with enough chocolate to shut her up.

"I respect the Hootiecackle Police Department. Why would I lie?" Serena crossed her arms over her chest and tapped the furry scuffs on the hardwood floor. "Why would I hurt my best friend? Hmm?" Her gaze dared him to argue the point.

"People do strange things at times. Maybe you—"

The open back door slammed against the wall with enough force to make everyone jump. A breeze blew into the room with the scent of tobacco smoke in its wake.

****

Lachlan didn't believe in hocus-pocus crap but the door, mixed with the flash of violet fire in Serena's narrowed eyes, would've made a lesser man rethink things. Evidence spoke louder than a gust of wind or a door with bad hinges.

"Anyone could be an accomplice." He wasn't about to let the fact Serena was one of Rory's friends get in the way of good police work. "Nobody is—"

"Sergeant Donovan!" Nick's excited yelp drew all of them to the front of the store.

"What is it?"

Nick crouched, and though the shop lights were on, he pointed his flashlight at a spot on the floor. A small puddle glistened in the beam. "I think Agnes was right about scaring the pee-waddin' out of the guy." He pulled a couple of plastic tubes with swabs from his kit and meticulously took samples of the liquid. "If it's urine we can get a DNA sample."

"Eww," Rory and Serena said in unison.

It looked like luck was with them. Glen probably jumped at his own shadow while stumbling around in the dark and his bladder let go. The mental image of the guy pissing himself satisfied Lachlan's sense of justice.

"Do you have a hairbrush, toothbrush—anything with Gavin's DNA?"

Rory looked at him as if he were mental. "Why would I keep his stuff?

"Who's Gavin?" Serena's confusion replaced the glare she'd been leveling at him. "Are you dating someone else?"

"No. He refuses to get Grover—I mean Glen's name right." Rory cast him an exasperated glance. "It's so childish."

"But entertaining. The man is an assho—idiot." Lachlan didn't care if it ticked her off that she found herself doing it as well. "Nick, send the bill to me if the chief reuses to pay for the DNA analysis." The faster Glen was out of the picture it would be better for all of them.

It was hard to explain, even to himself, why he wanted to protect Rory from her ex, or the past hurt caused by Chief Nolan. He wasn't sure if they *had* a relationship, but he wanted to see where things could lead without a lot of outside interference.

His first concern was to get past Serena's cockamamy story. It was clear he'd have to handle her differently than other suspects. Rory eyed him, daring him to bad mouth her friend.

"Just give me the facts." He gave both women a level stare. He took his job seriously, ghost, or no ghost.

Rory's lips quirked on one side. "You sound like a rerun of Antique Antenna's *Dragnet*. The Aunts won't miss a single episode. You do Joe Friday proud."

"She knew the passcode to your lock and then tells me a ghost told her?" No matter how he rolled it around in his head Serena's explanation made no sense. "I'm not buying it."

"Believe it or not." Serena crossed her arms over her breasts, her eyes and stance defiant. "I was watching my favorite KDrama, *Moon Lovers: Scarlet Heart Ryeo*." She turned to Rory with a sigh. "Agnes interrupted right in the middle of my favorite scene. Wang So had just stopped the princess from beating Hoo Soo. That's when Agnes *whoosed* in in a panic. Henry was upset that the dude downstairs scared her. He said you and Rory were down here and I decided to see what was going on. I looked out the window and I saw the police cars. End of story." She huffed. "Thank goodness for pause on the remote."

"And he told you the code?"

Serena nodded.

"Do you know how demented that sounds?" The words popped out of his mouth and a quick glance at Rory told him she was about to lose her shit. He couldn't tell if it was him or Serena who would set her off first.

Serena nodded again. "I wouldn't believe me either, but you can hook me up to a lie detector. I don't care."

Maybe it might be better to go along with Serena. It might be the only way to get information he could use that made sense. "How does Henry know the code?"

"He walks Rory to her car every evening. Told me he watched her punch it in a couple of times." He glanced over at Rory in question. She hunched her shoulders upward in puzzlement.

"Why didn't he open the back door?" He'd nearly come to the end of his patience. Playing along made the situation impossible.

"It was locked. He can't do it himself." Serena gave him a look that said the answer was obvious. "Besides, he was upstairs comforting his wife."

"I mean, if he knows the code, why can't he go through it, or do whatever spirits do?"

She glared at him again, her voice strained, her tone snarky. "One, it's hard for them to manifest. Agnes was only whole from the waist up because she wanted to pick up the pipe, hence Grover wetting himself. Two, they don't go through solid doors. Ectoplasm, you know."

He didn't know, but he let her continue.

"If there were an old-fashioned keyhole or a gap

they could slide through, that might be different, but Rory has this place secured tighter than my Granny's girdle."

"Except for the front door." He pointed toward the shop door.

Rory rolled her eyes heavenward. "I thought it would be okay since it faced the street and you guys patrol the square every fifteen minutes." She turned to Serena. "Besides, your Granny's dead."

"See, point taken. A keyhole."

Lachlan noted the old keyhole along with a newer lockset.

Serena saw the direction of his gaze. "Hey, the truth is the truth. Try to disprove it."

"Moondancer women are all shamans." Nick packed up his kit and stood. "My eomeoni," He leaned against the counter. "my mother," he explained. "She comes in here all the time for talismans."

"I thought your mom was Catholic." Lachlan was more confused than ever.

"She is." Nick's dark eyes danced, and he gave Serena a wink. "She buried a St. Joseph statue in her front yard when she and Dad wanted to sell their house. And my grandmother is Buddhist, but she couldn't find a shaman nearby, so she bought one of Miss Serena's talismans. One St. Joseph statue and one talisman later, the house sold in a week. Who's going to argue with that?"

"Me!" Chaos whirled in Lachlan's brain. He'd traded a charnel house in St. Louis for a Hootiecackle madhouse.

"Don't tell my mom—or grandmother." Nick hefted the case in his hand and headed toward the door. "I'll send this stuff off to the lab ASAP and email you the pictures of the crime scene. See you tomorrow afternoon."

Lachlan waved him away.

"Help me to understand this. One more time." He ran his hand through his hair. "You see ghosts, sell talismans, and read fortunes with tarot cards?"

"No, I give people the information they need to make decisions. Henry and Agnes are busybodies. They know all the good poop brewing in town. I use the cards to focus. The Purcells give me information and I'm very intuitive." Her knowing smile didn't give anything away. It was as if he were being pulled forward. "Body language and micro expressions are my thing. Like right now, you'd like to give me a whoopin' because I don't fit into one of your mental boxes. However, you don't believe in raising a fist to a woman." Her voice became slightly sing-song. "It makes you feel good to pigeonhole people. Your wife died. Now the grief is ebbing away. You want to hold on to it, but you can't. It irks you that Rory blasted into your life. She's hard to figure out. You can't figure *yourself* out." She took a step closer. The dark, musky scent of her perfume filled the air between them. "You don't know where you stand, you're on shaky ground. The spiritual side of your life is in limbo, but life is returning no matter what you do to hold it back." She came closer until all he could see were her eyes her eyes glittering in the room's bright light.. "Don't take her ex for granted. He's a nasty piece of work. Keep her safe—and cut back on your salt intake." She gave him a friendly pat on the shoulder. "It's bad for your blood pressure.

It took him a couple of blinks to break away from

her gaze. "Wow, you're good. I could use you at the police department." His snarky response hid how close she'd come to the mark. He'd heard of people who were able to read other's micro-expressions, but this was the first time he met one. "You have a gift."

"That's why I get paid the big bucks." A smile tugged at the corner of Serena's mouth.

"That doesn't mean I buy the ghost act."

****

Rory watched their interaction with surprise. Her friend was good, but she'd skated too uncomfortably close to the truth, at least Rory's truth. Serena always understood her emotions and could tell when she was unhappy or lying about being happy. Goosebumps prickled her skin.

Serena gave Lachlan a long look and shrugged. "Whatever." She turned to Rory with concern in her eyes. "You okay?" She put her arms around Rory and gave her a hug. "Weirded you out, huh?" The comforting strokes on her back asked, *Are we still friends?*

"I'm fine." Rory returned the hug before stepping back. "Really." Her friend had flayed Lachlan wide and left him exposed. She wasn't sure Lachlan even understood what had happened, that she'd heard his innermost emotions. They were both going through the same thing—grief and confusion about their relationship. He'd lost his love, and she no longer was with a man she thought loved her. There was the bewilderment of meeting someone who might fill up the emptiness. Was this what Serena saw when she looked at her?

Between Serena's woo-woo act, the break-in, and ghosts, this evening would probably go down as her number one strangest first date.

Chapter Sixteen

Lachlan walked into the dispatcher's office to see Chief Nolan frowning while Theo put his cane next to his chair.

"I don't know why the mayor made such a big deal about hirin' that boy." Nolan took a sip of coffee from the mug that announced "The Best Cops Have Big Guns." "Don't figure." He shook his head in what Lachlan could only construe as annoyance.

"I wouldn't call a guy who'd got his foot blown off in service of his country a *boy*. Some people would say that was a racist remark." Lachlan was never known to pull his punches while in St. Louis and he wasn't about to let Nolan get away with shit. He might be the newbie, but people needed to know where he stood.

Nolan gave a snort of disgust. "I can't stand all the political correctness bull crap. Now it's Me Too, You Too and Who the Hell Knows Too. Fifteen years ago, when I became chief of police this town was different, or it used to be until undesirables came here."

"Who would that be?" Lachlan decided to figure out which way to tack when the winds blew. He wanted to suss Nolan out, to substantiate Rory's claims. He believed her but others might not.

"Oh, we always had people on the wrong side of town—take the Tally's there," he pointed at Theo with his mug, not bothering to keep his voice down, "—

162

always nothin' but trouble. Whole family is a problem" He picked up a file from the neat rack on Lachlan's desk. "This B&E over at the Callahan woman's place. We're never goin' to find the perp. You know that, don't you? Waste of the department's resources."

"I don't know. We got some DNA."

"I don't give a shit about the pee that Nick found. Those tests are too expensive. Give me fingerprints. Science screws things up all the time."

"Fingerprints are based on science."

"No—they're based on *fingerprints.*"

"Don't worry. I'll pay for the analysis if that's the case," Lachlan closed his eyes and sucked in a deep breath. It was useless to argue with the man. "We have a suspect in mind. Rory's ex is giving her trouble."

"Good for him. Someone needs to bring that red head to heel." Nolan winked. "I hear you might be in line for the job."

Lachlan held his anger in check, barely. "My private life is off limits." His voice came out slow and steely. It was satisfying to see Nolan take a step back, his face pale.

"Well, I just heard it from Jenny."

No doubt the police's daytime dispatcher had already spread the news about his date with Rory being interrupted by the break-in.

"She said you two were takin' in a movie when Serena called. You can't take half of what that crazy woman has to say—or Rory, seriously They were in cahoots together in junior and senior high school and time hasn't changed them a bit. Nothin' but walkin' trouble with ti—"

Lachlan raised a brow and Nolan was smart enough

not to finish the sentence.

"I mean I don't understand how Chandra Barrett ended up runnin' around with those two. Nick sure got himself a sweet little woman. Mighty sweet." Nolan shook his head. "Now Nick's a good kid, even if his mother is Korean."

Lachlan decided to pick his battles. Let Nick have this one. He hoped there would never come a day when Nolan had to go up against Nick. Lachlan would put his money on Nick.

Nolan was right about one thing. Nick was a good man. Young, in love, and good. Sometimes it made a bad combination for a cop. Maybe luck was on Nick's side.

"About the B&E?"

"Wrap it up."

"It's a break-in."

"Was anything taken?"

"No, but Rory has filed with her bank and credit card companies about identity theft. We think it's the same person."

"You *think*? Show me some evidence. In the meantime—" Nolan threw the file onto Lachlan's desk, "—can this. Wrap it up in a bow and call it a day."

"The FTC will be calling on this." Lachlan picked the folder off his desk and put it back where it had been. "Rory's filed a complaint."

Red suffused Nolan's face. "Damn it to hell. That woman is pissin' in my Cheerios because she can."

"Does she have a reason?"

"What? No! She's just—" The coffee in Nolan's hand splashed over his hand. "Why? Has she said anything?"

"We've been on one date and that was interrupted

by the burglary. We don't share late night calls, or pillow talk, but she likes to reminisce about her early days in Hootiecackle."

Nolan's face paled. His mouth twisted.

Let the guy sweat.

Nick walked through the back door and waved at them. He stowed his stuff in a locker and ambled toward them with an affable smile on his face. "What's up?"

Nolan hunched his shoulders and headed toward the door. "I'll leave you to it."

"Ooo. What's got his shorts in a knot tonight?"

Lachlan's gaze followed Nolan. "He's ordered us to forget about Rory's break-in. He thinks we have more pressing business."

"Like what? Tracking down where Amos has set up his still?" Nick waved at Theo. "How's it going, man?"

"Quiet."

"I like quiet."

"Except someone saw the lights flickerin' at Serena's place again. She's down at the Cow Catcher Lounge with Rory. They're waiting for some producer guy from Hollywood."

"Hollywood?" Lachlan raised a brow in surprise. "Rory never said anything about going out with her."

"Serena wanted back up in case it was a hoax, at least that's what Chandra told me."

"Did she say what show. We can check it out."

"Ghost Reckoning." Nick picked up the call sheet. "I'll check out the store for Serena." He handed the clipboard back to Theo. "It's the biggest thing on The Destination History Channel."

"I've had enough weirdness in my life working in St. Louis. I don't need this shit."

"Welcome to Hootiecackle."

"Are you ready for the wedding?" It was a couple of days away. Rory told him Chandra had decided on pale pink and lime green as her colors. The dresses were something to behold, according to her. He couldn't tell if that was good or bad.

"Oh, yeah. I can't wait to have a whole week alone in Hawaii with Chandra."

His eagerness to marry his fiancée is palpable. Lachlan could see it was more than just being able to have a woman for sex. Nick's love was so apparent that some of the officers and dispatchers poked fun at him.

Lachlan knew the feeling, although his desire to have Kate close hadn't come near Nick's enthusiasm. For a moment he wondered if his love had been nothing more than familiarity and that she'd been comfortable living with that. Kate had her own career, made no demands on him. It wasn't until the last six months that she became clingy, depressed, and irritable. She'd been dying and he willingly switched roles from companion and lover to caregiver.

He'd been with Rory once, but it was not enough. He looked forward to their next encounter, wherever it led them.

"Nick, the chief told us to table the B&E over at Rory's place."

"Why?" The astonished expression on Nick's face echoed his own irritation and confusion.

"He thinks it's a waste of time."

"Anything concerning Rory is a waste of time according to him. She made his life hell for six years before she left town and went to college." Nick smiled and shook his head. "She was as my Grandpappy would

166

say 'a ring-tailed snorter.' "

"Snort what?" Lachlan's street beat days made the hairs on his neck stand to attention.

"Not what you're thinking." Now Nick laughed. "It means she was a troublemaker, but it was never anything bad. Just kid stuff that she always got caught doing while everyone else scurried out of detection. The biggest thing was the skinny dipping while everyone was at a party down by the lake."

"I heard about that. Wondered if it were true."

"Yeah. Bobby Joe Henry never got to home plate with Rory. Turns out he was wearing an aftershave that attracted wasps. Nothing like a swarm of horny stingers to take the starch out of a guy."

"Rory—"

"No one got a good look. The girls had a tablecloth ripped of the picnic table and wrapped around her at warp speed."

"You and Chandra dating all this time?"

"No. I was more into Frankie Stanley. All I could see was a pair of big brown eyes and—let's say I thought more with my dick as a teen. Chandra was way out of my league." He frowned. "Back then everyone teased her because she wouldn't date. She told everyone she was waiting for the right guy. I guess that's me." Nick beamed with pride.

They headed back to the employees' lounge for coffee. Nick filled up a thermos and Lachlan took a large to-go cup for his rounds tonight.

"I hope it's quiet tonight. The break-in shook Rory and I don't know what to make of Serena." Lachlan leaned against the counter and took a sip. He wanted to feel Nick out about Rory and her friends. His disquiet and well-honed senses told him there was more going on than either woman was telling him. It didn't have to do with the events of last night. If those two were possibly involved with Nolan, it was likely Chandra was as well. Three young girls, and now women, who were so close probably kept the others' secrets.

"Serena and Chandra are best friends. Rory is a good friend as well, but she lost contact with them when she went to school and then to New Orleans. Oh, they talked on the phone occasionally and sent birthday cards to each other, but Serena and Chandra are—" he crossed his fingers, "—like this."

"I'm new to town. It's hard to keep track of everyone."

"You'll fit in before you know it."

"In twenty-five years." Lachlan laughed at the memory of Deputy Parker's remark that she was still a newbie after living in the area for twenty years.

Nick gave him a knowing smile and a mock salute. "That's about right."

"Dating is an obstacle course of old ladies and people whispering to each other." Lachlan smiled then took a sip of his scalding brew. "I've never been in a place where you can sneeze on one side of town and someone on the other yells, *'gesundheit.'* Rory doesn't like cops but so far, so good. Does Chandra mind that you're working on the force?"

Nick's expression grew sober. "She's not thrilled. We've worked it out, but she refuses to go to any family activities hosted by the department."

"Any reason for that?"

"Chief Nolan and his wife aren't her favorite people. Why all the questions?"

"Hey, I'm just trying to figure out the players." He clapped Nick on the shoulder. "I'm the newbie, remember."

The next few hours were the standard driving around town and keeping an eye out for anything suspicious. All the while his brain worked on a puzzle no one else could or wanted to see. Was he painting a picture using the wrong colors? Time would tell.

Amos Cunningham, the town purveyor of "medicine," leaned against the brick wall of the Funky Junk Shoppe, drinking from a bottle. No one needed to be anywhere close to Rory's shop in the dead of night—not after what had happened the other day.

Lachlan stopped the car and got out. He ambled over to Amos who raised his bottle in salute. Instead of booze, Amos was guzzling from a cola. Something dodgy floated on the top of the liquid.

"What's up, Amos?"

Amos tapped the side of his forehead. "Now that's one of the big questions, right up there with the meanin' of life." His long gray hair was held in place by a red banana. He wore a stained green tank top and tattered jeans. A variety of tattoos covered his scrawny arms. Time had smeared them together into a smudgy mess. He hefted the bottle, took another swig, and then chewed.

"You're up early." Lachlan inspected the things floating in the brown fluid. *Peanuts. Why?* "What's with the peanuts in your soda?"

"I can't do that coffee shit. Too bitter or too foo-foo. I'll take a cola with peanuts any day."

"But, why peanuts?"

Amos shook his head with a combination of disappointment and annoyance. "Why not?"

169

I guess that answers everything.

"So why are you hanging around Rory's store at this time of night—er—morning."

"You see a lot of interestin' things." Amos took another swig of his concoction and finished with a satisfied sigh. "I can't sleep at night. PTSD from Desert Storm. Gotta walk that shit off. Sometimes the streets are dull as dishwater, but other times, whooee."

"Like what?" A surge of anticipation filled Lachlan. Maybe Amos had seen something the night of Rory's break-in.

Amos gave a little chuckle and scratched under his headband with one gnarled finger. "Well now, I seen Betsy Palmer, the organist over at the First Baptist Church getting it on with Charlie from the gas station. They were goin' at it like rabbits behind the diner."

"Oh?" Lachlan didn't know either party, so it didn't matter who was knocking boots. Jenny, the police dispatcher would relish this tidbit, but he could care less. He decided to give Amos a nudge and see if anything popped. "Were you on walkabout the night Rory's place was broken into?"

"Sure. I was sittin' on the bench across from the Funky Junk Shoppe when all the hubbub started."

"What did you see?"

"A man in a black hoodie on a warm June night is kinda hinky. Didn't make sense. Now if he'd been wearin' a wife beater and cutoffs, I'd never thunk anything about it, so I decided to keep an eye on him. Used to do recon and fly sorties in Desert Storm, you know."

"Yeah, Nick told me. What did guy look like?"

"Blond, longish hair. Lean. Looked like his clothes

didn't come from Target. No socks and black sneakers. Walked hunched down. Hands in his pockets. He kept lookin' around like he was nervous."

Lachlan was impressed by Amos' observance. "Anything else?"

"Well now, hey do I need to have a lawyer or somethin'?"

"No. I may have you come into the station to fill out a witness report. That's all."

"You sure?" Amos' eyes narrowed. "I want no truck with the law." He turned to face the shop window. "Why did Rory put an extra P and E on the end of shop. Looks wrong." His hand rested on his forehead as he peered in. "I got up when the dude decided to go into the alley. Just curious you know. Got nothin' better to do. Well, I stared into the store, and I could see that guy movin' around. He had a flashlight, one of those small gizmos that fit on the head. I think he wasn't expectin' a lady to be in the shop. I saw them in the light comin' from the fixture over the counter and his headlamp."

"Lady?"

"Yeah. Some lady with a short black— whatdayacallit—" he made a slashing motion from his ear to his chin, "—oh, yeah, a bob. She looked like one of those flapper gals. Wonder if it was Agnes."

Agnes again. Why was it always Agnes? "Maybe it was Serena?"

"No. Miss Serena's got that long black hair all the way past her butt. Seen it once when she was on the balcony above her shop. I was in the alley makin' a del— I was hangin' around and saw her brushin' it in the sun. Let me tell you, that's a sight to make the sap rise. I got all kinds of respect for that gal, though. Sweet as pie and tough as old boots."

Lachlan's patience ran dry at Amos' ambling stream of consciousness. "You saw a lady and the guy…" He motioned for Amos to continue.

"I done told you that." The exasperation in Amos' voice mirrored his own frustration.

"What happened next?"

"They both screamed, I ducked down. I saw the dude come waddling out of the alley as fast as he could and get into a black SUV." Amos gave a snort of derision. "I think he must've shit himself."

"What about the lady?"

Amos moved away from the building and gave the peanuts a swirl in the bottle. "I had my eye on the guy. She was gone when I looked back."

Had Serena lied about Agnes being a ghost? Was she hiding a suspect? He'd have to have another talk with her.

"Do I really have to go to the police station? I don't want to set off my PTSD."

The panic in Amos' eyes was real.

"Tell you what, I'll meet with you somewhere else and take a statement if we need it, okay?"

Amos' body visibly shuddered with relief. His hands trembled. "That's good. Real good."

"Meanwhile, let's not make any more deliveries around town."

"Gotcha." Amos gave him a thumbs up. "I'm thinkin' about retirin' anyway. I get enough off a social security and my rathole money so I'm good." He sighed. "Those Callahan Twins will be disappointed. Especially Miss Daisy."

"They can go down to Harley's Liquor if they feel

their bones start to ache."

"Suppose so." Amos gave him a big smile. "Well, I got to go home and get some shut eye." He waved as he walked away. After a few steps he turned. "Hey, officer. Do you know the best rock and roll song in the world?"

Lachlan shook his head. "I have no idea."

" 'Stairway to Heaven.' I wonder if Miss Serena has one of those in her building?" With that he began singing and making his way down the sidewalk.

Hootiecackle was supposed to be a quiet, boring little town, full of peace and sunshine. Somewhere along the line he was sure he'd stumbled into the Twilight Zone.

Chapter Seventeen

Rory pulled into her drive and glanced over at Lachlan's property. His truck wasn't in the drive. She breathed a sigh of relief. It gave her a few precious minutes to get her thoughts together before he came home. For the past two days she'd remained upset by the break-in of her shop. Not only had the intruder violated her business, he'd robbed them of more than that. All through the movie she'd been anticipating a goodnight kiss, to see if the heat she'd experienced with Lachlan was real. It had been on her part. Why she couldn't say. She'd been determined to ignore him, but despite her best efforts, she'd succumbed to his smile, the dimple that graced one side of his mouth and the twinkle in his dark eyes. She needed to find out if he felt the same about her. One way or another she planned to get a kiss before Lachlan tucked himself into bed.

Two boxes of Elmer's Donuts sat on the seat next to her. No one made donuts like Elmer and these were the first batch of the morning, still warm and smelling of yeasty goodness. She figured she'd leave a half-dozen on the kitchen counter for The Aunts as a sop and take the other box to Lachlan. Warm, sugary, deep-fried goodness was a good way to warm up a seduction.

As quietly as she could she closed her van door and snuck into the house. The clock on the wall in the dim light said it was five thirty. Lachlan should be home any minute. Giddiness filled her. Memories of their wild night suffused her face with heat. She hadn't been looking for a relationship but the idea of waking up with Lachlan in the mornings, or late afternoon, had its perks. Oh, yes, it definitely made her perky.

She leaned over the sink of the darkened kitchen and peeked out the window. The headlights from Lachlan's truck swept across the road and he finally pulled into his drive. She picked up one of the boxes of donuts and took two steps toward the door.

"I thought I heard someone down here." Aunt Maisie yawned and turned on the light.

It took a couple of seconds for Rory's eyes to adjust. She blinked a couple of times before she could focus. It might have been better if she hadn't. Her aunt stood there in a neon yellow nightgown that sported a psychedelic print from the Seventies. It was enough to give her an instant headache.

Aunt Maisie sniffed the air and spied the donuts. "Oh my, you are so thoughtful. Elmer's makes the fluffiest donuts in the world." She waddled to the overhead cabinet for a small plate. "I can taste it already."

"Taste what?"

"Those lovely donuts."

"Sure. Sure." Rory put one six-pack of the pastries on the kitchen table. "Here you go."

Aunt Maisie spotted the other box behind Rory on the counter. "You're not going to eat the rest of those are you?" The longing and resignation in her voice meant she had her eye on at least four donuts. The woman could eat enough of Elmer's to choke an elephant.

"Well—I—"

"Oh, my sweet Lord, I smell Elmer's." Aunt Daisy ambled into the kitchen, looking around for the treats. Her gaze landed on the box on the table. She breathed in the enticing aroma. "Why did you get these? I'm not complaining but it's O-dark-thirty outside. You normally don't get up before sunrise."

"I—ah—wanted." Why was it so difficult to tell The Aunts she wanted some alone time with Lachlan? They started this with their shenanigans, now, they should let it play out naturally. It wouldn't if they didn't keep their noses out of her business. "I thought I'd take them over to Lachlan as a thank you for helping me with the break-in." There. That was partially the truth.

"That's a wonderful idea." Aunt Daisy scrambled around the kitchen. She got out her hoarded gourmet coffee from the pantry. She was the only person Rory knew that still used a stove top percolator. Aunt Daisy insisted that was the way God intended coffee to be made. It usually tasted like hell. No amount of sugar or creamer could salvage the resulting sludge. "Let me get this started and we'll all go over."

"No!"

"Why not?" The Aunts turned their heads with identical questioning stares. A chill ran through Rory. It reminded her of a horror film she'd once seen as a child where children, who were aliens, moved in unison in exactly the same way. It scared the pee-wadding out of her then and they were doing a pretty good job of it now.

"Uh—sure—let's make it a party." Rory's good mood deflated. If she weren't such a chicken shit when it came to her aunts, she'd tell them to back off—but they were her family, at least the only ones that counted.

Once they were dressed for visiting, Aunt Daisy

filled up a thermos and they headed out to Lachlan's property. Rory unlocked the fence on their side and went to his back door.

He answered after two knocks. Rory had half-hoped he'd already gone to bed since she had her entourage in tow. Instead, he stood there in a white t-shirt, cargo shorts, and bare feet with a smile on his face. He held a large, steaming mug in his hand.

Her heart pounded and the giddy feeling increased tenfold. The sun came over the horizon to bathe him in a golden glow. It was so cheesy that she had to suppress a giggle.

He squinted against the early morning light. "What do I owe the pleasure?"

Aunt Maisie held up a box of donuts. "We want to thank you for helping Rory out with the break-in."

"Not a problem. I was just doing my job." His gaze swept over her, and the dimple popped out. Her stomach flipped in anticipation. She couldn't explain it, even to herself. Sex with him had given her a new perspective on desire compared to the mediocre encounters with Glen. *Was that it? Sex was better. No. No. No. The way just holding his hand makes me feel more than I'd ever experienced before. Damn. I hate it when The Aunts are right.*

"Where do we go from here? First the intruder, Callie couldn't do anything about our intruder." Aunt Daisy slowly shook her head. "I'm so disappointed in her. Now the break-in"

Lachlan frowned. "It's not her fault."

"Well, I told her it was that no good Glen Peters." The martial gleam in Aunt Daisy's eye flared. "What more does she need?"

"Evidence?" He opened the door for them. "Come on in ladies."

Rory led the way inside. His kitchen was spotless. It was a clear difference from the Callahan's clutter. Their counters were filled with half-finished scrapbook projects, well-used recipe books and cards that never produced an edible meal, and fossils that Aunt Daisy found while gardening. An interesting group of kitchen gadgets covered his.

The man liked to cook.

Aunt Daisy looked around the kitchen, taking in the changes from a couple of months ago. "Oh, this is nice. Different, but nice." Her gaze took in the items on the counter. "I know you can grill, but you cook as well? Really cook?"

"It's a matter of survival."

Rory took in the sage green wall and the darker green cabinets with white counter tops, old-fashioned brass hardware and white tile backsplash. Light entered from a new set of windows over the sink. Herbs sat in a neat row on the large windowsills. She hadn't noticed the changes so much the night she spent with Lachlan. Her attention had been on him the whole time.

"Well, I must say. It's an improvement from the old red linoleum and white walls. That window adds a lot more light." Aunt Daisy nodded her approval. "I saw the carpenters coming and going."

"I guess I should've given you a tour the other night. My mind was on grilling rather than the house."

"Oh, no. This is your home." Aunt Maisie peeked into the dining room from the kitchen doorway. Her curiosity was palpable. "I'd never thought to use sage green and gray together. It looks so inviting. I like the gray dining table and checked chairs. It works."

"Thanks. I went to the IKEA in St. Louis and pointed to what I liked. The rest is dumb luck."

"No. It's very homey but not frilly." Aunt Maisie glanced over at Rory. "I think you could give Rory a run for her money." She put the box on the table and opened it. "They're not warm, but Rory bought them right out of the fryer so at least they're fresh."

Lachlan leaned over to inspect the yeasty goodness. "Why don't we sample those donuts. I heard Elmer's is legend but never tried them."

"I brought along some coffee in case you didn't have any made yet." Aunt Daisy held up the thermos as if it were a trophy.

"I'm drinking an herbal tea. Too much coffee late in the day keeps me from falling asleep."

"Oh, that's too bad. My Marvin always loved my coffee." Aunt Daisy's shoulders drooped, and a small pout graced her mouth. "Well, I understand—about needing to get a good night sleep and all."

Aunt Maisie glanced around his kitchen. "Where are your cups and plates? I can't wait to dig into these."

He went to a cabinet and pulled out three extra mugs, along with four small plates.

Rory took a napkin from the holder on the table and pulled out a donut and handed it to him. "Here you go." She leaned closer to put it on a plate and lowered her voice so her aunts, who were busy ogling the dining room and living room combination from the doorway, couldn't hear. "You lucked out on the coffee. Aunt Daisy brews it sharp and bitter. That's the way my uncle drank it. He had taste buds of steel but did most of the cooking to save his stomach."

"Good on me then." He took a sip of his tea and bit into the pastry. His eyes grew round and sparked with pleasure. "Everyone's right. These are great." He bit into it again and groaned. It sounded so much like the noises he made when they were tangling under the sheets that her mouth went dry.

"Uh—yeah—Elmer's never fails."

The Aunts turned around at the sound.

"Oh, he's started on the donuts." Aunt Maisie waddled over to the table with urgency as if she'd miss her share. She grabbed up a napkin and two donuts in a sleight of hand that would've made a magician look like a piker.

"Sister! Don't be a pig." Aunt Daisy's admonishment held little sway because she helped herself to two as well.

"Okay." Her aunt heaved a sigh and began to put one of the donuts back. "It's just—"

Aunt Daisy opened the thermos and started to pour three cups of coffee.

"None for me." Rory held up her hand. "I had a cup on the way back from Elmer's." It was a lie but one designed to save her internal organs from being mummified by Aunt Masie's coffee.

Aunt Maisie gave a quick glance from one side to the other and reached for another donut.

"We have a whole box at home." Aunt Daisy gave her sister the side-eye.

Her aunt stiffened her spine and gave her sister a haughty, nose in the air, glare. "Who made you the donut police?"

"Don't worry about it. I appreciate the thought and the company." Lachlan waved a hand toward the table.

"Enjoy."

Aunt Maisie beamed. "I will. I will." She wriggled with joy at the first bite. "These are the best with coffee." A quick sip was followed by another mouthful of fluffiness. "Oh, my God! I think my mouth just had an orgasm."

Lachlan's tea shot through his nose. He began coughing and dabbing at his damp shirt with his hand. Rory grabbed up a hand towel from a hook next to the stove and gave it to him. His eyes watered and he mouthed, *"help me."*

"Sister! Language." Aunt Daisy scowled and helped herself to the treats on the table. "What's with the potty mouth?"

"Hey. Get off my back, Sister. Weren't you the one that called our intruder a, well I can't even say the word," her aunt said around another bite. "Don't come between me and Elmer."

Rory thumped Lachlan on the back. "Can't you two see he's strangling?" She was distressed to see how watery and red his eyes were and the way he struggled for air.

There was only one donut left in the box. The last thing she needed this morning was to have her aunts fighting over a single pastry like a couple of hyenas.

"Ladies," Lachlan gasped. He sucked in a wheezing breath. "I need to talk to Rory about something."

"About the break-in?" Aunt Daisy glanced from Lachlan to Rory and back to Lachlan. Her eyes widened in understanding. "Oh, oh yes. I'll leave the thermos here. Rory can bring it back with her later. Come on Maisie." She pointed to the box on the table. "Bring your lover with you."

****

Lachlan never had hot tea spurt out of his nose, but it wasn't an experience he planned on repeating any time soon. He finished wiping up the mess as the two old ladies toddled back to their home with Maisie clutching the box in her pudgy hands.

"I'm so sorry." He could tell Rory tried hard not to laugh but failed miserably. She went to the sink and moistened another paper towel before handing it to him. "Here you go." A smile nudged the corner of her mouth. "Are you all right?"

He wiped his face." I'll survive, but I can't unhear your aunt." The mental whiplash had nearly killed him. Death by herbal tea.

"Aunt Maisie doesn't have any filters." Rory held her hand over her mouth as the giggles erupted loud and long. "Sometimes I think she does it to get Aunt Daisy's bra in a knot."

"That's another image I didn't need."

"Sorry again." She sat at the table and dashed the tears away. "I tried to sneak out of the house to talk to you, but I got outted by Elmer's. Aunt Maisie has the nose of a bloodhound."

"I noticed she has a deep affection for him."

"They thought we should have a party. I really think Aunt Maisie was afraid we'd eat all the donuts."

"It's okay. I don't normally go to bed until about nine or ten. It gives me a chance to get some business done before I call it a day." He held his mug up toward the sunny morning sky. "You don't have to make excuses to come over. You're my neighbor."

Rory's face flushed but she met his gaze head on. "I'm confused."

"About what?" He poured hot water in a mug and handed it to her, along with a tea bag. "Breakfast tea. Decaffeinated."

"Thanks." She dunked the teabag for a few seconds. "I'm trying to figure us out."

"There's an us?"

"Well, I don't even understand myself—why I jumped you the night of the barbeque. The lust monkeys were throwing emotional coconuts all over the place that night. I think one might have caved in my head because I don't do that—go to bed with strangers."

"We've already established that's not our normal M.O." He put a saucer next to her mug for the teabag. "I don't regret what we did." A flash of worry shot through him. "Do you?"

She shook her head, making her ponytail swish across her shoulders. "Lord, no. It was the most amazing night of my life."

"Good to know." He couldn't help the satisfaction that buoyed him up. No one had ever said he'd given them the most amazing night of their lives. He tried to be a generous lover.

"Oh, I dabbled with sex in high school. Most disastrous, disgusting thing ever."

"The mayor's son?"

"Ugh—don't even go there."

He didn't bother to hide his chuckle. "I think that tale lives in Hootiecackle history."

"There was only one other person before Glen, but I found out he was a dick. As you know, Glen turned out to be an even bigger dick. I should've realized it when I never had an orgasm with him."

"That's the second orgasm I've heard about this

morning. You're making it hard for me to go to sleep."

It was her turn to laugh. He loved the abandoned and full throaty quality that made him ache to touch her again.

"Sorry." She took a tentative sip of her tea. "I'm going to just say what I need to say, and you're not obligated to do anything, okay?"

"Okay."

"I really like you. I mean *really* like you. It's not anything I expected or wanted, but there it is." She sucked in a deep breath. "All of The Aunts' fancy footwork paid off—and I hate it."

"Why?"

"Because I feel manipulated."

"They have good hearts." He held out his hand. She put hers in his and stood. "If it makes you feel better, I've been wondering the same thing about *us*. What I had with Kate was good. I came to Hootiecackle to get away from the memories in St. Louis. I wanted an uncomplicated life. I was happy until one kiss blew the doors off." He touched the side of her face, tracing the little line of freckles that marched across her nose. "I feel a little shortchanged that we didn't get a goodnight kiss after the break-in."

Rory's eyes grew wide until there was a green ring around huge pupils. "I second that." She licked her lips, and he was lost. He lowered his head to taste her, to feel the warmth of her breath mixing with his.

There it was, the kick to the heart that grew until his body hummed with longing. She wrapped her arms around him, pressing closer. Every part of her body molded to his. Her breasts, the way she cradled his hardness against herself urged him to deepen the kiss. He wanted more.

"How long until you have to go to work?" he whispered against her mouth.

She smiled. "I don't have to be there until eight-thirty to open up."

A quick glance at the clock said it was seven o'clock. "That gives us and hour at least."

"Give me thirty minutes. Any more than that and The Aunts might get nosy."

He loved the mischievous smile on her face. Her eyes were wide and inviting. "Challenge accepted."

Chapter Eighteen

"Miss Rory," Josie pointed at the display Rory was making, "you've been doin' that over and over. Is something wrong?"

Rory stared down at the antique watch in her hand. "No. I'm fine. Better than fine." She smiled as she rearranged the items once again.

"This doesn't have anything to do with that fine officer Donovan, does it?" She gave Rory a knowing smile.

The kid was too perceptive. "Maybe." This was silly. It wasn't as if she'd never been with a man before, it was nothing new, and yet, Lachlan made her so aware of herself as a woman. This morning was everything she'd hoped. For the few precious minutes they had before she had to leave, they lay in bed, intertwined talking about the simplest and silliest things. It was strange that their relationship began in a frenzy of heat and now they were getting to know each other. It was too soon for anything more. Holding each other would have to be enough for now. That's what she kept telling herself.

All day her mind had been on Lachlan instead of her job. He said he'd drop by before he had to go to the station. Each moment until she could see him again wound her tighter and tighter with anticipation. *Lord, I'm a mess.*

She glanced at the clock. It was five thirty. Half an hour from now he should be coming through the door. *Obsessed much?* She laughed at self. *This is so high school.*

Her phone rang and she picked up, still thinking about Lachlan. "Funky Junk Shoppe."

"It's good to hear you, Rory." Glen's voice came through, sweet and melting like powdered sugar on a hot beignet. It sent a ripple of disgust and unease through her.

She closed her eyes and steeled herself for the argument she knew would come. Glen was tenacious if nothing else. "What do you want now? Your shenanigans aren't going to work."

"Now, be sweet. You know you belong in New Orleans, not in that podunk town with those senile old women."

The Callahan temper rose hot and fast. "I know you're trying to ruin my business. It won't work. My life is here in Hootiecackle."

"Even the name is so—rural."

"I don't care. You can quit being a jerk and leave me alone," she ground out. "And, I won't go back to you."

His soft laugh chilled her. "You're wrong. I always get what I go after. You're the best thing that ever happened to me. I know I messed up, but we belong together. You deserve the finer things in life. And yes, I was blinded by Fiona. She was—."

"You mean someone who wasn't able to come through with money and influence."

"Fiona and I just didn't work out. Have dinner with me tonight." It wasn't a request. It held a command. "We'll talk things over."

"When will you understand I have nothing to say to you."

"It might be wise."

"Is that a threat?"

"No, just some advice."

"I thought you high-tailed it back to New Orleans." She forced herself not to hang up. His voice held confidence that she would sit across a table with him. He had to be closer than she thought. "Where are you?"

For a moment he hesitated. "I'm—I'm in Branson on business. Checking out some of the antique places. I thought dinner wouldn't hurt. I want to prove coming back to New Orleans is the right thing to do."

"For you, maybe. I have a good life here. There's nothing for me in New Orleans. Not even you." She ended the call before he said anything else. His business was his problem, not hers.

The door chimed and she looked up from the phone to see Lachlan standing in front of her with a questioning gaze.

"Looks like you're holding a snake instead of a phone."

"I might be. It's someone that slithers like one."

"Peters?"

"Yeah." She gave him a smile and saw the familiar Elmer's bag. "More Elmer's?"

"I only got a couple of bites before your aunts made off with the box." He shook the white paper bag with the familiar blue logo. "Come on, you know you want one," his voice tempted.

Josie rolled her eyes. "Should I leave you two alone?" She made kissy noises at them.

"Stop that." Rory gave Josie a playful swat on the

shoulder. "Or you don't get any."

"I don't need any." Josie took a little skip back and gave a little twirl. "Those things are the mortal enemies of my hips. Gotta keep my girlish figure."

Lachlan put the bag on the counter with a laugh. "Well, your hips called and ordered two."

Josie ran her hands over said hips. "Traitors. Okay, I'll take these and put them in the office so you can make mookie eyes at each other." She grabbed up the bag and left them alone.

The heat in his eyes and the way the dimple popped out on his left cheek made Rory's heart stutter and bump. "What is this? Seduction by Elmer's?"

"Hey, you started it." The feigned innocence on his face made her laugh.

"So I did."

He took a step forward with a smile that made promises he couldn't possibly keep with Josie in the office. "Do you want coffee, my place tomorrow morning?"

"I'll do my best to ditch The Aunts." She couldn't resist putting her hand on his chest, hoping her touch left him aching for more.

She leaned forward to give him a quick kiss. Her mission was thwarted by her phone ringing. She put up her finger for him to keep his place. "Funky Junk Shoppe."

"Hey, Rory, it's Callie—no, Mikey, go the other way," she yelled. "Head it off before it gets hit by a car." The sounds of yelling and screaming blared over her phone. "You've got a situation at home. The chain on the gate to the fence between the farm was cut. Matt Turner's cows are loose and running all over the place."

Rory held the phone away from her ear when Callie bellowed another command at her partner. "Sorry about that. You better get here. Your aunts are about to go apoplectic."

Rory squeezed her eyes shut and rubbed the bridge of her nose. She took a deep breath. "I'll be there as soon as I can." She sighed and looked at Lachlan. "There's mayhem at home. Someone let out the neighbor's cows. My aunts rent out that pasture behind the backyard."

"Who would cut the fence?"

"I've got an idea." Her lips curled at the thought of Glen being anywhere near her home.

"The snake?"

"Yeah. He said he was in Branson on business."

"I don't like the idea that he's so close. Let me know what Deputy Parker says, okay?"

"I will, and thanks for the donuts." She gave him a wan smile. "Coffee tomorrow morning?"

"You got it." He gave her a quick kiss on the cheek and waved as he went out the door. "Catch you later."

She nodded and waved back. "Later." A quick glance at the clock said there were only fifteen minutes to closing, but she knew it was imperative she get home. "Josie," she called out.

Josie came running, wiping the evidence of glazed sugar from her mouth. "What is it?"

"You need to close tonight."

"I don't know if I can do it." Josie's eyes were full of concern. "You've never had me close out before."

"There's an emergency at home. Just lock up and I'll take care of everything else tomorrow morning. I'll be sure to show you how to close up later in the week."

"Okay." Josie nodded. "I can do that."

It took ten minutes to get home and pull into the drive. At least ten large, black and white cows ran around the yard, bawling and going every which way. Matt Turner was desperately trying to keep them out of the road. Chipper, his border collie, nipped at the cow's heels and zipped back and forth to keep them in a group.

Her aunts raced around surveying the damage. "Rory!" Aunt Maisie came hurrying at a fast waddle toward the car. Her face was red from the heat and anger. "My tomatoes are ruined. The garden is trampled, and some of Daisy's roses are now cow fodder."

****

Lachlan dialed his phone.

"Deputy Parker."

"Hey, Callie. This is Lachlan Donovan."

"Why, hello, Sergeant. What can I do for you—wait, don't tell me. You want to know what happened with your neighbors."

"Yeah."

"Nothing much. Someone cut the chain on the fence. Turner's cows got out and made a mess of things. Everything is set to rights now."

"Good. Was there any evidence at the site?"

"You're asking about her ex?"

"Peters is a loose cannon. I don't trust him."

"I told Rory I'd canvas the neighbors if they saw anything unusual."

"Thank you. Let me know if you need anything from me."

"Will do."

After the call he was more than ever convinced it was Peters causing trouble again. He'd promised Rory he would contact his friend, Caleb McGuinness in the St.

Louis FBI office about the identity theft. Now it was imperative to follow through.

A minute later Caleb picked up. "Hey, Lachlan, how goes it in, what was it—Hootiecackle?"

"It's going."

"Very informative. Are you bored out of your skull yet?"

"No. Hootiecackle is a weird little town with a lot of interesting characters. That's why I wanted to talk to you." He went on to explain about Rory and the identity theft. "I need some ideas. She's being victimized by her ex-boyfriend."

"And you're the new guy?"

"I want to be. Right now, it's too new to tell."

"It shouldn't be hard to find out how the theft was done. Just give me a couple of hours with a computer."

"Great, come down, spend the weekend. There's a steak with your name on it. I'll invite Rory over along with her aunts but beware of the Callahan twins. They'll likely want to set you up with a potential wife once they find out you're single."

"They can try." A snort conveyed his hubris.

"That's what I said. You've been warned." He sorted out the details for the weekend and ended the call. He immediately called Rory to tell her what Caleb planned. "I want to invite you and your aunts over for another cookout. I'm sure they'll love him."

"Should we bring anything." The laugh in her voice said he better say no.

"Only if it comes from the Sunny Supermarket."

"Message received."

"Oh, dress like a frump. Once Caleb gets a good look at you, he won't be able to concentrate on finding how Peters did it."

"Are you jealous?"

"He's got a hipster, nerdy vibe that some woman like." He tried to sound nonchalant but a part of his wondered if he was just a blip on her radar. "I've seen him charm babies, old ladies and every female in-between."

"My, my, that *is* a talent." There was a pause before she gave him a slow, throaty chuckle. "Iguess I'll have to tell you what I like over *coffee*."

Chapter Nineteen

Lachlan took his coffee to the patio table and sat across from his friend, Caleb. He closed his eyes for a moment, enjoying the soft morning breeze on his skin, the smell of his coffee and the heat of it in his hands. The moment he opened his eyes, the sun began to rise over the horizon throwing a palette of color over the sky.

"It's been a long time since I was up at the ass-crack of dawn." Caleb stared down at the mug of coffee. "How do you handle the graveyard shift?"

Lachlan laughed. "I'm used to it." His gaze drifted over to the Callahan property. Caleb was good company, but he could never compare to Rory. "It was a challenge at first, but worth it." He remembered the horrific banging of Rory's nail gun and the saucy way she'd greeted him. "Yeah. Way worth it."

Caleb sucked in a deep breath. His eyes widened. His nose wrinkled. "Nope. Don't take offense but this isn't my jam." He motioned in a wide arc with his mug. "I smell cow shit."

Lachlan sniffed the air. "I don't smell anything."

"You're nose blind. That's one kind of pollution we don't have in St. Louis."

"I'm sorry if your dainty nose is offended." Again, he stared over the fence, wondering why Rory was late. She was supposed to be here as usual, but this time to talk with Caleb.

He sincerely missed her company this morning. Around this time, they'd sneak in a tumble between the sheets and have a quick breakfast. His heart sped in anticipation. He needed to see her and touch her again. Desire grew stronger each day.

It was surprising how much they had in common but also how much they differed. She made him laugh. It was something he hadn't done in a long time. He'd managed to slough off some of the grief that belonged to Kate. He'd tucked her away in a part of his heart no one could reach, yet Rory's presence in his life made him feel new.

Their early morning trysts were as important as breathing. He knew he teetered on the edge of falling in love. The need to protect Rory grew each day.

As for Rory, she'd given up trying to bamboozle her aunts that her early morning dates were just for coffee. Every so often he would catch one of the older Callahan women giving him the hairy eyeball, followed by a knowing smile.

Caleb cleared his throat. "Something interesting in that direction?"

"Not yet."

"I'd think small town life would get dull."

"So did I." Lachlan sipped his fast-cooling coffee. He launched into the story about Rory's bachelorette party. "And then the town librarian grabbed me by the gonads. The stripper Rory hired showed up, ripped off his clothes, and yelled he was the long arm of the law."

Caleb coughed and coffee shot out of his nose.

"That happens a lot around here." Lachlan tapped the side of his nose. "Don't get me started on Rory's friend Serena. She's like Wednesday Addams and Elvira rolled up into one. She swears she has ghosts in her building."

"She sounds interesting."

"Rory or Serena?"

"Serena."

"Don't go there. If Henry or Agnes, her resident ghosts, don't like you she'll stick pins into a voodoo doll."

"Ouch."

"Ask Rory's ex." Lachlan gave a quick snort. "He swears Serena put a hex on him."

"Isn't he the one causing her problems?" Caleb stared at him over the rim of his mug.

"We're pretty sure, but there's no evidence."

A honking in the sky interrupted their conversation.

His friend stared up at the loud noise. "What the hell?"

"Canada geese. I hope they didn't poop-bomb our cars, but I wouldn't count on it."

"More greetings from Mother Nature? I thought I came here to work a case, not be a part of an Animal Planet documentary." Caleb settled back in his chair, watching the geese. "What's happened so far with the identity theft?"

"Rory's done what she could—contacted the banks and so on."

Caleb shook his head. "It's pretty damned hard to find a hacker when it comes to identity theft."

"She keeps receiving merchandise she never ordered." Lachlan stood and paced his patio. He jammed his hands into his shorts' pockets. Frustration ate at him. "Her ex has all of her personal information. She used to work for him."

"That would make it easier."

"I found out last week, after the break-in at her business, that she still uses the same passwords on her locks and computers that she had in New Orleans." It was embarrassing to admit the woman he admired and was half in love with could be so careless.

Caleb whistled between his teeth. "Ouch. A lot of smart people make the same costly mistake."

Lachlan didn't know if he should broach the subject of Chief Nolan. He knew he was a good detective, but Caleb might be able dig in places that wouldn't send out any red flags. He blew out his breath and decided to go for it. "I need another favor."

"O-k-a-y."

"Rory mentioned something about the local Chief of Police that's troubling me."

"You, not her?"

"The man asked for sexual favors from her when she was fifteen. She's put it in her past, or so she says."

"How do you know she wants this?"

"I don't. Could you check on your own, not through the Bureau? I need a starting point. He's probably done this more than once—he might still be doing it." He thought of the station's dispatcher, Jenny. "I can't ask around because it would have the town gossips working overtime. I can't tip him off."

"What if it's not true?" Caleb took a sip of coffee.

"I'll face that as well."

A flash of red caught Lachlan's eye. It was Rory, stomping her way to his gate. Her voice rose in volume until the birds perched on the birdbath took flight.

"Glen Peters, I hope your balls shrivel up like rotten black walnuts." A blue cloud of swearing accompanied Rory as she threw open the gate.

A vengeful Queen Boudica could've been storming toward them. Green eyes flashed and her long cape of curly red hair flowed in the wind. "He's gone over the line." Righteous anger rolled over them. "I got a call from an appraiser last night. He's from a lending company concerning a mortgage on the farm. The man wants to stop by this morning. To look over the property."

Caleb's mouth twitched with a hint of a smile. "Well, she's really chipper in the morning."

"You have no idea." Lachlan's appreciation of his lady grew by the second.

Rory stood, hands on her hips, eyes closed, and sucked in a deep breath. The red cherry blouse and the white capris covering her long legs looked like armor instead of Hootiecackle business casual. She was magnificent.

"You must be Caleb McGuinness." She held out her hand with a forced smile. "Lachlan says you're the best at finding identity thieves."

"I'd like to think so." He scooted his chair closer to the small patio table, motioning her to sit. "Depends on the case."

"My ex is a piece of work." She sank into the chair. "I didn't find out how much until this last year. My bad on that one."

"Tell me about him."

She leaned across the table in her enthusiasm, causing a slight gap in her blouse to show a bit of cleavage. Lachlan wasn't sure if the glint in his friend's eyes was of professional or personal interest. Suddenly, Lachlan's skin became too small and itchy. He stepped closer to keep tabs on Caleb as she regaled him with the details of her relationship with Peters. Jealousy slithered in his guts. The rare emotion staggered him. He'd never been this way with Kate.

"Are you sure you're not trying to get back at Peters?" Caleb leaned back in his chair. "I have to ask to get that out of the way."

"No!" She recoiled. "Although I wouldn't be sad if he broke out in genital warts. I hear his most recent ex is on the wild side. There's no way I'd return to New Orleans. He's harassing me with this latest trick" Lachlan was glad she sat back in her chair and crossed her arms over her breasts.

"You didn't apply for a loan?"

"The farm is paid off. We don't need a mortgage."

"I should've punched Grover the first time I saw him—" Lachlan had had enough of the pissant's tricks. "—smug asshole."

"I thought you said his name was Glen."

"He's always calling *Glen* Grover. It was funny at first, but now—" Rory glared at him. "—it's getting old."

"Believe me, he's a Grover. I used to think he *was* an annoying joke. There's no way I'll let him hurt—" he pointed toward Rory's home, "—them."

"The Aunts can't know what's going on. They'd freak out." Red flushed her cheeks. Tears of anger glimmered in her eyes. She stood and joined in Lachlan's pacing. "What did I ever see in him?"

Lachlan put his arm around her shoulders to stop her restless movements. It frustrated him to see her so upset. "He's the past."

"But he's making my life a hell right now, and he knows it." She stiffened for a second but relaxed under his light hold. "He's capable of worse. One of the reasons

I left him, besides finding out he was an unfaithful jerk, he was coercing people to use our business."

"Blackmail on the side?"

"I'm not sure. He said he was good at ferreting out their secrets. When you run in that crowd it uses up a lot of high octane. I couldn't go on living with him."

"Did he ever say anything about his clients?" Caleb narrowed his eyes.

"Only that they shouldn't do stupid stuff if they didn't want it to end up on social media." She bit her lip. "I never saw anything unusual about them on Facebook, Instagram or the other sites."

Lachlan grew angrier by the moment. "Maybe he didn't need to let it get that far if they were willing to buckle. Did an investigator dig around for him?"

"If he did, I never knew about it."

"What about any strange files on the company's computer, yours or his." Caleb crossed his arms over his chest, his eyes narrowed.

She shook her head. "No. He hated technology. Everything was old-school. I had to input all the receipts of the day into the computer at night. He had copious notebooks."

"I thought designers used special programs to show their customers what the finished interior would look like." Lachlan was surprised Glen was so technologically inept. "Nothing like that?"

"He had elaborate sketches with swatches. Like I said, old school."

"What about you?" Caleb asked.

"I used the company computer to do my designs."

"Did he ever touch it?"

"I took care of all the techy stuff. He didn't know

squat about installing programs. His two-finger pecking drove me nuts. It took forever for him to be able to find what he wanted in our files. Even his phone gave him fits." She gave Caleb a wan smile. "I once caught him trying to use the tray of the CD drive in the desktop computer for a cupholder."

Caleb rolled his eyes. "You're shitting me, right?"

She shook her head. "Nope."

"What about his personal laptop?"

"He didn't have one, or at least, I never saw him with one."

"Okay. Not helpful."

"Sorry."

"That means he had someone do it for him." Caleb looked like the gears were turning in his head. "Do you know of anyone who might be able to help him?"

"There's a kid who used to deliver food to the stores. One day I came back from lunch early. He was using the office computer while Glen looked over his shoulder." Her lips canted to one side. "I thought they were watching porn from the way they jumped when they saw me."

"Is it usual to have non-employees in the office?" Caleb's brow went up in question.

"Glen isn't the trusting type. I'm surprised he let the kid back there."

"Do you remember his name?" Lachlan had hoped this would be easy. His bubble burst when Rory shook her head.

"What about where he worked?"

"Better Bagel Deli and Po'boy Shoppe. I put in the lunch orders every day." Before he could ask his next question, she piped up. "He still worked there when I left. I know because I stopped to get a bagel on my way out of town."

"Let me do a little detective work and I'll find out who he is." Caleb gave her a speculative glance. "We still might not be able to find him if he uses a VPN."

"Oh." Rory looked as crestfallen as Lachlan felt. She dropped into the glider. Lachlan sat next to her and took her hand for comfort.

"What should I do about the appraiser?"

"Send him over here. We can explain things and let him get back to his company. It's up to them about what they want to do. It wouldn't look good for them to be a part of real estate fraud." Caleb's smile made Lachlan glad he wasn't in Peters' shoes. "Maybe we can get them to cooperate, especially if they know you plan to go to the FTC." He gave a little snigger. "I'll bet Peters hired the kid to hack into your accounts. Real estate fraud is trickier than playing around with credit cards. Residential mixed with agricultural property will trip them up. I have a way to check for his hackers IP address that could nail him to the wall. If this is a side gig for the kid he might be willing to testify against Peters."

"I hope so." Rory raked her fingers through her mass of curls. "I've done everything I could think of to stop him—contacted my bank, changed my passcodes," she wrinkled her nose, "—I'd like to think I'm smarter than the average sleazeball, but I really messed up this time."

"Some of the smartest people I know have done the same thing," Caleb said.

"That's not very comforting. However, I did get new email addresses when I moved back. I didn't want him contacting me."

A new thought made Lachlan uneasy. "Peters

probably found her new email address after he broke in."

"That's not hard to fix. What we need is the email address from the person who asked for the mortgage." Caleb stood, picking up his coffee mug. "I'll talk to the appraiser when he comes over. I'm sure he'll be able to find out for us. There's a lot of information most people never see in an email."

"I'll let you know when he shows up." She turned to Lachlan with a radiant smile that never failed to get to him. "After I get finished with the appraiser, I need to run into town to get a few things. Serena is hosting a sleepover the night before Chandra's wedding. I won't have time for morning coffee." She cast a surreptitious glance at Caleb. It was her way of saying no sex while his friend was here.

"Don't miss coffee on my account." His brow rose in question as he gave them a knowing smile.

Lachlan didn't know whether to laugh or give his friend a hard Dutch rub.

"We'll have plenty of time for coffee later." She turned and glanced at them over her shoulder. "Have fun catching up. I'll see you tonight at the cookout."

She leaned over and took his mouth. The kiss revved him up faster than the caffeine in his mug. He cupped her head with his free hand to bring her closer.

She stood and gave them a little wave. "See you tonight." With that she walked away with a bounce in her step that sent her long hair swinging from side to side.

Lachlan narrowed his eyes as his friend kept his eyes trained on Rory's retreating backside.

"I can see why you've taken a liking to the lady." Caleb smiled.

****

Rory walked back to her house with a spring in her step. Not only were they going to get to the bottom of her problem with Glen, but she also discovered that Lachlan was jealous. Not with the screaming, finger pointing suspicion Glen had exhibited, but letting Caleb know in a *this is my woman* way. She had to admit she'd feel the same if another woman came on to Lachlan.

She walked the rest of the way back home, still amazed that Lachlan was everything Glen wasn't. He supported her business, argued the merits of movies, and listened to her thoughts. She relished the lazy moments after they made love. Her strength didn't threaten him. A smile tugged at her lips. His jealousy wasn't aggressive but sweet.

The back door squeaked when she opened it. The Aunts' heads turned toward her, green eyes staring at her in scary unison.

"How was *coffee*?" A hint of a smile tugged at Aunt Daisy's mouth.

"I just dropped in to say hi. He has a guest for the weekend and wanted me to meet him." She tried to sound nonchalant. It was difficult when, if Caleb's planned worked, Glen would soon be dead meat.

"Oh?" Aunt Maisie nibbled at the corner of her toast.

"Yes, and Lachlan invited us to another cookout this evening."

Aunt Daisy crinkled her forehead in thought. "Doesn't he have to work on the weekends?"

"He took a couple of personal days off." Rory leaned against the kitchen counter. "Nick is taking his shifts because Lachlan is trading with him on his normal days off. That way Nick can take a week off for his and

Chandra's honeymoon."

"That's so thoughtful," Aunt Maisie beamed. "You said a cookout—tonight? I planned to freeze some of the green beans that didn't get trampled by Matt's cows." She looked conflicted.

Rory suddenly realized she couldn't talk to the appraiser with her aunts around. "I'm sure he's got the steaks marinating right now. I need you and Aunt Daisy to run some errands for me."

"I've got to salvage the tomatoes and beans." Aunt Maisie daintily slurped her orange juice. "There won't be enough for cannin'." She sighed and picked up her toast. "At least the kitchen won't be so hot this year. Even with air-conditioning it's like a sauna. It's not even worth it because we end up throwin' half of it away. Sister cans as well as she cooks. One of these days her cannin' will kill us."

"Please." Rory went to her aunt and knelt, throwing her arms around her shoulders. "Please, please? I've got some work for the shop I need to do from home. Josie is taking care of the store, so I won't have a lot of interruptions." It wasn't a lie.

"Well, I don't know."

"I need to get things for my sleepover with Serena and Chandra. I've made a list." She stood and went to her purse she'd left on the counter last night. "Aunt Daisy can go with you. Isn't there a new nursery in Holloway?" She pulled out a couple of crisp one-hundred-dollar bills and the list. "Here." She handed it to her aunt. "Pay for the supplies with one and take the other for helping me out. Maybe they have something to add to your rose garden."

Aunt Daisy took it, her eyes round. "Maybe we can

stop off at the Dinner Bell for breakfast. She stared at the runny eggs and burnt bacon on her plate. "Maisie's been cooking for Sam and Ella's restaurant again."

"If you don't like it, dump it." She cast a sour look at her sister. "Better yet, let Rory cook it."

"I value my life too much." Aunt Daisy went to the waste can and scraped her plate. "I need my strength to prune my roses. Not one is fit for the county fair and I'm sure Lotta Charles is dancing naked under the moonlight at their demise. Dinner Bell it is."

"Why on earth would Lotta do that?" Rory was fascinated and appalled at the image of a skinny Lotta dancing, let alone naked.

"Because she's a witch."

"She's a god-fearing Christian." Aunt Maisie reminded them.

"Maybe—" Aunt Daisy narrowed her eyes and thinned her lips, "—maybe not. Last year I'm sure she conjured up a big case of black spot."

"Aunt Daisy!"

"Well, it's true." Her aunt glared at her.

"What is?"

"No matter what I did, I got black spot over all my roses and those Japanese beetles came in droves," she huffed. "And what about Matt's cows?"

"You can't blame that on Lotta, too." Rory tried to set her aunt straight, but she knew it was next to impossible to get rid of whatever bug was wriggling around in her brain.

"Cows can be familiars, can't they?"

"That's cats you dipshit." Aunt Maisie stood. "I've had enough of this. Things happen."

"Language!" Aunt Daisy blew up like a puffer fish.

"Ladies, quit bickering." She had to get her aunts out of the house. The appraiser and Caleb would be here in an hour. "Come on. I really need you to help me out. I want to bring something for the cookout, and I don't have time."

"Well," Aunt Daisy warmed to the prospect. "I'd planned to give Toots a crew cut, but it can wait until tomorrow."

"Oh, I'll bake something," Aunt Maisie squealed in delight. "Let me crack out my cookbooks. What about—"

"No, no, no." Rory rushed to cut Aunt Maisie off at that culinary pass.

"Okay." Aunt Maisie's crestfallen expression pulled at Rory's heart.

"Why don't you go to Holloway to that fancy French bakery. I'll bet the guys would love some cream puffs after you check out the nursery and do the shopping? You won't have much time left for baking after you get back."

"You have a point," Aunt Maisie conceded. "I'm going to get dressed."

Aunt Daisy stood and put the dirty dishes in the dishwasher. "I better get going, too."

"Thank you. I'm sure I can count on you to keep Aunt Maisie from buying out the bakery?"

"Know what you mean. There isn't an éclair or pastry she doesn't like."

It was less than a half-hour later they came down, dressed to take on the town. Aunt Maisie wore a white lacy top with hot pink capris and sparkly, flowered flip-flops. The camouflage cargo shorts, and olive drab t-shirt Aunt Daisy wore said she was going rose hunting.

"Is there anythin' else you need besides the fruit and veggie trays? Crackers?" Aunt Daisy stared down at the list.

"I forgot crackers. Good catch." Rory was anxious to get them out the door.

They got as far as their truck when Aunt Maisie turned to her. "I forgot to ask what Lachlan's friend is like."

"He's very nice and smart." Rory herded them to their car.

"But what's he *like?*" This time it was Aunt Daisy who chimed in with a glint of cupid in her eyes.

"Keep your match making tendencies in check." Rory huffed out a sigh. "He's cute in a Chris Hemsworth sort of way. Very Thor-like with glasses."

Aunt Maisie's eyes went round, while Aunt Daisy's squinted

"Young Thor or Fat Thor?" Aunt Daisy probed.

"Young Thor."

"Good," they chimed in together.

"I wonder if we could bring a guest?" Aunt Daisy pulled out her phone and slid into the passenger seat of the truck.

They chattered away without paying her any attention.

Aunt Maisie got in the driver's side. "What about Tanzy, or Francine Yoder?"

Rory watched the truck take off down the road. "We're doomed."

Chapter Twenty

The doorbell rang. Rory glanced over at Lachlan and Caleb for any last-minute advice. "Well?"

Caleb sat in Aunt Maisie's big floral armchair, his butt on the edge as he leaned over the laptop on the coffee table. "Bring him in and I'll do the rest."

"You've got this. Go get him." Lachlan's thousand-watt grin went straight to her heart and gave her the last bit of confidence she needed. "Just don't eat the poor guy alive."

She did a little fist pump. "Consider him got." Glen was about to go down and tied up with a big bow of legal hurt. The time had come to put an end to his spitefulness. She could handle anything he threw at her. Except this time, he'd involved her aunts. If things went as planned, she'd put grease on his skids, maybe all the way to the stony lonesome as Aunt Daisy would say.

Rory opened the door to see a man in his fifties, fluffy around the middle and sweating like crazy. He mopped his bald head with a handkerchief and huffed in exertion. She stepped outside, closing the door behind her.

The logo on his blue polo shirt read *Donnie Jones Appraisal Service.*

"Ms. Callahan?" His red face looked like he was two heartbeats away from a heatstroke. Even the veranda couldn't mitigate the ninety-five degrees showing on the thermometer by the front door.

"Yes." Her emotions ran hot but she had to be cautious and polite. It wasn't the man's fault he was there because of Glen's petty revenge.

He held out his hand that had recently held the sweaty handkerchief. "I'm Donnie Jones." The appraiser pointed to his shirt. "I'm the appraiser for my client, Golden Aspen Finance Service. We talked on the phone earlier." He noticed his damp hand and pulled it back. "Sorry about that." He wiped his hand on his pant leg. "Anyway, I'm here about appraisal. There seems to be some problems and I—"

"Problems?"

"Yeah." His face grew redder. "Could we go inside to get out of this heat?"

Even with Lachlan and Caleb inside the house, a sudden burst of distrust filled her. Had Glen possibly sent this "appraiser" as part of a scam? "Could I see some ID and a business card?"

Mister Jones looked nonplused for a second. After a couple of blinks, he shoved his handkerchief in his pocket and pulled out his wallet. "Here you go."

"Just a second." He looked like his driver's license picture, but she wanted more verification. She went into the house and gave the business card to the men. Lachlan made a call and gave her the thumbs up. The appraiser was legit.

Poor Mr. Jones looked ready to pass out by the time she reopened the door. He'd sat on the porch swing, redder than before. He mopped harder at the sweat pouring down his face.

"Come on in. Sorry about making you wait. A girl can't be too careful. It's something I'm learning day by day."

"It's okay, honey, I'd want my daughter to be just as careful." He had stood when she opened the door.

She forced a smile at the endearment and led him into the living room.

His eyes grew round at the sight of Lachlan and Caleb.

"These are my friends. This is Sergeant Lachlan Donovan. He's on the Hootiecackle police force." She then pointed to Caleb. "This is Special Agent McGuinness with the FBI."

"What's going on here?" Mr. Jones' glance went from one man to the other, uncertainty filling his eyes. "Is something wrong?"

Lachlan rose from the couch and held out his hand to Mr. Jones. "Hi. Ms. Callahan's business has been a victim of identity theft. She filed a complaint with our local department." He handed Mr. Jones his ID. "I contacted a friend of mine from the FBI."

Caleb followed suit and greeted, also showing his ID as well. "I'm with the cybercrimes division."

"I'm just the appraiser here." Mr. Jones took a step back. "I don't have anything to do with identity theft."

"We understand that." Caleb sat back down and began typing on his laptop. "We're trying to get to the bottom of this case and find the hacker. We could use your help in tracking this guy, or woman, down."

Rory was afraid Mr. Jones would bolt. "Why don't I get us some iced tea and cookies? Mr. Jones looks positively frazzled." She pulled out every southern belle trope she could think of to put the man at ease. "Why don't you take a seat? Working in this heat takes a wind out of a person."

Lachlan rolled his eyes behind Mr. Jones' back. His compressed lips were either to hold back a laugh or tell her not to lay it on too thick. She batted her lashes at him over the man's bald head. Lachlan might know the law, but she had a lock on handling middle-aged southern men.

She led Mr. Jones to Aunt Daisy's matching chair. "Have a seat. I'll bring that tea out in a jiff."

"Thank you, honey," he wheezed and settled into the overstuffed chair. "It's a bit hot today." His briefcase rested at his feet.

A few minutes later she returned to find the men chuckling over whatever they found funny about the situation. She set the tea and store-bought shortbread cookies on the coffee table and handed a glass to Mr. Jones. She put coasters on the table for each one and gave Lachlan and Caleb their tea. "Here you go."

Caleb's eyes rounded and his face screwed up after the first sip. "It's sweet." It was hard to tell if it was a statement or an accusation.

"I can make some unsweetened if you don't like it."

"It's—fine. I just wasn't expecting the—"

"I've gotten used to sweet tea during my time here." Lachlan came to Caleb's rescue. He raised his glass to her in salute. "Now unsweetened tea tastes funny."

Mr. Jones took a long gulp. "Thank you, honey. I really needed that after doing a quick walkaround to get a feel for the property."

"Really?" No wonder he was exhausted. She didn't mind the man doing his job, but Glen's fraud made her hackles rise.

Thank goodness she had Lachlan and Caleb for backup. She walked a tight line of worrying about looking like a damsel in distress or trying to do it all herself. It took a while for her to realize it didn't weaken her newfound self-esteem to ask friends for help.

"Yeah. I like to get a head start on these things." His forehead scrunched up until he looked like a round, Shar Pei puppy. "To tell you the truth I think a two-million-dollar loan is more than the land and house is worth."

"Oh? He wanted two million?" she croaked. Glen was going all out for revenge. She sat next to Lachlan and took his hand, trying to keep her voice sounding normal. "Can you believe it? Two million."

"The guy has bigger balls than I thought," Lachlan whistled between his teeth.

"He wishes." Rory sat back with her arms crossed over her chest. "I'll have Serena make a voodoo doll of him. I'll rip its nuts off."

Mr. Jones expression was one of someone who thought they'd fallen into The Twilight Zone. He pulled his briefcase onto his lap as if he planned to leave the first chance he got. "What? I don't understand."

Caleb raised one brow. "Inside joke." He straightened and gave Mr. Jones a level stare. "I need the original email requesting the loan. It could lead to the hacker."

"I told you. I don't have anything to do with that."

"But you could contact the loan company and ask?" Rory picked up the plate and offered Mr. Jones a cookie. "Please."

Mr. Jones' eyes rounded again. "Honey, wish I could help, but I drove all the way from Springfield. I have two more places to see this afternoon."

"My name is Victoria, not honey. The guy who did this has all my personal information. He used to be my fiancé." She sucked in a deep breath. Slashes of heat rose up her neck, but she had to stay calm. "It was a hacker not me."

Mr. Jones sat back into his chair and pulled a tablet from his briefcase. "Here you go. This is all I have." He swiped the screen and held it out to her. It was bad enough that Glen was stealing from her but now he was forging her signature and doing a damn good job.

"I didn't sign this," she insisted and took the tablet from him. Lachlan glanced down at the screen. "Look. It's a good attempt but not me."

"Go get a pen and some paper." Lachlan gave her a small pat on the shoulder. "Write your signature down several times and give it to Caleb so he can do a comparison."

She went to the end table where the aunts kept a spiral notebook to keep their canasta scores. Three signatures later, she handed the paper to Caleb. "Here you go. What do we do next?"

He pulled a black cylinder from his bag and plugged it into his laptop. "I'll scan this in, and we can tell in no time." He fed the page through the scanner. "Let me set up a file and I'll compare these. Mr. Jones, I know you are a contractor for the finance company, but it would help for you to contact them about this fraudulent loan."

"It's not my place—"

"It would be helpful." Caleb's no-nonsense tone held a command rather than a request. "I need all the original emails they have on file concerning the loan." Caleb unplugged the scanner and put it back in the computer bag. "Once I have those it should point us in the right direction. Did I mention she'd filed a complaint with the Federal Trade Commission? The loan company should be made aware of this."

"The FTC?" Mr. Jones went white.

"The Chief of Police wants the case closed ASAP." Lachlan took Rory's hand. "He doesn't think it's possible to catch the thief, but Special Agent McGuinness believes differently. I'd put my trust in him."

"Okay, okay." Mr. Jones stood and fumbled in his pants pocket for his phone. "Let me talk to my contact."

A half-hour and several phone calls later Caleb sat staring down at his laptop, his fingers racing over the keys. A frown of concentration puckered his face. Rory leaned into Lachlan to whisper, "What's he looking for?"

"I don't know but I'm confident Caleb will sniff out the hacker."

As if on cue, Caleb hooted in victory. "Got you!"

Mr. Jones ran over to stand behind Caleb. "What? What? Who?"

Rory sizzled with excitement. *Maybe this nightmare will be over.* She and Lachlan joined Mr. Jones to stare down at what Caleb found. The screen was filled with enough gobbledygook to make her eyeballs cross, and her brain turn to mush. She was used to dealing with computers, but this was way beyond her abilities. "I don't understand—you can find the hacker with that?" She pointed to the cryptic lines on the screen.

"Your ex's friend isn't very smart. We're in luck he didn't use a VPN."

Mr. Jones looked confused.

"Virtual Private Network. It's designed to hide the origin of the email. That was my biggest worry." Caleb grinned and highlighted a line of text. "Here's our culprit. Really sloppy work. I'll contact the New Orleans office and have them check it out. Hell, I'll even go there myself."

Rory sighed in relief. The weight that had pressed her down for the last few days became lighter. It was easier to breathe and think. "Thank you, thank you." Lachlan slid his arm around her waist, and for a moment, she allowed herself to lean against him. She looked up at him. "Thank you for calling in reinforcements."

"I knew Caleb could sniff out the culprit. Peters will regret starting this." He reached over to tug at one of her curls. "Chief Nolan will be eating crow as well."

Mr. Jones beamed. "You two have saved my company's butt—er—you've kept me from getting involved with fraud."

"We couldn't have done it without your help." Caleb exited out of his computer and shut the lid. "I'll email the finance company with the particulars once we make an arrest. They may want to file charges." He stood and picked up his laptop. "I'm going to go make that call."

A few minutes later, Mr. Jones had gone as well. Rory sank onto the couch with another sigh. Lachlan sat next to her and took her hand. The way their fingers linked together was so right. It had taken a lot from her to allow him to help. She'd worked hard to be independent, to be strong again. The realization that there was a true friendship behind this budding relationship surprised her. Glen had either praised or belittled her—Lachlan was a pillar to lean on, but he was there even when she didn't need help.

"I'll be so glad to have Glen out of my hair for good." She would be getting her life back on track and could concentrate on the man sitting next to her.

"Don't get your guard down." Lachlan's thumb

traced little circles over the top of her hand. Such a little act shouldn't make her feel so reassured and giddy at the same time, but it did. She settled her head on his shoulder.

"I know." She nestled closer and grinned. "It's one step closer to hanging Glen by his thumbs."

Lachlan sat up and turned to her. "Vengeance, thy name is Rory." His expression was comical.

"Oh, yeah." She giggled and gave him a little pat on the knee. "Remember that for the future." Lachlan didn't resist when she stood and pulled him to his feet. "Let's celebrate." She wrapped her arms around his neck and whispered against his mouth, "There's a carton of Mint Chocolate Chip ice cream in the freezer with our names on it. You've earned an extra dip today."

Chapter Twenty-One

Rory rolled over and ran a finger down Lachlan's chest. "I think I should've given you three dips." The heat radiating from his body, the scent of sex and the feel of his heartbeat under her hand made her ache for another bout. "Maybe we should've invited Caleb over for ice cream instead of sneaking away like this and letting him do all the work."

"He can get his own damned ice cream." His arm wrapped around her waist to hold her tight. He caressed her face before tangling his fingers in her hair and bringing her closer for another kiss. "I'm really partial to mint chocolate chip."

It tickled her that Lachlan was a bit jealous. The giddy sensation of being in love filled her. She lay her head on his shoulder just as a niggle of doubt popped into her head. *Am I going too fast? Is this just lust?* Whatever it was, she would take it. A quick glance at the clock on her bedside table said they were cutting it close. "The Aunts will be home soon." She rolled over with a sigh.

He pulled her back to his side. "Think of the thrill." The quick kiss on her nose was as earthshaking as the others they'd shared earlier.

"The thrill?"

"I might have to escape out the window."

"It's a two-story drop."

"Ouch." He let her go and sat up. "I guess I'll have

to think of another way."

"Not unless you can fly. Uncle Marvin put me in this room when I was a kid because there are no trees nearby." She smiled at the memory of her beloved uncle. "Aunt Daisy had nagged him to fix the squeaks on the stairs until he told her they would rat me out the minute I stepped on one. It really put a kibosh in my wild child days."

"I'm sure you found a way." A look of seriousness settled in his dark eyes. His lips thinned, dimming the rosy after-glow of sex.

"What is it?" A knot of anxiety settled in her chest. She settled her hand over her heart as if she could push it away. Whatever he had to say couldn't be good.

"I asked Caleb to do a deep dive into Nolan's background." He stared straight ahead, his chin out. "I don't think you and Serena are the only ones he's approached."

His admission stole her breath. She stared at him in disbelief. "I told you what happened because I thought you'd prejudged me." She didn't hide the burst of anger that fired her words. "Maybe it would've been better to let you believe the rumors. It's on me that I outed Serena but I didn't expect you to go Lone Ranger on me." Her agitated fingers raked through her hair, pushing it out of her face. "Why didn't you ask first?" Before he had time to answer the hurt burrowed deep and hard. "Did you say anything to Serena?"

He shook his head. "I wanted to tell you first before I talked to her." His body language said it all. He planned to investigate Chief Nolan, regardless of what she said.

"It's over and done with for me, but I don't know how she feels about it." Rory scooted against the headboard with the sheet pulled tight over her breasts. "What happened to us was a long time ago. It'll be hard to prove a thing."

"Believe me, I've seen cases like this before. The man won't be able to help himself. He'll keep preying on young girls."

"Do you think anyone will admit to being his victim?" She rubbed her eyes with the heels of her hands as if it would erase everything. "This is a small town. No one will come forward."

"You and Serena would be a start." His eyes bore into her, both pleading and demanding.

"I need you to ask her to talk to me."

"I have to do your dirty work?" She couldn't believe what she was hearing. "No. If you decided to dig into this, you can ask her yourself." Her stomach clenched and she had to work to hold back the tears burning in her eyes. "Nothing good will come from you poking around. Who's going to talk to the newbie on the force? No one will trust you."

The muscles in Lachlan's jaw clenched. "I have to investigate and enforce any proven allegation of sexual abuse on the force. A sexual predator won't stop. If he'd only propositioned you, it would be creepy enough, but you said he did the same to Serena. I told you before, he's a man in power, and mixed with a predator mentality, well, I can't let it go."

"It's bad enough that I have to live in this town with the reputation pinned on me when I was a kid. Do you think people will say, 'Poor Rory. The bad man made a pass at her.' No. They'll say I tried to seduce him."

"I'll be discreet."

"Discreet? The minute Jenny hears a faint whiff of

scandal it'll be all over town." Jenny was only the first of many who relished good gossip. "Aunt Maisie says her tongue flaps so much they use her for a fan at church."

"Why do you think I asked Caleb to help? The FBI isn't involved in this. It's just fraud and ID theft. He's doing it as a favor—he has more connections than I do. If need be, I'll pay for a private investigator."

"What!" She spiraled down into a black hole of despair and anger. "Why not place a flashing neon sign over their head when they show up? If they won't talk to you, they sure as hell wouldn't talk to a stranger." She didn't want to talk about this anymore. "Just go."

In one swift move she bundled her clothes together and headed for the bathroom. The door became a barrier between her and the man she thought she could build a relationship. Maybe even love. The sounds of him dressing on the other side of the door slammed like the hammer on the coffin nail. Her mind churned as she showered. There was no way to wash away the painful betrayal.

A half-hour later she sat at her uber frilly vanity Uncle Marvin gave her when she was thirteen. Her parents had dumped her here without a backward glance. He had no idea she wasn't into girly stuff, but she hadn't the heart to hurt him. She ran her hand over the white surface graced with gilt curlicues along the edges. His face had beamed at the vanity and matching canopy bed.

He'd never said he was disappointed in her wild behavior but gently guided her with love and Aunt Daisy's common sense. The hole he left in her heart after he died never closed. Lachlan had come close. Now the hole was bigger.

How were her aunts going to react to Lachlan's newest crusade? Things always had a way of getting out, especially with Jenny at the police station. It wouldn't take long for everyone in town to say she'd tried to lure the police chief into a compromising situation. No one would believe her.

A knock on her door had her dashing the tears from her eyes and jumping up to smooth the bedspread. She didn't want the slightest hint that she'd been with Lachlan.

"Yoo-hoo." Aunt Maisie knocked again. "Can I come in?"

Rory inspected her face in the mirror to make sure her eyes weren't red and swollen. She opened the door to see her aunt giving her a questioning stare. "What's up?"

"I put everything you asked for in the front hall, except the ice cream cake. We had the decorator put a badge on it that said FBI. I pulled up a picture on my phone," she chirped with pride. "I made Sister hot foot it home before it melted and ended up looking like the butterfly tattoo on her butt."

Rory's stared in disbelief. "Aunt Daisy has a butterfly on her backside?"

"It used to look like a beautiful swallow tail but now—" Aunt Maisie gave a delicate grimace, "— I'm sure it hasn't weathered well with the time."

That was one image Rory wanted out of her mind. She had to ask, "How do you know?"

"Oh, we went skinny dipping in the hot tub out back a couple of years before your uncles died. It wasn't looking too chipper then, I'm sure it looks more like a cockroach by now." Aunt Maisie's grin faded. Her gaze bore into Rory until it was hard to keep eye contact. "What's wrong?"

"Wrong?" Rory gave her the best smile she could muster.

"That's what I'm asking you." Aunt Maisie eased herself into a butter yellow armchair and pointed to the bed. "Sit."

Rory did as commanded.

Aunt Maisie pursed her lips. Her eyes demanded an answer. "Now tell me what's happened. I saw Lachlan leaving. He looked as broken as you do. You two have a fight?"

For a second, Rory wondered if Aunt Maisie's concern was for her or tonight's steak dinner. Shame made her push the ungrateful thought away.

"That's between us."

Aunt Maisie shook her head. "Not if it's about Glen trying to run us off this place, it isn't. Daisy was about to get her gun when she found out."

Rory shouldn't have been surprised but she had to ask. "How did you—"

"Jenny cornered us in the ice cream parlor. I'm sure half the people of Hootiecackle knows it by now." Aunt Maisie *harrumphed*. "She said Chief Nolan wanted to shitcan the whole investigation until Lachlan called in his buddy at the FBI. Apparently, they had a powwow with the chief yesterday afternoon. He didn't take too kindly to *the Feds getting in their faces*, as Jenny put it, but there was nothing he could do once the ask was made, and the FTC got involved."

"I'm surprised the cake didn't melt before she got all that out." Irritation egged Rory on. "Can't someone do anything about her gossiping?"

"Good Lord knows we've tried at Sunday school. Hasn't taken yet and if He can't do anything about it, who can?"

Rory stood and began to pace. "It's not right. None of this is right." Her personal life had turned into a nightmare and entertainment fodder for everyone in town. If this was such a scandal, Lachlan's investigation would be nuclear.

Aunt Maisie's eyes narrowed. "Why do I get the feeling this isn't about Glen?"

"I don't know what—"

"Oh, I've been around long enough to know when you're hiding something." She drummed her fingers against the arm of the chair. "If I can tell there's more than that jerk botherin' you, then Daisy will eat you alive."

A cornered animal couldn't feel as threatened and pushed to its limit. Rory wanted to lash out until she saw Aunt Maisie's eyes soften. "I-I…" She didn't know how to say the words that ripped from her when she thought Lachlan hadn't believed her.

"What is it, sweetie?" Aunt Maisie stood and led her to sit on the bed. She sat beside her. A time worn hand reached up and pushed a stray curl from her face. The gentle touch undid her.

The tears she'd held back rained down her face. "I can't—"

"Yes, you can." This time Aunt Maisie turned slightly and drew her into a billowy hug. "Tell me why you're so upset." Warm circles of comfort rubbed up and down her back. It was hard to get her hiccupping sobs under control. She prided herself on being strong, but it was so hard to tell the truth that she thought she'd put her pain to rest years ago. Lachlan had picked at the scab, and she found the festering mess underneath.

"I did—no, someone did something to me when I was a kid. It wasn't my fault really. Chief Nolan caught me drinking a beer when I was fifteen."

"A lot of kids do that. Not that I condone it but—"

Rory sucked up a snot bubble that threatened. "He wanted me to give him a blow job. If I did he wouldn't tell you or put me in juvie."

"What?"

Despite her now pounding head, Rory nodded. "A blow job. I told him to fu—I called his bluff. He did the same thing to Serena, and she told him to go ahead. She told me she did some mumbo jumbo chant, so he'd think she'd hexed him." She wiped at her eyes with a watery giggle. "Serena imagined he probably checked his dangly bits for quite a while after."

"Why didn't you tell us?"

"And have the Uncles take pot shots at him?" She shook her head. "I thought I had it under control. Now Lachlan is investigating Chief Nolan. He didn't ask. He said his job demands it be investigated. We had a huge disagreement and I told him to get out. After he left I Googled the statute of limitations for underage sexual offenses. It's thirty years."

"Oh, sweetie." Aunt Maisie's hand wiped the tears from Rory's face and a few from her own. "We would've believed you—stood by you. Daisy and I will stand by you now."

"What are we going to tell her?"

"The truth. She'll be home in a half-hour."

"This will be all over town once Jenny sniffs out an inkling of what happened."

"Don't fret about that. I'll personally tie a knot in her tongue. If that doesn't work, I'll let Daisy lop it off with her gardening shears."

The vicious words made Rory's heart jump. She threw her arms around her aunt. "I don't know why I was more afraid of The Uncles going after Chief Nolan. Fifteen minutes with you and he'd be eating dirt and asking for seconds."

Chapter Twenty-Two

The minute Lachlan closed the kitchen door, Caleb nailed him with a stare. Why did he feel like a kid caught playing hooky by the school's principal? It didn't help the anger and disappointment in Rory at her unwillingness to understand him. He thought he had something special with her, but now he wasn't so sure. Why couldn't she see he was in an untenable situation? Hurt warred with his sense of honor and justice.

"Smells like earthquake weather." Caleb closed his laptop and leaned back in his chair with a sigh.

"What?" Lachlan hadn't a clue what he was talking about.

"Maybe it's more like *I sense a disturbance in the Force.*" His friend gave a wheezing imitation of Darth Vader. He held out his hand as if choking someone and made gurgling noises.

Leave it to Caleb to be a walking cliché. "Cut the crap."

"Is there a hiccup in our plan? Hope not, because I have some promising news from New Orleans."

"About Glen? No." Lachlan got a beer out of the fridge, twisted the cap off and threw it in the trash with more force than it warranted. The sooner he got that rat bastard out of Rory's life the better. There were bigger issues that needed to be addressed. "I told Rory we were running a background check on Chief Nolan."

"Oh." The single word said it all.

How could he get her to see that a sexual predator was out there, possibly still pursuing young girls? He couldn't let it ride.

Even if it meant losing her.

His gut clenched at the idea of never making love to her again. Some things came with a high price, and this was one of them. "Yeah. She wasn't happy."

"Why do I get the feeling that's an understatement."

"Want a beer?" Lachlan pointed at the fridge with his thumb. The last thing he needed was to be asked a bunch of questions right now.

"Okay, I get it." Caleb waved his offer away. "No beer. I just finished off a pot of coffee while I was working."

"You said you had good news from the New Orleans office?" Lachlan settled in the kitchen chair opposite Caleb. "I could use something positive right now."

The smile on Caleb's face gave him a bit of hope. Maybe one thing would go right today. He'd taken a calculated risk with his investigation of Chief Nolan, and it blew up in his face. This had better be something to show for all their hard work or his newly decorated kitchen would have a fist-sized hole in the wall.

"They found the hacker without any problems. I'll head down there tomorrow and talk to the dude."

"I hope he's willing to give Peters up."

A smile tugged at Caleb's mouth. "Oh, he'll be shitting diamonds by the time I'm done with him." He got up to rinse out his coffee mug. "Are you sure you want to go ahead with your background search on Chief Nolan?"

It would be easier to forget the whole thing, but he

couldn't. "Yeah. I do."

"Okay then, I have a friend who's a private investigator. He owes me a big favor for getting his son out of hot water. Some kids at his high school hacked his social media account and bullied a girl using his name. Smug little bastards thought they'd get away with it—but nope."

"Will he be discreet?" Lachlan didn't want to tip his hand too soon. "I need some solid evidence."

The smile returned. "He's already in town just waiting for the word."

Lachlan nodded and released a sigh. "I have to know. Oh, and tell him to avoid Jenny Meyers. She's one of the police dispatchers and the worst gossip in town."

His phone rang and he looked at the caller ID. It was Maisie McDermott's cellphone.

"Hello." Why did he get the feeling he was about to be reamed out by a professional?

"Listen here, Lachlan." He'd been right, from the tone of her voice.

He manned up. "I'm listening."

"We've got things to discuss. Don't even think you can get out of the barbeque or listen to what we have to say. You've upset Rory. You went about it the wrong way, but we got to take this pervert Nolan out."

For an instant he wasn't sure he heard right. "O-k-a-y." He drew out the word to give his mind time to wrap itself around Maisie's words.

"Rory's is still mad, so you better watch your step."

"Got it."

"Oh, we're bringing a guest." Her tone didn't brook any discussion.

"Who?"

"Serena. I hope you have a tofu burger or something. I don't understand turning down a good steak, but that kid was always a bubble off plumb."

"I might have something in my freezer to fit the bill."

"Good, good. We'll see you in a bit." A clatter sounded over the phone. "Rory," she shouted so loud that he thought his ear drums must be bleeding. "Get your aunt under control. We're all going to end up in jail if she keeps this up." An aggrieved sigh *whooshed* through the phone. "It's a good thing I hid the double-barrel. Sister is so hot-headed."

"You want me to come talk her down?"

"Nah, we got this, but if Nolan is still doing this crap then I might give it to her." The call ended and Lachlan stared down at his phone.

"What did you say about earthquake weather?"

"That bad?"

"Imagine your worst nightmare and crank it up to eleven."

Caleb whistled through his teeth.

"Yeah, Daisy Callahan will make a berserker took tame. Her sister Maisie said she hid her double barrel shotgun after Peters damaged her roses."

"That bad?"

"She shot him."

"What?" Caleb's eyes went round.

"Rock salt. I'm afraid she'll opt for the real deal over this."

The next few hours were spent getting the food ready for the grill while Caleb made several phone calls and later helped him set the table. Soon raised voices could be heard coming over the fence.

The gate opened.

Maisie Callahan pushed through with a cake box in her hand and wearing a neon orange blouse that threatened to melt his eyeballs.

"Where can I set this?" Maisie pushed the box into his hands. "It's an ice cream cake. It'd be a shame for it to melt now."

Everyone else followed behind, Daisy looking bullish, Rory cool and aloof. No one could possibly tell what was going on behind Serena's violet eyes. It surprised him to find her dressed in a lace top, albeit black, over lavender capris. She looked *almost* normal.

Luckily, he had enough space in his garage freezer to accommodate the box. "Everyone, this is Caleb McGuiness, my friend from the FBI. Rory, you do the introductions while I stow this in the freezer."

"Yeah, do that." Caleb absently waved him away and stared at Serena as if he'd been pinned between the eyes like one of her voodoo dolls. "Put the cake in the freezer. It's hot out here."

Lachlan had no doubt the heat was Caleb's own doing. Serena gave his friend a smile that touched the corner of her lips, tilting them up ever so slightly. She was as cool as Daisy McDermott was steaming mad.

"Get going, Lachlan. That thing is melting by the minute." Maisie shooed him toward the house. "Rory, you go with him. We can make our own introductions."

"We don't have time to worry about the cake, Sister." Daisy stood in front of him, blocking his way to the garage where he kept his chest freezer. "Our girls have been accosted by that pervert Chief Nolan. I always thought he was a little dodgy, and never went to church. He better be right with the Lord before I get my hands on him."

"Aunt Daisy, you can't go off like that. It's been fifteen years. There's no proof." Rory did the dutiful thing and followed behind. The coolness radiating from her could keep Maisie's cake from melting.

"Go on." Maisie urged Rory forward. "You two have some talking to do."

Rory heaved a sigh of exasperation but accompanied him to the garage.

"I guess you told your aunts, huh?" He winced at how stupid his question was.

She gave him a little nod. "Aunt Maisie caught me at a weak moment, and it spilled out."

"Maybe it was a good thing." He opened the freezer, slipped the cake into it, and closed the lid. "What did she say?"

"She sicced Aunt Daisy on me. Once she found out what happened it was game over."

"How do you feel about it?" He'd been worried they'd overwhelmed her. Rory didn't do overwhelmed.

"Isn't it a little late to be asking that question? I'm boxed into a corner." She gave him a side-eye. "I wouldn't do this except this was the only way to keep Aunt Daisy from taking her shotgun after Chief Nolan. Have you ever had the Callahan Twins tag team you?"

He raised his brow in answer.

A little smile tugged at the corner of her mouth. "I guess so." She leaned against the freezer. Her hands gripped the edges of the lid. "I hate this."

"I hate that I have to do this." He reached out to touch one of her hands. She slowly moved it away. "Believe it or not, I care about you. No, I do more than just care, I—"

She shook her head, making the long ponytail swish against her shoulders. Not more than four hours ago he'd been kissing the same pale skin her hair now caressed.

He ached inside.

"Don't say anything." Her eyes darkened with misery. "I couldn't handle it right now—not after you betrayed my trust." She covered her face for a moment and then she pushed away from the freezer. "And now you've outed Serena as well." Her lips thinned and she sucked in a deep breath. "The thing that kills me is that you're right."

His victory tasted raw and sour. "Does this mean—"

She rounded on him, her voice low even though her words were hot and angry. "I'll help you. Nothing more than that. I will go back out there—" she pointed in the direction of the patio, "—I will be sociable and polite, but that's all. It doesn't mean I forgive you."

"I never meant to hurt you."

"But you knew it was a possibility."

"Yes."

"There it is. We'll get through this, but I don't want to see you anymore. I knew it was wrong to get involved with a cop."

The world folded inward, locked onto her face, the sadness and misery tearing at him. All he could do was nod. "Got it."

She turned to leave. It was as if she were the ice queen freezing everything in her path.

He grabbed up the cooler with the drinks for something to do, to keep his hands steady while he went to greet his guests.

Around the corner of the garage Lachlan heard

raised voices.

"Your word's good enough for me. Serena's too." The boiling anger in Daisy's voice brought Rory's own words to mind.

"Miss Daisy, everyone in town thinks I'm tetched in the head. They have me lumped with Amos Cunningham." Serena's voice was soothing like iced tea on a hot day. "The poor man has PTSD."

Lachlan placed the cooler next to the grill and popped the top. "I don't know about you, but I need food if I'm going to figure out a plan. Beer, soda?" The cold ice bit his hands when he reached in for a couple of cans of each. A quick glance at Rory confirmed his suspicion. She didn't bother to hide her anger. It made the cooler's contents feel tropical.

It was a struggle to speak over the knot in his throat. "Caleb, why don't you throw those steaks on the grill while I pass these around?" He tamped down the hurt and emptiness and smiled at his guests.

Caleb unglued his eyes from Serena long enough to jump to his feet and pick up the package of pseudo-burgers. He turned them over in his hand. "How long do I cook this?"

"I don't know. Check the instructions."

Serena stood and strolled over to the grill. "I can help."

Caleb's face lit up. "Sure. Steaks I know but this stuff is—"

"Strange?" Serena took the package from him. "Let me."

Lachlan watched the two together. The laws of attraction could be bent, twisted, and turned into something totally different than what one expected. No matter how angry Rory was with him, or how upset he was that she didn't understand his stance, he still wanted her. Not just her body but her smile and laugh. Her aloof attitude killed him slice by slice.

"How does everyone like their steaks?" Caleb called out.

"Miss Daisy likes hers warmed through, Miss Maisie wants it very well done, and Rory is medium. You know how I like mine."

"I came over here to put Chief Nolan's balls in a wringer, not eat steak." Daisy's mouth turned into a wrinkled pout. Red flushed her round cheeks.

"Sister! How come you admonish me for language and you're swearing now?"

"Because I'm five minutes older, that's why," Daisy snapped. "We got to get him."

He glanced over at Caleb for help, but his friend and Serena had their heads together. His last hope was Rory. She leaned back in her chair, arms crossed over her chest. No help there.

"We'll think better with full stomachs. Caleb and I have a plan to put a stop to Chief Nolan's activities. It'd be a shame to waste those steaks."

Daisy calmed down a bit. "You have a point." She spent the rest of the meal grumbling about Chief Nolan, but a steak and baked potato went a long way to pacify her.

Rory remained distanced from him and treated his friend with coolness.

Was she embarrassed about Caleb knowing about her secret or that he'd exposed Serena's? He tried his best to make her smile or show some sign she'd forgiven him. Still, she remained distant.

Caleb played host to Serena while the Callahan Twins made themselves at home. He filled her plate, got drinks, and made sure he was there in case she needed anything. His friend was usually the cool, collected type when it came to women. It was strange to see him fumble around like he was in high school. "Do you need anything else?"

Serena's smile never slipped.

"No thank you." She turned to Lachlan. "You did a great job on the burger."

"I bought the Best Burger Ever plant-based 'meat' the other day. Thought I'd check them out."

"I'll have to get them when I go to the store." She lifted her hard lemonade for a sip.

Caleb's eyes were trained on her lips.

It was time to get some work done before his friend melted faster than the ice cream cake. He sat back with his iced tea and mulled over several ways to approach the subject. Daisy McDermott took matters into her hands. Her eyes narrowed and lips thinned.

"What about Chief Nolan? How are we going to prove he's actually a sexual predator?" Her elderly hands clenched together until her fingers went white. It was a good thing Nolan wasn't within grabbing distance. "It took a lot for me to convince Rory to talk to you again, but I made her see Chief Nolan can't get away with this."

"I told her the same thing."

"Well, you messed up big time." Daisy sucked in a deep breath and spread her hands over the tabletop. "That doesn't mean you aren't right."

Maisie held up her hand. "Now I'm all for taking this asshole off the streets—" she pointed at her sister, "—and don't give me any guff about my word choice.

The man is an asshole, pure and simple. How do you plan to go about this because Chief Nolan has his fingers in a lot of pies from Hootiecackle to Holloway. He's got friends in the state capital. I heard he's even plannin' on runnin' for state office when he retires next year."

"I know." Lachlan rubbed his chin with his hand. "Caleb has a private investigator on this."

"You got to keep him away from Jenny Meyers." Maisie's panic spread through the group, all except Serena.

"No, I think we need to bring her in on this." A quirk touched the corner of Serena's mouth.

"What?" Rory's cool left her. "Why? We all know what she's like."

Lachlan wasn't sure where Serena was going with her suggestion. "We've got to be careful. If the chief gets word of this he can cover his tracks."

"She knows more than anyone in town and I can assure you she'll keep her tongue between her teeth." Lachlan saw an unholy glint in Serena's eyes.

"Oh, I think she won't be able to turn down a free reading. Jenny comes in several times a month although she swears me to secrecy." She tapped her long purple nails on the glass patio tabletop. "I see a bad card throw in her future about gossiping."

Daisy clapped her hands. "It could work. The girl's as superstitious as she is a loudmouth."

Lachlan was impressed by the supernatural guerilla fighters. "I'll talk to Jenny about gossiping after your reading with her."

"Put the fear of the Lord in her too." Maisie nodded. "Proverbs 21:23."

Lachlan was stumped. "What's that?"

"Those who guard their mouths and their tongues keep themselves from calamity."

Lachlan pondered their plan. These women knew Jenny better than anyone here. They knew the whole town and how it functioned. "That just might work."

"We'll make it work." Rory smiled for the first time today. "We'll make it work."

Chapter Twenty-Three

Rory's mind whirled. Between Glen and Chief Nolan, the sense of betrayal sat bitter in her heart. Glen had twisted her heart and mind to believe his lies about her abilities and talents, took credit for what was hers alone. It sickened her to realize she'd allowed it to happen. Had she been so needy for validation that she'd abdicated her strength and will? She'd been helpless as a child.

Out of the corner of her eye she saw Aunt Daisy pull a silver flask from her cargo shorts. With the sleight of hand she added a dollop of liquor to her iced tea. Rory knew she should say something but didn't want to out her aunt in front of everyone. Instead, she leaned over the table and patted her aunt's hand.

Aunt Daisy gave her a look of innocence that said this wasn't her first addition to her tea.

It was her fault her aunt was so upset. No amount of "medicine" would take away the trauma to her family. They didn't blame her for what happened with Chief Nolan. They were supportive but their world had been shaken. Hootiecackle was no longer the innocent small town they'd grown up in.

"I don't want to believe something like this happened in Hootiecackle."

"We've had a lot of scandal in this little town. Good Lord, Jenny should know every one of them." Aunt

Daisy gave a not so delicate hiccup. "The next to the last minister at church had an affair with his secretary and don't forget that Arnie Andrews embezzled a hundred dollars from the feed store." Tears welled up in her eyes. "There's a lot of other stuff but no one in town, at least that I know of, has been propositioning kids for vile sex acts." She took a sip of her tea and glanced around at them. "I mean, they're not vile in the bonds of matrimony." Her lower lip wobbled. "No one even has an idea of how many young girls there might be. It's so wrong."

"Miss Daisy, I need to investigate this." Lachlan sat beside her at the patio table. "We won't accuse him until we have something solid."

Rory resigned herself to the investigation, but it didn't let Lachlan off the hook. Her heart still hurt, lacerated by his betrayal.

Aunt Daisy pointed first at her and then Serena. "That monster violated these two over fifteen years ago. Who knows how many more babies he's ruined?"

"I'm not ruined." Rory reached for Aunt Daisy's glass. She pulled it away before Rory could wrest it away. "Neither is Serena. He wasn't a match for us."

"Who else could've fallen for his lies and threats? He's an evil man." Her aunt's green eyes burned laser bright. "We've got to get him, no matter what."

Rory sighed. How many times had she said the same things over and over? It would be cowardly to let this slide. It would also be the worst thing she'd ever faced. Did her aunts even know how much notoriety this would bring?

"Rory, Rory!" Aunt Maisie called out to her. "Your phone's ringing. You going to answer it or not?"

Rory stared down at her phone and it took another ring for her to register the caller. It was Glen. She held up her hand to stop the chatter around the table and made a zip-it motion to silence her aunts. She put her phone on speaker.

"Hi, Glen. What do you want?" It amazed her that she sounded so nonchalant. She tamped down on the urge to throw the phone on the concrete and watch it shatter to pieces.

"You sound strange." Suspicion clouded his voice.

"I'm outside enjoying the afternoon. I'm hands free so I can get a few things done."

"Call off your hounds." he snapped.

"What hounds? Lucy, Einie?" She couldn't help the sarcasm that crept out.

"The cops, feds. Geez, are you stupid?" A shot of heat flared in her face, but she remained calm. Lachlan glowered and held his hand out for the phone. She waved him back down with a glare, daring him to interfere. This was her fight.

"Well, it's out of my hands now. Hmm," she sighed in mock contentment. "You should've thought of the consequences when you began to play games with my life."

"And you're not doing the same?" His voice was strangled. "I've got people crawling all over my business. How am I supposed to get any work done with cops at my front door?"

"That's your problem. I've merely reported identity theft and fraud." She sucked in a deep breath and smiled. Glen couldn't see her smile, but she knew it was there and it gave her a boost of confidence. "I've learned a lot from you. I don't trust as easily as I used to, *and* I make sure to document all my work. Unlike you, I don't have to lie and cheat to be a success."

"You bitch."

Lachlan sprang to his feet and stood behind her. So much for trying to fight Glen on her own. It irritated her that he took away her authority.

"I'd watch what you say, Peters." Lachlan leaned over her shoulder. "There's a police officer and a federal agent here."

It wasn't a lie. Caleb opened the gate and ambled across the patch of pavers nestled in the lawn. He raised one brow in question. Lachlan put a finger to his mouth before Caleb could ask any questions.

"Yes, they're here to go over the case." It was true she needed their help. She wanted it to be at her insistence instead of one of them taking the ball and running with it.

"You can't do this!"

"I have." She was curious. "You could be arrested. Your partner has spilled his guts." She cringed at sounding like a Forties film noire heroine.

"No." He paused. She knew him well enough to envision his hands shaking. "I heard people are asking a lot of questions."

"You mean your hacker." She might as well go for broke with the Forties theme. "Or should I say snitch. Keep watching over your shoulders, Glen. They're closing in on you. The state is willing to give you room and board with a nice burly roommate named Bubba." She disconnected the call and heaved a sigh of relief. "That was—delightful."

Aunt Daisy snorted. "Well, that's the first time I've ever heard of revenge as delightful. That's a letdown after all the drama." She gave Rory the stink-eye over her glass of reinforced iced tea. While Aunt Maisie became overly friendly and loud when she'd dipped too deep into her stash of booze, Aunt Daisy turned into an Amazon psycho war-bitch from hell. "The Bubba scenario works for me. The jerk almost killed Toots. Do you know how much I pampered that rose? She climbed over the trellis like a champ until she was—" Aunt Daisy sniffed and sipped, "—Matt Turner's cows wouldn't have trampled her if Glen hadn't opened the gate. I'll never forgive him."

"It's so close to being done that it's closure." Rory stared at her phone. "Maybe he won't be convicted or put in jail, but it'll take a long time for him to recover his business or reputation. He hates losing face."

"I'll take care of his face," Aunt Daisy mumbled into her tea.

Aunt Maisie *tsked* and took her sister's tea. "Sister, Rory is the one who's been hurt the worst. I'm sure Toots will come out of this just fine. We need to concern ourselves about Rory."

Aunt Daisy speared Lachlan with a glare. She leaned forward and pointed at him. "You screwed the pooch with Rory. Handled it all wrong. We got to do something. This is going to be a clusterf—"

"Sister!" Aunt Maisie, who sat next to Aunt Daisy, clapped her hand over Aunt Daisy's mouth before she could finish.

Aunt Daisy blinked and didn't protest when Aunt Maisie hauled her to her feet. "Tell us what you decide to do. I've got to get Sister to bed. She must be having a reaction to her 'medicine.' but she's right about one thing. You're a jerk, too." She wrapped her arm around her sibling's shoulders. "Let's go."

"Wait, he didn't have a choice." Caleb stood and hooked his arm through Aunt Daisy's. "He's mandated by law to report Nolan's crime, but he wanted to investigate it first."

"You don't believe my girl, either?" Aunt Daisy stared up at Caleb pie-eyed. "I'll have you know she's honest, well if you don't count lying to us about the skinny-dipping incident with the mayor's son." She wobbled on her feet, and it took both Aunt Maisie and Caleb to keep her upright. "Said she was going over to Chandra's to study."

"I did," Rory bit the corner of her lip. "We just ended up at the quarry with everyone else."

"Why don't I help you take Mrs. McDermott home?"

At first Aunt Maisie narrowed her eyes and sized up the situation. "Normally, I'd just take her home myself."

"Not a problem, Mrs. McDermott." Caleb's lip twitched but steadied. "Can't be too careful when it comes to drugs."

"Not drugs." Aunt Maisie gave a horrified squeak. "Medicine."

"Medicine." Caleb nodded. "Got it."

Aunt Maisie gave him a little sniff of acceptance. "I guess the others have stuff to talk about."

With Caleb's help they headed toward the Callahan/McDermott house. Aunt Daisy wobbled a couple of times, but they made it past the gate. A rousing chorus of "Everything's Coming up Roses" rang through the warm evening air.

"They've got their hands full." Serena stared at Caleb closing the gate behind him and the aunts. "I think he's up to the task."

"There were a couple of times he dragged me back to our apartment when we were in college."

"I can't imagine you overindulging in anything." Rory caught his gaze. Longing and desire heated his eyes. She lowered her lids to steel herself against the same emotions beating against her heart.

"At least not on duty." His deep voice rolled over her like warm honey.

She relived their times together, not just the wonderful physical part but talking, sitting on the bed and eating lunch while discussing their lives and goals. He'd told her about his life with Kate, her death and the reason he'd come to Hootiecackle. She told him about how her desire for success allowed Glen to gaslight her. She'd mixed love with career approval. She'd discovered how to open up to another human, something she never had with Glen. So much time wasted.

"Are you okay?" Lachlan's concern broke through her mental meltdown.

Rory closed her eyes and took a slow breath. "Fine. No, that's a lie, but nothing I can't handle."

"This can of worms has been truly opened." Serena rested her chin in her hand. She stared at each in turn. "There's a lot of hurt to get past—on all fronts. I didn't like to be thrown into this without notice—" she held up a hand, "—no, I'm not psychic despite what the townies think. I use tarot cards and I can't read my own throw. I see the dead. Most of my information comes from Agnes and Henry. Don't roll your eyes at me." She pointed at Rory. "Him, I understand his skepticism, but you should know better."

"Serena—"

"Nope." Her friend shook her head. "I told them to see what they could find."

"They aren't stuck at the shop?" Lachlan stared at Serena. It wasn't clear if he believed her or not, but she caught his attention. "I've heard of psychics helping the law."

"I'm not a psychic. I don't know how they get their information, but I get the deets faster than Jenny Meyers."

"I can't believe I'm saying this—let me know if they have any leads."

Chapter Twenty-Four

Lachlan cursed himself for forgetting his thermos this afternoon. There was no way he'd drink the coffee at the station. Jenny made the coffee each morning and afternoon before the shift change. It tasted of stale cigarette and smelled like ass. So many things occupied his mind that he forgot to be mindful of the now. That was a dangerous thing in his business. Especially when it came to coffee.

In the few months he'd been here he hadn't had a decent cup yet.

He walked into the lounge, watching Nick stare down into his cup. He picked a clean mug out of the dishrack and started toward the coffeemaker.

"I wouldn't do that." Nick continued to scowl at his cup.

"Why not? Besides the fact it makes my tongue numb?" Lachlan sniffed his cup. He'd been right about the smell.

"Just take my word for it. I found out why this tastes so bad." Nick grimaced. "I found out Jenny is putting new coffee over old grounds. The coffee filter hasn't been changed in four days."

No wonder Nick had been staring at his cup in horror.

"I plan to put a stop to it. No telling how many new lifeforms are growing in that pot."

It didn't matter how many bloody crime scenes Lachlan witnessed. The idea of drinking fungi infested coffee made his stomach lurch. "What do you plan to do?" Nick had a history of pulling pranks and Lachlan wasn't sure what to expect.

"Just go along with me." Nick glanced at his watch. "Wait a minute. She should be here in—three—two—one."

Jenny walked into the lounge and headed toward her locker.

"Bingo," Nick muttered under his breath.

"Another dull day in Hootiecackle." She sighed and pulled out a huge purse.

"They only come out at night." Lachlan shook his head at Jenny's lament. "Be thankful you don't have to dispatch in a big city. It's non-stop."

"Jenny?" Nick waved her over to the table.

"What is it?" She stood, hands on her hips. "I've go to get home. Dave doesn't like it when I'm late gettin' supper on the table."

"I wanted to ask you about the coffee." He swirled his mug and sniffed. "It tastes off."

Her nose wrinkled in disgust. "I wouldn't know—don't touch the stuff. Tea's my drink."

"Then why do you make it?" Lachlan's curiosity got the better of him.

"Chief Nolan asked—er—made me do it. He said it was part of my job description."

Lachlan closed his eyes and shook his head. Rory would have a field day with that remark.

"I noticed you put new coffee on top of the old grounds. Why?"

"That's the way my mom makes it. She said that's

the way her family made it during the Depression."

"Do you know what happens when you do that?"

"Doesn't bother Dave, or my Dad and Grandpa."

"Let me show you something." Nick pulled out a lighter.

"I didn't think you smoked," Jenny queried.

Nick shook his head. "I don't, but I keep one in case of emergencies. I'm about to save the lives of your fellow officers." He held the light over the cup and thumbed the flame. A whoosh and flash of fire burst from the cup and sputtered out.

Jenny screeched, wide-eyed and dropped her purse. Her hands flew to cover her mouth as she did a two step back.

"What the hell!" Lachlan's coffee splashed over the top of his mug when he jerked in surprise.

"The Chief is pretty strict. He told you to make coffee, sobeit. Why don't you make a fresh pot every day? The city can afford it and your co-workers would thank you."

Jenny blinked a couple of times and nodded. "Okay."

"New pot every day." Nick gave Jenny a smile and winked.

"Every day," Jenny repeated.

Lachlan picked her bag from the floor and handed it to her. "I'll bet you'll make great coffee from now on."

"Oh, look at the time." Jenny slid her purse back onto her shoulder. "Dave will be drinking his supper if I don't get home." She trotted out the back door to the parking lot.

"Did I go too far?"

"Maybe a touch, but it was for the greater good."

"I didn't want to hurt her feelings. She's kinda thick sometimes. Her good nature makes up for it—if only she'd quit gossiping."

"Yeah. There is that." Lachlan looked mournfully at the black sludge in his mug. "I think I'll stop by the Daily Grind and get a to-go cup. It's time to start work."

Nick rubbed the back of his neck and winced. "Chandra wanted me to ask if everything was okay between you and Rory."

"She'll have to ask Rory." The last thing Lachlan wanted to discuss was his love life—if he still had one.

"Jenny told Chandra that you two had a falling out over the old boyfriend."

"If Rory wants to discuss it with Chandra, she will," he snapped harder than he intended. "Sorry. Every couple hits a rough patch now and again. Let's just say mine was black ice." He rose and got ready to leave for the evening. "I'm scheduled to work your shift, so I won't be at the wedding, so it's all good."

"I can't believe I'll be married in a couple of days." Nick's smile changed to frown. "Chandra is getting so antsy and uptight before the wedding. She's never been like this. I hope you and Rory can come work it out. I'm not letting her worries about her friend ruin our wedding day."

Lachlan gave him a quick pat on the shoulder. "She'll be fine. It's wedding jitters."

"Maybe." The expression of uncertainty filled Nick's black eyes. "I feel like she's keeping something from me."

"Could be you're overthinking everything. She's got a lot to do before the wedding. It's less than a week away."

Nick's face brightened. "Yeah, you're probably right."

****

Lachlan spent the next few hours doing his regular beat around town. Sometimes hours spent just driving around or walking the streets of Hootiecackle gave him time to think. Tonight, he wished he could get the racing thoughts out of his head. Rory was right—he should've gotten her permission, but regardless, he had to investigate the sexual assault of over fifteen years ago. The fact he was doing it on his own was like walking a tightrope. If he messed up there was a chance the chief would walk free. Even if he lost it meant Rory and Serena were exposed to the townspeople and the media.

"Man, you're screwed," he mumbled to himself. He walked down the main drag and found himself in front of the Funky Junk Shoppe. It was as if his feet knew where he wanted to go. Rory wasn't there but he could feel her personality radiating from the window display.

A soft summer breeze blew with a smell of rain in the wind. It was sweet, full of expectation that tingled the nose and made the heart beat faster.

"Hey!"

He turned to see Amos Cunningham sitting on his usual park bench across the street. His musings burst like a bubble. It was going to be one of *those* nights. He ambled across the street and sat next to the man.

"Whatcha need, Amos?"

"I want to report a crime." Amos tipped a large can of energy drink to his mouth and took a healthy swig. "Damn. I sure miss my hootch."

Lachlan stared down at the can Amos rolled between his hands. "I'd say that was better for you, but it'd be a lie."

"You're right. Too much sugar. I'll end up with that diabetes instead of a rotten liver."

It was hard not to laugh but Lachlan managed to keep a straight face. "You have a point there." He reached over and tapped the side of the can. "This won't land you in jail."

"I've been in the stony lonesome more than once. It'd be worth it for one good eye-burning, gut rotting drink. I'm goin' to have to call my sponsor when I get home." He took another drink. "So what you goin' to do about my crime?"

"You committed a crime?"

"Hell, no. I'm reportin' one." He pointed across the street. "See that light. It shouldn't be on. Someone is messin' with Miss Serena's house. She never uses the third floor."

"Maybe she has merchandise up there?"

"Nope. I unload her merchandise when it comes to the shop. I do it for a few extra dollars. She keeps the inventory in the back room like Miss Rory. Speakin' of which, I hear you two are on the outs."

"Why is our relationship the talk of the town."

"'Cause Jenny Meyers is faster than social media." Amos squinted at him. "You better do right by Miss Rory."

"It takes two, Amos."

"Right now, you better get your butt across the street and make sure Miss Serena is all right."

Lachlan stood and gave Amos a quick nod before heading toward the old bank building. Sure enough, a lone light shone through a window on the third floor. The rest of the building was dark. Serena had called it a night or was upstairs. He'd never been upstairs in the building, but Rory had told him Serena only used the second floor for her home. The third floor was empty.

The hairs on his neck stood. Was someone upstairs?

He decided to check it out and went around the building to the wooden stairs at the back. He went up the stairs and knocked.

Serena answered, blurry-eyed and dressed in lightweight purple cotton pjs printed with little black skulls. She blinked a couple of times before opening the door all the way. "Why the early morning call. I don't do readings at this time of the morning."

Lachlan scanned the area around the landing and glanced up to the third floor. Everything appeared normal, or as normal as it could be concerning Serena. "Amos saw a light coming from the upstairs window and flagged me down. He wanted me to check to see if you're okay."

"Isn't that sweet. Poor guy is at loose ends since he tore down the still." She motioned him in. "Let's go upstairs and check."

He followed her upstairs to the upper floor. She flipped on the lights. Instead of a dusty mess was a room that looked like it was frozen in time. He wasn't great with periods of interior design, that was Rory's field, but his late wife, Kate, was into silent movies and late Twenties black and white. He recognized the "modern" design with its angled, geometric lines. The walls were painted a light sand color with a pair of deep padded, darker camel-colored armchairs, a cream-colored ladies' chaise lounge sat along one wall. He knew what it was because Rory had one in her shop in red velvet that was butt ugly as sin. This one was white leather and streamlined with what he recognized as burled walnut legs. A white baby grand sat in end while a radio, with the same gold walnut casing sat opposite the chairs.

A lone lamp lit the room. It looked like two amber saucers stacked on a long slim rod. It sat on a brass and marble table between the chairs. A book with a bookmark looked as if someone would pick it up and begin reading at any time.

"Wow. This is—amazing."

"Yeah," Serena yawned. "It's not my jam. Although Rory says Henry had good taste. The lamp is Danish, some guy that sells for thousands of dollars now.

"Why did you leave it like this?"

"It's Agnes and Henry's place," as if it were the most obvious thing in the world.

Inwardly he groaned. Agnes and Henry again. "How did the piano get up here?"

"Don't ask. I don't know. It was already here when I moved in. I got the place at a bargain price. I didn't know I'd have landlords." Serena sighed and looked around. "I had everything reupholstered and the electrical redone when I remodeled the building." She leaned down and turned off the lamp. "I'm going to have to talk to them about leaving the lights on."

As much as he hated to give her ghosts any credence, he decided to bite down on his skepticism just this once. "Is it possible to for me to talk to them—er—face to face?"

Serena shrugged. "There's no telling what they will or won't do. Don't get your hopes up. They don't usually *talk* to me. It's more signs or impressions."

Lachlan's brain had a problem processing what she said. He did know he needed to address the most pressing issue. "I want to apologize again for involving you in the investigation. I have no choice."

"I get it. Unlike Rory, I don't feel betrayed—not really. It's something I never thought about after it happened, unlike Rory. Don't believe her when she says it's in the past."

"So," he cleared his throat. He picked up a double frame with a photograph on each side. One was a flirtatious woman, with elegant features, dark eyes and an equally dark bob.. The other photo was of a man with a strong jaw and face. Lachlan could see drinking a beer with him. The wire-rim glasses didn't make him look weak. "How do I talk to these ghosts?"

Serena stared at him as if he'd eaten a bug. "They're won't talk to you if you keep referring to them as ghosts. They like to be called TBs."

He's more confused than over. "TBs?"

"Transcended Beings. They come and go as they please but usually TBs are fond of particular places. However, a NVTB, a non-voluntary TB is usually stuck in one spot, going over the same thing over and over.

"You know you sound—"

"Like a whack job?" She gave him her Mona Lisa smile. "We all have a little crazy in us. Mine's just out there for everyone to see."

His patience was running thin. "So what do I have to do to talk to the TBs?"

Just then the radio blared to life.

"I think you have your answer."

Chapter Twenty-Five

The strains of "The Long and Winding Road" from the Beatles *Let it Be* album filled the room. Kate's favorite song washed over him. It speared him through the heart and took his breath.

"Stop it," he ground out. It had to be a malfunction of the radio, a short circuit—anything except those damned ghosts.

The radio went quiet. It was even worse than the music. A heaviness settled in the room and a slight chill flittered on the air. The hair on his forearms and neck stood at attention, waiting—for what?

"You wanted to talk to them. They're willing—in their own way." Serena motioned for him to take one of the chairs. She must have seen his uncertainty. "Sit down. You have their permission."

This was too much. His rational mind was twisted into knots. His initial willingness to go along with Serena's nonsense got a big shot of *nope*. He shook his head. "I've got to get back to work."

"Aren't you working now?" She leaned over and patted the arm of the empty chair. "This will only take a few minutes."

He stilled his feet from making tracks for the door. "This is—"

"Weird?"

"Insane." The word slipped out before he could stop

it. "Sorry."

"Most of the people in town have kept the Moondancer women at arm's length unless they want their fortunes told, so on and so on. I inherited their talent."

"What about the voodoo doll you used on Glen." Rory's telling of the events in the Funky Junk Shoppe had been so hilarious and compelling that he could *see* Glen's reaction to Serena.

She giggle-snorted. "I played on his fears. I usually refuse to do anything harmful but his was a special case. He shouldn't have gone after Rory." She motioned to the chair again. "Let's get this over with, okay?"

He had to be three parts crazy and one part desperate to even consider speaking with the dead. This was untried territory. The guys back in St. Louis would throw him in a padded cell and hide the key if they saw him dealing with a psychic. No, Serena had declared more than once that she wasn't a psychic. Whatever she was, he didn't know if he could be a part of this craziness. "I don't think I want to do this."

"Didn't you want to talk to them?"

"I was only half serious."

She crossed her arms over her chest. "Well, the serious half won. You've got their attention."

There was no getting out of this gracefully. He was already in hot water with Rory and no telling, even if he believed this stuff, what sort of paranormal jam he'd end up in. He sighed in resignation. "What do I do?"

"*You* don't have to do anything but listen."

Serena settled back in her chair and gripped the arms as if she were a nervous plane passenger waiting for take-off. "This isn't easy for me either. Once Agnes gets to talking, she won't stop. She loves to visit. Henry on the other hand is a man of few words but all of them neat and elegant. Now sit."

He did as commanded.

She closed her eyes. Her head drooped. Each breath she took echoed through the silence in the room.

He was itchy and uneasy watching her do her *work*. "What are you doing?"

"Nothing if you don't stay quiet." She gave him a side-eye that would've peeled the hide off most people. Once again, she settled herself. Her head lolled back. A small moan escaped her a moment before her eyes popped open. She rested her elbow on the arm of the chair and supported her chin in her hand. The Mona Lisa smile was replaced by a saucy grin.

"My, my, you are the cat's pajamas." The husky, slow southern drawl caught him off-guard. Her lashes fluttered as she sighed in appreciation.

He was stunned and a bit uneasy. This was the first time he'd ever seen a flirtatious Serena. "I—ah—"

She interrupted him and stared over her shoulder with an exaggerated huff. "Don't be such a blue nose, Henry. I can see why Rory is keen on the guy. He's a regular Sheik. Don't get your shorts in a bunch. I married you—didn't I?" Once again, she turned her attention back to Lachlan. "Don't worry about him."

He was more confused than ever. Was Serena supposed to be Agnes or Henry?

"He's a smidge jealous. How could I pass up his chiseled features and cornflower blue eyes? However, I do tend to flirt with men whenever I can, which hasn't been at all over the last, what is it sweetheart, 97—98 years? Anyway, as I was saying. Rory is a lucky woman."

"She might disagree." He'd go along with the charade and see where it led.

"Oh, don't worry." She motioned his comment away with a small wave of her hand. "She's still over the moon for you. Don't let her get away."

"It's for her to say."

"Coward," she tittered.

Lachlan bristled. "Coward? I did what I had to do." Now he was trying to reason with a *ghost*.

"Oh, I know, I know. Rory is tough. She can deal." She crossed her legs and leaned forward, clasping her hands over her knees. "Most men think we can't handle the tough stuff. You wouldn't be here if your mama was a wilting daisy."

"I'll give you that. Regan Donovan didn't suffer fools." For an instant he forgot he was talking to Serena and not Agnes.

"I could give Rory some advice if you want me to." She leaned back in her chair and bounced her foot up and down. "She needs—"

Serena's foot stopped mid-move. She gave a shuddering breath and slumped for a second before sitting upright.

This time her voice took on a deeper, steadier timbre. "Agnes just had to say her piece first. Strange, I don't know how I feel about this. Should I be jealous?"

"No."

"There's no stopping her when she gets the bit between her teeth but—er—life is never dull. Now about this Nolan chap. We've been around awhile—"

"Ever since those bank robbers fitted us with wooden kimonos." This time Serena's mouth turned into a little pout. Lachlan recognized Agnes' voice. "We were closing the bank and heading out to the petting pantry to see the new talkie, *Broadway Babies* and a double with *The Son of the Sheik*. I never pass up a chance to see Rudi and besides, the Gem Theater in Hollaway is—was cooled by the caves below. So-o-o divine. Is it still there?"

"I—ah—don't know."

Serena's eyes narrowed. "Agnes, I'm talking to the man. We have some serious business to discuss." There was a huff and she mimed adjusting a pair of glasses. "And quit using slang. It's unlady like."

"See," Agnes scrunched up her shoulders, then let them down, mouth pursed and with her nose in the air. "Blue nose, through and through."

It was like watching a tennis match in fast forward. His head spun from trying to figure out the Serena/Agnes/Henry dynamics.

Serena sat a little taller, adjusting her pajama top downward. "As I was saying, we've seen a few things. We can go outside but it requires too much energy, but I did see the chief getting fresh with a young lady, oh about fifteen years ago, behind the building. It was abandoned at the time."

Lachlan thought he'd follow along the rabbit hole for a while. "Who was it?"

"I don't know for sure. All I could see was the back of her head. She was frightened. He forced her to her knees and—well, I don't think I have to be explicit."

"What can you tell me about the woman? Tall, short, color of hair—that sort of thing."

"Blonde, about five two—oh, she had a little heart-shaped mole on the back of her right arm. Poor kid was scared to death."

"Kid?"

"Yes, about thirteen or fourteen. I got hot under the collar and wanted to punch him out."

"Why didn't you materialize?" The rabbit hole went deeper and deeper. "That might've stopped him."

"Don't get the idea we're like that Casper fellow." Serena shook her head. "It's not something I can do. Agnes has the lock on manifesting and even she has to rest several days afterward." She leaned toward him over the table. "Come by again. Do you play chess?" she whispered.

"Er—ah—no."

"Too bad? Gin—poker?"

"Both."

Serena leaned back with a sigh of satisfaction. "Good, good."

"Why?"

"Do you think I want to be stuck up here with two women all by myself without another man?"

"I—ah—"

"Exactly." She slapped the arm of the chair. "Drop by when you feel like you need a guy's night out. A good game of poker it is. I'll make sure Agnes is occupied."

"Right." Lachlan didn't know what to say. He didn't have to worry about a response.

"Dear Heart, you're a party pooper but I love you anyway." Serena's eyes squeezed shut and she blew a kiss.

Lachlan wasn't sure if it were at him or the invisible Henry. *Hell, Serena's roommates were both invisible.*

"My offer still stands, sugar. I'll have a talk with Rory."

"Don't. She doesn't believe in this, either." He knew Rory well enough to foresee what she'd say about tonight's meeting with the beyond.

"Regardless, someone wants to talk to you. Toodles."

"Lucky me." He wondered what Serena had planned. "Have you ever considered psychiatry? Maybe you have Dissociative Identity Disorder."

"Don't be a dick, Donovan. The lady is trying to help."

Serena's words set him back. He became defensive. "I'm not a—"

"Sure you are. You're being one now, and you made a dick move with your new girlfriend." She looked him up and down, this time the grin was sly and knowing. Her expression eerily familiar. "It wouldn't be the first time. Remember the night I dumped a big plate of spaghetti in your lap?"

His chest tightened. Anger warred with uncertainty. "Kate?"

"Bingo." Serena tapped her fingers on the arm of the chair. It was a small habit of Kate's that used to drive him crazy.

He wasn't buying this. Maybe Rory had let it slip about Kate's fiery temper and how she'd left a warm plate of pasta in his crotch after he'd made what he thought was a witty remark about PMS. *No, I never told Rory about the spaghetti incident.* "You can stop this right now."

"Oh, come on, Donovan, it was hard enough to get here. Don't you dare push me away."

Kate had been strong, opinionated, yet held a softness within her that helped with her job as a 911 dispatcher. She'd saved people every day. Her composed voice had soothed frightened children, helped women through labor, and calmed accident victims. Now it washed over him. The sound was Serena's, but the cadence and phrasing was all Kate.

"This isn't real."

"It's as real as you want it to be." Serena stood and came to kneel in front of him. She took his hand and stared up at him. For an instant it was as if Kate were there. "I'm at peace, Donovan. You helped to give me that." A scent of lilacs, Kate's favorite flowers wafted in the air. He'd brought them for her bedside table the day she passed away.

"You died." He squeezed her hand so hard that he could feel her fingers crushing in his grip. She never made a peep. He loosed them and smoothed the reddened flesh. "You fucking died."

Serena's expression softened. "I want to thank you for making my passing beautiful. I'm at peace now, but I'll always remember the way you held me, sang "The Long and Winding Road" to me through your tears."

He was sucked into a world of confusion. It had only been the two of them at home. He'd taken over for the hospice nurse when Kate had reached out for him, telling him it was time to go. All he could do was to sing and cry while she faded away.

Hope and disbelief warred within him. He couldn't move or speak. It hurt to breathe and his whole being wanted to shatter.

"It's time to start over—to go on with your life, Donovan. Do it for me. Do it for yourself." Serena gave a little laugh. "You've got a good woman. I know, I've been watching, so don't make me chuck another plate of spaghetti in your lap." She reached up to touch his face, to smooth away the hot tears blistering his eyes. "The heart knows what it wants, but first you have to let go."

"No." The pain in his chest split his soul in two. "I can't let you leave, again."

She stood and sat back in the chair. "It's time to go. Goodbye, Donovan."

Serena's face twisted. She stiffened. For one second he thought she was going into a seizure, but instead, she blinked her eyes and relaxed. "That was strange."

"How did you know that stuff about Kate?" He had to understand. No one had been there when Kate had died in his arms, of that he was certain. "How does this work?"

"I hear them, feel them and the whole time, I'm lost in a—a—I don't know. I'm there, but not." Her eyes took on a dreamy quality. "Kate just showed up. I've never had anyone besides Agnes and Henry come through."

His frustration grew. "That's really helpful."

Serena froze, her posture became defensive. "You don't have to believe me, any more than I have control over what they say."

"I'm sorry. That didn't come out right." He ran his hand through his hair. "Was it real?"

"That's for you to decide."

Panic gipped him. He hadn't told Kate he loved her. "Look, I need to talk to Kate again."

She rose and headed toward the door to the Purcells' apartment. "Party's over. I need my sleep if I'm going to get any work done later this morning."

He had a million questions, but she opened the door and pointed to the stairs leading outside. "Tell Amos I'm fine and not to worry about the lights up here."

"Please."

She shook her head. "I'm beat. Good night, Sergeant Donovan."

Step by step he argued for and against what had happened up there in the Purcells' living room. There had to be a logical reason for what happened, yet it was Kate. It *was* Kate.

Once outside, he stared up at the sky. The warm night was now humid and the sky turbulent. The stars that had been out a half-hour ago were now obliterated by clouds. Streaks of lightning flitted across the sky while a low rumbling followed in their wake. It would storm before he got off work.

His radio blared to life and Theo Tally's voice came through.

"Ought to let you know we're in a tornado watch until 8:00 a.m. It looks a bit dicey right now so keep your eyes peeled if you see anything."

"Ten-four." Ghosts, a crazy lady, and the sinking sensation he'd really spoken to Kate nagged at him.

A fork of lightning, immediately followed by a crack of thunder, made him jump. The wind whipped the tree limbs into a frenzy. A gust blew past him, then eased with the softness of a kiss, followed by the smell of lilacs.

...Your heart knows what it wants. Let go, Donovan...

Chapter Twenty-Six

The early morning storm left Rory tired and uneasy. Wind and hail had buffeted the house. Everyone had pitched in to make sure the chicken coop and the other outbuildings hadn't suffered any damage from the 60 mile-per-hour winds. A few panes of polycarbonate covering the greenhouse took a bit of damage and the garden looked bedraggled. Several shingles on her workshop had gone MIA.

She came inside, leaving The Aunts to prune, and inspect the veggies. Neither was her forte.

The couch beckoned to her. She curled up on the comfy cushions and nibbled on the last baby carrots and celery sticks in the house. They were down to raw vegetables and there was one frozen pizza left. The Aunts would have to go to the grocery store instead of her. She wasn't in the mood to face people in town. Everyone probably knew she and Lachlan had split and the last thing she needed or wanted was to dodge probing questions disguised as concern.

She'd decided the only thing that would numb her to all the drama swirling around was to binge watch *Bridgerton,* followed by a couple of Korean dramas.

It hadn't worked.

She reached for the remote the moment a hot and heavy scene reminded her too much of her mornings with Lachlan.

Aunt Daisy wondered in, still wearing her gardening gloves, and carrying her pruning shears. She spied the scene unfolding on the television. "Oh, my." Her head cocked to one side while her eyes went round. "Oh, my!"

Rory quickly turned off the TV.

"What they get up to nowadays." Aunt Daisy shook her head and flopped into an armchair. She set her gloves, along with the clippers, on the end table next to the chair. "I swear, the good Lord is out to get my roses this year. Maisie is staking up the new tomato plants. Only three or four out of the twenty she planted are savable. Luckily, I had a few heirlooms out in the green house. I don't know why she has to plant such a big garden when she can't cook or can. Go ahead and watch your show."

"No, I have a table and a chifforobe to bring up to snuff before I put them in the shop." She got up from the couch and headed to her room to change into work clothes when the doorbell rang.

Glen stood there, hands in his pockets, looking sheepish. It was his "ah—come on—I didn't mean it" demeanor he used to charm her out of being angry that sent out a red flag of warning. No more. Now she was past anger, or revenge, she wanted justice.

"What do you need?" She was weary and bored with the man. He had nothing she wanted.

He had the gall to look surprised.

"I've decided to stay in Hollaway until you come to your senses. You belong in New Orleans." His tone was a cross of cajoling and pissed off. The scent of alcohol wafted through the screen door. "Look, I'm sorry I messed up. You can't blame me for being a little angry." He waved his hands in the air in a half-drunken attempt to wipe out the past. "No, really, I just wanted a little harmless revenge, and it got out of hand. You can tell the feds it was a joke. Get them off my ass—please?" He sighed and looked everywhere, except at her. "Come back."

"I don't know how many times I have to say this. No. It's too late, and besides, everything is in the authority's hands. I can't help you."

His eyes took on the familiar glint he got when he was angry. "You mean you won't help. I'll bet you got that cop so whipped that he'll do anything you want—even throw me in jail."

"I'm going to go down to the courthouse and file a restraining order if you don't leave me alone."

He gave a drunken laugh. "They're not worth the paper they're written on. You'll be sorry. The whole lot of you will be wishing you never tangled with me."

In the background, Rory could hear Aunt Daisy on the phone but couldn't make out the conversation.

"You haven't changed. Take your narcissistic ass back to New Orleans. You're on your own."

"Listen here—"

Aunt Daisy appeared behind her. She gave her pruners a couple of snips in the air.

"Unless you want to keep your 'bud' blooming, you'll leave Rory alone." She came to stand next to Rory. "I called the sheriff's office and Callie is on her way out."

A sheriff's cruiser pulled into the drive before Glen could spout anymore nonsense. Callie got out and loped up to the porch.

"I was just a half mile down the road when I got a dispatch to stop by your place." She turned to Glen, hand on her holster. "I'm Deputy Callie Parker. You need to leave."

"Don't think I don't know you're friends with her." Glen pointed at Rory. "I'll call my lawyer."

"Go right ahead. From what I understand, you're going to need one. I didn't make a suggestion. Leave."

"Screw you." Glen tried to stare down Callie and lost. His glare went from her to Rory. "Okay, okay. I'll leave but remember what I said."

Aunt Daisy pushed past Rory and made a couple more snips of the clippers. "You remember what I said."

He left, got into his car and headed down the road in the direction of Hollaway.

Callie glared. "Are you okay?"

"I'm fine." Rory swept an errant curl from her face. "Let's just say I've had better days.

"I should follow him. He's been drinking." Callie waved goodbye. "Can't have him harming the good citizens of the county."

Aunt Daisy looked down at her pruning shears. "I was sure hoping to give him a Callahan Clip."

****

Lachlan clocked in for his shift and wandered into the staff lounge to see if the coffee was drinkable. Jenny sat at the small table. Usually, she was out of the station before he checked in. A frown puckered her freckled brow.

"Something wrong?" He picked up the coffee carafe and gave it a sniff. It would do.

Jenny motioned him over and pulled a chair close to hers. "Have a seat."

"Okay." He wondered what had made her so worried. "I've got to get going pretty soon."

"I know. I know." She bit her lower lip. "Someone suggested I stop carrying stories but when does something change from gossip to what needs to be told? I'm confused. It concerns Rory."

"I'm not sure I'm the one to answer that question."

Jenny clasped her hands on the tabletop. "I heard someone over in Hollaway has been asking questions about her, and a couple of other people. You know how I got friends and relatives everywhere that are *true* gossips. Anyway, Gertie Champion, she's my second cousin who works over at the Hollaway Holler said some guy came to the paper yesterday wanting to look at back editions on microfish."

"Microfiche."

"That's what I said." She gave him a look of exasperation. "He was looking for stuff over twenty-five years ago. He was asking about the chief's family."

Lachlan decided Caleb's P.I. was ham fisted and didn't understand small towns. He glanced at the perplexed woman next to him. The grapevine was strong with this one. Hootiecackle and Hollaway weren't like St. Louis where a detective could fit in and ask questions.

"I heard the chief's retiring at the end of the year and thinking about running for state government." He decided not to lie but to steer Jenny in a different direction.

"Oh, like a reporter or maybe the opposition." For a moment Jenny acted mollified but sidled closer. "But why would he be asking about Rory and Serena, too? Jasper over at the bar inside Hideaway Hotel said the same guy was there the other night." She wrung her hands. "I don't know what to do. I know you and Rory are on a break, and that's all it is, believe me, that girl is mad for you, but don't you think it's odd? All these questions?"

"I think a lot of people need to keep their noses out of things they know nothing about." He didn't want to lie to Jenny but had to skirt around her questions. "Tell you what, I'll talk to Rory after work. Okay?"

"What about the chief and Serena?"

"Rory can talk to Serena and the chief is on his own."

"On his own about what?" Floyd Brennon, one of the other officers getting off duty walked into the lounge. He brown nosed the chief with abandon. There was no telling how long he'd been outside the door or if he'd heard everything they said.

"Oh, nothing," Jenny piped up. "Just some nosy guy asking questions about him running for office after he retires—at least," she glanced up at Lachlan, "that's what I think it was about."

"But you don't know that's why he was asking questions." He stared down at Jenny trying to assess her expression. Floyd was an avid crime show watcher and believed he was a premier sleuth. "Do you?"

Jenny rose and grabbed her purse. "What I do know is my husband will be eating the carpets if I don't get home soon." She gave Lachlan a quick wink. "We just had them installed a few weeks ago." She double-timed it out the door before Floyd could ask any more questions.

"Is there something I should know about?"

"Why would there be?" Lachlan poured coffee into his metal go-cup."

"It concerns the chief."

"He's a big boy. He's able to handle his own

problems."

"Yes, but—"

"I've got to go, Floyd." Lachlan gave him a salute with the cup and left before the man could ask any more questions.

The entire night he alternately fumed over the P.I's clumsiness and worry about Rory's story being outed. They needed positive evidence the chief had been propositioning minors for years. Caleb would get a call first thing after Lachlan got off his shift.

He couldn't stand the idea that Rory would be shunned by the people of Hootiecackle. They'd let her down once before—he hoped it wouldn't be repeated.

Once again his beat took him to the park across the street from the old bank building. He parked and got out of his vehicle. Amos wasn't there tonight. Maybe he was able to sleep through his demons. It didn't stop Lachlan from sitting on the bench and looking at the third story window.

There were no lights in the second story, but it was four in the morning. Upstairs was equally dark—except for a faint shimmer at the window he knew was next to the radio. Out of curiosity he went to the front door of Funky Junk Shoppe. The faintest notes of "Singin' in the Rain" came from above. It was both jarring and comforting at the same time.

He remembered what Kate, he was sure it was Kate, said.

His heart was with Rory. It might take a long time to win back her trust, but he had to make the effort. He'd talk to her today—not about the chief, but about how he should've given her the benefit of the doubt. It was time to climb off his white horse and fight the dragons alongside Rory, not for her.

****

Rory decided to get an early start on the chifforobe and headed out to her workshop. The dawn was bright, filled with so many colors. The day smelled new from the morning dew and filled with possibilities.

She had tossed and turned the whole night. First about Glen and next Lachlan. Handling Glen was nothing next to the whirlwind of emotions when she thought of Lachlan. He'd stepped on her toes, left her aching with hurt, but he hadn't done it maliciously. The moment she woke she decided she'd talk to him. They could work this out.

The sound of his car pulling into his drive made her stop oiling the wood of the large chifforobe. Her heart pounded, her hands sweated, but she knew she could do this. It was time to grab some happiness. He was in for a fight if he thought he would let her go.

She stood and wiped her hands on a rag and checked the mirror to make sure she didn't have oil smudges on her face. It was hard to breathe. One step, then another took her out the door and over to the gate.

He stood there in the morning light, on his side of the chain-link gate. His hand was on the latch. His dark eyes looked tired, yet filled with—hope?

She had to tell him before she lost her courage.

"I'm sorry." They said in unison.

Chapter Twenty-Seven

Rory didn't know who opened the gate first, not that it mattered. She was in Lachlan's arms. His hands cupped her face, and his mouth covered hers in delicious urgency. A deep well of desire bubbled up until it was difficult to think or breathe.

"I missed you." He whispered and brushed her cheek with his thumb. "How about a *cup of coffee*?

"I wouldn't say no." She wound her hand in his and he led her toward his house.

It was a crazy race to the bed. Clothes flew in every direction. She was hungry for his touch, the taste of his skin and the way her body reacted to the way he traced each part of her with his kisses. It was selfish to feel so giddy and feeding her need to be with him. She couldn't help it. H n /e brought out a wild, primal part of her she never knew existed. Glen had never left her shaking with need.

"I love you." He picked her up in his arms and whirled her around in dizzy wonder.

She squeaked in surprise and clasped her arms around his neck to steady herself.

"I love you," he said again with a mix of joy and orneriness.

The words washed over her, leaving her surprised and speechless. His smile captured her heart. At first she was self-conscious—then she laughed in wonderment.

Maybe it was spinning around the room in the arms of a naked guy, but she couldn't help the words that popped out of her mouth. "I love you, too." She planted kisses on his chin, feeling the stubble on his jaw and the salt of his skin. "I love you so much."

His chuckle rumbled in his chest as he stopped moving and set her on her feet. He captured her face in his hands and gently brushed his lips against hers. "How about that cup of coffee."

"I've worked up a thirst." She grabbed his hand and led him toward the bed. "You know how I take mine."

****

The room was quiet except for the sound of birds singing and squawking around the birdfeeder outside Lachlan's bedroom window. A soft morning breeze, full of the scent of dew and greenness, filtered through the pale gray curtains and over their cooling bodies.

"Someone told me the heart knows what it wants. I want you—no, I love you." He pulled her closer. "Does that scare you?"

"I'd be a liar if I said I wasn't nervous. Glen told me he loved me. I believed him, but now I know it wasn't real. I had to earn every morsel he threw my way. For two years I forgot who I was. Not with you." She looked up at him and smiled. "Even when I'm pissed-off at you I'm strong and know who I am. So, who is the wise person who told you to follow your heart?"

He gave a little half-smile. "Kate. Kate told me."

"Before she died?"

"No." He shook his head. "Just the other day."

Confused, she stared at him. "How is that possible."

"It's a long story. I'm not sure I even understand." He kissed the tip of her nose. "I'll tell you about it someday."

"O-k-a-y." She was curious but decided it wasn't the time to push.

"I'll always love Kate, but I feel free to love you—Rory Callahan."

"Love can be hard. I guess my heart knows what it wants, and that's you."

He ran a finger along her nose to the tip. "I'm glad" He sighed, deep and long. "We may have another problem."

"What's that?"

"Jenny asked me about a rumor from a friend of—"

"Of a friend, of a friend. I know how this works." A smile tugged at her mouth. "So he's been sniffing around."

"Both in Hollaway and Hootiecackle. If Nolan has a past this guy will find it. He's checking the local newspapers, and the county seat records, but the investigation might be harder if people decide to be tightlipped."

She chuckled. "All he'd have to do is to buy a few rounds at the local bars. Good ol' boys around here chin-wag worse than Jenny. Gossip works both ways."

"I'm hoping he'll come up with solid evidence to back up your and Serena's allegations."

She clutched the sheet to her chest and ground out, "They're more than allegations."

"I know you're telling the truth." He sat up, hands behind his head before turning his head to look at her. "Do you know of anyone else who had a run-in with the chief?"

She shook her head. "No, at least nobody said anything to me."

"I wish the PI hadn't been so careless." He sighed. "I should've warned him about small towns and their own brand of social media."

"Don't worry. I can handle anything the chief or the town throws at me. Serena will deal as well."

"You shouldn't have to be strong."

"I'm used to people in this town." She gave a little shrug. "They'll say I'm trying to badmouth him for getting on my case when I was a kid, especially since he plans to run for state office." A sudden thought hit her. "What worries me is that this might come back on you."

"I've come to really like Hootiecackle, but I can always find another job if the chief decides to fire me." He took her hand and kissed it. "You come first."

"No," she put her other hand over his. "*We* come first, together.

He stared down at their hands for a few seconds. "Kate always got on to me for my WKS—White Knight Syndrome. You know, trying to fix everyone's problems."

Rory could relate to Kate at that moment. "The world needs people like you. I'm getting used to this uncontrollable tendency of yours, but I need to make my own decisions. Not alone, though. I'll take your advice into account. It's good to know I'm not alone."

He held out his hand. "Deal."

"Oh, you can do better than that." She leaned forward and took his mouth in a kiss.

****

Lachlan pulled her closer, enjoying the feel of her in his arms. She suddenly stiffened.

"Oh, lordy, look at the time. I've got to get back home." He tried to pull Rory back into bed. She gave him a light slap on the shoulder. "You need to get some rest."

He eyed the clock. "There's enough time for a *small* coffee."

"I'll pass if it's small." She frowned and sat up against the headboard. Her lower lip caught between her teeth. "Glen stopped by the farm today."

"Oh?" His question held a wealth of curiosity and concern. "Everything okay? What did he want?"

"The same old, same old. He wants me to stop the investigation." She snuggled closer to him. "I was so angry that I wanted to punch him out. He'd been drinking."

"What happened?"

"Aunt Daisy called the sheriff's office and Callie came out." She went on to tell Lachlan how Callie noticed that Glen had been drinking and he followed him out the drive. "She pulled him over and made him do a sobriety field test. Unfortunately, the breathalyzer came in just under the legal limit. She gave him a warning. He's staying in Hollaway. They said they'd keep an eye on him."

"He's lucky he left with a warning."

"You're right about that." A slow smile dimpled her face. "Aunt Daisy had just come in from pruning her damaged roses and wanted to give him a nip and tuck."

"Ouch." He cupped himself over the covers. "You Callahan women are fierce."

"Yeah." She gave him a saucy smile. "Don't you forget it. Oh, before I forget it," she said as she wriggled into her panties, "Serena and I are having a security system put in at the building. They dropped by yesterday to check things out and give us an estimate. It should be in by tomorrow." A quick yank of her t-shirt covered her breasts.

"I wondered. I saw the van outside the store."

A smile quirked at the corner of her mouth. "Did you do a background check on them?"

"They're rated one of the best," he said before he caught himself. He winced. "Busted, huh."

"Bad case of White Knight Syndrome." She leaned down and kissed his mouth in a short but sweet kiss. "It's okay. You're worried about my safety. I'll feel better when Chandra, Serena, and I have our sleepover the night before the wedding. Last girls' night out and all that. I have to admit the building is a little creepy at night."

"I'm glad you're taking your safety seriously."

"There's no lights to indicate it's recording so if Glen tries to monkey around with my shop, I'll know. We're doing cloud storage." She pushed her legs through her shorts and gave him another quick kiss. "I'll see you tomorrow morning?"

Sleep eluded him after she left. He made a call to Caleb.

"What did your PI find out?"

"The chief has a juvie record. It's sealed but he went into the military at 17—with his parents' approval. Also, some serious money changed hands somewhere. His parents took out $20,000 but there is no indication they bought anything or invested it."

Lachlan's mind went into overdrive. "The parents probably paid somebody off."

"People at the local watering hole didn't say much." Caleb sounded frustrated. "You know, school jock, the popular guy, heavy drinking in high school, but nothing to hang anything on."

"Damn."

"A couple of guys said the chief hit on the younger girls in high school."

"I wonder if the money might be a cover up for a sex crime?"

"Even if it was we don't have any real evidence."

He ended the call and tried to go to sleep again. It didn't come easy. He tossed and turned until an insistent ring brought him out of his troubled sleep. He opened one eye to see the illuminated numbers on the clock. It was only ten in the morning—three hours sleep. The caller ID said it was the chief. *Great. Just what I need.*

"Umm, hello." He pushed himself up and rubbed the sleep from his eyes. The grittiness echoed his mood. "What you need, Chief?"

"We need to talk, ASAP." The growl in the chief's voice sent out red flags of warning. It didn't take a soothsayer to predict he'd heard about the private detective.

"What's this about?" It didn't hurt to find out for sure.

"I'll tell you when you get here." The call abruptly ended.

Lachlan jumped out of bed, went into the kitchen to turn on the coffee maker. The command was for ASAP, but he was determined to get one cup of coffee to clear his brain. He padded into the bathroom, letting the hot shower brush away most of the cobwebs. His shift didn't start until 6:00 p.m. so he opted for comfort and threw on a pair of cargo shorts, a black t-shirt, and a pair of sandals.

Cherry Banks, the receptionist, buzzed him in. He waved as he shut the door and noticed Jenny's guilty face on his way back to the chief's office. Yeah, she flipped faster than a flapjack at the local VFW's pancake breakfast. The chief wouldn't have to use truth serum to get Jenny to spill.

He gave a quick knock on the chief's office door.

"Come in."

The Chief sat behind his desk reading a report. He motioned Lachlan to sit but kept his eyes on the papers before him.

Lachlan pulled out a chair on the other side of the desk and eased into it. He sat, relaxed yet respectful while the chief continued to read. He wasn't in a mood to play games.

"You wanted to see me." It wasn't a question. His statement made Chief glance up and put his papers away.

The Chief took a pack of cigarettes from his shirt pocket. He made a show of tapping one out and lighting it with a silver Zippo with a golden Marine logo. He inhaled before blowing a puff of smoke.

"There's a no smoking sign on the wall behind you."

"Who's going to stop me?" The Chief smirked and took another drag. "Let me get right to the point."

"That'd be good. I can still get in a couple hours of sleep if we make this quick."

A flash of red stained the chief's face. "A private detective is asking questions in Hootiecackle and Hollaway?"

Lachlan kept studying his boss's face. It was going to be tricky to tell the truth without giving away the true intent of the investigation. He snapped his fingers as if the answer came to him. "He has to be the PI recommended to Rory by my friend from the FBI cybercrimes unit."

"Why the hell does she need a detective?"

"The PI is checking on anyone who might have an issue with Rory's return to Hootiecackle." Lachlan shrugged. "The break-in, the ID theft, and anyone who might have a grudge against her."

"I thought it was the ex-boyfriend."

"She wants to be sure. Whoever broke into the shop didn't take any money or valuables. They did turn on the computer—looks like they went through the files." Lachlan leaned back in his chair and laced his fingers together. "Rory felt she wasn't getting any cooperation from the HPD since you decided to shitcan the investigation. That's why she turned the evidence over to the FBI."

"It didn't seem important."

"The perp took information from her computer onsite and used it in the ID theft. The PI might come up with some other leads. She said she and her friends were harassed in high school. Some people never forget old slights—or rejections."

The Chief got red in the face. "I don't like the guy sticking his nose in my town." His eyes narrowed. "Why are you helping that piece of tail that dumped you? It doesn't make sense." He stood and paced behind his desk. "She's always been trouble," he sneered. "Nothing but a damned trouble."

Lachlan's gut reaction was to plow his fist into the chief's face. Instead, he stood and smiled. "Jenny didn't tell you the news? We're back together. It was a misunderstanding. Good communication can work wonders in a relationship. We talked about our pasts and got to know everything about each other."

The chief's face turned stone hard. "Don't be too

sure."

"Oh, I'm sure." Lachlan pulled his car keys from his pocket. "I got to go home and catch some Zs."

Chapter Twenty-Eight

Rory tip-toed through the back door and into the kitchen trying not to make any noise. Her morning with Lachlan left her body tingling from his touch. She could still taste his kiss, but the last thing she needed was for The Aunts to catch her looking like she'd just tumbled out of bed. It'd be true.

First she needed a shower and a big cup of coffee. She'd had one cup before she left Lachlan's, and she could get another at the shop. Josie made a mean pot of coffee and the idea of Aunt Daisy's gourmet blend made her stomach jump.

"Where do you think you're going, missy?" Aunt Daisy sat at the kitchen table next to her sister. Their arms were crossed over their ample bosoms. Two sets of green eyes bored into her.

"Oh, good morning," she chirped on her way out of the kitchen.

"Victoria Shoiban Callahan, sit down."

Damn. All three names. They meant business.

She decided to ignore the command. "I need to take a shower."

"I'll bet you do, missy." Aunt Daisy narrowed her eyes. "Now sit."

She did as commanded. "What's wrong?"

"Sweetie," Aunt Maisie reached over and patted her hand. "You know you can't hide anything from us. You

284

were with Lachlan."

"Well, yes." It was no use lying. She figured they already knew where she went so early in the mornings. It wasn't to the workshop.

"I may not look like it now," Aunt Maisie ran her hand over her brightly floral covered breasts and downward, "but I remember being young and in love with a hunky guy. You may only picture your late Uncle Albert as bald and with dentures but let me tell you—that guy rocked my world."

"Sister!" Aunt Daisy's shocked expression would've normally been laughable, but Rory knew better than to crack a smile. "We're not interested in *your* sex life." Her chest heaved and she tapped the table with a blunt finger. "Now, when is that young man going to pop the question?"

Rory blinked a couple of times. She didn't know what to tell them. "I—ah—"

"I thought we agreed to broach the subject slowly." Aunt Maisie made a slow, downward motion with her hand as if to cool her sister's enthusiasm.

"Oh, come on, Sister, you know the Jacksons are leavin' town. Sally Anne Schrock will be snapped up in a jiffy." A hint of panic touched Aunt Daisy's voice.

"I know, but we can't afford to get a cook until—" Aunt Maisie turned to face Rory with shock on her face. "I mean—"

"You mean you want me to get married so you can hire a cook? I thought you wanted my happiness, although that doesn't mean it's right to push me into a relationship—but just to get a cook." She'd thought they were only interested in getting her and Lachlan to the altar.

"Well," Aunt Maisie quickly looked away. "I—ah—ah." She pinked with guilt.

"That's about the size of it." Aunt Daisy gave the table a light slap. "Not that we don't have your well-being at heart. We really do. The moment we saw Lachlan we knew he was the one for you. So nice and—"

"Yummy lookin'," Aunt Maisie added with enthusiasm. You have to admit that, but," She hung her head and looked down at her folded hands. "I'm tired of frozen dinners and fast food."

"We'd love a maid who can cook. Sally Anne is used to a live-in situation and the Jacksons were transferred to Kansas City. The family leaves at the end of the month," Aunt Daisy said. "My knees aren't what they used to be. It's all I can do to prune the plants in the green house and yard—but we can't afford her because we *do* live on a fixed income."

Rory narrowed her eyes. "What happened to the money I paid you for rent?"

This time they squirmed in their chairs.

"You put most of your money into your business. How could we ask for more?" Aunt Daisy eyes darted everywhere except to meet Rory's. "Besides, we had to buy some essentials."

"Essentials?"

Aunt Maisie fluttered her lashes and waved her hands in emphasis. "Oh, you know, I needed a new wardrobe for the spring. We paid the bills of course, but I was so tired at shopping at the thrift store."

"That was useless junk." Aunt Daisy snarked. "I needed some new tools for the roses and garden."

"And shoes." Aunt Daisy raised a plump foot to

display a pair of hot pink wedgie flip-flops with bright yellow flowers between the toes.

Rory squeezed her lids shut for a moment before giving them a little rub. "I see. You're selling me into slavery to keep from eating your own cooking." Rory didn't know whether to be mortally offended or shake her head in disbelief.

"Laud a mercy, why, we'd never deal in human trafficking." Aunt Daisy patted her chest with a pudgy hand in indignation. "Never."

"We love you to bits, Rory but that good for nothing excuse of man put a big dent in your heart." Aunt Daisy sucked in a deep breath. "You need us, and I figured we lucked out when Lachlan bought the other house."

Rory knew when she was licked. "Why don't you call Sally Anne and I'll pay her wages—whether I get married to anyone or not. I can bunk in the workshop. To tell the truth, I wouldn't mind a breakfast I could eat."

"We didn't want to burden you with another thing while you were going through so much." Aunt Maisie's eyes watered up. "To tell the truth it would be a good thing for Sally Anne, too." She perked up as if a thought hit her. "We could fix up the room for her, you know, the one on the third floor. She jogs several times a week. Her knees are in good shape so she can maneuver the stairs. You can keep your room."

****

Rory's arms ached from holding so many shopping bags.

The talk she had with her aunts this morning played over and over in her mind. She could understand their motives, but they should've come right out and told her what they wanted. Still, she had met Lachlan. He was the

287

one. They were right about that, however, she wanted to take things slow.

She chuckled. *Taking things slow isn't Lachlan's way of doing things, except when it comes to making love.* What was it Aunt Maisie said, he rocked her world.

Rory just about made it to her van when someone called out her name. A quick glance over her shoulder confirmed her worse fears. It was Jennie. The last thing she wanted was to have a gabfest in the middle of the sidewalk.

"Rory," Jennie shouted once again and waved her hand to catch her attention. "Yoo-hoo!"

Unable to stand the weight straining her arms, Rory put the bags on the sidewalk next to the parked van. "Hey, Jenny. What's up?"

That was the wrong question to ask.

"Oh, nothing much." She gave an eloquent shrug. "Amos was put in jail overnight for getting into the park fountain last night."

"Wading in the fountain isn't a crime."

"It is if you strip off naked and try to take a shower."

"Oh."

"I heard Rudy Smith got kicked out of the house. Alicia decided she'd had enough of dealing with two toddlers by herself while he was at the Cow Catcher Lounge all the time. A skillet upside the head. A quick trip to the ER and all that. I'm surprised Lachlan didn't tell you."

"Can't say I blame her—and Lachlan never tells me who he gives tickets to or arrests."

"Oh." Jenny sounded disappointed and peeked at the bags on the grounds. She eyed the party decorations and bottles of champagne. "Having a do?"

"Well tomorrow is the day before the wedding. Chandra and I are going over to Serena's for a slumber party. You know, last day as a single girl. We decided it would be fun. We'll rent a limo to take her back to her parents. That way they can do the rest of the preparations. I'll have to get home to wrangle The Aunts." She hoped that was all the information Jenny's greedy ears could handle at once.

"That's wonderful. I was wondering if it was going to be a big party." She jabbed her hands in her uniform pants pockets. It was clear she was fishing for an invitation. "Carolyn over at the party store said you bought the place out."

"Nope. Just the three of us." Rory opened the van's side door and began loading up her packages. "The bachelor party was for everyone else."

"But that was ages ago." The whine in Jenny's voice grated on Rory's nerves. She should be more considerate of Jenny's feelings, but she had a long list of things to get done.

"It was the only time everyone on Chandra's list could get together. Serena couldn't go because of a family thing. Joy Nowell was working the night shift at the nursing home." She closed the van door. "I've got to get going before the chocolate melts."

"Oh, okay." Jenny brightened up. "I have to pick up lunch at the Dinner Bell for the station. The Chief will be upset if his hot beef sandwich is lukewarm. He hates nuked food—refuses to use the microwave in the breakroom. He probably doesn't know Mikey uses instant mashed potatoes and canned gravy." She wiggled her fingers. "Bye-di-o."

Rory hurried into the van and started the engine

before Jenny could think of something else to impart. She headed to the shop. Once there she parked out back to unload her party haul. Serena must have spotted her because she came out of the front door of her apartment and raced down the stairs.

"Whatcha' got here. Let me help." She picked up a bag containing the champagne. "Oh, poor Chandra will have to soak her head in the morning to sober up."

"I plan on doling out the drinks. The last thing Nick needs is a maudlin bride."

"Party hats!" Serena's squeal of delight came close to bursting her eardrums. "If you have party crackers in here I'm going to die."

"I've saved you from certain death. The only crackers in here are for the cheese tray." Rory picked up the rest of the bags and followed Serena up the long flight of wooden stairs. "The only excitement I want tonight is to watch three-hankie movies and eat a ton of junk food."

Serena opened the screen door and sidled past it. The bottles clanked as she put the bag on the table. She pulled out three bottles of champagne, along with one rose wine. Her nose lifted in the air. "What's that I smell?"

Rory hefted an aluminum take away carton in her hand and held up another. "Jasper Jack's Famous Pulled Pork." She unloaded several more from the bag. "Along with Barbeque Jack Fruit for you. Cole Slaw, country style green beans minus the ham, and potatoes au gratin."

"You went all the way over to Hollaway to get Jasper Jack's?"

"That's how much I love you and Chandra." She gave Serena a big smile. "I want this to be a night to remember."

Serena loaded the food into her fridge. "Agnes and Henry have been restless. I think it will do them good to have other people around."

Chapter Twenty-Nine

Rory brushed her fingers over Lachlan's face. Even blindfolded she knew she could pick him from a lineup of guys. She reveled in his kiss, the taste of him, the scent. Her heart ached with a sense of loss when he pulled away and tugged a curl that had escaped her ponytail. "I'm glad you stopped by before the party."

"I need to get going. I'm doing my shift as well as Nick's today. The Chief decided to monkey with the schedule, and I got the short stick. Things will even out after tomorrow." He brushed his lips along her cheek. "I'll have to make do until Monday morning."

She couldn't stop the giggle. His lips tickled and the little touch sent her desire skyrocketing. "Nick and Chandra better get back from their honeymoon as soon as they can. Maybe we can convince them to cut it short by a few days?"

"Would you?"

"No." She sighed and stepped back but still holding on to him. "You better go before I—"

He stiffened. His eyes scanned the upper floor of the building.

"Is something wrong?"

He relaxed, shook his head, and smiled. "I thought I saw something upstairs but it's probably a flash from the sun reflecting off the window."

"I see a couple of peeping toms at the kitchen

window." She patted his shoulder. "You're right. You better go."

Lachlan laughed and headed down the stairs.

She leaned over the railing to throw him a kiss. He reached up and pretended to catch it.

Her heart was still tap dancing against her ribs when she went back inside Serena's apartment. Chandra and Serena stood next to the window trying to act innocent.

"That was so romantic—like Romeo and Juliet," Chandra cooed giving her a sly smile.

Rory went to the fridge and pulled out a cola. "I don't plan on ending up like them." She popped the tab. "My experience with Glen made me understand my worth. So has Lachlan. Being really, I mean really, in love is scary for both of us. He's suffered through loss, and so have I. We want to take things slow unlike Shakespeare's unlucky pair."

"Enough of being serious. Why don't we get this party started?" Serena clapped her hands. "Everyone into the living room."

A few hours later, Rory sat on a cushion on the floor, eating popcorn and watching a sloppy tear-jerker. They were three quarters into their second bottle of champagne. Through the soft muzzy haze of the wine, Rory decided, like the kitchen, this room was Serena. Soft gray walls and lighter gray woodwork surrounded them. Deep gray carpets covered the floor. The sofa was a wonder of deep purple with an ornate gray frame rubbed with silver. Light purple gauzy drapes of cloth hung from silver rods with crystal balls at either end. Instead of being creepy, Serena managed to make it very inviting.

"I wouldn't want to spend the day before my

wedding with anyone else—except Nick." Chandra giggled and poured another glass. "A sleepover was a good idea." A goofy smile settled on her face.

Rory could sense a touch of maudlin slipping into her speech. Tears wouldn't be far behind. Typical Chandra. Loveable Chandra. She glowed with inner strength and Nick's love.

"I wouldn't be here without you two." Chandra snagged up a large strawberry from the fruit and cheese plate on the floor in front of them. She dipped it into the champagne and took out a big bite. "You paid for my therapy sessions when my insurance wouldn't cover them. Anxiety is awful. So is low self-esteem. I wouldn't be able to let a man into my life, even someone as special as Nick, if not for you both."

"Are you still going to make us wear those hideous dresses?" Rory threw her arm over her friend's shoulder. "The colors are—er—okay, but the ruffles. I feel like I'm a Barbie cake topper."

"Hey, it's my wedding, and the dresses aren't that bad."

Serena filled up her glass and scowled at Rory. "If I can wear it, you can wear it." She held up the champagne flute. "Here's to our noble selves, there's damned few of us left."

"Amen," Rory and Chandra echoed.

Chandra suddenly stiffened and grew quiet. She placed her glass on the ornate table by the couch. "I'm scared."

"Of what?" Rory removed her arm and turned to face Chandra.

"I've got a secret. It could ruin Nick's and my lives." Her friend stared at the floor.

"The wine is making you over dramatic." Serena giggled and poured herself another glass. "What is it? Did you spend too much on the wedding?"

"Hey, I thought you were the wine monitor." Rory took the bottle away and set it on the coffee table. "What is it, sweetie?" The paleness of Chandra's cheeks sent out a red flag of warning. "You can tell us."

Serena blinked a couple of times and sat her glass down. "You're serious." She rubbed her temples. "Damn it, I'm supposed to be able to pick up on stuff. Rory's right. We're here for you."

Chandra sucked in a deep breath. "Do you remember when we were in junior high?"

Both Rory and Serena nodded.

"Back then I tried to kick my good girl image. I was so tired of it. One night I went out with Billy Ray Thornton."

"Oh no, not the worst biker in town." Serena's horrified expression echoed her own surprise.

"I know, I had second thoughts the first time I got on the back of his bike. He took me out to the edge of town, in back of the old Red Barn Restaurant. Several of his friends were there. He made me drink a beer and before I knew it they—"

"Oh no." Serena put her hand to her mouth. "Please, don't tell me."

"Chief Nolan showed up before they could do anything." She gave them a wobbly laugh. "Being a good girl didn't seem so bad after all."

"You don't have to be afraid to tell Nick. He'll understand." Serena reached out to put her arm around Chandra's shoulder and pull her into a quick hug. "It's in the past."

Chandra's eyes brimmed with tears. "That's not the worst of it."

The way Chandra paled even further made Rory worry she would faint. "Are you okay?"

"No." Chandra shook her head. "No. No. I'll never be okay. I thought Chief Nolan was my savior. He was so kind, until he pulled behind this building."

Serena's eyes went wide.

The air in the room suddenly chilled and a faint breeze fluttered past Rory.

"He gave me a choice to…"

"Give him a blowjob or tell your parents."

Chandra shuddered. Her eyes looked as shocked as Serena's. "How do you know?"

"Because he tried the same thing with us."

"Did you—you know?"

"Hell no." Rory couldn't keep her contempt for Nolan from her voice. "I told him to go ahead."

"He tried the same with me," Serena took Chandra's hand, "but I threatened to curse his manhood. He believed I would do it."

This time it was Chandra's turn to look shocked. "Oh no." She violently shook her head. "I did it. I did what he wanted. I couldn't let my family find out what happened." Chandra broke down in hard sobs. "My father was running for mayor. Mama had her church group."

"What if Nick finds out?" Of the three girls Chief Nolan had propositioned she was the only one to submit to his demands. She'd accepted the devil's deal. "My parents—I couldn't hurt them." She hugged herself. "I tried to forget about it, but it didn't let go. One minute my mood was up, the next down. My parents didn't know what to do."

"Oh, sweetie." Rory gave her a soft pat.

"I can't. I know the therapist said to tell him, but I couldn't."

"He has the right to know." Serena's eyes narrowed. "Damn Chief Nolan."

"I've come to terms with what I did, what I felt I was forced to do, but it will kill Nick."

"He's a grown ass man." Rory wanted to jump up and go to Nolan's house to call him out. All it would do was to hurt her friend against her wishes. She forced herself to stay still and choke back her anger. She was as much to blame as Nolan. If she'd said something this might not have happened to Chandra. Guilt chewed into her like a hungry rat. How many others had he propositioned?

"I don't want Nick to lose his job. It means everything to him." Chandra took a deep breath and smiled. "This is a new start for me. Now I can be who I want."

They knew Chandra's dream was to be a wife and mother. Most would say her goals in life were old-fashioned but up until now she had given her love to other people's children. Her daycare center was one of the best in the county. Her eagle eye kept guard for any signs of abuse. She embraced each child as her own. No one beyond the three of them and Chandra's therapist knew the way Chief Nolan molested her.

"We won't say anything." Serena glanced over at Rory. "Right?"

"It's your decision." It irked Rory to say it, but hadn't she and Serena kept quiet?

"Nick and I are going to have a beautiful wedding,

a wonderful honeymoon and life." She pointed to each of them. "And yes, you do have to wear the bridesmaid dresses."

"Damn." Serena's head dropped to her knees, and she gave Chandra a side-eyed glance. "I'm wearing black jet combs in my hair, not those roses."

"Please," Chandra pleaded.

"Okay, okay, but one of these days I'll make you pay." She gave Chandra a light poke on her shoulder.

"Hey, what about me? Those colors are going to clash with my red hair." Rory gave Chandra a gentle nudge. "Whatever possessed you to choose pink and lime green?"

"They're my favorite colors and I've always wanted big poufy skirts. Hey, it's my wedding." She smiled a little smile that held a bit of wicked to it. "I know how much both of you hate big southern belle dresses."

"We wouldn't do this if we didn't love you." Rory sipped at her drink. "We hang tough no matter what— even with your wedding dreams." She reached out to give Chandra a fist bump.

"Hang tough, girl." Chandra passed the fist bump along to Serena.

"Only for you, kiddo."

The room grew warmer. It wasn't uncomfortable but, in the way a balmy night blankets the land. A peaceful glow settled over the group. Rory smiled thinking how this was the way life was supposed to be. Glen was forgotten for the moment, and it was impossible to keep from thinking about Lachlan. She hummed with anticipation at seeing him. She sighed as the champagne worked its magic.

Later in the night they settled down to sleep. Rory

opted for a pallet on the floor with a camping mat underneath. Not too bad. It wasn't long before the wine and barbeque did their job. Sleep welcomed her.

A flash of light filled the room. It filtered through her eyelids as if someone had turned on the overhead light. It was enough to make her blink awake. A chill covered her. Wisps of smoke rose above her. The word *fire* screamed out. She wasn't sure if she heard it or imagined it, but the smoke was real. A ruddy glow filled the room.

The building was on fire.

Chapter Thirty

Lachlan glanced at the clock mounted on the dash.
3:00 a.m. The evening started out quiet but rocketed out
of control before he could take a sip of coffee from his
travel mug. Deescalating a fight outside the Dinner Bell
Diner was the beginning and it went downhill from there.

His radio blared to life. "Officer Lachlan, you need
to get back here." The panic in Theo's voice and lack of
radio protocol made the hair on Lachlan's neck rise.

"What's going on?"

"The old bank building is on fire. Amos
Cunningham alerted us to the fire. I've called the
Hootiecackle Volunteer Fire Department. You need to
get here. Rory, Serena, and Chandra are inside. I'll call
Sean to cover your shift."

Lachlan's guts turned to water. Rory was in danger.
Myriad images raced through his mind. Rory laughing,
angry, reaching pleasure, and the thought of never seeing
them again sucked his breath away.

The sound of sirens blaring jerked him back to
reality.

He had to go. "I'm on my way."

Time stretched and shrank in the ten minutes it took
to get to Serena's building. Flames shot from the roof
next to the firewall of the joining building. Local
firefighters raced to position three ladders under
windows on two sides of the building. Ronnie Baxter, the

volunteer fire chief directed the action when Chief Nolan showed up. They talked a bit, although Lachlan had other things on his mind. All he could think of was Rory and trying not to imagine the worst. He turned toward the park at the sound of tires squealing and a car door slamming shut.

It was Nick.

"Chandra," he shouted as he ran toward the fiery building. "Chandra!"

Lachlan bodily stopped him before he ran into the inferno. The taste and smell of smoke, the heat, encircled them. "Nick. Nick." He held the struggling Nick tight. The man echoed his own desire to push the firemen aside to get to Rory. "Let them do their job."

"They're bankers and mechanics, not real firemen," Nick ground out.

"And they've trained for this." Lachlan led him to the park across the street. "We'll just be in the way."

Nick dropped to his knees. "We're supposed to get married today." He rocked back and forth in his agony.

"Don't you think that way." He crouched by Nick and held him by the shoulders. "I understand man. Rory's in there, too. They'll make it." The words came even if he wasn't sure he believed them. "They'll make it, man."

Nick glanced at him with tortured eyes. "You don't know that."

"Yeah, but I've got to have hope."

Amos sidled up to them and whispered. "I tried to tell everyone." He turned in tight circles twisting his hands together until the knuckles glowed white in the light of the flames. His voice grew agitated. "Fire. Fire. People burnin'. It's not right but the tanks kept rollin' toward the enemy. Rollin' over them." Amos pressed his hands, his eyes shut tight as if it would take way the images in his mind. "The woman in the buildin' kept poundin' on the glass. She kept yellin'. I couldn't hear her over the tanks."

"What lady?" Lachlan wondered if she might have set fire to the building.

"You know. The one who lives there."

"Serena?" He stood.

Amos' expression was one of exasperation. "No. The one with the short black hair. Her!"

Agnes? No, it couldn't be.

"She tried to tell me, but the enemy kept comin'. The man ran from behind the buildin'. He ran. I thought I recognized him. Couldn't be. What to do? What to do? Tell Theo. That's right. I told Theo, but the ladies are inside." He started to sob with his hands wrapped around his body. "The ladies are inside."

Lachlan looked to the second floor. One of the windows shattered and flames poured out.

Chief Nolan, who'd been talking to the fire marshal, stopped in front of him. He pulled his ball cap off and swiped the sweat from his brow. He was the last man Lachlan wanted to see.

"Those three have always caused trouble." His eyes scanned the crowd that helped in the rescue. "Shows what happens when a town pulls together." He stared up at the burning building sounding more aggrieved than hopeful. "I'll bet it was that boyfriend of hers—I mean ex-boyfriend. Glen something—or—other. I heard he was stalking Rory. It's going to take damned miracle if they make it."

"I have to believe in miracles." Lachlan's jaw

clenched and his fists tightened. "Rory will come out of this alive."

"Well, miracles ain't worth shit." The Chief stalked off to talk to someone else in the crowd.

This was the second time in his life he'd been helpless to save someone he loved. First Kate—her loss had been devastating. He'd barely survived— now Rory. This time the unthinkable would kill him.

****

Rory heard the voice again. A man yelled, "fire" much louder now.

Her lungs burned. A coughing fit shook her while her eyes stung with smoke. She looked around for the fireman who woke her up but couldn't see him in the smoke.

She managed to get to her hands and knees and glanced toward the kitchen. Flames glowed through the window of the kitchen door. The stairs were involved. No one could escape that direction. She could barely make out Chandra sleeping on the couch and Serena on a blow-up mattress by the coffee table. They'd decided to bunk here together tonight while they'd giggled and reminisced.

Chandra was the closest. Rory tried to rouse her, but she wouldn't open her eyes. A quick check for a pulse said she was alive. Relief made her already weak knees shakier. "Chandra, honey, get up." Her strangled words were barely audible. Tears rolled down her face. She swiped them away. "Chandra!" *Shit, shit, shit.*

She stumbled over to Serena and gave her a hard shake. "Serena," she shouted over the crackling of the fire. Her friend opened her eyes and coughed.

"What?" Serena began to choke. Her nostrils flared.

Her eyes widened in sudden understanding. "Smoke. Fire!"

"Can't get Chandra up." Serena was okay, or as well as someone could be surrounded by flames and heat.

The smoke grew denser.

They were both alive—but the smoke grew thicker.

"Chandra's unconscious." Rory helped Serena to her feet. The acrid smell burned her lungs as she stumbled back to Chandra. "We—have—to—get—her—up."

The room crackled with heat and smoke. Small embers flew like vicious fairies around the room.

Serena coughed and held her pajama top to her mouth. "Escape ladder—under—bedroom window. Wicker basket," she panted. "I'll stay—with Chandra."

Rory fought her way to Serena's bedroom. The door was hot, and the knob burned her hand. She'd seen movies to know this was bad. Really bad. They couldn't make their way out of that window. Fire was on the other side waiting to get at them.

"Can't go—that way." Smoke filled her lungs with each word. That left the two windows in the living room. They had a choice of a sixteen- or twenty-foot drop to freedom.

The front of the building was the shorter drop and held the least probability of serious injury. It proved hard to open. Her wet hands slipped as she tried to open the catch. It took two attempts, but she was able to unlatch it. She pushed up at the bottom of the window. It groaned in protest and stuck a fifth of the way up. *Damn.* She yelled in frustration and pounded against the bottom of the frame with the palms of her hand. It didn't budge. A breeze of fresh air came through the small space. She pulled in a deep breath until she heard a crackling coming from behind her. A quick glance set her heart racing.

A ripping noise caught her attention.

The fire ate its way from the kitchen to the living room. It merrily crawled up the wall behind Serena's entertainment center and across the ceiling.

"Serena, help me."

There was no answer.

Panic set in. Her heart raced faster than before. She couldn't breathe. Her lungs burned and vision blurred. She'd never felt such heat before.

A loud crack filled her ears. She turned to see the ceiling in the kitchen come down with the roar of an angry animal. It was intent on devouring them.

Embers and flames came closer. The heat was overwhelming. She collapsed in front of the window with a cry before darkness took her.

****

Lachlan watched the fireman tear away the window screen. Smoke poured from the small opening at the bottom of the window. Twice he hit the glass and wood with an axe to make an exit for the women. The first man went through the window. Two other firefighters waited at the foot of the ladder ready to move once they were given the go ahead.

"Won't take long now." The Fire Marshal came up and clapped him on the shoulder in comfort. "Some of my men tell me this might be a case of arson. One of them was sure he smelled gasoline. We won't know until we can sort things out." His gaze fixed on the flames. "God willing they're safe. My men are good at their job." He left to direct the operation, shouting commands.

Lachlan sucked in a breath of relief. His respite was short lived.

The roof gave a loud crack, followed by a *whoosh*. It came down with fire and sparks shooting up into the night sky.

"Chandra!" Nick howled in anguish. "Chandra."

Devastation curled inside Lachlan with the ferocity of a raging beast. It was ready to destroy him at the first sign of weakness. Rory had to be alive. He'd feel it if she were—it didn't bear thinking about.

****

"Come on. Get up." She came to, feeling hands gripping her from under her shoulders.

Was she dead? No. Smoke still burned her lungs. Water rained over her. Hungry embers bit her arms and legs.

"Get up. He's waiting for you." Rory saw a handsome man with glasses leaning over her. His voice sounded strange, as if filled with static from an old radio. "You can do it."

Her lungs were clogged with smoke. Coughs racked her body while acrid fumes burned her eyes. She blinked and the man's face morphed into that of Mike Johnson.

"Are you able to get up?" Mike asked, his voice muffled by his masked helmet.

She nodded. Her hands and legs were burned but she could still stand. "Serena? Chandra?" Two other men came through the window.

"Bobby and Ben Fisk are taking care of them. Hold steady." Mike assisted her to her feet. "We have to get down."

Soon she was helped over the windowsill. The journey down the ladder and being put on a gurney was a blur. The world refused to focus until a familiar face came into view.

Lachlan.

She could breathe again with the oxygen mask the paramedic placed over her face. The sweet taste of the air rushing in her lungs couldn't be any better than the sight of Lachlan at her side. She reached out for his hand. "Hey, you," she croaked.

"Hey, you." He brought her hand to his mouth for a kiss.

"Serena? Chandra?" She coughed and stared up at him.

"Chandra is on her way to Hollaway Memorial Hospital with Nick. She had the most smoke inhalation. Serena is headed that way as well."

The paramedics came by to put the gurney into the ambulance.

A familiar truck roared down the street and screamed to a halt. The Aunts tumbled out, Aunt Maisie uncaring that she was in her robe and her nightgown, both which rucked up to her plump thighs as she slid from the seat. She ran toward the gurney as fast as her knees would let her.

"Rory," Aunt Daisy yelled out, tears streaming from her eyes. "Oh, Lachlan, tell me she's okay."

"I—the paramedics could best tell you."

Aunt Maisie leaned over her. "Oh, baby." Her hands hovered and shook as if afraid to touch her. "Your face is so swollen—" Rory took her hand even though it hurt from the burns. Aunt Maisie burst into loud sobs. She held Rory's hand to her bosom. "—And your hair is half-burnt off." Her other hand reached out to touch the singed, red tresses.

"I'm okay," she managed to rasp out.

The paramedics raised the gurney and placed Rory inside the ambulance.

Lachlan jumped in beside her. "I'm going with you."

"No. No. Take my aunts to the hospital." She sucked in a deep breath of oxygen and grimaced at the roaring headache. "Aunt Daisy has bad night vision. Aunt Maisie can't drive because of her bad knees."

"Okay. We'll be there as soon as we can."

"I'll be fine" She knew he wanted to be with her, but she had to think of The Aunts. "I love you."

The paramedics closed the doors of the ambulance and soon they were off running hot.

Her eyelids fluttered shut from the rhythm of the ambulance wheels on the road. The image, not of Lachlan, but the man with the glasses lulled her to sleep.

Chapter Thirty-One

"Dear, can't you go any faster?" Miss Maisie yelled through the opened plexiglass partition between him and the back seat of the cruiser. "Anything could happen before we get to the hospital."

Lachlan glanced in the rearview mirror and saw Miss Daisy give her sister a little swat on the shoulder.

"Will you shut it?" Miss Daisy flopped back against the seat, crossing her arms over her bosom. "We don't need gettin' pulled over before we get there." Her loud huff filled the cruiser.

"Duh. We're in a police car," Miss Maisie snapped and rubbed her arm. "Who's goin' to stop us? We could still floor it, run hot." She leaned through the partition and tapped him on the shoulder. "How about lights and sirens. It's an emergency."

"I'm already ten miles over the speed limit." He understood the women's need for haste. Rory was too far away. He needed to see her, touch her to reassure himself all was well. A glance at the speedometer showed it was actually twenty.

"Sit down sister. You keep botherin' him and we'll end up in the emergency room as well."

"I can't help it," Miss Maisie sniffed. "Everyone says it was arson."

"We don't know that." Lachlan needed to deescalate the high emotions. "You've got to let the fire marshal's office and his team make that decision."

"Chief Nolan said it was Glen—that Amos saw him skulkin' around the building earlier on." Miss Maisie sobbed, bouncing between urgency and despair. "That bastard will do anything to hurt Rory."

"Language, Sist—never mind. I don't know if it was him, but whoever did this is goin' to get a backside full of buckshot. I'm done with rock salt." Miss Daisy leaned forward toward Lachlan. "You didn't hear that."

"Deaf as a post, Miss Daisy."

"All I got to say is no one will convict me if it was him. Lyin' on his stomach for a good long stretch will be a small price to pay. That fire almost killed those girls." The normally rough and ready Miss Daisy's voice wobbled. "Poor Chandra and Nick won't be able to get married this afternoon, Serena has lost her home, and Rory, poor Rory's business is gone."

"Now don't you think that way, Sister." A sniff came from Miss Maisie. "We have to be positive."

"I'm positive. Their home, business and weddin' are gone."

"They're alive, ladies." Lachlan refused to think of any other outcome. "We *will* find out who did this." He knew their chatter was because of stress but it made it harder for him to contain his own worry and anger.

"Believe me, this town don't take kindly to people who burn someone out." Fury radiated from Miss Maisie. "Especially strangers."

Lachlan gripped the steering wheel tighter and sucked in a calming breath. "The fire marshal will get back to me once they have any evidence."

"Take my word, it'll be that good for nothin' Glen," Miss Maisie muttered.

"You don't know—" Her sister's admonition was cut short when he pulled up to the emergency room entrance of Hollaway Memorial Hospital. Miss Maisie was out of the car, feet hitting the pavement as fast as her plump legs could manage.

"Oh, sweet baby Jesus. I better go after her." In a move that would do The Flash proud, Miss Daisy ran after her sister.

Lachlan got out of his cruiser and leaned against the vehicle to get himself emotionally ready to face the sights and smell of the hospital.

You can do this.

Rory was inside. She needed him. He needed her.

He went through the automatic doors, trying to ignore the antiseptic smells and sounds surrounding him. Old memories entangled him like so many spider webs, but his steps were measured and sure. Each one was a journey away from the past. His future was inside the ER fighting for her life.

A woman sat at the reception desk, head down, concentrating on typing.

"Excuse me."

She looked up, her eyes widening when she saw his uniform and badge.

"What can I do for you, sir?"

"There were three women brought here from Hootiecackle. I know it's not visiting hours but these ladies are family to the McDermotts."

"Oh, yes. The fire victims." She looked at her computer. "Ms. Moondancer and Ms. Callahan are in the ER and Ms. Barrett is in ICU. "Just take a left through the double doors."

"Thank you." He made his way to the area that held

several small rooms. A nurse hurried down the corridor, but he didn't have to flag her down to get directions. He followed Miss Maisie's sobs.

"Sister, I swear they can hear you all the way to Hootiecackle." Miss Daisy's attempts to control her sister were as loud as the wailing of her twin.

The women were upset but the last thing Rory needed was more stress.

He pushed the door open.

The glaring light of the room revealed her injuries in merciless starkness. She lay against the pillows, her face swollen and covered with soot, and nasal cannula feeding her oxygen. Her eyes were closed. Was she in pain or trying to shut out the circus playing out in the room?

All he could do was wait. Wait. Wait. Wait. No matter how many hours had passed with Kate the result had been devastation. Would this be the same? His heart pounded so hard he was sure the nurse could hear it.

"Are you family?" The nurse sat on a rolling stool typing away on her tablet. "Or on official business?"

"I'm her fiancé." The words came out without thinking and easy as silk. It was true. He'd wait as long as it took.

Miss Daisy gasped while Miss Maisie began sobbing and lifting her hands in the air. "Alleluia! Our prayers are answered, Sister. The Lord *does* work in mysterious ways."

The nurse glared at Maisie. "Ma'am, you're going to have to go outside if you can't calm down."

"You hear that, Sister. Now hush." Miss Daisy patted Miss Maisie's hand. "Lachlan's here. Let's give him have some time with Rory."

Sniffing, Miss Maisie wiped away her tears. "You're right. After all, they're engaged." She glanced up at him. "Take care of her." She turned to her sister. "She's all we have."

"I'll do my best."

"Why don't we get some coffee or something in the waitin' room?" Miss Daisy led her sister from the room. "A shot of caffeine will do us good."

The older women left with Miss Maisie making wedding plans.

Rory opened her reddened eyes. "Are they—gone?" Her voice was husky and thick with smoke.

He wanted to laugh, cry, and grab her up. Holding her would heal all the worry and doubt scaring his soul. If she hadn't been covered here and there in burns, he'd do just that. "Yes." He allowed himself the luxury of stroking one of her remaining long curls. "It's just you, me and the nurse."

The nurse gave him the thumbs up.

"Thank goodness."

He stood by Rory's side, pushing down the desire to crawl in the bed next to her. "It looks like you do throw one hell of a party."

She nodded. "Lot of fun—until—fireworks—started." She looked around the room. "Serena? Chandra?"

"They're pretty tight lipped around here." It was like her to be worried about her friends rather than herself. For a brief second his eyes burned with tears of pride, but he blinked them back. Rory didn't need to worry about him as well.

"Oh." Rory's brow puckered. "Serena—her mom—on the road—in a RV."

"We'll find her. Theo can call different agencies to help." She reached out and took his hand in hers. His heart clenched when she grimaced and then smiled.

"I'll check in on both of them for you."

The nurse stood. "The doctor should be here in a few minutes." She gave Rory a small smile. "Ring the bell if you need anything."

"Fiancée?" Rory's reddened eyes twinkled. "You're walking—in—dangerous territory, big guy."

"It's the adrenaline rush. That's why I'm a cop." Lachlan leaned down and picked up one of Rory's curls. He kissed it despite the odor of burnt hair and smoke that permeated everything. "I'll go in a few minutes. I just want to spend some time with you."

Rory's nod was followed by a grimace. It took everything Lachlan had not to touch her.

"We wouldn't—be alive—if—" she gasped. The nasal cannula under Rory's nose delivered oxygen to her starved lungs. "—if the man hadn't warned me." Tears flowed down her cheeks. She reached up to wipe them away, streaking the soot. "Stupid tears. He saved me twice."

A suspicion curled around Lachlan's brain. "What did he look like?"

"Hard to see. Handsome. Glasses. But he was really Mike Johnson. I'm so confused."

Henry? It couldn't be. He said Agnes was the only one to manifest. However Henry managed it, Lachlan owed a huge debt to a ghost. This night rattled him more than usual. A ghost? He ran his hand through his hair. He'd barely wrapped his brain around the Kate *thing,* and he wasn't about to say it wasn't her he kept hearing. The mind could do strange things in a moment of stress, but

Henry?

The nurse knocked on the door. "I'll take you to Miss Moondancer's room."

"Could I have a few more minutes?" He didn't want to leave Rory.

"Go find Serena—Chandra." Rory pulled in a deep breath of oxygen. Her voice was husky. "Please."

"I'd rather stay here." He was afraid to leave but he knew Rory well enough that she would get out of bed and search for the others on her own. "Okay. Stay put. I'll be back in a bit."

"Better." She managed to smile. "Talk—about—fiancée business—later."

"You betcha."

Serena was a couple of cubicles down the hall. He opened the door to find her drumming her fingers against the white sheets. Her hair worse than a Rory's, the long tresses gone, but her face still had smudges of soot.

"Hey, there. Rory sent me to find out how you're doing."

"I don't smoke anymore—now this." She pointed to the mask covering the lower half of her face. "Rory saved us," she said with a hint of a wobble in her voice.

"She said there was a man there."

Serena frowned. "Man?"

"Handsome—" He worried his mind, trying to come up with something, anything that didn't sound crazy. Earlier he thought he'd had everything that happened the other day sorted out. Rory's experience threw all his suppositions out the window. A chill ran through him. The hair on his arms rose as familiar fingers touched his face. Kate always loved to—he turned left and right to find the culprit. No one. He drew in a deep breath to calm

315

his racing thoughts. "—she said he wore glasses."

"Oh my." Serena's eyes rounded over the top of the mask. "Henry?"

Lachlan grimaced. That was the last thing he wanted to hear. "I *knew* you were going to say that." He paced in a small circle before stopping at her side. "He said—you said he couldn't do that. I'm grateful he did, but…"

"It might have been the fire—" she stopped to catch her breath. "Maybe it triggered him to act."

"What am I doing talking about ghosts, excuse me, TBs?" A knot formed in his chest. Years of resistance cracked bit by bit. "But I heard Kate. Smelled lilacs more than once."

"I don't have the answers." She shifted in her bed and sat upright. "Everyone is bound by their own beliefs." Her hand pressed against her chest as she breathed deep. "How is Chandra?"

"She's next on Rory's list. By the way, Rory wants me to contact your mother. She's worried about you."

A coughing fit shook Serena's body and she pushed the mask closer to her nose. "Selena Moondancer will make the fire—look—like—a—weenie roast." Her voice had a Darth Vader vibe.

"That bad?"

She nodded. "Overwhelming."

"Got it." He took her free hand. "Thank you for being—you. Get better, okay?"

She nodded as she waved at him when he left her room.

He rode the elevator to the ICU floor. It was difficult. Memories of the times spent in one of these rooms while he held Kate and felt her life slip away. He stopped at the nurses' station.

"I heard Ms. Barrett is in ICU. Can you tell me which room?"

"No more than one person at a time in the room. Her family is with her right now. The waiting room is around the corner."

He went to the waiting room. Nick's mother and Chandra's family filled the chairs and sofas. Her mother was huddled against Mr. Barrett, sobbing. Her husband sat still and dazed, absently patting his wife's shoulder. Nick leaned against the wall with his eyes shut.

"You okay, man?"

Nick opened his eyes. They looked hollow and unseeing.

"They're goin' to intubate her—put her on a ventilator." His words came out distant and bewildered. "They'll put her in a coma and—"

Lachlan understood the place Nick found himself in at. "You still have her. She's alive. Don't forget that."

"What if—"

"Forget the what ifs." How many times had he asked the same questions over and over? "They don't help."

"I—"

Nick didn't get to finish his sentence. One of the nurses sprinted into the waiting room. "Nick Davis?"

He pushed away at the sound of his name. "Yes."

"Miss Barrett wants to speak to you before we intubate her. She's insisting and we can't lose much time."

Nick nodded and went to speak to the Barrett's in hushed tones. Mrs. Barrett sobbed and nodded. He finally turned to the nurse. "I'm ready. Lachlan? Will you go with me?"

"Sure." He gave Nick a pat on the shoulder. "Not a

problem."

"I'm going with you." Chandra's father followed because he was the next of kin and would have to make any ultimate decisions concerning his daughter. No matter how much in love, no matter the fact the wedding was to have been held later in the day, Nick had no say.

The three men waited outside Chandra's room. The nurse motioned Nick inside but stopped her father. "She won't talk to anyone except her fiancé."

Agony twisted Mr. Barrett's face. "I'm her father."

"We have to get her intubated. She won't let us do the procedure until she talks to Officer Davis.

Nick squared his shoulders and followed the nurse to the ICU where Chandra lay.

Lachlan waited outside the room. He knew the emotions wracking Nick. They were new for his fellow officer and scratched at the scabs on his own soul. He could see the two through the window to the ICU. Nick leaned down to Chandra. Her hands clenched at Nick's sleeve while the nurses hovered over her, ready to spring into action the moment she was done talking or things went egg-shaped.

Lachlan debated staying. It hurt to watch the two lovers and what the world had thrown at them. He wanted to go to Rory, but knew she'd bombard him with questions as long as her voice lasted. If that went, she'd resort to pencil and paper. He didn't have to wait long. The blinds to the ICU closed and Nick came out.

Pain and anger radiated from him. A light of fury stamped out the worry in his eyes. "I'm goin' to kill him." Nick's fist clenched. "I swear to God, he's a dead man."

Chapter Thirty-Two

Nick shot past Lachlan with deadly intent.

"Wait. Wait!" Lachlan's shouts caught the attention of everyone in the hospital except Nick who headed toward the elevators.

"What's wrong," Chandra's father called out. Commotion broke out in the waiting room with panicked questions coming from every side. The man grabbed at Lachlan's arm. "Something is wrong."

"I don't know. I've got to stay on Nick." Lachlan didn't have time to stop. "Your daughter needs you." He watched the elevator doors close behind Nick.

"But—"

"I've got to go." He hated leaving everyone in confusion, but Nick was his priority.

He raced down the stairs trying to beat Nick to the ground floor. Flight by flight, he ran until he made it to the lobby. He pushed through the door in time to see Nick leave the hospital.

"Damn it, Nick. Stop!" Lachlan called out to the retreating man, dodging people heading to the emergency room and nearby benches.

Nick ignored him and went to the police SUV parked nearby, under a light.

Lachlan grabbed him by the arm before he could open the door.

Fire glittered in Nick's black eyes. "Let go." He

pulled back his free arm, his fist ready to strike.

"Don't do it."

"Then get out of my way," Nic growled and pushed Lachlan hard against the SUV. "I'm warning you."

"No." It was a risk. Devastation glittered in Nick's eyes. Whatever had happened in Chandra's room tore at him and Lachlan understood the need to lash out.

A guttural growl rumbled from Nick. He jerked away from Lachlan's hold with a howl. His arm shot past Lachlan's head to contact the driver's side window of the SUV. Nick's next cry was one of frustration, hurt and pain.

Lachlan *whooshed* in relief that Nick had decided to bash the car instead of his face. A quick side glance showed a blossom of shards in the tempered glass.

"I swear, Lachlan, I mean it. I'm goin' to kill him." He turned to pace the parking lot, flexing his bloody knuckles.

"What the hell is wrong? Who's a dead man?"

"Nolan, chief of fuckin' police Nolan." Fury poured from Nick like sweat with each step. "He can't get away with it." He sucked in a deep breath. "She's in there, thinkin' she's goin' to die, and she had to tell me—"

"Nolan? What did he do?"

"I can't tell you." Nick's pacing grew more agitated. "Get out of my way." Nick tried to push him aside, but Lachlan refused to move. "He's got to pay."

"What has Nolan to do with Chandra?" Lachlan pressed. Nick kept trying to get past him to get in the car. Lachlan pushed him away.

"Didn't you hear me? I can't—now let me go."

"No. Don't do something stupid." Suddenly the pieces of the crazy conversation in Serena's upstairs apartment snapped together. A young, blonde girl of about fourteen or fifteen servicing Nolan behind the bank building. It had to be Chandra. "Wait. Did Nolan demand she give him sexual favors when she was a teenager?"

The shock on Nick's face matched the anger. "How—I mean, I—"

Lachlan ran his fingers through his hair while he tried to figure out how to tell Nick the truth. "She's not the only one."

"He's done this before?" Nick's body sagged. He went to the bench in front of the hospital entrance and dropped onto it as if his bones were pulled from his body.

"Yeah. Rory and Serena were both propositioned by him when they were fifteen."

Lachlan sat next to Nick, his hands hanging between his knees. "I wanted to take Nolan out as well. Rory said it was too late."

Nick's gaze snapped to his. "Sexual offenders don't just stop. You know that. I know that."

"He's probably still doing it but who's going to speak up in a small town like Hootiecackle."

"Chandra was so afraid I wouldn't love her anymore." Nick's shaky sigh was worse than a scream. "I've been after that girl from the time we were in elementary school. She was so bright and sunny until she turned fifteen, then she shut down for a while. You know," Nick wiped his face, "I thought I'd done somethin' wrong and left her alone until last year. I decided to take a chance and didn't know how I got so lucky. She finally said yes. Now she says she's damaged, not good enough for me." He frowned. "I feel guilty that I didn't see somethin' was wrong a lot sooner. She'd been nervous and anxious, but I assumed it was about the weddin' preparations.

"What about now?"

"No matter what happened she's still Chandra." Nick's jaw tightened. "No matter what you say, Nolan deserves to pay."

"The last thing Chandra needs is for you to do something stupid." Lachlan thought about how badly he'd handled the situation with Rory. "Believe me, I've been there."

"I can't face Nolan as if nothin' has happened? How do you do it?"

"It sucks." All the pent-up frustration that ate at Lachlan over the last two weeks boiled over. "You think I don't want to expose him? I need solid evidence."

"Maybe Rory and Serena could file charges against him." Nick sounded hopeful. "We can leave Chandra out of it. This would kill her family."

Lachlan shook his head. "He'd just say it's their word against his. Rory hired a detective for another reason but—"

"The ex-boyfriend?"

"What?" Lachlan was caught off guard. "How did—"

"Small town, and Jenny Myers."

"You'd think everyone would know about Nolan's extra-curricular activities."

"Again, small town. Some things are better buried deep." Nick gave a shaky snort. "You can't just go up to someone and ask if the chief of police solicited them for sex. He's usin' the fear of scandal against his victims."

"That's why Rory's detective is looking into him, but I think he's on to us."

"Shit."

"Yeah, we have to take this one step at a time, but we can't let emotions rule us. I understand where you're coming from, especially when I think how much this has messed up Rory. I'm not sure about Serena. She threatened Nolan with a bunch of hoodoo."

"I'm pickin' up what you're throwin' down. I'll hope he keeps lookin' over his shoulder."

"More like checking his privates."

A small smile quirked at the corner of Nick's mouth. "I can imagine—knowing the Moondancer women."

"How are you doing now?"

"I still want to put Nolan away, but Chandra and her family come first. There's no way I'm leavin' her side until she's better." Nick sucked in a deep breath. "I've got to believe everything will be all right."

A surge of relief washed over Lachlan. The situation had been defused for now.

"You were supposed to be on your honeymoon, so your shifts are already covered.

"Some honeymoon." Nick's eyes glistened in the early morning light. "What if—"

"She's alive. Don't forget that. Every minute is precious. It's not the time to grieve. Go on." Lachlan clapped Nick on the shoulder. "Chandra may not be awake, but she'll know you're there."

"Thanks." Nick nodded and turned to leave. He stopped and shoved his hands in his pockets. "I've been thinkin'—"

"Lachlan, Nick." The fire marshal strolled up the walk and waved in greeting.

"Bill, what brings you here?"

"Checking on our casualties." Bill shoved his hands in his pockets and squinted at the sun beginning to peak over the trees. "It didn't take the Division of Fire Safety long to determine the fire was arson."

"Who was it? Chandra's layin' in there," Nick pointed to the hospital, strugglin' for her life. I want to kill them."

The fire marshal took a step back. "Now that won't solve anything."

Lachlan's first reaction was the same as Nick's—a primal need for violent revenge. It flared for a moment to be replaced by deadly calm. "The best thing to do is to let the arson investigators do their jobs.

"Who knows what happened." Nick's body shook with agitation. "Why would anyone want to hurt them?" He grew more restless. "Everyone in town knew about their sleepover tonight. It wasn't a secret."

"I know. The arson team even floated the idea that Serena may have hired it done for insurance, but that don't make no sense. Those girls have been tight since junior high. She'd never harm them, especially while she's inside." Bill pulled a piece of paper from his pocket. "All we know is someone threw a shit ton of gas on the wooden stairs. I told Serena about those steps, but she showed me the escape ladder she had in her bedroom during the inspection I did earlier this year. I shouldn't have let it slide."

"What about Glen Peters? He's Rory's ex-boyfriend." Lachlan knew Peters was a loser, but he didn't see him as a murderer.

"He's got the best alibi in the county. Hollaway PD has him locked up tighter than my great aunt's virtue." He pulled his phone from his pocket. A few seconds later he handed it to Lachlan. "Look familiar?"

It was a picture of a Zippo lighter with a Marine

Corps logo. The picture on the reverse side had the engraving of *to Donnie from Betsy*.

The world imploded into a single moment.

Chief Nolan!

Chapter Thirty-Three

Rory's aunts fluttered around the room, much like the Fairy Godmothers in Disney's Sleeping Beauty. Aunt Daisy gathered the bouquets that filled the room and set them by the hospital room door.

"Here, let me help you with those." Rory started to rise from her bed. She was dressed in a pair of her late Uncle Marvin's blue plaid lounging pants and a red jersey with St. Louis Cardinals emblazoned on the front.

"I swear, Rory, you stay put until Lachlan comes by to pick you and Serena up." Aunt Maisie pointed her finger at Serena, who made a move to get to her feet as well. "You too, young lady. Sit down. You barely survived that fire." She tied a green scarf around Rory's head to cover the fire damage.

Serena sported one of Rory's bright yellow tank tops and raspberry pink exercise pants. They were way too big for her friend. The Aunts had supplied a green scarf, like the one Rory wore. She started to slip it into her bag, but Aunt Maisie pointed at Serena. "Put that over your head. You didn't fare any better than Rory in the hair department."

"Aunt Maisie—" Rory couldn't hide her impatience.

"Don't sass me." Aunt Maisie fluffed the pillow behind Rory's head for the third time. "Lachlan will have my guts for garters if you so much as stub your toe."

"After everything you went through," Aunt Daisy's bosom heaved and her green eyes glinted with anger, "It's a wonder he hasn't been kickin' butt and takin' names. We know who did this. Lord knows, I'm a Christian woman but it's all I can do not to tackle Chief Nolan and spit in his eye."

"You can't go around accusing him of anything." Rory closed her eyes and rubbed the spot between them where a headache coiled, ready to strike. "There's no evidence."

"Oh, I got a sixth sense about these things." Aunt Daisy crossed her arms over her bosom.

"Since when?" Rory was stuck between annoyance and laughter.

"When it comes to assholes." Her steady gaze dared anyone to contradict her.

Aunt Maisie and Rory stared in disbelief while Serena snickered.

"You aren't the only one with intuition, missy."

"Sorry, Miss Daisy." Serena managed to look suitably contrite. "I forgot myself."

"Well, that's all right." She stuffed a robe in Rory's bag. "You've got a lot on your mind with rebuildin' the old bank and all."

"I appreciate you and Miss Daisy letting me stay at your place until I can get something worked out. The insurance company said my policy covers lodging until my home is restored." Serena started to get up again, but Maisie gave her the Callahan Stare again. She sat back in the chair with a sigh. "Fire Marshal Bill told me everything was ruined."

"It looked pretty sad." Aunt Daisy gave Serena a little pat on the shoulder. "We drove around the square for a peek along with all the other neck-craners."

"I feel like I'm putting you out."

"Oh no. It'll be like when we were teenagers." Rory smiled at the memories of them sneaking out at night and getting into mischief. "We're older now. You might need an air mattress for your back."

The sound of wheels on the tile floor outside their door stopped the chatter. Lachlan came through the door with a dazzling smile on his face, a wheelchair, and a young, blonde nurse on his heels. She pushed another chair, chattering away. Her eyes ate him up.

Rory's hand went to the green kerchief covering her burnt hair. Her heart gave a twist that twined together low self-esteem and jealousy. She didn't like the sensations rattling around in her head. Never once had she wanted to tell a woman to get away from her man when they glommed all over Glen. Now, one little nurse made her ache with uncertainty.

"Here we are." Lachlan stopped the wheelchair by her bed.

"Oh, Lachlan," Aunt Maisie fluttered around him like a sequined covered moth. "You came just in time. Rory's about ready to bust outta here."

"I'm tired of lying down and being fussed over." Rory knew it sounded ungrateful. "Chandra should be the one leaving today."

"Nick said they want to keep her for a little while longer. She had the worst of the smoke in her lungs." Lachlan positioned the chair so all she had to do was to slip into it.

Rory sat in the chair and watched the nurse assist Serena. "We're all lucky." She gave a small shudder when she realized how close she'd come to losing her life. She gazed up at Lachlan. In two short months he'd gone from an irritating neighbor to a man she could believe in. It wasn't a fantasy to think she could build a life with him. Her heart was no longer hers and as scary as it was, it was exciting as well.

"There you go." Aunt Daisy put a flowered afghan over her legs. It was heavy and so colorful it made her eyes water.

Her hands ran over the nubbly yarn. "It's August. I'll bet it's over ninety degrees outside."

"You can never be too sure." The frown on Aunt Daisy's face brooked no discussion. "All it takes is a sudden shift in the wind. Your throat and lungs took a beatin'."

"Serena, your ride is here as well." Lachlan motioned to the nurse with the other chair. Her name tag read Karen. She flashed a super white smile at Lachlan before she scooted the chair next to Serena. "Sergeant Donovan made sure you had someone to take care of you, too. Not everyone gets such personalized service." She helped Serena take her seat. "But how could I refuse when he asked so nicely?"

"Yes. How?" The words slipped out before Rory could stop them. A tinge of regret that Lachlan saw the flash of jealousy. She tucked the afghan tighter. "Let's get out of here."

"I'm taking you and Serena back to the farm. I can go over a few questions while I drive." He picked up her bag, slung it over his shoulder. "Here we go. Hold on." He maneuvered her through the door into the hall. Serena followed close behind thanks to Nurse Karen.

"Okay." Being wheeled through the corridors of the hospital was an odd mix of vibrations rumbling through her body and antiseptic air, tinged with the smell of disease ruffling her hair.

"Did something happen?" Aunt Maisie followed behind, her round piano legs doing their best to keep up with Lachlan's pace. Did you find out who did it? We have our suspicions, but—"

"Don't go there." Rory didn't want the latest Callahan Conspiracy Theory to get out. They had enough troubles without a lawsuit for slander.

"What do you know?" Aunt Daisy prodded. She huffed and puffed but kept up. "You might as well tell us because Jenny will be spillin' the beans before you get out of the hospital."

Lachlan merely smiled at her. "She doesn't know these beans."

This time Aunt Maisie piped up. "Don't be too sure. I remember one time Elvira Hinkle's panties lost their elastic and they fell to her ankles while she was walkin' down the street. Talk about embarrassment. She just toed those suckers up in the air and caught them without breakin' her stride. The Hinkles are always strapped for cash, you know. Thanks to Jenny, everyone in the grocery store was talkin' about it by the time I got to the grocery store from the Knotty Place. Three blocks I'm tellin' you. Three blocks."

A snort of muffled laughter came from Serena.

Rory buried her head in her hands. She couldn't get to the car fast enough.

They made it to the hospital entrance without any other stories or incidents, except for Nurse Karen's incessant chatter.

"Ladies, we'll see you later." Lachlan flashed her aunts a smile and gave Nurse Karen a nod.

"You know somethin'. I've half a mind to bake some oatmeal raisin cookies." Aunt Maisie shook her finger at him. "Maybe even some banana bread. That'll make you think twice for keepin' stuff to yourself."

The threat of her aunts baking only made him laugh. "And maybe I won't bring over the lasagna I made last night. I thought you ladies might want a break from 'cooking.'"

"Okay, I take it back. No bakin'."

"I'll pick up a French silk pie on the way back," Rory offered. Aunt Daisy gave her the stink eye. "Okay, I'll have Lachlan run into the bakery for me."

"Oh, get goin' and don't forget that pie, or the lasagna. If I can prune roses, I can throw together a salad."

"Make sure there aren't any thorns in it." It was the last bit of advice Rory gave before Lachlan whisked her away to the car.

****

Before long Lachlan had Rory and Serena settled in the back of the cruiser.

A couple of minutes later Serena leaned forward. "Is it possible to stop by the bank building? I need to see it for myself. Closure, you know."

"Sure." He guided the cruiser through Greene Summit toward Hootiecackle. "I wanted to tell you there's been a breakthrough in the case."

"What—who?" Rory piped up.

"There's nothing that says it's Chief Nolan, but the arson team found his lighter at the back of the building where the fire started."

"He'll have a logical explanation." Rory huffed in dejection. "He's always careful."

Serena's excitement filled the cruiser like the vibrations of a tuning fork. "But it puts him in at the arson scene."

"Right now, he's the only suspect. The problem is there's no motive."

Serena's excitement died. She sat head down.

"Yes there is. He hit on me and Serena. Chandra— Chandra was—" Rory stopped and bit her lip,

"Nick told me. It's going to be up to you, and Serena,"

"To what?

"Say something. Tell the truth." Lachlan knew that was the last thing Rory wanted to hear. It was the truth.

"Whose truth? Ours? No one will believe us."

It was necessary for him to keep on her about coming forward, no matter how it made either of them feel. This was for the greater good. "You have to take a chance."

Rory leaned back in the seat with arms across her chest. "Do you think people will believe he tried to kill us to cover up his crimes?"

"He may have done it to more than you three. That's a good enough motive if he thinks you might talk."

"That puts a target on us."

"Exactly."

"I don't know—I—" Rory stumbled over her words.

Serena broke her silence. "I need to I see my home first." Her hands twisted together. "There's something I need to do."

"What?"

"I don't know." Serena stared out the window. "Yet."

Rory threw her hands up in exasperation. "How can

you not—I don't understand."

"Neither do I." A slight testiness filtered through Serena's voice.

The last thing he wanted was for the two friends to get into an argument. "We'll get there ASAP."

The next few minutes were spent driving and watching in the rear-view mirror as Rory put her arm around Serena. The mini spat was forgotten. The women were quiet, except for a few whispered words from Rory. Serena nodded.

He caught Rory's gaze in the mirror and saw worry and confusion. An ache squeezed his chest. The need to protect Rory swelled with the intensity of a tsunami. If what he suspected was true, she would be the center of a furor. Some people in town still considered her reputation dubious, but she'd been working hard to overcome their prejudice. This would open old wounds. The only thing he could do was to be there for her. It felt inadequate at best.

He guided the cruiser into Hootiecackle and onto the city square. Serena's gasp at the sight of the ruins tore at him. The burnt husk of her home, the bricks, and charred skeletal fingers of the wooden framing, vied with the acrid smell of wet ashes. Everything that had been in the entire three stories was now a pile of debris in the basement.

Serena got out of the car and slowly went to where the dumpster stood. Tears flowed down her face so hard she had to swipe them away.

It was hard to watch her pain and not know how to make her hurt go away. He didn't know her that well, but she'd helped him through the last part of his grief.

Rory gave her another hug and patted her back. "It's

okay to cry. You can buy another house or rent a space for your business."

"This is so—so—" Serena shook her head in distress, her eyes averted to the ground. Her crying stopped. "What's this?" She pointed at several items by the dumpster.

Lachlan crouched to inspect the pile. The familiar UFO lamp lay haphazardly on the gravel, along with a couple of picture frames. "How did these survive?"

"I don't know." Serena stared down at them. "Maybe one of the fire fighters saw them in the ashes and put them here?"

A shiver caught him off guard. The hair on the nape of his neck prickled. "They're all from the third floor."

"How do you know that?" Suspicion crowded Rory's question.

"I told you I was over here talking to Serena."

Lachlan agreed with Rory. They continued to sort through the rubble. Why was everything else destroyed but these remained, a bit of smoke damage but intact. He stared at the damaged building. "It doesn't make sense."

Chapter Thirty-Four

Rory stared down at photos in the silver frame. A pair of familiar eyes peered through the sooty glass. Curiosity drove her to pick it up. She pulled a tissue from her pocket and ran her hand over the grimy photo to uncover a familiar face—the face so familiar it made her hands shake. "Who is this?" She grew more agitated by the second. "Who the hell is this!" She shoved the man's picture toward Serena. "Please. Tell me."

Lachlan glanced down at the picture. "Henry," he whispered in disbelief.

Serena took the photo from her. "He's right. It's Henry Purcells. He used to own the bank building in the Twenties and he and his wife, Agnes, were gunned down during a robbery." She ran a finger to remove some of the soot from the other photo. "That's her."

"No, it can't be." Rory shook her head in protest. She pointed at the movie star perfect portrait of Henry. "He's the one who saved me—us."

Serena sucked in a deep breath. Her eyes rolled up into her head. She went lax.

"Serena!" Rory's lungs refused to work. Her heart hammered at the sight of her friend fainting. The picture fell from her hands. The glass shattered and the frame came apart.

"Whoa. Hold on." Lachlan caught Serena and held her close until she tried to push him away.

"Back up. Give a man some distance." Gone was Serena's usual enigmatic expression. Now her body language said she was filled with purpose. Her voice was deeper, huskier.

Lachlan dropped his hands from Serena's shoulders. "Henry."

Serena, now acting like the so-called Henry nodded. "It's good to meet you again. Yes, I'm Henry.

I hear from those around the investigation that your friend Nick's fiancée is still on the mend. So sad."

"Ah—okay," Lachlan didn't appear to be very surprised at Serena's transformation. "I hear she's doing great. Nick will take her home in a few days."

"Good, good." Henry paced.

Rory looked to Lachlan to explain what was happening. She got nothing. "Serena?" She'd never seen her friend like this. Angry, happy, depressed—yes, she had even put up with her New Age Gothic phase during junior high and even now. That was one she never grew out of. This was different. Serena took the Moondancer Legacy to heart and ran with it. This went beyond anything Rory had experienced before.

It scared her. Tears burned her eyes. Her friend had gone over the edge. She didn't know what to do. The impotence made her angry and frightened.

"Serena. Please stop this," she cajoled. "Please."

"You're a lucky woman, Ms. Callahan." Henry stopped pacing. "Lachlan is a good man. Right to the point. I like a man who doesn't dilly dally around." Serena tugged the bottom of her tank top. "Officer, I'd like to report a crime."

"What crime?" Rory couldn't believe Lachlan was going along with Serena's nonsense. He might be doing more harm than good if her friend had a mental breakdown because of the fire. "Both of you—quit it. Now."

Lachlan didn't look at her but held his hand out for her to be silent.

"Arson. It was the same villain who molested that young girl fifteen years ago."

"Chief Nolan?"

"If you mean that pot-bellied thug with the piggy eyes, well, yes." Henry gave an impatient sigh. "It was your chief of police. I saw him douse the steps with gasoline and start the fire."

"Wait a minute." Rory put her hands on either side of her head. "I can't believe this. Stop it, Serena. This isn't funny. I know you want to blame someone." She stepped forward and grabbed Serena's shoulder to give her a little shake.

"Don't." Lachlan stopped her before she could rouse Serena. "Let him—Henry, tell us what he wants to say."

"I can't believe any of this."

"This doesn't require your belief." Serena came out of her spell and gave her a smile before furiously batting her lashes. Once again, her eyes rolled back and went white before returning to normal. Her body grew languid. "Hello again." Her attention was focused on Lachlan. This time Serena's voice changed to a woman with a velvety, southern belle accent.

"I'm Agnes. Henry's wife." Agnes' gaze raked over Rory. She gave a little sniff of disapproval. Her gaze drifted back to Lachlan. "How did you get hooked up with a regular Mrs. Grundy?"

Rory didn't need a dictionary to figure out that Agnes considered her a non-threat.

Agnes bent down to touch her things. "Oh, Lachlan, you saved the lamp. I gave it to Henry for our fourth wedding anniversary." She dusted her fingers off and touched Lachlan's shoulder to brush a bit of imaginary lint away. "You know of course that Henry is never wrong. It's so maddenin' at times. Anyway, Nolan is wrong gee, a real highbinder."

"What?" Lachlan's brow furrowed in confusion..

"He's crooked. You know, a bad cat." Agnes gave him a slow, easy smile. She dropped her hand.

Rory's hackles went up. Her best friend was hitting on Lachlan. "Where's Henry?" She asked.

"Oh, he's a bit weak from manifestin' for the first time. Nothin' like takin' his maiden voyage durin' a fire. He had just enough juice to talk to you." She examined her nails and glanced at Lachlan from under her lashes. "Anyway, that night Henry went down to investigate some racket goin' on outside. He told me Nolan was in a lather, talkin' to himself and pourin' gas all over everything."

"Did Henry tell you what Nolan said?"

"Something about gettin' rid of trash. Henry was awfully upset when the man used a Marine lighter to set the fire. Henry was a Marine in his day." She closed her eyes and smiled as if lost in memory. "Henry was so dashin' in his uniform. Got to love a man in uniform." She smiled at Lachlan "Anyway, Henry instantly recognized the lighter."

"A lighter with a Marine insignia?"

"Didn't I say so?" She gave a pretty pout.

Lachlan yelled in victory, reached out, pulled Agnes forward, and laid a big, fast kiss on her lips. "You are a doll. Tell Henry not to get upset."

"If that was a little kiss—whoa." Agnes giggled. "Thank God, it's me and not Henry that popped in."

Rory grabbed Lachlan by the arm. "Why did you kiss Serena?"

"Not Serena, *Agnes*. She's given me enough to mess with Nolan's head." He gave Rory a big hug and swung her around before putting her on her feet. "I plan to see the chief after I drop you and Serena off at the farm."

Agnes gave him a smug smile. "Well, honey, you better get a wiggle on." She wriggled her fingers in farewell, sighed, and stumbled back a few steps.

"What happened?" Serena touched her forehead and winced.

"Well, it was a repeat of the afternoon you showed me the third floor."

"Agnes and Henry?" She stared at the things on the ground. "I'll get new frames and—" she glanced at Rory. "Can the lamp be restored?"

"That's what Agnes asked." Rory couldn't be mad. This was her friend—not some mental delusion. Relief took her breath away. Tears of relief burned the back of her eyes. She was concerned that whatever happened hadn't harmed her friend. "Yes. I can check around for someone to repair it for you. Agnes said it was an anniversary gift for Henry." She put an arm around Serena. "But don't go kissing my man again. Got it?"

"Technically, I kissed her." Lachlan's smile held a hint of orneriness.

Serena's eyes widened in shock. "What!"

"I couldn't help myself. You may have broken the case. It's nothing we can use in court, but I can use it against Nolan." Lachlan helped them into the back seat of the cruiser. Once they were settled, he got in and started the engine.

Serena leaned against the window and stared at the fast-moving landscape. "I've never done this before—well once in the third-floor apartment." She squeezed her arms around herself. "Lachlan said I channeled something, or someone. I see them, hear them, but this is different."

"Who did you *channel*?" Rory had to know.

"Agnes and Henry—and one other."

"There's three?" Rory's thoughts ran down a rabbit hole until she thought she'd hitched a ride with Alice to Wonderland. Three? What other revelation would send her into a tailspin of craziness?

Serena nodded.

"Start from the beginning." Rory wasn't sure she really wanted to know. "Please."

"Well, only Agnes and Henry. The other—" she glanced at Lachlan. "He'll have to tell you about the other. I don't mind using my gifts for making a little money, but I hated it when I found out that the ghosts use me for their—mobile phone—I guess." Serena rubbed her face. "Agnes and Henry liked talking to Lachlan. That's all I know, because it's like I'm watching a fuzzy movie, I can't hear everything I say. I was channeling Henry when someone else pushed through, a stranger."

"Who was it?"

"Someone named Kate who wanted to talk to Lachlan" Serena's shaky sigh didn't stop Rory's worries. "I didn't like it when that happened. I felt wrong, not myself."

Kate. The name of Lachlan's late wife shook her. It became hard to breathe. She put her hand to her racing heart to still its frantic beating.

"You know Kate?"

"No. That's what bothered me. Agnes and Henry had been at the Bank for ages. They leave little signs from time-to-time. Sometimes there's a hazy mist and cold spot. I think that's Henry. He's more reclusive. I see Agnes all the time. Kate came out of nowhere."

Rory cleared her throat as if readying herself for a firing squad. "What did she say?"

"I don't know. That was the foggy part. I couldn't make out what they said. Lachlan can tell you."

"Lachlan?" She caught his gaze in the rearview mirror.

"We'll talk later."

"I'd talk to the devil himself if it nails Nolan's ass to the wall." Serena squared her shoulders and held her head high. "I'll file a complaint with the police. He's a molester and we need to keep him off the streets."

"So will I." Rory knew it was past time to speak out. She couldn't let Serena do this on her own. "Chandra said she can't tell her family what happened. We need to honor her decision."

"That's okay. I'd say your testimony is a start." Lachlan was a world of strength. She needed to hear his confidence and conviction. Being independent, doing things on her own, and finding her own power was good, but it was also nice to have someone else to lean on.

Lachlan pulled into the farm driveway. The Aunts were on the porch waving them forward.

She was home.

"Don't be disappointed if this doesn't work out" She reached out for Serena's hand. "It'll be uphill all the way. Remember, we have each other's backs."

They got out of the cruiser. Lachlan wrapped his

arm over Rory's shoulder. "I'm persistent. You should know that by now." His kiss on the top of her head was what she needed from him. It was both affectionate but reassuring as well. "Come on. Let's get you two inside."

Rory was ready. There were so many things to do between the ID theft and now the fire. She was worried about Serena. The incident at the bank building left them unsettled. And, she had to have a long talk to Lachlan about Kate. She was a little ball of snow that rolled down the hill, building in size as the speed of things that made her life heaven and hell.

Chapter Thirty-Five

"What do you think?" Rory looked at Miriam Jones, the attorney recommended by Caleb. The expression on the woman's face was disconcerting. She gave nothing away.

The sunshine coming through her aunts' big living room windows and the homey smell of lemon furniture polish didn't take the edge off Rory's worries. She and Serena took a leap of faith that this case would go the distance. It had been two days since the fire. Taking her life back was the first step.

"I won't lie." Miriam glanced from her to Serena before making a few notes on her tablet. "This will be difficult. However, cases of sexual abuse from years ago, especially by the church or other organizations and public institutions are getting more tread."

"We knew this wasn't going to be easy." Rory squared her shoulders. A rush of anticipation mixed with a hint of trepidation. "This is a fight I don't intend to lose."

"Let's say I know it's going to be bumpy, but things will take an unexpected twist." Serena's smile was as inscrutable as ever.

Aunt Daisy settled on the couch next to Serena and gave her a little swat on the shoulder. "Quit talkin' like a fortune cookie. This is serious business. No one messes with my girls and gets away with it."

Her friend leaned over and gave Aunt Daisy a kiss on the cheek. "I call 'em like I see 'em."

Aunt Maisie waddled in with a tray of iced tea and passed the glasses around. "Everyone is workin' so hard. Do you think there's any chance we can win?"

"Let me be upfront. Your case will likely be thrown out by the judge. The incident, or incidents, happened so long ago and there's no evidence" Mariam folded the cover over her tablet and replaced it in her briefcase. "I want you to be prepared. Both of your reputations could be irreparably damaged."

Rory thrust out her chin and gave a little laugh. "My reputation is—shall we say is questionable in this town. I'd hoped to start over. I'm not afraid of Chief Nolan even if the judge shitcans my case."

"Language, Rory. You know we don't swear in this house." Aunt Daisy wagged a finger at her.

"Since when?" Aunt Maisie took a delicate sip of tea.

"I give up. You're right. Go on." Aunt Daisy waved her hand in dismissal. "Swear like a heathen." She huffed in exasperation. "Even if we can't make the charges stick, the man won't be able to show his face in town. The one I feel sorry for is his wife but not enough to keep from makin' his life a livin' H. E. Double Hockey Sticks."

"That's not the point. He won't be able to target any other girls." Rory ran her fingers through her new, cropped hair. It felt weird, alien, and made her feel unlike herself. Her whole life had changed in a matter of minutes and seconds. She didn't recognize herself anymore. The fire burned more than her hair. It charred her soul until the thick walls surrounding her turned to ash. It sifted from her to float away on the winds of the inferno. What remained was solid Rory. No fear or regrets.

"Why didn't you tell someone when it happened?" Miriam leaned forward in her chair to

Rory stared out the window covered with lace curtains. "I worked hard to shove it in the past, to forget about it. I couldn't tell my aunts and uncles because—

"Her Uncle Albert would've killed Nolan." Aunt Maisie piped up. Amos may have given up his still, but she decided her aunt had fortified her tea with something stronger than sugar.

"And Marvin would've disposed of the body." Aunt Daisy stood and started to play a demented game of charades. "*Thud chugga-chugga splat*." She looked around as if expecting an answer.

Miriam's eyes widened. "I—ah—what?"

Aunt Maisie sighed in disappointment. "*He would've dumped him in the woodchipper*. I hope you're a good lawyer because you suck at charades."

"See, this is what I have to deal with." Rory closed her eyes and sucked in a deep breath. Her aunts meant the best, but they weren't helping her case.

Miriam shook her head. "I'll pretend I didn't hear that."

"Nolan should know better than to mess with the Callahan Women is all I'm sayin." Aunt Maisie gave a delicate hiccup. "Especially after he's already tried to kill you and Serena."

"He did what?" Miriam stopped mid-sip of her tea. "He tried to kill you?"

"The man set fire to the buildin' where she, Serena, and their friend were stayin' two nights ago." Aunt Daisy plopped down on the sofa again, her face pinched in anger. "Take out two witnesses at the same time."

Rory caught Serena's quick glance. She didn't plan to out Chandra to anyone.

"Let's focus on filing the sexual abuse charges."

"Now, Miss Daisy, we don't know if he's guilty or not. It's all just fanciful thinking at this point." Serena turned to face Rory's aunt. "We'll catch the arsonist— soon."

"Right. The fire marshal said they found Chief Nolan's lighter at the crime scene and a gas can in his car."

"And he'll have a good excuse for everything."

"That dog don't hunt." Aunt Daisy crossed her arms over her chest. "Amos saw someone runnin' from the back of the bank buildin'. That's where the lighter was found."

Rory had had enough. The only thing to get her aunts to change the subject was food. She stood and clapped her hands. "Ladies, get gussied up and we'll go to Tonio's Italian Restaurant."

Aunt Maisie's eyes lit up and Aunt Daisy knew a deflection when she saw one.

"Okay." Aunt Daisy took her sister by the elbow and led her away but not before her expression said they'd talk later.

Miriam stood, slung her purse over her shoulder, and picked up her briefcase. "I'll have these ready by nine tomorrow morning. Let's meet at the police station and get the charges filed."

The war was about to start. Rory held her hand out to Miriam. "Thank you so much for taking this on. It won't be pretty."

The smile Miriam gave her said she had a sister in the fight. "I don't do pretty. Caleb said you were strong. I'm looking forward to the fireworks."

****

The next morning, Rory ran a host of scenarios in her head during the trip to town. None of them ended well but she wasn't going to let any of the possibilities stop her. She had to do this. Her conscience wouldn't let her do otherwise.

She stopped the car in front of the police station. Sunlight sizzled against her skin when she got out and little eddies of heat flirted with the hem of her sundress. The stifling humidity didn't stop her from sucking in a deep breath to calm her nerves.

"This is your last chance to back out." Miriam set her face in an expression designed to let everyone know she meant business.

"No. Let's do this."

Serena got out of the back seat. "I've been sending out positive vibes to the universe." She patted the knit bag slung over her shoulder and opened it just enough to reveal a voodoo doll tucked inside. It was adorned with a badge and a pin stuck in its crotch. She settled a large straw hat on her head and adjusted her cat-eye sunglasses. "But I believe in backup."

Miriam leaned over to whisper in Rory's ear. "Is she for real?"

In the past Rory would've been the skeptic in the crowd but after the last few days she didn't know what to say. "Uh—I'd let the universe answer that question."

"O-k-a-y." The attorney pointed to the police station. "Let's blow the lid off the town."

Rory inwardly groaned at the sight of Fred Brennon

at the duty desk. Fate was against them from the beginning. The man had his nose up the chief's backside from the first day he joined the force.

"Well, well, what have we got here?" Fred eyed them with curiosity touched with condescension.

Miriam stepped forward. "We'd like to report a crime."

"Oh?" Fred glanced at each of them in turn. "What's the crime and who's it against?"

"Sexual abuse of a minor and the perpetrator is Donald Jeffrey Nolan." A hint of a smile touched Miriam's lips. She laid the report on the counter.

Jenny, who sat at a desk on the other side of the room gasped. "Oh my God. Oh my God," she whispered under her breath like a mantra.

"I'm not gonna do that. No one in this town will believe it." Fred's voice grew in pitch with each word. "Now get out of here. I don't have time for your jokes, Rory Callahan."

"And Serena Moondancer." Serena pulled her sunglasses half-way down her nose and stared at him over the top. She tapped the papers with a black polished nail. "See, it says Serena Moondancer right here." Her eyes never left his face.

He took a step back. "You are out of your fuckin' mind."

"No." Serena's smile didn't reach her eyes. "All my synapses are firing just fine. Now it would be a good idea to file this thing."

Fred's face grew red and mottled. "You're talking shit. Take your complaints and stuff them."

Rory closed her hands so tight her nails bit into her palms. "Where is Chief Nolan?" The little crescents of pain helped her focus. She was ready to fight.

"He's with—it's none of your business." Fred bulled up and puffed out his chest. She half-expected him to start beating his chest with his fists.

"Very well. We'll take our case to the county prosecutor's office. They'll decide the merits of our complaints." Mariam radiated confidence. "If they refuse to see us, well, we'll contact the FBI."

Serena smiled and readjusted her sunglasses. "I hear that wilt is really bad this year. I hope those prize pumpkins of yours are okay."

"Are you threatenin' me?"

"Why no Fred. I'm just giving you some gardening tips."

"Come along, ladies." Miriam gathered up her files. "Next stop is the county prosecutor."

"Wait, wait." Fred put his hand out in the classic motion to stop. "Let's not be hasty. Jenny, take them to the conference room. I'm goin' to get the chief."

"What's goin' on?" Jenny's question turned Fred's face an even brighter red.

"It's none of your damned business," he snapped and left them at double time. "Now do what I tell you—and keep your mouth shut."

Jenny led them down a hall and to a room that smelled of musty upholstery, unknown body fluids, and old floor wax. "Here you go." The minute Fred was out of earshot she turned to Rory. "Is what she said," Jenny pointed to Miriam, "true?"

"I—ah—" Rory didn't like being put on the spot. It was clear from Jenny's expression that any denial would be seen as a confession.

Miriam jumped into the fray. "I'm advising you as

your attorney not to say anything."

Relief filled Rory. She didn't want to answer any more questions. They'd be flying all over town soon enough and they didn't need to be jet propelled by Jenny.

"You heard her, Jenny. No more fuel for the fire." Rory settled in a hard metal chair. It was a good thing they weren't planning on being here very long. She hated this place. Memories of getting a mug shot for smoking grass, the leers of a couple of the officers, including Nolan. The walls closed in with each breath and she fought to remain calm. Her breathing slowed and strength returned.

"Got it." Jenny shrugged. "The whole office is goin' nuts anyway."

"What happened?" Rory regretted the words the instant they were out of her mouth.

Jenny sprawled in the chair next to her and crossed her hands over her middle-aged tummy. "The City Administrator's secretary called the chief. I put the call through and the next thing I know is the chief racing out of here like a scalded hound."

****

Lachlan finished the report on the upcoming yearly budget for the department. Violet Nowell, the city administrator's secretary, had called to remind him it was due—even if there'd been a lot excitement in town of late. The Administrator's secretary was in her seventies, full of sass and a force of nature.

City Hall was divided into two parts. One half was the police department, while the other side belonged to the city administration and held the council meeting room at the back.

He came through the door, and Violet put a finger to

her lip and motioned him to sit. "Things are about to get real interestin' around here."

Before she could say more Lachlan could hear Nolan's bellow. "I didn't start any fire and you can't prove it."

"Now all we're saying is there's evidence linking you to the fire. Your military lighter was found behind the bank and the empty gas can in the back of your car don't look good. The fire marshal suggested an administrative leave."

"Like hell."

The door was paper thin. Lachlan and Violet might as well be in the room with the city administrator, Paul Townsend, and Chief Nolan.

"You don't have a say in it."

"Like hell. You know I could make things uncomfortable for people in this town—a lot of important people. Most of them wouldn't give a rat's ass if those sluts were dead."

Lachlan rose from his chair. He'd had it with Nolan. No more.

Violet moved with lightning speed. She rushed from behind her desk and stood in front of the door. "Sit back down." She hissed and pointed to the chair. "He's greasin' his own skids." He reached around her skinny body, searching for the knob. Violet hustled like she was blocking a shot in a basketball game. "Nope. Not goin' to happen. Sit."

Word had it she might look like a sweet grandmother, but she could be mean as a snake.

He knew when he'd been bested. "Yes, ma'am."

"Good." She patted his arm. "I've never liked—"

Voices rose again before she could say more.

"That will do Nolan."

"I'm just sayin' it's the ex-boyfriend."

A rustle of papers filled the silence for the next few minutes. "Well, I must disagree with you there. I have a report from the county jail that shows Glen Peters was arrested for driving while intoxicated. Deputy Parker followed him to Holloway, and he went off the road into some trees. There was also a warrant out for him for identity theft and wire fraud. The feds don't take too kindly to cybercrimes either. They've already hauled him away."

"Damn it."

"Don, I'm sorry but we've got to put you on administrative leave until we can get to the bottom of this." The men came out of the administrator's office. Paul Townsend looked apologetic. "We'll get this sorted out. Until then—"

Before anymore could be said, Fred barreled through the closed door. "We got big trouble, sir." His remark was aimed at Nolan instead of the city administrator.

"What's going on?" Paul demanded.

"You're not goin' to believe this. Rory Callahan and Serena Moondancer have filed sexual assault with a minor—" Fred glanced around the room. "—they're filin' against the chief. They got a lady lawyer. She said if we don't allow them to be filed here, they'll go to the county prosecutor."

"What!" Paul Townsend's shock turned his face white then gray. "Don't leave." His command was aimed at Nolan. "Stay here until the city attorney shows up." He turned to Violet. "Make the call. I want to see Grayson in here in less than a half-hour."

"Got it." Violet hustled to her desk and picked up her phone.

"It's a lie. Tell them to go to hell." Nolan tried to leave but Lachlan stopped him.

"I'd stay and listen to Mr. Townsend if I were you." Lachlan could tell Nolan could feel his world closing in on him.

"Go to hell. This was your doin'." Veins stood out in Nolan's neck. His face took on a purple hue.

"I don't molest minors."

"Go to hell. All of you." Nolan looked ready to stroke out. "That bitch of yours will do anything to make my life hell."

"I'd watch what you say, Nolan." He took a step forward, ready to strike.

Violet grabbed Lachlan by the arm. "Not the time and place." It was only her words that tore away the haze of red-hot anger that enveloped him.

"Shit." Paul paced the crowded anteroom to his office. "Sorry for the profanity, Violet. Did you get a message to Grayson?"

"Sure did." Violet's eyes glimmered with anticipation. "He'll be here in twenty minutes."

Townsend turned to Nolan. "You better get an attorney of your own."

"To hell with that. I'm innocent."

"First the fire, now this." Townsend turned to Violet. "I'll call a closed council meeting. We can't let this get out until we know more."

"Oh, you can bet it's already the latest topic of conversation at the Country Kitchen Coffee Shop and the Dinner Bell." Violet piped up. "I'll get hold of the councilmen for you. What time to you want the

353

emergency meeting."

"This evening. Seven sharp."

"I want a public meeting. I want this out in the open," Nolan shouted. "I'm not afraid to take on those bit—" He glanced around the room and his gaze settled on Lachlan. Nolan was lucky Violet had talked Lachlan down enough to keep from decking the guy. She looked ready to step in and do it for him. "—women or the fire marshal. I want to set the record straight. All the councilmen know me. No one can run me out of *my* town." He glared at Lachlan, his eyes filled with a challenge before he stomped out the door.

"Shit, shit, shit." The city administrator went back into his office.

"Ooo. I do believe Chief Nolan is a little pissed" Violet's mouth quirked to one side. "I think that's his version of 'I'll get you and your little dog, too.' "

"I'll be sure to bring a bucket of water to the meeting."

Chapter Thirty-Six

Lachlan surveyed the crowd from the back of the room. The individual murmurs blended into a tidal wave of sound. It bounced off the wall in a tinny concerto that pierced his eardrums until he could swear they were bleeding. Tonight he was on security detail—just in case someone got rowdy. The city administrator hoped it would be cut and dry. He was wrong. Half the town showed up once word got out about the chief's suspension.

Rory was in the front row with Serena and their attorney. He could easily pick her out with her now short red hair and the square set of her shoulders. She was ready for battle. He'd give anything to fight it for her, but she wouldn't appreciate him slaying monsters she needed to handle on her own. His role would be there for her, no matter if she won her fight or failed.

"Yoohoo, Lachlan are we too late to get seats?" Miss Daisy's voice cut through his *knight in shining armor* fantasy. She surveyed the crowded room. "Maisie made us late." She glared at her sister through slit eyes.

"I couldn't find my lucky shoes." Miss Maisie pointed to a pair of bright pink sneakers with sparkly, rainbow laces. "Let me tell you, I win every canasta game when I wear them."

"Well, if you—"

He was saved from a sibling squabble fest by

catching sight of Rory, raising her arm, and pointing at two seats on the front row. "Ladies, Rory has your seats saved for you. She's up front."

"Thank you." Miss Maisie patted him on the arm. "You're such a good young man. I—"

Miss Daisy pulled her by the arm. "Come on, Sister. This isn't the place to be flappin' your gums. You're holdin' up the line. People are tryin' to get in."

The two women waddled down the aisle, arguing the whole way until they sat next to Serena.

The chatter in the room rose when the councilmen filed in and took their place on a raised dais. Paul Townsend sat in the middle of the councilmen. Chief Nolan strolled in with them and took a place at the end with his attorney at his side. He was at ease as if he were at a local VFW dance rather than a hearing to decide his future.

The city attorney rose. "We have convened a special session of the council to consider a temporary suspension of Chief Donald Nolan. The arson team discovered several items at the scene that belonged to Chief Nolan. I've passed a copy of the file to the council members, and we'll show whatever photos are pertinent to the case."

Lachlan frowned in confusion. There wasn't any mention of Rory and her case against Nolan.

The room filled with chatter once more.

The City Administrator raised his gavel. He gave several hard raps against the sounding block with his gavel. The crowd continued to talk over him. He finally resorted to giving a sharp whistle. Everyone went silent.

"Good. Now are we goin' to hold this special session in a mannerly fashion? I know there's a lot to get through, but it will go faster if you're quiet. If not, I'll have Sergeant Donovan escort you from the building."

"Like that's gonna happen," a large, orange-red haired woman called out with a chuckle from the middle of the crowd. The owner of one of the town's mechanic shops flexed her arm to show a large bicep.

"Now, Connie, I'm going to say this once. No more interrupting." The City Administrator pointed his gavel at her. "You can either be sitting or leaving—take your pick."

"I hear there's goin' to be fireworks." Connie sat back in her chair. "I'd hate to miss them."

Paul half stood and leaned against the table. "And I'd hate to think you got all your news second hand from someone else." His eyes settled on Jenny. He sat back in his leather padded chair. "Now, as you know the city council has made a decision to temporarily suspend Chief Nolan."

The crowd's displeasure rose in shouts, scuffling and scraping of chair legs against the vinyl tiles of the floor. A few rose to their feet.

"Why? He ain't done nothin' wrong," one man called out. "He didn't set no fire."

One after another rose to shout out their opinion of the proceedings. Lachlan prepared to show a few people out if need be.

"I'm sure the chief appreciates your support, but we have important stuff to get to tonight." The gavel thundered again.

Everyone sat down with grumbles and mutters under their breath but soon the room was quiet.

"Now, as I was saying," Paul continued, "The fire that destroyed the old bank building *was* arson. The arson team found a few things, bits of evidence, or at least they're calling it evidence, that belong to the chief. We wanted to do this in a closed session, but he insisted everything was out in the open."

The crowd murmured their approval.

The Chief couldn't hide his smug smile.

Lachlan narrowed his eyes and stared at the man. Lachlan's sense of impotence grew stronger. He knew the man was guilty and had the gut-sick knowledge that he would go free.

The City Administrator opened the folder that lay in front of him. "Now you," he pointed to the other council members, "have the same files, but we will also project the images as we see fit."

The city council studied the evidence and shared photos. The people squirmed in the hard metal folding chairs. An underlying energy, a jumpiness filled the room.

"I think it's time for Police Chief Nolan to have his say."

Nolan leaned into the microphone. "I'm innocent of any crime. All my life I've served this town and its people." His eyes scanned the crowd, settling on one person than another. Even though he was in the back of the room, Lachlan watched them fidget under the chief's scrutiny. *Did Nolan have something on them?* "Why would I even burn down the old bank. I don't own it. There's no insurance in my name." He stared at Serena. "Unless someone else needed the money. As for the lighter, well I could've lost it when I saw someone runnin' from behind the bank. I chased the guy as far as I could but lost him. As for any other so-called evidence, well, that's all easily explained like I told the council.

Right, Herb? Larry?"

The councilmen stared at the papers in front of them instead of the crowd and nodded.

"See, that's all I need to say. I'm sure the council will see I'm innocent and undo the suspension."

A murmur worked its way through the crowd— some in agreement, others uncertain.

"Our attorney said you'd have to remain on paid suspension until all the evidence is sorted out. It's proforma, nothing else. I'm sorry but consider it a small vacation. Do you agree, Chief Nolan?"

Lachlan knew then that Paul wasn't compromised like others either in the audience or some of the council members.

Nolan frowned. "I don't mind, as long as the council and *my* town have faith in me." He smiled at the crowd. "We hang together in Hootiecackle. Right?"

A cheer and clapping rose to fill the room.

"There. I don't think we need any discussion from the crowd. With that, do I have a motion to adjourn this meetin'?"

Lachlan took a step forward. This wasn't the way the meeting was supposed to go. What had been done to Rory and Serena's complaint? There was no mention of it. *Damn them. They're trying to cover up Nolan's crimes. Not only the fire, but they haven't mentioned the sexual abuse charges. If Paul isn't under Nolan's thumb, then why?*

Councilman Herb Meyers lifted his hand. "I make a motion that—"

Lachlan made a move to speak.

Miriam Jones beat him to it. She stood. "Might I have a moment of your time?"

359

"We're in the middle of making a motion to—"

"I understand, but I would like to discuss a serious issue." Miriam charged ahead before Paul could have Herb restate his motion. "It's concerning a complaint against Donald Jeffrey Nolan. I tried to file with the police department this afternoon. Unfortunately, the Hootiecackle police department refused us. The complainants are Victoria Siobhan Callahan and Serena Moondancer against Donald Jeffrey Nolan. The charge is for solicitation for sex with a minor."

****

The room gasped. Shock waves of disbelief rolled over one person after another like a tidal wave. The murmurs grew to a roar. Rory's heart fluttered in sick anticipation. Her breath left her lungs. This was it—the beginning and the end of the old Rory. It was hard to maintain a neutral expression when she was shaking inside. She had to admit there was a touch of trepidation, but she shooed it away. She was no longer a victim.

A quick glance at Serena showed her friend as calm as ever on the outside but her violet eyes burned with fire. She wasn't going to go down easy, either.

Her aunts were yelling at Paul Townsend. Aunt Maisie stood, her round face red and her fist raised. "You're tryin' to hush everything up. First the fire and now this. You know," she pointed at Chief Nolan, "you did it. You set fire to Serena's house, and you demanded sex from when they were just girls. You can't hide your sins, Donnie. It won't work."

"Sit down, Miss Daisy." The City Administrator let loose with his gavel and glared down at Ms. Jones. "You can't do this. We're about to adjourn."

"Oh, shut up, Pauly." Aunt Daisy joined the fracas.

"This is gonna come back and bite you on the butt. See if it don't. God's got eyes everywhere." She gestured at her own eyes with her fingers and pointed them back at him. "*Everywhere*."

"Ms. Callahan, can you get your aunts to sit down?" Miriam asked out of the side of her mouth. She glanced at Rory's angry aunts. "Please."

Rory was proud of her aunts for jumping to their defense, however, she saw Miriam's point.

"Sure." She leaned over to Aunt Daisy. "You're hurting our case, so pipe down. Pass it on."

Aunt Daisy's mouth thinned but she nodded. "Okay." She turned and whispered to her sister. Aunt Maisie's huff of indignation could be heard over the noisy courtroom.

"Sergeant Donovan, kick out the next person who so much as sneezes." The gavel came down harder and louder.

"That's my job." He stopped by The Aunts. His swift smile of approval soothed out the moment. Both calmed down and sat once more. He turned to the council. "I think you better listen to Ms. Jones."

"What did you say?" The City Administrator sputtered in surprise.

"You heard me." Lachlan crossed his arms over his chest. "Things are about to blow up in your face if you don't."

Rory wanted to push through the crowd and kiss him then and there. Love swelled in her heart. She might balk at his knight in shining armor routine at times but tonight she adored his steadfastness.

The City Administrator covered his mic with his hand. He turned to one side and the other to convene with the other members of the city council. He turned to Miriam. "We need to set a time for you to meet with our attorney."

"Delay tactics. I'm not letting you hide behind legal counsel. Like I said, I was told I couldn't file my client's complaint with your police department, but my clients have a right to justice." Ms. Jones held up papers in her hand. "I told Mr. Fred Brennon at the police department that I'll go to the county prosecutor or the FBI if you can't or won't file our complaint."

The members of the council went white while Nolan turned red and rose from his seat. His attorney grabbed his arm, pulled him down, and whispered in his ear once he was seated. Anger still burned hot in his eyes. He shook off his attorney's hand and pointed to Rory and Serena. "These two are doin' their best to make my life a hell. One's a slut and the other is a witch. They think I tried to burn them out."

"Why would they think that?" Paul Townsend frowned. "You said you chased the arsonist away."

"I—"

"Because he's afraid of the truth." Serena stood, her stare boring into Nolan's face. "His political career is on the line. The Callahans are right about the fire."

"You don't know anything. There are no witnesses." Nolan sat back in his chair with a smug sneer on his face. "Everyone here knows you're a psycho—" he pointed to Serena and then to Rory, "—and so is your *friend*."

"We'd like to make a statement." Nick's voice boomed from the back of the room. He turned to Chandra who clung by his side. "Are you sure, sweetheart? You don't have to do this." She gave a small nod and together they made their way down the aisle.

"You keep your mouth shut if you want to keep your job." Nolan growled.

"Why?" Nick challenged. "You don't even know what I'm goin' to say."

Chandra came up to the podium in front of the council. "I'd just turned fourteen and Chief Nolan found me and a boy petting. He gave the boy a warning, but he demanded I give him—he wantcd —" her voice trembled, and she sucked in a shattered breath.

Rory couldn't stand it. She stood and went to Chandra. Fear rolled off her friend in deep, unending waves. Rory understood. She knew the horror of losing everything. If it hadn't been for the man, Henry, she wouldn't be here to help Chandra. It was time to pass it on. She took Chandra's hand.

Serena came to stand with them. She took Chandra's other hand and nodded at her. "Go on."

Chandra sucked in a deep breath. "He wanted sex. I gave in because I was scared."

"You're lyin' you bitch." Nolan stood.

"I'm tellin' the truth." Chandra's smoke damaged throat made her words sound like a scratchy record.

"You tried to kill us." Rory's voice shook with outrage.

"They could've ruined me." He looked from one person to another. "I took my chance to get all three of them at once. It was too good to pass up." His face went from red to purple. "They should be dead," he screamed. His frustration bounced off the walls. "All of them!"

The crowd lost control. Shouts filled the room.

Lachlan had to physically hold Nick back from attacking Nolan.

"He raped me when I was fifteen." The bellow

overrode the noise. Everyone turned to see who'd made the accusation. "I said he raped me when I was fifteen." It was Connie Yoder, the mechanic.

"What?" Henry Shoals, one of the councilmen asked in confusion. "You said he raped you?"

"Yeah, behind the Dairy Freeze." Connie's expression said she dared anyone to disbelieve her.

"I was sixteen." Tanzy, the librarian, stood.

Five more women gave testimony of Nolan's abuse.

Tears rolled down Rory's cheeks. She grieved over what the women had suffered, yet she was grateful for their confessions. She hugged Chandra and Serena.

This wasn't the ending, but it *was* the start of a new beginning.

Chapter Thirty-Seven

"You're lyin'." Nolan stood, rushed around the table and down the stairs of the dais. "You're just tryin' to get back at me for throwin' you in juvie." He gestured to the crowd. "Tell them," he shouted.

Rory watched in disbelief. Anger gripped her with each step he took toward her. Lachlan stiffened beside her. His arm around her shoulder tightened. "Don't," she whispered. The last thing she wanted was for him to do anything that would hurt his career. Bashing his superior to mush would be a mark against him.

A wheezing sound drew her attention. Chandra had drooped in Nicks arms. "I—I—need—" Her eyes grew wide and unfocused. The beginning of a full-blown panic attack stole her words. Nick pulled her closer.

Rory's heart stumbled. All of this was her fault. Her stomach twisted in knots at the thought she caused this by being so sure she could fix this horrid situation. She was wrong. Guilt tore at her. She'd forced Serena and poor Chandra into a no-win situation.

"Let's get out of here." Nick leaned down to Chandra, gently touching her cheek. "I love you. Don't forget that—okay?"

Chandra nodded as he picked her up and took her out of the room.

The unflappable Serena took a step back but remained smiling.

"You." Nolan pointed at Serena. "You witch. You put a spell on me, seduced me back then. Now my career, my family, my life is goin' to hell. It's all your fault." His voice rose in volume and pitch. "The three of you together did this. You made me set fire to the old bank buildin'. It was almost too easy." His breath came hard and fast. "Get rid of the town menaces all at once. Everyone should be thankin' me."

"That doesn't make a lick of sense." Serena turned her pinpoint violet stare at Nolan. "Rory already told Lachlan about what you did. I think you were worried about Chandra spilling all those nasty beans to Nick." Her arm motioned across the room at the other women. "Believe me, I think it will be more than these women who will have similar stories to tell." She took Rory's hand. "We may be the first, but we won't be the last."

They stood their ground in the face of his anger.

"Bitches," he screamed. His face turned purple with rage. "Why didn't you die?" He shrieked and lunged for her and Serena. She pulled back but his hands closed over her shoulders to give her a vicious shake.

Serena kneed him with lightning-fast speed and precision. Nolan dropped to the floor with a gurgling scream. Spittle drooled in a stream onto the carpet. She knelt beside him. "Didn't I say I'd make your balls shrivel and die if you touched me?" Nolan gasped in the air but couldn't speak. A dark stain spread across his pants and down his legs.

The man who thought he controlled the town had wet himself in front of everyone.

Lachlan moved fast and sure before Nolan came to his senses. He had Nolan on the floor and handcuffed. The man rolled around on the floor and gave Lachlan a feeble kick.

"Don't you fucking move. You've added another charge against you—hitting a police officer." Lachlan pulled him to a sitting position. "You have the right to remain silent. Anything you say may be held against you in a court of law. You have the right to consult with a lawyer before and during questioning and have a lawyer appointed to represent you if you can't afford one, and these rights can be exercised at any time. Do you understand your rights?"

"Go to hell." Nolan wheezed trying to catch his breath.

"Do you understand your rights?"

All Nolan could do was nod.

Applause broke out, along with shouts to throw Nolan in jail.

"Serves you right, you perv." Aunt Daisy shouted over the crowd.

"They're conspirin' together." Nolan groaned and clutched himself. "Like that You Too, Them Too—whatever movement."

"You'll be havin' another *movement* to worry about if you don't quit runnin' you mouth." Aunt Daisy leaned down and showed him her chubby fist. "Don't forget, I'm a Callahan Woman and we protect our own."

"Come on, Sister." Aunt Maisie pulled her back. "I think Lachlan has everything under control." They went back to their seats, chattering like cats at a birdfeeder.

The sound of everyone talking over each other became unbearable. Rory grew claustrophobic with each second that passed. She sat next to her aunts, who immediately surrounded her with concern and love. It was hard to breathe, and she hated herself for feeling so weak.

"Quiet." The City Administrator shouted into his microphone and pounded his gavel.

The room stilled with a few comments petering out until the room was silent, except for Nolan's whimpering. "Take Nolan to the police department. Call 911. They can check him out. Call the prosecuting attorney and Judge Sanders, whoever else we need to get hold of. We'll want to file charges of arson, attempted murder, and what is it, six charges of sexual abuse and solicitation of a minor—so far."

"You got it." Lachlan hauled Nolan to his feet and marched him out of the council room.

Rory's knees began to shake. It wasn't time to break down, to cry with relief but she had to sit. Serena settled in the chair next to hers.

"We did it."

"Yes, we did." Rory drew in a deep breath. "I'm so proud of Chandra. That was the bravest thing I've ever witnessed. And you," she gave her friend's hand a small squeeze. "When did you learn the kung fu stuff."

"Krav Maga." She patted Rory's hand and leaned back in her chair with a grin. "If you can do it, I can do it. I started taking lessons in Branson a couple of years ago. There's a lot of crazy people out there and I tend to draw the craziest."

"Wow, I see I'm going to have to take up a new martial arts. Where do I sign up?"

****

Lachlan stepped out the backdoor of his house and onto the patio with a steaming cup of black coffee. The concrete was cool under his feet with a slight dampness left by the pre-dawn showers. The sun painted the clouds with the colors of his grandmother's favorite rainbow sherbet. He closed his eyes and breathed in the fresh air. It was as if the whole world had been scrubbed of Nolan's filth.

The man sat secure in a holding cell awaiting whatever justice came his way.

Lachlan figured he'd be there for a while because Nolan's wife refused to pay the ten thousand dollars to keep him from taking off for parts unknown. During his booking, he'd spewed hatred and threatened to divulge all the dirty secrets he'd gleaned over the years. Nothing worked. No one stepped forward to help him. His alleged crimes were too great for him to be let out on his own recognizance.

The weight on Lachlan's shoulders, his worry for Rory, the people who'd come to be dear to him drifted away on the morning breeze. For a town that was supposed to be his ticket to easyville, Hootiecackle had proved to be nothing such. He found he didn't resent the intrigue or the policework involved in crime solving small town style. Deep down he was still a detective.

He took a sip of coffee, relishing the dark, slightly bitter heat on his tongue. His ears perked at the sound of the back screen door of the McDermott/Callahan house slam shut. He glanced over the fence to see Rory letting the dogs out for their morning run. Rory ran after them in the early morning light with her nightgown flapping around her knees.

"Yo." He called at her over the fence and waved his hand.

She returned his greeting. "Back at you, big guy." Her smile was a creation of beauty. She came up the path with a walk that stripped him of breath.

For the last two weeks it had been hard to have a moment alone and she stood there with the morning light filtering through the thin cotton of her gown. He knew every curve, every inch of her skin. The taste and scent of her was embedded in him, body and soul.

The dogs followed her to the fence, yapping and bouncing around her feet. She snapped her fingers. "Quiet you two." The corgi and dachshund behaved as any hyper dogs and ran after a squirrel that bounded in front of them. Rory laughed. "I swear."

"What do you swear?" He opened the chain link gate and let her in.

"That I—no—I—" She shook her head and leaned into him, resting her head on his chest.

"Coffee," he cautioned and raised the mug out of splashing distance. His other arm went around her. "And I swear you're a walking menace, Rory Callahan."

She straightened herself. "Sorry. It feels like a year since I saw you last night. You disappeared. I never saw you again." There was a hint of a pout to her words.

"I texted you about what happened." He stepped back and held the mug with both hands, even if his first instinct was to throw the damn thing away and kiss her silly. "A cop's hours aren't predictable and there are times I have to focus on the job."

"Oh, I got the text. I might be jealous if it wasn't Nolan you were throwing in the stony lonesome as Aunt Daisy calls it." She patted him on the chest and went to sit on one of the patio chairs. "I already figured out you're dedicated to the job—just don't hound me for banging on nails early in the morning." She gave him a smile that drew him with the intensity of a spoon to an electric magnet. "I'll get used to it."

He put the mug on the table and placed a hand on each arm of her chair. "Oh, you'll get *used* to it?"

She nodded, cocking her head, her eyes gleaming with mischief. "Umm, sure will."

He leaned down and took her mouth in a kiss that turned lust, friendship, and love into a gordian knot of desire. There was no sword strong enough to cut through the way she'd worked her way into his heart. "How about a cup of coffee?"

"Oh, yes, yes, yes." Her hands came to rest on either side of his face. "I thought you'd never ask."

Epilogue

"Winter weddings are the best, don't you think?" Maisie fanned herself with the wedding program. "It's so cheerful and colorful."

"Speak for yourself, Sister." Daisy huffed and pulled at the neck of her red velvet blouse. "It's 70 degrees outside in the middle of December. That ain't right." Sweat poured down her face. "Even with the doors open, I'm goin' to pass out before they say their I Dos."

"I agree." Maisie gave her makeshift fan another go. "It's all that climate control they talk about on television. They say we're in for a blizzard right before Christmas."

"That's climate change, global warming. It's—"

"Whatever you call it, I think Mother Nature is goin' through menopause and she's havin' a hot flash." Maisie pulled a tissue from her purse and gently patted her face to keep her makeup from running. The last thing she needed was to look like a dyspeptic clown. "She's just makin' sure she's not goin' through it alone."

"The heat in here has nothing to do with the weather." Daisy held out her hand for her sister to give her a tissue as well. "Blame Pastor Mansfield's cold feet. He's got the heat cranked to 78 and he has the only key to the little plastic box covering the thermostat."

Organ music started and everyone stood for the bride. Pachelbel's Canon in D Minor flowed over the crowd. Chandra stood at the back door of the church with her father. She made a beautiful bride with her hair pulled back into a smooth knot with her veil attached with sparkling white rhinestones. Her plain white satin gown was elegant. She looked cool despite the heat.

A nervous Nick stood next to Lachlan shifting from one foot to another until he saw his bride. He stared in gob smacked surprise. Loved bloomed on his face.

It did Maisie's heart good when things turned out the way they were supposed to. Tears welled in her eyes at the sight of Nick taking Chandra's hand. The squeeze in her heart was one of pure joy.

One of these days it would be Rory's turn—if Lachlan would get off the stick and propose. The Plan had to work. At this rate Rory would be gray-haired and she and her sister be nothing but skeletons if they couldn't get a proper meal.

She turned her attention back to the service. It went off without a hitch and everyone headed over to the VFW for the reception. The afternoon turned hotter by the minute. Maisie went outside to catch a breath of fresh air. She ambled through the pretty garden the VFW installed around the gazebo. She stopped at the sound of familiar voices.

Unable to resist, she peeked through the branches of a lilac bush to see Rory and Lachlan sitting on a bench at the back of her destination. Her hand went to her mouth to stop a gasp at the sight of Lachlan dropping to one knee.

"I look corny, don't I?" Lachlan's quick grimace changed to a smile.

Rory dashed tears away and smiled. "You look like the most handsome man in the world. Maybe little corny, but I love it."

"Okay, let's see if I can do this right. Victoria Shoiban Callahan, will you do me the honor of taking me on and drinking coffee with me for the rest of our lives?"

"Oh, yes." She placed her shaking hand over her mouth and nodded vigorously. "Yes. Yes, I will."

Lachlan stood and took Rory into his arms for a kiss that was better than anything Maisie had ever seen in the movies or TV. He swung Rory around and ended by giving her grandniece another kiss that Maisie was sure would blister her eyes if she kept watching.

Maisie left her hiding place with as much speed as she could hustle in heels and a girdle. She found Daisy eating wedding cake at the closest table to the front door. "Sister," she panted, "Go, find Sally Anne right now."

"I'm eatin' here." She pointed to her plate. "I just found the only place to catch a breeze in this sauna. Why do I have to get up and find Sally Anne—" Comprehension lit her eyes. "Are you sayin'—I mean—did he—did they?"

Masie nodded. "Sure did. Right outside in the gazebo."

Daisy lay her fork down and stood. She grabbed Maisie and hopped up and down. "The Plan worked. Our plan worked."

"Yes, it did." Maisie couldn't help but beam and rub her hands in anticipation. "Now head me toward the weddin' cake."

A word about the author…

With the maiden name of Love, how could I not write romance? I was a voracious reader in my teens and early twenties thanks to my mother buying load of books at garage sales. The first time I read Tarzan of the Apes I was confused by the flutter in my thirteen-year-old heart. As I got older I understood. It was after I married my greatest supporter and cheerleader that I realized I wanted to write as well. I mean, how hard could it be. Lesson learned on that one.

Now I've retired and reside in the Ozarks with my husband and two large marmalade cats--Aka and Jinja. Although there is a bevy of birds and squadrons of squirrels in our yard, I don't consider them family. Well, maybe a little. 636 W. Commercial St.

Thank you for purchasing
this publication of The Wild Rose Press, Inc.

For questions or more information
contact us at
info@thewildrosepress.com.

The Wild Rose Press, Inc.
www.thewildrosepress.com